6/02

The Judas Tree

Also by D. J. Delffs
in Large Print:

The Martyr's Chapel

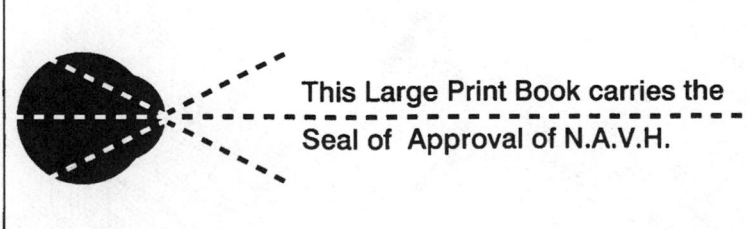

This Large Print Book carries the
Seal of Approval of N.A.V.H.

The Judas Tree

D. J. Delffs

Thorndike Press • Waterville, Maine

Published in 2002 by arrangement with
Bethany House Publishers.

Thorndike Press Large Print Christian Mystery Series.

The tree indicium is a trademark of Thorndike Press.

The text of this Large Print edition is unabridged.
Other aspects of the book may vary from the original edition.

Set in 16 pt. Plantin by Myrna S. Raven.

Printed in the United States on permanent paper.

Library of Congress Cataloging-in-Publication Data

Delffs, Dudley J.
    The Judas tree / D. J. Delffs.
      p. cm.
    ISBN 0-7862-4245-0 (lg. print : hc : alk. paper)
    1. Tennessee — Fiction.   2. Clergy — Fiction.   3. Amish — Fiction.   4. Large type books.   I. Title.
PS3554.E4423 J84 2002
  813'.54—dc21   2002022886

To G. K. Chesterton,
Father Brown,
and the mysteries of Faith

ACKNOWLEDGMENTS

As Father Grif continues on his journey, I am thankful for the many people who contribute to making the adventure so worthwhile. Many thanks to my dear friend Jerri Kayll for her insights into Amish and Mennonite culture. Thanks, too, to Jerri's mom, Mrs. Maxine Miller, for her kindness in loaning books and experience. Connie Tawwater answered questions and kept me informed from The University of the South. Thank you, Connie.

I'm consistently grateful for the rich community of students, colleagues, staff, and friends who comprise Colorado Christian University. Thanks to the many SPS students who reinforce my calling and the support and encouragement of colleagues like Dr. Elaine Woodruff, Dr. Stan Dyck, Dr. David Oakley, Dr. David Williams, and many others. I'm equally grateful for my new community of peers and students at the University of Denver. Dr. Margaret Whitt has been especially kind and supportive in sharing her concern and expertise. Professor Brian Kiteley has also enriched my return to graduate school through his contributions to me and my writing.

Friends like Phyllis Klein are hard to

come by; I am most grateful for her support and sharing of her own spiritual journey. Old friendships grow dearer: Bill and Lisa Reagan, Doug and Cindy Skelton, Nancy Todd, Darlene Hayes, the Pierces, the Thurmers, the Raders, the Broomes, and Berthiaumes. New friends contributed so much to this endeavor: Mark DeVerter, Mark and Sarah Wakefield, Len Tamura.

Dave Horton challenged me to make this a better book. His help with plotting and revising, along with his patience and encouragement, proved invaluable. Once again, Barb Lilland provided thoughtful suggestions and professional support. Her patience and gentle spirit are most appreciated. Kathy Yanni continues to amaze me in her ability to provide vision and direction for me and my writing. She remains a dear friend and much respected professional. Thanks and thanks again to Kathy.

None of this would be possible without the love and sacrifices of my wife, children, and family. My parents remain my biggest fans. Thanks to my wife's family for all their love and support: Jim and Libby, Lee and Malissa, Andrew and Tracy, Dennis and Sydney, David and Jamie, and John Christian. Finally, thanks, Dotti, for loving me so well. You continue to inspire and encourage me beyond words.

CONTENTS

*"The Son of man goes
as it is written of him,
but woe to that man by whom the Son of man
is betrayed!
It would have been better for that man
if he had not been born."
Judas, who betrayed him, said,
"Is it I, Master?"*

MATTHEW 26:24–25A

Chapter One

The Outsider

Spring break was only two weeks away when Simon Hostetler's body was found hanging from a legendary oak in the woods a mile outside of Tremont. Nothing in the light snows and mountain frosts could have prepared me for such a crime. The winter months after Christmas had encased our lives with the comfortable tedium and slow-paced familiarity of my small hometown.

I had not seen my old friend Dr. Simon Hostetler, professor of cultural anthropology at Penn State University, in years. So when his present research sabbatical brought him back home to the Amish community in nearby Tremont, I thoroughly enjoyed catching up with him and comparing the different turns we had each taken since seminary days.

Simon's was not the first untimely death to mar the tranquility of the community that I loved and served in the quiet parish of Avenell. Some effects of the murder that had occurred in our midst the previous autumn continued to linger like stale smoke. One consequence in particular consumed my past two months: I'd been drafted for the Presidential Search Committee after Avenell University President Franklin Milford resigned at the end of fall semester.

Our parish church, the Divine Cathedral, was undergoing a thorough cleaning and face-lift, a compromised restoration overseen by Mrs. Joan Dowinger, a widowed millionaire with too much time on her hands and not enough good taste. My beloved Martyr's Chapel, the original university sanctuary where so much evil had transpired, had been restored to its prior status. Yet despite numerous cleanings and a service of blessing, the place still troubled me. I had not returned there alone since last November. Echoes of inhuman voices and gunshots reverberated through the old stone works of my mind.

On the surface, however, my parish life resumed its normal routine that was as familiar as the liturgy itself. The Ash Wednesday services had been especially well attended this year, and the Lenten Missions Committee had sponsored a spaghetti dinner that raised over a thousand dollars. A few parish families battled the flu, but there had been no serious illnesses or deaths. My young curate, Peter Abernathy, continued to infuse his passionate faith into the growing body of college students and young adults in our parish.

In fact, by March the only conflicts in our community were of the relational variety. My sister, Beatrice, had taken up with a newcomer in our small town, the Reverend Lyle Slater, senior pastor of the First Christian Church of Avenell. While she was clearly smitten with the eloquent, silver-haired widower, his approach to ministry did not particularly appeal to me. He immediately made sure his Sunday services were broadcast on our county radio station, WVNL, "1330 on your AM dial." His sermons included visual aids, sound effects, and tailored suits. He was impressive, all right, but somehow I was not used to the idea of him and my sister becoming a couple.

I continued to counsel Peter regarding his romance with Leah Schroeder, the beautiful Amish woman whose love of art had intersected with the murder investigation last fall — one of the only redemptive outcomes I could see so far. However, my role as counselor forced me to sift through my own tensions between my grief over the loss of my wife, Amy, to cancer almost five years ago and new feelings of attraction toward Caroline Barr, a professor of Restoration drama in Avenell's English department.

While Caroline and I continued to become better acquainted, Peter and Leah quickly reached a stalemate. Both acknowledged their love for the other but could not reconcile their cultural differences. Mr. and Mrs. Schroeder offered the young couple an ultimatum after Peter's hasty proposal last Thanksgiving. They had until Easter — now less than a month away — to make decisions that would affect the rest of their lives. If they proceeded to marry, then Peter would have to join her Amish community in Tremont. If he refused, then she would no longer be allowed to see him.

The only other alternative remained unspoken by her parents: Leah could revoke her baptism and commitment to the Amish Church and basically become an outsider. Peter assured me that this was very rare, and he could not imagine his beloved making such a life-altering choice. Although she would still be permitted to see her family occasionally, for all practical purposes she would be forever separated from the close-knit community. Based on my curate's winter listlessness and the approach of Easter, Bea and I knew that some turning point, one way or the other, was imminent.

Our anticipation, however, turned to shock the second Thursday in March. Nothing in the day betrayed the news beforehand. The groundhog had not seen his shadow in February, so our recent weather delighted us with fulfilled expectations. The morning sun bleached a handful of stubborn gray clouds, and a slight breeze emboldened Bea to hang sheets on the clothesline. The air smelled moist and rich with pollen. Spring had indeed arrived early in the rural Tennessee backcountry along the Cumberland Plateau.

By that afternoon, Bea had nagged me into helping her weed last year's vegetable patch. We were debating the merits of raspberries over blackberries when Peter came dashing round the corner of the rectory.

"Just in time!" Bea exclaimed, about to arm the twenty-six-year-old with a hoe.

"Grif, Miss Bea, I'm so glad I found you," he panted.

"Peter, are you all right?" I asked.

"I'm fine. It's Leah." His breathing evened out and his voice returned to its rich tenor. He brushed a blond cowlick off his forehead and took one last deep breath. "She just called from the sheriff's office. It seems she . . . she found a dead man this morning . . . in the woods . . . about a mile from her family's barn outside of Tremont. She was out drawing and found a man hanging from that old oak tree."

"Good heavens!" Bea shrieked, as if the man's body dangled before her now. "Can you believe humanity?"

"Indeed," I said. "The poor girl must be in shock. Was it someone she knew?"

"Sort of. The man was dressed in a traditional Amish suit — black homespun. But he was so disfigured from the . . . rope around his neck that Leah didn't recognize him. At the police station, however, they identified him. Turns out . . ." Peter swallowed thickly and his Adam's apple knotted.

"Someone we know?" Bea questioned, clasping her palm around her own thick neck. "Heaven help us! Who was it?"

My curate looked me in the eye, and I felt the weight of his announcement like a tremor before an earthquake. His eyes told me that it was someone *I* knew.

"It was Simon Hostetler. The professor from up north."

"Oh my!" whispered my sister. "Poor Simon! What in the world happened?"

Peter simply shook his head, still trying to gauge my reaction. My eyelids suddenly felt leaden. The sun, which had seemed so cheerfully bright only moments before, now seemed harsh and alien.

"Grif! Are you all right? Do you need to go inside?" Bea shifted into maternal mode, and I felt her hand on my shoulder as I struggled to open my eyes, as if just awaking. "Peter, help me get him to the porch," she commanded.

The two of them led me for a few moments before I came back to myself and negotiated the steps on my own. "I simply cannot believe it," I murmured. "What happened, Pete? Surely he didn't kill himself. Things were going so well for him. He was so — so vibrantly *alive* when I saw him last weekend."

"I knew you'd take it hard, him being an old friend of yours and all," said Peter, leaning on the porch rail. "They're not sure what happened exactly. There was no suicide note, only a Bible verse carved into the trunk of the tree —"

"Oh, good heavens, no!" interrupted Bea. "Surely this doesn't have anything to do with Simon's research of the Amish."

"Dan Warren said they're not ruling anything out at this point. It's hard to tell." He sighed and the three of us fell silent. Some detached part of me immediately wanted to know which Bible verse, as if knowing the epitaph would explain something. Instead, my senses seemed to linger outside myself. The sloping hillside behind the tree line shimmered with new tufts of grass and the creeping tendrils of jade kudzu. One of the first bottle-green flies of the season buzzed about and landed on a spade handle next to Bea's work gloves. A fire-breasted robin chirped from the left side of the grape arbor. There could not have been a more incongruous setting in which to assimilate the news of my friend's death.

"I wondered if I could borrow your car to take Leah back home," said Peter. "She had to go to the station to give her statement and Dan Warren assured her that he'd take her home, but since she's so close, I thought she might be more comfortable . . ." His emerald eyes seemed to burn brighter at the thought of seeing his beloved.

"Of course, Peter. Always. We weren't going anywhere, were we, sis?" I asked.

"Not at all. I promised Berthy Weismuller that I'd go over to the hardware store with her for some new seed catalog, but we'd planned to walk anyway. Amazing that woman can get around so well for someone in her seventies! I hope I'm that spry when I'm her age." I had no doubt about that whatsoever. Despite her short attention span, Beatrice was nothing if not spry for her six decades.

"Peter, tell Dan that I'll call later and that I'd be happy to help out with any arrangements that need to be made." I handed him the keys to my six-year-old Buick LeSabre, the silver key ring embossed with the Episcopal seal glinting in the sunlight.

"Give our best regards to dear Leah," said Beatrice. "Poor Simon," she echoed and hugged my shoulder.

Several hours later as the light began to fade behind Eaglehead Mountain and spring-fevered students tossing Frisbees retreated back to their dorms, I sat in my office pondering the loss of my friend. It was almost five o'clock and Bea had returned from her walk with Berthy just in time to remind me that my dinner was last night's leftover pork chop and Jell-O salad. She had to attend the Ladies' Auxiliary potluck meeting at our church next door and needed to leave early to help set up. She offered to stay, concern palpable in her tone, but I waved her off and welcomed the time alone. I had called to tell Caroline of the news — she had only met Simon once — but got her machine instead. In the jagged mountain shadows of twilight, alone in the wingback chair of my office, I finally began seeking God's comforting presence.

It wasn't that I was so close to Simon, that the loss was deep. In fact, he and I had lost touch until a month ago when he showed up at Sunday service and invited me out for lunch to explain about his latest research project among the Tremont Amish where he'd grown up. Sure, we had been friends at Union Seminary twenty-five years ago, but not the kind that attempt to maintain the relationship over distance and time. We belonged to the same study groups, shared rides home to Carroll County, exchanged news of common acquaintances, but back then we had never quite connected at a heart level. I liked him and he liked me, and we were both content with the casual friendship.

I'd been delighted to see his familiar face, smudged by age but not diminished, in the vestibule at church only a month ago. The receding hairline had given way to a close-cropped oval just covering the top of his head, the wrinkles of five decades complementing his ruddy complexion and sharp nose. Translucent gray eyes as inquisitive as ever. A smile and firm handshake after a quarter-century.

In an odd way, we seemed more connected now, in a shorter period of time, than we had for the two years in New York at Union. Perhaps it was that we found ourselves in similar situations: just on the other side of fifty, single, devoted to our work's calling.

Simon was a good man. I liked the direction our reunion was taking, the almost instant feeling that I could trust him. When we had lunched last Saturday at the Corner House down in the valley, we had discussed our jobs, talked about the potential of our current relationships. He told me about his life of scholarship and students at Penn State, about his first four books on various religious sects and cultures. I recalled then that Simon had diligently sent me copies of all of them while I could only remember reading the first two. He had disclosed that there was an Amish woman — someone he knew from his childhood — with whom he hoped to reconnect while he was here. I shared some of my fears about my relationship with Caroline and ended up describing Amy and all that I missed about her.

And then there was that moment where Simon seemed odd. I had almost forgotten it. We were finishing up the conversation, waiting on the change from our tab, when I asked how much longer his research would require. He looked at me curiously, then leaned in to whisper, "Not much longer, Grif." He looked around at the other tables, at the assortment of couples and white-haired ladies, and leaned in farther. "I'm on to something that must be exposed in Tremont."

"What? What are you talking about, Simon?" I'd asked, grinning. In seminary, Simon had an infamous sense of humor, and I anticipated a punchline within his dramatic tone. But just then our waitress came bustling up to the table with our change and some final patter about our clean plates. Simon shut down immediately, retreated back into his slatted chair, and smiled up at the college-aged server as if he knew her. I calculated the tip and we headed out. In the parking lot I tried to resume the conversation, sensing that he had not been joking after all.

"What were you saying — exposing something about the Amish in Tremont?" I asked.

His eyes pierced mine for a fleeting second, his irises the color of the wind-churned clouds above us, and then he smiled and shrugged my query off. "Oh, nothing, Grif. You'll hear more about it soon enough. You know how we professors are — always talking to ourselves when we should be listening."

We shook hands and made plans to talk by the end of the week. An appointment we would never get to keep.

When the phone interrupted my reverie a few moments later, I hoped it might be Caroline, but Sheriff Sam Claiborne's hoarse voice answered mine instead.

"Sorry to bother you, Grif. I . . . I hate to ask, but could you come down to Tremont tonight?" he questioned. "I need your help." His voice echoed curiously, and I suspected a cell phone.

"What's wrong?" I asked, automatically lowering my voice.

"You know about Hostetler's death, right? I'm down here at the Schroeders' with the bishop and his elders. I can't say much, only that they're not being very cooperative."

"What have they told you?" I asked eagerly.

"Well, that's just it. They refuse to answer most of my questions about their relationship to Hostetler. They're not too happy about your curate's presence either, but he's been allowed to stay as a kind of moral support for Leah. She suggested to her father and me that perhaps you could come down and help us gather some information."

"Well, I . . . uh . . . I don't know what to say," I stammered. Resistance surged within my heart at being forced into another circumstance where a life had been taken. I had never wanted to be involved with last fall's horrid events in the Martyr's Chapel. The Lord pulled me into it nevertheless, silently kicking and screaming like C. S. Lewis at his conversion. And now another one. This time the victim was someone I not only knew, but cared about. "What makes you think they'll open up to me any more than you?"

"No guarantees, Grif," replied the sheriff. "But I don't know what else to do. I've been here for over two hours and know less than when I got here. I thought about calling in the Mumford department or even the state, but Mr. Schroeder assured me that it's nothing personal. They'd be just as tight-lipped with anybody else. Except maybe another man of the cloth, I figure. Look, Grif," he was growing impatient, "I'd consider it a personal favor if you'd give it a shot."

I paused to think for a moment. A dog barked in the background, and suddenly I could see the sheriff standing there next to his squad car in the shadow of the big white farmhouse, annoyed that the Schroeders did not even possess a phone for him to use inside.

"I understand you knew Hostetler?"

"Sam, you're really pulling out the stops, aren't you? Yes, Simon was an old friend from seminary days. . . . I'll be down soon as I can borrow a car," I sighed.

"No need. I radioed the office and Dan can pick you up in half an hour. Then you can ride back with us or with Pete." He immediately sounded relieved.

"I'm not exactly sure what I can do," I cautioned. "I have tremendous respect for the Amish, but I'm not sure they'll be willing to open up any more for me than for you. I'm still an outsider."

"I know. But Leah seems to think a man of your age and standing would be respected by her people more than me with my guns and badges. If you're willing, it may be our only shot to figure out what happened to Simon Hostetler."

"I'll see you around seven then," I said.

"Father Grif —"

"Yes, Sam?"

"Thank you." He hung up.

"You're welcome," I said into the static void.

I had only a few minutes to wolf down my pork chop and a few bites of gelatin before

Dan's squad car pulled up. Annoyed that what Sam requested of me somehow interrupted my personal grief, I suddenly felt rushed and uncertain of what I had agreed to, like a student who enrolled late for a class that started weeks earlier. Dan knocked solidly and entered at my reply.

"Good to see you, Sherlock," my friend said and shook my hand firmly. "You ready to solve another case?"

"None of that now. I'm just helping out Sam by trying to mediate a difficult situation."

Sergeant Dan Warren's dark face beamed. "Didn't I see Hostetler at church a couple of times? Did you know him?"

"Yes. We attended Union at the same time. We weren't close, but we had remained friends. We hadn't seen one another in years until he showed up last month. . . ."

"I'm sorry, Grif. I didn't know. . . . Look, I was just kidding about the Sherlock and all." My friend's countenance showed concern.

"I know," I said. "Let's get on the road."

"Sheriff is mighty relieved that you're coming. Said to be sure to thank you. He's totally buffaloed. He's trying to be respectful, but you know Sam. When someone doesn't cooperate, he can lose patience fast."

"Yes, he's not one to suffer fools. And even though the elders of Tremont aren't fools, their reluctance to answer his questions probably appears foolish to Sam. Like I told him when he called, I'm not sure that I'll have any better luck."

"Miss Leah seems to think so, and it's worth a shot." Dan turned back toward the door while I scrawled Bea a brief note and flipped on the porch light. The mountain air retained the cool scent of winter despite the springlike afternoon. Old Man Cunningham assured us at the last vestry meeting that we would have at least one more snowstorm before spring was here to stay.

Inside Dan's squad car was a mess of faxed bulletins, bulging notebooks, and empty coffee cups from the Kwik-Stop. He pulled down Southern Avenue and onto Highway 64 before accelerating beyond the speed limit.

"Looks like you're staying busy," I commented.

"Yep, but nothing major. We've been workin' on a stolen car ring and a little drug activity, but it's actually pretty quiet. Now this."

"How're Diane and the girls doing?" I asked. Although Dan and his family were parishioners, his work often kept him from attending services regularly. Last year our summer fishing trips had kept us connected, but I realized then that I hadn't really seen him much since Christmas.

"Oh, they're doing real fine, Grif. The girls are eager for school to be out, already making summer plans for basketball camp and swimming parties. Diane's stayin' busy at the hospital." I smiled thinking about his junior high-aged twins and his lovely wife, a nurse at Carroll County General.

"How are you doing, Dan?" I paused for a moment as we began taking the lazy-eight curves down the mountain road. "How are things, you know, with you and God?" I never knew how to ask that question gracefully, and when I first entered the ministry, my awkwardness often kept me from asking at all. I'd learned, however, that I often had to risk a little embarrassment in order to share in another human's growth.

Dan smiled as if reading my thoughts and took his time in replying. "We're getting along pretty well, I reckon. I've been trying to make more time to spend praying and reading. That Nouwen book you gave me for Christmas is good stuff. It helps me keep my faith simple, more honest."

"I'm so glad you're enjoying it. *The Road to Daybreak* is one of my favorites. It's funny you say that about keeping faith simple. I've been trying to think about what I know about the Amish, specifically this community at Tremont. Simplicity of faith and purity of heart are hallmarks of their people."

"Is that what drew Simon Hostetler back to them after all these years? Sam told me that he grew up down there among the Amish." The dark valley highway rose up to meet us like the throat of a tunnel, and Dan accelerated the large sedan toward our destination.

"I'm not exactly sure what drew Simon back here. He's a cultural anthropologist, you know, specializing in religious cultures. He never talked much about his Amish upbringing when we were in school together — I remember being shocked at the discovery. He seemed so . . . well, normal. I'm not as ignorant now as I was then about seeing through the stereotypes of the Amish, but I'm still not sure I know how to characterize them."

"This is the first suspicious death in the community that's ever been reported. Some record for over eighty years," said Dan.

"Yes, I believe Tremont was founded by several families from Lancaster County right before World War I. Then after the war more families moved down and the community thrived. I wish I'd asked Simon more about them now."

My vital question could be contained no longer. I inhaled deeply and turned toward my driver's dark profile. "Dan, did Simon kill himself? Or was he murdered? I can't imagine that this was any sort of accident."

"Doc Graham's ruling it a murder by asphyxiation pending the autopsy results, which we should have by tomorrow afternoon. There were no props to indicate that Hostetler rigged himself up in that tree. Not sure till the autopsy, but Doc's estimating that he'd been hangin' there since last night at least, a good twelve hours before Leah found him. No, I don't think your friend took his own life, if that makes you feel any better."

"I'm not sure it does," I said.

"Leah found Hostetler dressed in traditional Amish garb — an oversized black suit. Did he typically dress like them while he was here?" Dan continued, trying to objectify the case.

"Not when I saw him, no." I envisioned my friend in the uniform of these people we were about to question.

"The clothes have no labels, of course, since they're homemade. Hard to tell if he was wearing them because he wanted to fit in or if someone did this to call attention to the fact that he wasn't really one of them."

"But if that's the case, then why dress him up at all? Why not leave him in his own English clothes?"

"Good question. Perhaps to mock him? I don't know, Grif."

"Or maybe to remind him of his roots, since he grew up here in Tremont."

"Maybe. Somehow, I've got an uneasy feeling about this. Seems strange that a peace-loving group of folk like the Amish could find itself with a murdered man in its midst."

"I think I share your feeling," I said.

The remaining minutes of our journey passed in silence. Perhaps we were gathering courage for whatever we were about to face.

Chapter Two

Appointment with Death

The dark, polished wood of the Schroeders' parlor gleamed in the blaze of kerosene lamps. Stern-faced men, many with hoary beards, sat rigidly in cane-bottomed chairs, their black hats in their laps. Empty coffee cups and saucers with pie crumbs were the only indication that the group had attempted to get along.

Leah Schroeder appeared momentarily, accompanied by my weary-looking curate. The young woman who had discovered Simon Hostetler's body still looked shaken. Her flag of bright copper hair was bunned and tucked neatly beneath her small white *kapp*. Her eyes looked troubled.

Introductions were made by Benjamin Schroeder, Leah's father. He began with Bishop Thomas Zook on his left and proceeded around the broken half circle. Zook was younger than I expected — mid to late-thirties, with his own black circle of wiry beard, high cheekbones, and a sharp nose. His eyes did not leave mine as the others were introduced. Most of the other names and faces blended together — bearded men in dark clothes with Dutch-German names. Not one of them smiled, but two nodded politely.

"We are all very upset by this tragic accident in our community," offered Bishop Zook.

Sheriff Claiborne sniffed from the other side of the spartan room. "Like I said before, this isn't an accident. A man doesn't hit himself on the head and then rig up a noose, climb to the tallest tree in the woods, and finish himself off. Simon Hostetler was murdered."

Most of the Amish men, especially the one who appeared oldest, flashed lightning eyes toward Sam.

"Sheriff," I began, "would you mind talking to Dan outside for a few minutes? I believe he has something in the squad car to show you."

Dan Warren eyed me complicitly. The sheriff sighed and muttered "might as well" under his breath as he rose and accompanied his deputy outside. Officer Andy McDermott lingered in the sheriff's shadow until Dan motioned him to follow.

Leah brought me coffee, and I was offered a seat next to her father. Peter stood in the background, between the parlor and dining room, clearly agitated.

"Gentlemen, I regret the circumstances that bring us together. May I pray for us before we begin?"

Nods and grunts of assent. I kept my words simple and direct, asking for wisdom and discernment, and the restoration of peace to this family and community.

I decided to maintain my direct approach. "What can you tell me about Dr. Simon Hostetler? I understand he spent his boyhood here in Tremont?"

Leah's father stroked his dark, beardrounded chin. "Yes, Brother Reed. He was an outsider, though. Someone that we do not worship or fellowship with. He was staying in the little motel up in Mumford, but most days he was down here trying to interview our people, examining our fields and farm implements. Writing everything down in that little book of his."

"Yes," nodded a white-haired, wizardlooking man. "He was not welcome here, but we tried not to be unkind. Some of our people hoped that he might return to us."

"So Simon was not forbidden to come and go in your midst. He was not shunned, but he was not particularly welcomed either," I summarized.

"That is correct," Bishop Zook said. "Shunning is reserved as the severest punishment for members of our own body who transgress against the Lord. Although Simon grew up here, he chose the world's path instead of our own. He was treated courteously but not familiarly." His words sounded rehearsed and edged by a defensive border, a professor justifying an exam grade to a complaining student.

"Do any of his family still live here?" I asked. Leah and Peter shifted nervously just inside my field of vision. The misshapen shadow of a house cat expanded in the candlelit kitchen doorway.

Silence. No one answered.

"I understand his sister remained in the community," I answered my own query.

"That is correct," stated Zook in the same pedagogue's tone.

I moved on. "When was the last time any of you remember seeing or talking to Dr. Hostetler?" I wasn't sure how I would react to their stonewall tactics.

More silence. An uncomfortable cough. One of the younger men, perhaps my age, leaned forward and locked eyes with me. But no one spoke. Even Benjamin Schroeder avoided my glance.

"Please. I realize that you are disturbed by

such a brutal crime in your midst. That makes it all the more imperative for you to tell what you know about this man. No one's accusing any of you. And I know you're all just as eager to get to the truth and move on. . . ."

I pleaded with my eyes to the dozen men seated around me. Most kept their heads bowed and their line of vision nailed to the floor. I decided to deliver my only ace in the hole. "I attended seminary with Simon many years ago . . . he was my friend. Please tell me anything you know that might explain this horrible event."

My syllables floated up to the dark rafters and dissolved like a pagan prayer.

"I'm sorry," said Bishop Zook. "It's just that we want no interference from the English. We will investigate this situation and determine if there is a punishment to be meted. Surely you can understand?"

"Yes, I can. But what if Simon's death does not involve any of you? Or what if Simon was mistaken for one of you? If we work together, justice will be accomplished sooner," I replied.

Suddenly, Leah Schroeder began to whimper in the dark shadows of the doorway. Peter refrained from embracing her, but I could tell he was worried about her. Nervous eyes shifted her way. Her father rose to console her.

"Is Leah all right?" I asked. "Perhaps she should see a doctor."

"She's fine!" clipped Mr. Schroeder.

"No, no, no!" she cried in response. "I must tell you, must tell you all. *I* am responsible for Dr. Hostetler's death. I can bear no more. . . ."

She sobbed uncontrollably and Peter abandoned decorum and held her in his arms as the room exploded in excited voices. All I knew to do was pray.

Leah's heart-shaped face shown feverishly in the lamplight. Tears converged to form small rivulets like rainwater across her pale, freckled cheeks. As her sobs subsided and she gradually composed herself, she removed a white handkerchief from an apron pocket and wiped her eyes and nose. I wasn't sure what upset Mr. Schroeder and Bishop Zook the most, Leah's burdened secret or the comfort she seemed to find against Peter's shoulder. The murmurs among the elders and deacons faded into the shadowed planes of the solid wood walls and floor.

"I will not believe that my daughter had anything to do with the death of Simon

Hostetler," snapped Mr. Schroeder. "Leah Rebekah, speak with the truth of one who has been baptized in the fellowship of God's children."

I heard a sharp scrape from the staircase around the corner and suspected Mrs. Schroeder and her oldest sons were listening with the same suspense as the rest of us.

Bishop Zook stood and offered his ladder-back chair to the young woman. A serene expression graced her face now, and she looked up at my curate for support before seating herself and straightening her long dark skirt over her lap.

"I had agreed to meet Dr. Hostetler at the Judas Tree this morning after breakfast. I saw him in the bakery yesterday and agreed to show him some of my sketches and paintings. He thought he could use some of them to illustrate his new book. . . ."

The blood in Mr. Schroeder's face rose like mercury in a thermometer. "Once more, your precious art has gotten you in trouble. Once and for all, I forbid you to lift a brush to canvas! Do you understand me? The devil uses such vanity, and now a man has died from it!"

"But that doesn't prove anything!" blurted Peter.

"Benjamin, release your anger without sinning," said Bishop Zook firmly, but calmly. "We will discuss the matter of Leah's artwork at a later time. Right now we must determine how her appointment with Hostetler led to his death."

A screen door creaked and a barn owl screeched somewhere across the dark countryside. Dan Warren and Sam Claiborne tried to enter quietly, like a pair of latecomers to the church business meeting, but Dan's size and the sound of their boots on the hardwood floors made them conspicuous once more. To their credit, neither the sheriff nor his deputy spoke.

After moments of silence, Leah spoke clearly and deliberately, her words almost visible in the confined room. "I agreed to meet Dr. Hostetler at the Judas Tree this morning around nine o'clock. Like I said, he wished to see some of my paintings. I was late getting there —"

"How late?" I interrupted.

"Oh, about twenty minutes, I suppose. I had to help Mother finish the wash and hang the sheets on the line out back. I didn't leave the house until almost nine, so I may have been delayed a half hour."

I nodded and saw Dan scribbling in his notebook out of the corner of my eye.

Leah continued. "On my way, I thought I heard someone coming toward me. You know, distant footsteps, snapping twigs. I thought maybe Dr. Hostetler had grown impatient and was coming to the house."

She cleared her throat and Peter placed a glass of water before her on the table.

"Were you frightened at all when you sensed someone coming toward you?" I asked.

"No." She hesitated, as if in thought. "I wasn't afraid for my safety. But I did fear that Dr. Hostetler would want to come back to the house to see my work. I know that he had come to visit Mother once. . . ." Leah averted her eyes.

"What? Here in my house? Dear Father in heaven, please help me," prayed Mr. Schroeder. "Sarah did not tell me of such a meeting. How many more secrets is my family keeping from me?"

The bishop placed his hand on Benjamin Schroeder's shoulder.

"So you wanted to keep your parents from discovering your appointment with Dr. Hostetler. Did you see the person you heard coming toward you?"

"No. The sounds faded, as if the person had turned around or taken a turn off the path. I assumed some children were playing or looking for spring ferns, so I continued on my way. When I got to the clearing where the old tree is, no one was there. I was about to leave, assuming Dr. Hostetler grew tired of waiting when I happened to look up . . . and there it was. I thought it was a prank that Nathan and Mark had pulled. But then I could tell it was not a scarecrow or ragdoll . . . it was a man . . . flies were buzzing around his head . . ." An involuntary shiver telegraphed the grotesque horror of her discovery.

"It's a tragedy that you had to find such a scene." I paused to respect Leah's trauma but didn't want to lose the focused momentum of her disclosure. "But you didn't recognize the man as Dr. Hostetler at first?"

"No," she said softly. "Other than realizing that it was an actual person and not a prank, I did not recognize any familiar features. It didn't even register that the man was in Amish clothing at first. I was so shocked . . ."

I leaned toward her. "Leah, you must listen to what I'm about to say. You are not responsible for Simon Hostetler's death. Even if someone overheard your appointment with him and decided to show up before you arrived, it is not your fault." It seemed important to alleviate the young artist's guilt since her father would likely discipline her for the clandestine appointment.

Sheriff Claiborne could keep his silence no longer. "Miss, we'll want you to walk us back out to the crime scene tomorrow. We'll take the same route you took today and write down everything that you might remember as we go. I know it will be hard, but something you saw or heard may be able to help us find out what happened to the victim."

Leah nodded silently.

Her father boomed, "I will not have my daughter subjected to the horror of violence that has already shocked her so today. She had nothing to do with this man's death and knows nothing further to help any of you."

The other Amish men began talking quietly among themselves. Dan and Sam exchanged stoic glances.

Bishop Zook finally turned to the rest of us, as if to explain that a group consensus had just been reached among the competing voices.

"We value human life as a precious gift from God," he said. "We do not believe in violence as a means to resolve conflict. For this reason we do not participate in the military draft. Our community has been here for over eighty years and we have had no murders during that time. What sins have been committed have been handled by our church in accordance with God's Word. We take care of our own. This discovery is an unwelcome intrusion into our peaceful community. Since Simon Hostetler was an outsider, we believe therefore that an outsider must be responsible for his death."

"You must realize, however," countered the sheriff in the same measured tone, "that this was not a random incident or an accident. It was murder. Hostetler grew up here and had ties to some people still living here, his sister's family included. And even if the murderer was an outsider, your people may still be in danger. Since Hostetler was dressed in Amish garb, it may have even been a hate crime against your community. Someone could've spotted the victim, assumed he was Amish because of the way he was dressed, and killed him to make a statement. Do y'all have many enemies outside the community?"

Bishop Zook quickly returned the volley. "No, we do not have enemies. Neither inside nor outside of our community. As I have explained, we are a peace-loving people."

I did not watch the religious leader as he

spoke but instead caught an ominous exchange of dark glances among the older Amish men. One in particular, the wizard, looked as if about to speak, but then did not.

I recalled something one of my own deacons, Jack Taylor, had told me some months back. He'd heard down at the Mumford Co-op, where natives exchanged stock prices and local gossip, that Riley Peterman had been trying for years to buy up some Amish farmland that bordered his own thousand acres. Jack said that some new farmer had also been pressuring the Amish to sell some land. There was even talk that the Carroll County Industrial Recruitment Council was negotiating with Nissan about locating a plant in the area if they could find a suitable site. Once again, the unincorporated farmland of Tremont was coveted for its central location and access to the Jackson River.

Of course, there was the trouble back in the sixties when the Department of Defense forced the Tremont Amish to sell their western parcel of land for the expansion of Dolby Air Force Base. I remembered seeing Amish protesters praying and fasting on the site. The Amish were finally forced to sell off several thousand acres to the government. While they are a forgiving people, we all have our human limitations.

No, it seemed to me that the good Amish folk of Tremont might have quite a few enemies — at least perceived enemies. Despite their best attempts to remain peace-loving, could they actually hope to escape the clash of faith and contemporary culture? One of the Proverbs sprang to mind, reminding me that it was possible. "When a man's ways please the LORD, he makes even his enemies to be at peace with him." Then I wondered, *Do these people's ways please the Lord? Do their ways please Him more than the way my congregation lives for and worships Him?* It's a question I've held for some time, an issue I had hoped to discuss with Simon leisurely, over coffee in my study some lazy afternoon. Perhaps each faith community thinks it's pleasing the Lord more favorably than all the others. Such is the pride of humans.

During my chain of thoughts, a slow movement began as the elders stood and stroked their beards. For now it was clear that the leaders of this community wanted us to perceive that they had no enemies. I would take up the discussion with Dan and Sam, perhaps, at the next opportunity. In the meantime, all in attendance seem to agree that tonight's interrogation had ended. I could tell it was going to be a continual battle with Bishop Zook and the elders. As Peter and Leah cleared the table of cups and saucers, the wizard-looking elder approached me.

"May I speak to you, Brother Reed?" asked the man. Up close his eyes were much younger than his white beard and balding head indicated. I allowed him to guide me through the small throng of men toward the front door. He led me to the end of the porch and leaned in carefully toward my right ear. His shirt smelled of the sun and wind absorbed from a clothesline, his breath of coffee.

"I am Joseph Yoder, and I know I speak for my bishop as well as the other elders in thanking you for coming. And it is out of the same mutual respect for your faith in our God that I ask a tremendous favor from you." I tried to find his eyes, but they were shadowed by his furrowed brows like storm clouds hiding twin moons.

Peter and Leah's relationship came to mind, and I wondered if somehow my curate's involvement with her was viewed suspiciously as the cause of the outsider troubles.

"Yes, please ask. I will do what I can."

"Please, you must convince your friend the sheriff to close his investigation as quickly as possible. There are too many . . . He does not realize how difficult it is for us to have something like this happen in our community. May we count on you to assist in expediting this matter?"

There are too many what, I wondered. *Too many secrets? Too many complications?* I inhaled deeply to consider what he was actually asking and why I felt uneasy. A moist breeze ruffled my loose shirt cuff. Looking upward and away, beyond the silhouette of the wooded tree line plump with spring foliage, I marveled at the expanse of stars prickling the sky above. It was only a feeling, but if I didn't know better I would think there was something the elders of Tremont wanted to hide.

"So what did you tell him?" Peter asked as we turned my car onto the two-lane state highway that would take us up Eaglehead Mountain and back to Avenell. Dan had returned with the sheriff and promised to call first thing in the morning.

"I told him that solving this crime quickly was something that 'my friend the sheriff' desired just as much as they did. I said of course I'd do whatever I could to help. Mr. Yoder seemed frustrated then, almost scoffing under his breath as if I had missed the true message he was sending."

"Which was?"

"I don't know, Pete. Something to do with the 'too many' statement he left unfinished. Based on my gut response, I think he wanted me — all of us — to stay away."

"Do you think there's really something to hide? Or do the Amish just resent any kind of intrusion?" my curate asked.

"They certainly seem to resent any kind of government intrusion. That's why they don't participate in the military draft, social security, or use public utilities. They prefer community dependence. They may have nothing to hide at all. But somehow I don't have a good feeling about all this."

I shared my recollection about the forced land sale to Dolby Air Force Base and the recent rumors about encroachment and buyouts.

"Maybe it's not as easy being Amish as I thought it was," mused Pete. We navigated the twisting highway through the dark, chilled night. It was after eleven.

"Don't you have a friend down there? Someone your wife knew? You mentioned her to Leah a few weeks ago when we were discussing the Spring Arts and Crafts Festival," said Peter.

"Yes. Mary Lapp. Since Tremont is so

close, Amy sought her out after reading an article about her quilt patterns in a sewing magazine. They struck up a unique friendship that lasted until Amy's death. Mary became a kind of grandmother to my wife, a spiritual mentor."

"Have you stayed in touch with her?" he asked.

"Not like I want to," I explained. "We exchange Christmas cards and notes. She sends me apple butter and chow-chow on my birthday. She also invites Bea and me to the annual quilt show. . . ."

"It might be a good thing to have an ally in Tremont. That is, if you're going to assist with the investigation," qualified Peter, aware of my misgivings.

"No, I wouldn't use that term. I was willing to come down tonight because Sam asked me. And because Simon was my friend. But I'm no detective, Peter. I'll gladly pray for Sheriff Claiborne, for Dan, for Simon's sister and friends, for the killer and his family. But I'm not so sure there's anything else I can do."

We wound up the final corkscrew curve toward the outskirts of the university town of Avenell. Brackish light from streetlamps and a roadside tavern flitted through the canopy of spring-grown branches.

"But if there were something for you to do, you'd do it, right?" A note of personal urgency heightened my curate's rhetorical question.

"I suppose so, Peter. Why do you ask?"

He let out a sigh, a long extended breath like that of a sleepy child. "The look in Leah's eyes when I picked her up this afternoon, the way she described the man's body dangling from that old oak tree . . . She said it was perhaps the first time in her life that she realized what *evil* felt like."

Peter's face looked strained in the passing glow of another car's headlights, his tone uncharacteristically ominous.

Chapter Three

The Legacy of Judas

Friday morning, after a brisk four-mile run around the outskirts of campus, I filled my coffee mug and retreated to my study. I skimmed through the Carroll County *Clarion*'s account of Simon Hostetler's death. No mention of the hanging, no details to even imply murder, only that a young Amish woman in the quiet community of Tremont had discovered the dead body of Dr. Simon Hostetler, age fifty-two, in a clearing not far from her family's farmhouse. The body was "reportedly in close proximity to the legendary Judas Tree, an ancient oak that has figured centrally in other regional and historical tragedies."

Two additional articles covered my friend's demise. The first was taken from the AP wire service and was written by a reporter from the *Philadelphia Free Press*. It surveyed Simon's illustrious career, including his five academic degrees, numerous articles, and four books.

Another sidebar column by Sheldon Bly,

51

our county librarian and self-appointed historian, described the incidents that had caused the old tree to grow into a local legend.

LEGACY OF JUDAS

Judas Iscariot, the disciple who betrayed Christ for thirty pieces of silver, has left a legacy of betrayal, murder, and the supernatural right here in Carroll County. Just as Jesus left Christians with the cross as a reminder of His sacrifice, Judas also left us with a tree of remembrance.

Outside the county seat of Mumford near the Amish community of Tremont stands a stately oak. The proud tree must be at least two hundred years old, with thick branches that hide as many secrets as winter acorns for the squirrels. As a boy I listened to stories from my friends about how the tree was haunted, and I heard tales from my father and grandfather explaining the basis of such superstition.

According to legend, during the War Between the States the oak tree marked the boundary between two brothers' farms. One had slaves and the other did not. Both signed on for the Confederate

Cavalry and were stationed in the area. The slaveowner rose to become leader of a battalion while his brother remained a private in the same company. They were part of General Bragg's outfit sent to counterattack Rosecrans' siege of Chattanooga.

The brother who didn't believe in owning slaves, the humble private, turned out to be a Union spy. The night before the battle at Chickamauga, he appropriated a Confederate map with defense positions and managed to deliver it to his Union contact back near his own home. Supposedly the vital information was exchanged around midnight at the big old oak marking the property line between the two brothers' land.

The information came too late for Rosecrans' Army of the Cumberlands, and the Union suffered a major setback in two days of some of the bloodiest fighting of the war. However, during the battle the Confederate commander brother was killed in the fighting. His younger brother, whose betrayal now seemed in vain, was so overcome by guilt that he wrote out a confession to his newly widowed sister-in-law and then hung himself from the stately oak tree that had been his rendezvous only days before. Thus, the beautiful tree became associated with the tragedy of wartime betrayal, hence the nickname "Judas Tree."

Historical records offer some reinforcement for the tale. Records for Carroll County, Tennessee, in 1860 include the property deeds for two large farms, Twin Oaks and Shady Valley, to two men sharing the same last name, Josiah and Robert Wallace. Confederate infantry records list both men's names in the same company, the 27th Confederate Cavalry, from 1861–1863. Records indicate that Captain Josiah Wallace died in battle on September 20, 1863, at the age of 33, and that his brother, Private Robert Wallace, 31, died of self-injury three days later.

Nonetheless, the incident might have become another sad footnote to a terrible war and the tree might have recovered its dignity except for another incident that happened during the 1930s. Virgil M. Caulfield, a black man visiting from Montgomery, Alabama, was accused of raping and killing a white woman in the woods near the Judas Tree. Caulfield was apprehended, arrested for suspicion of assault and murder, and held in jail awaiting trial.

Several weeks later, he overpowered a guard and managed to escape. A county-wide manhunt turned up nothing and was called off after several fruitless weeks. It was suspected that he made it to Chicago and the safe obscurity of his many relatives there.

However, one year to the day after the white woman's murder, Virgil Caulfield's body was found hanging from the Judas Tree. It was ruled a suicide, although some evidence suggested otherwise.

Ever since, of course, schoolkids have claimed to hear Robert Wallace sobbing in remorse on moonlit nights at the Judas Tree. On Halloween, tricksters still like to rig up a dummy in Confederate dress to scare their friends and enemies.

Unfortunately, during the fifties and sixties, the Judas Tree became a popular meeting spot for local KKK activists. In the past few decades, campers and hikers have reported mysterious sounds and sightings near the old oak.

And now the tree has witnessed another victim. The details have not been released on the death of Dr. Simon Hostetler, 52, a Penn State cultural anthropologist who grew up in the Carroll County valley. Will his death prove to be as mysterious as his tragic predecessors? Does Robert Wallace's ghost haunt the tree? Was Virgil Caulfield punished by fate? Only the two-centuries' old massive oak known as the Judas Tree knows.

The legacy of Judas lives on.

Even our small-town newspaper had succumbed to tabloid sensationalism. It sounded just like something Sheldon Bly relished, a lot of antebellum moonlight-and-magnolias ghost stories with a dash of racial hate crime thrown in for good measure. Although nothing factually reported in the other accounts indicated foul play, it was clear that Sheldon was implying, and morbidly enough even hoping, for more fuel for the legend. Next thing I knew, he would be giving guided tours and serving mint juleps.

Sure, I had heard the stories, too. One couldn't grow up in a place like our county and not hear them. I'd driven out to Chigger Ridge Road and hiked to the Judas Tree as a teenager many times, scaring friends, telling ghost stories, toasting marshmallows around a campfire in the clearing beneath the tree. Once my brother, Tupper, and I took our double dates out there and pre-arranged for a friend of Tupper's, Quinton Sharp, to climb the Judas Tree and wait until we were all gathered beneath telling ghost stories. During Tupper's slow, exaggerated narrative recounting the betrayal of Robert Wallace, Quinton slowly lowered a homemade dummy left over from the homecoming parade from a noose. At the climax of the story, Tupper shouted, "And there he hangs!" just as the girls turned to see the form swaying from a long, almost horizontal arm of the tree. Judy Bishop and Tara Suddarth never did forgive us. I wondered if they ever thought of that incident. What became of Tara anyway?

My mind wandered around the local storehouse of memories, trying to catch up to the present. I couldn't recall the last time I'd been out to the Judas Tree. It had to have been over ten years at least. I seemed to recall taking a youth group down there back in the mid '80s.

A sharp, solid knock on the door was followed by the appearance of my sister, Beatrice.

"Grif? What's all this about you going down to Tremont last night? Is Leah all right? Did something else happen? And do you have this morning's paper?" Although still clad in her thick, fleecy robe, Bea looked alert and ready to face the day. Her long, braided hair cast a girlish aura that softened her silver-gray hair and sixty-plus features. Impatient with my uncertainty over which question to tackle first, she began to unbraid one long, silver cord. "Well?" she said.

"Good morning to you, too," I laughed. "I think 'yes' answers all your questions."

"Griffin Reed, honestly. Are you going to make me pull it out of you? So what happened in Tremont last night? Do we know who killed poor Simon?"

I folded the paper and handed it to her, seating myself on the corner of my desk.

"Sam Claiborne thought I might be able to help question the Amish elders about Simon Hostetler's death. For the most part, they were just as reluctant with me. The only new disclosure . . ." I hesitated. "And you really must keep this confidential, Bea. I wouldn't even tell you if it didn't involve Peter and Leah." My sister's eyes grew bigger as she unwound her other braid.

I summarized Leah's outburst and tearful confession, as well as her father's response.

"Poor dear," purred Bea. "I won't breathe a word of it, Grif."

Despite her propensity to indulge in gossip with her many friends in the Ladies' Auxiliary, I knew she would keep her word.

"So what now? Will you continue to assist

in the investigation?" she asked.

"I am *not* assisting with the investigation. Honestly, you and Peter think I don't have a full-time job already. I don't really see what else I can do."

A wide smile bridged the flowing tresses on either side of my sister's face.

"I see that gleam in your eye, sis. I know what you're thinking — that I warn you not to play amateur detective while I go out and do just that."

"That wasn't what I was thinking. What occurred to me was that I forgot to tell you that Joan Dowinger called last night and said that she'd be dropping by this morning about nine. Caroline called as well and said she'd talk to you this morning. I told her about Simon — she was so worried about you. She's such a gem."

"Yes, she is," I said absently. Mrs. Dowinger and Professor Barr, the two ends of the female spectrum. A wicked thought, but not without some accuracy. I smiled to myself and looked at the clock — just enough time to shower and dress. "What do you suppose Joan wants now? Did she say?" I asked.

"No, only that it's a personal matter. You know Joan. Since the restoration's coming to a close, she has to find something else to spend her time and money on."

Mrs. Dowinger had insisted last fall on a complete renovation of our neo-Gothic parish and campus church, the Cathedral of the Divine. We compromised and in January undertook a restoration — a complete and thorough cleaning along with a return to the church's original beauty. We had hoped the project would be completed in time for Easter, but it looked like at least May now before the new pew cushions and Italian marble replacement tiles would be in.

"Have you eaten yet? I've got muffins in the oven." My sister pulled back her long silver mane and retreated toward the door.

"Save the muffins for when Joan arrives — I'll have one then. And please call Janine at the office and tell her I won't be in until around ten."

Joan Dowinger was her usual punctual self. Her white Cadillac pulled up in our drive like a royal carriage and she rang the rectory doorbell at nine on the dot. If her attire was an indicator, Joan clearly had spring fever — lavender jacket and skirt with a fuschia blouse and an amethyst brooch featuring a Tennessee iris, our state flower. Bea welcomed her in, offering her hot tea and a muffin. She accepted the former, declined the latter, and requested to speak to me alone.

Bea restrained her curiosity and excused herself while Joan and I seated ourselves in my office in the tartan wingbacks that faced the view of Eaglehead Mountain's eastern slope.

"Griffin, so good of you to see me on such short notice," the wealthy widow began. "What I've come to discuss has been on my mind for some time. I've struggled to know the best way to put this. . . ." She sipped elegantly from my sister's best china teacup.

"Go ahead, Joan. You know you can speak candidly with me." I couldn't imagine her being at a loss for words or courage.

"Yes, I know. It's only that this . . . well . . . it's a personal matter. In fact, it's one of *your* personal matters. You see, I'm a bit concerned about your relationship with Dr. Barr, and I know others in the parish share my concerns."

"Concerns?" I echoed. My voice remained calm with some effort. "What concerns would those be, Joan? Dr. Barr and I are casual friends, I've made no secret of that. Nor have I made a pretense that there's anything more there."

Joan lowered her teacup and looked me in the eye. "Griffin, I know how lonely and bereft you must feel after losing that dear wife of yours. And I, along with everyone who loves you, want you to be happy. Dr. Barr is a very attractive *young* woman. The two of you seem to be together a great deal of the time — attending ball games, parish potlucks, faculty luncheons. I'm sure she's a very fine person."

I was growing impatient. "So what's the problem, Joan? I'm not allowed to have friends of the opposite sex?"

"Now, Griffin, please — hear me out. Of course you can choose your own friends. It's only that . . . well, some of us question whether it's prudent for you to date a non-believer."

I restrained my anger with every fiber in my being. But instead of counting to ten, I recited a silent prayer: *O God, you have bound us together in a common life. Help us, in the midst of our struggles for justice and truth, to confront one another without hatred or bitterness and to work together with mutual forbearance and respect; through Jesus Christ our Lord. Amen.* It was the best I could do under the circumstances, but I'm not sure that any of the words registered with *me* at that moment.

"Joan, you astound me! I'm not sure you are qualified to assess Caroline Barr's spiritual condition at this moment. Nor she, yours, for that matter. Our Lord is very clear in His Word that we are not to judge —"

"And just as clear that we are not to be unequally yoked," she countered. "Griffin, I did some checking, and while Dr. Barr's professional credentials are impeccable, she has never been a member of any registered church."

I laughed. "You did some *checking?* What does that mean? Did you hire some service to cross-reference Caroline's name against national church records? Joan, if you have that much time on your hands, we must get you more involved in the Foreign Missions Committee or the Deacons' Fund or something besides other people's business."

"Griffin, I'm only thinking of your best interests. And those of the parish, of course. Have you tried to share your faith with her? Have the two of you talked about why she's not a believer?" She twirled her amethyst brooch as if it were a magic amulet empowering her spell.

I ignored her question. The surreal quality of the conversation transcended my imagination. I paused to control my temper and produce some kind of response I would not later regret. The silent moment grew awkward as I turned my focus beyond my window.

Outside a lovely spring morning blossomed into a lush green, sunlit day. Pink dogwoods bloomed in the narrow stretch of lawn between the rectory yard and the mountain woods. They were a bit early this year; I'm sure Bea had noticed.

At length I decided that Joan's interest was really rather touching in that intrusive, invasive way of hers.

"Joan, on one hand I'm moved that you care enough about my happiness to go to so much trouble. On the other hand, I'm terribly angry at you for invading my privacy and that of Dr. Barr. I appreciate your gumption in coming here, and I will keep in mind what you have shared. But you must remember this: My relationship with Dr. Barr is not a matter of church business to be scrutinized like next year's budget."

Joan's expression now bordered on indignation. I rose, extended my hand formally, and escorted the tight-lipped woman out of my home.

At the front door she turned and unpursed her mouth into a tight smile. "Griffin, simply think about why you're so upset with me at this moment. Could it be that I'm willing to face something you are not?"

"Thanks for your concern, Joan," I replied and shut the door firmly. She descended the handful of porch steps to the sidewalk awkwardly — a sure sign her arthritis was acting up — down to her regal automobile. I suddenly pitied her and wondered if I'd been too harsh in my rebuke.

"Trouble in our parish paradise?" asked Bea entering the room in her work clothes. "Or simply more restoration plans?"

I sat on the navy camel-backed sofa. As stoically as possible, I recounted the entire conversation. My sister hung her dust cloth across a dining room chair and hurried over.

"Oh, Grif, I'm so sorry. You know how Joan is, though. She has nothing to do but shop and pry into other people's business. Don't let this inhibit your friendship with Caroline. I only hear good things from others in the parish. Just last week Roberta said that she's as pleased as punch that you and Dr. Barr have become friends."

I looked up at my sister's comforting hazel eyes. She placed her hands on my shoulder.

"You remember when I first wrote to you about Amy, about what she was like and what I enjoyed about her? Did I ever mention whether she was a Christian or not? Or did you automatically assume she was because I was seeing her?" Despite my annoyance, Joan's ultimate question haunted me.

"I don't recall that ever being an issue, Grif. I can't remember thinking, 'Hmm, wonder if Amy is another of Grif's wild, pagan women?' " We both smiled as she continued. "I guess I did assume that she was a Christian, that she had some level of faith, or you wouldn't be attracted to her in the first place." Bea stood, retrieved her dust cloth, and began polishing the oval coffee table before us. She added casually, "I suppose I assume the same thing about Caroline."

"Amy was certainly a beautiful, intelligent woman, and Caroline, too. Maybe I'm just —"

"Yes, but so much of their beauty emanates from inside. I've been pointing out attractive women to you for the past two years. Caroline's the first one you've ever paid a moment's notice since dear Amy. . . ." My sister vigorously massaged the antique table, releasing the luster of dark-stained wood.

"Grif, other than the fact the she's an enormous busybody with the chutzpah of Jacob, why has Joan upset you so? Are you still feeling guilty about caring for another woman?" The walnut table now gleamed before us like a miniature pond, morning sunlight reflecting off my sister's waxy strokes.

"No," I said finally. "Maybe I'm so upset because I share some of the same concerns about Caroline's faith."

Over at the church office Janine McCaffrey, my parish administrative assistant, was stuffing Sunday bulletins with flyers about our ongoing Lenten services and the approach of Holy Week, less than a month away. Peter was sitting at the small desk in the back corner of the basement office, pecking away on a computer keyboard.

While I maintained a large oak desk on the other side of the partition from Janine, I was fortunate that most of my work could be done from the rectory. Most of my biblical references and theological texts were in my study at home. The occasional counselees or pastoral visitors I saw were usually more comfortable in my study as well. The office here was more for the nuts and bolts of administration and official parish business.

Janine, a single mother with a young son, had come to us over two years ago and had quickly demonstrated her remarkable efficiency. Between her trustworthy capabilities and a host of parish volunteers, my time was considerably freed up for personal study and relational ministry. I was very blessed.

"Good morning, Father Grif. Here are

your phone messages — one's from Dan Warren. He just missed you. You have the PAC luncheon at the Pepper Tree at noon. This afternoon you . . . are you all right? You look upset." She smoothed a blond coil of hair behind her ear and looked like an inquisitive schoolgirl with her round wire-rimmed glasses and porcelain face.

"I'm fine, Janine, thank you. Just a bit preoccupied. I forgot all about that PAC meeting today! I'm glad you reminded me. What would I do without you?"

My assistant smiled demurely and resumed her engagement with the computer document on the screen.

The Pastors of Avenell Community, or PAC, as we all called it, was scheduled to plan the community-wide Easter service today. It would be a long meeting, atypical of our once-a-month fellowship and prayer time.

I shuffled through the handful of pink phone messages, noted one from my dear friend John Greenwood, a Baptist chaplain for one of the state penitentiaries, but placed Dan's on top.

At my desk I glanced at the wall clock. It was only ten-thirty but the mail had already been delivered. Newsletters from other parishes, a couple of magazines, the new *Semi-*

narian, a stiff, formal-looking envelope addressed to Avenell Parishioners in care of me, and a catalog of vestments and icons. I looked back toward Peter and called out a greeting. He nodded and said, "Hi, Grif," and continued with his work, likely a Next Generation youth group bulletin. I wanted to inquire about Leah but guessed that he had not communicated with her since last night; the Amish resistance to telephones could be both a blessing and a curse.

I opened the mail to find that the heavy parchment envelope yielded an engraved invitation: *The Parish of St. Anthony's Episcopal Church, Mumford, Tennessee, cordially invites you to a reception honoring the retirement of our beloved rector, the Right Reverend Philip Jackson.* So Philip was finally taking the plunge. Another inevitability I'd been dreading for some time.

Wondering how my old friend would occupy his time, I dialed the sheriff's office and Maria Alvarez put me through to Dan Warren.

"See the morning paper?" he asked after we had exchanged pleasantries.

"You mean the article about Hostetler's death and all the mythic legend nonsense from Sheldon Bly? Yes, I saw it. I'm guessing that won't help your case any. It only feeds the public's morbid curiosity and creates an appetite for more details," I replied. "And maybe attracts visitors to the site. Nothing a group of fraternity boys likes better than an old haunted tree."

"Yep. Sam wasn't too pleased . . . of course, nothing he can do to stop Sheldon from reporting ancient history. We may not be frat boys, but are you up for a visit to the crime scene? The sheriff asked me to take a state forensic agent and accompany Leah back out to the murder site. I thought you and Peter might tag along to make her feel more comfortable."

"Are you sure we wouldn't just be in the way? Did you ask Sam about this?" I glanced over at Janine's inquisitive eyes.

"He thought it was a great idea. The Amish seem to trust you more than us, and if this is a religious hate crime, Sam thinks your input could be valuable. Of course, if you're too busy, I understand."

I thought a moment. "What time? I've got a lunch meeting here shortly. I thought you would've already been down there by now." My curate stopped his typing and instinctively cocked his head my direction.

"Yeah, Sam wanted us down there first thing this morning, but the state agent, John Corey, couldn't get here — had to testify in

Nashville. If he finishes his testimony by the time the trial adjourns for lunch, Corey hopes to be here by three. If Corey doesn't make it down today, Sam still wants Leah to walk us through it before too much time passes. I'd take Corey down tomorrow then. He's one of the best."

I thumbed through the phone messages once more and glanced at the desk calendar. "Let me talk to Peter, but count on us for now."

"I'll pick you up around three in front of the Divine unless I hear otherwise."

Before I could replace the phone on the receiver, my curate hurried over, his blond hair in its usual disheveled state. "Count on us for what? Was that Sheriff Claiborne?"

"It was Dan. He asked if you and I would help take Leah back out to the Judas Tree."

My young friend's eyes sparked interest.

"A state forensic specialist is coming down as well," I added.

"Count me in. Do they know any more about Simon's death?" he asked.

"Didn't say. I guess we'll find out this afternoon. Dan's picking us up here at three."

"Perfect. I have to run now, but I'll see you then." He took a step back to his desk and then did a double take. "You okay? You look tired."

I chuckled to myself. This from the man who could coast on three hours sleep and still look like a teenager.

Without explaining the entire exchange, I lowered my voice and summarized my run-in with Joan Dowinger. I promised to fill him in more on the way down to Tremont. He sighed deeply and shook his head.

"Surely you're not taking her seriously, Grif. You should have expected something like this from her. Take it with a grain of salt," he called over his shoulder. "See you at three."

Oh, to have his energy again, I thought to myself. This day was not shaping up the way I'd hoped. The retirement party invitation caught my eye again. Something else that I'd been dreading would now come to its climax. My winsome curate, though young and headstrong, was the logical first choice for the rector's position down in Mumford. If Bishop Wilder did not offer it to him, both Peter and I would be disappointed. Still, I was old enough to admit that I did not like change. The idea of training and interacting with a new curate, likely fresh out of seminary, did not hearten me. Most of all, I would miss the daily interactions with a man who had become like a son to me. Selfish, I knew, but it's where I was that day.

It was not the idea of change that bothered me nearly as much as the prospect of loss. Even though Peter would only be a short distance away, his departure would mark the end of a sweet season. I would never totally reconcile myself to loss. Simon's death reminded me once again of the fragile bonds to others that we could not live without, but which always carried a price. The betrayal of mortality and memory. I recalled Sheldon Bly's article from this morning's paper. Yes, the legacy of Judas indeed lived on . . . an inheritance of betraying those we loved most for fear of them leaving us behind.

Chapter Four

Body and Blood

Slumping in my swivel office chair, I'm not sure how long I sat there ruminating in what amounted to self-pity. My brother, Tupper. My parents. Amy. Perhaps that's why the death of people I knew became so much harder the older I got. A present death triggered a domino effect of grief, compounding all the losses of a lifetime.

And I knew that this same issue lingered within my other impending concern: my relationship with Caroline. My conversation with Joan this morning only reinforced my growing apprehension, not just about the status of Caroline Barr's faith, but about the future of our friendship. I had meant what I said to Joan; Caroline and I really were just friends. We had not crossed the relational pivot that leads to romantic pursuit. Still, I was very fond of her. . . .

In the fall when we were first becoming better acquainted, Caroline had shared about her very trying ordeal with her former mentor, who had once plagiarized one of her plays. This man's betrayal led Caroline to embark on a journey of facing her fears and reinventing herself. As she described this transition period to me, she had once mentioned "finding her faith," but I had not pursued it. More than a few times she had acknowledged that she didn't consider herself the "praying type" and that she had grown up in an agnostic family that did not attend church services regularly. Her attendance at the Divine had gone from sporadic to regular in the last few months as we'd gotten better acquainted. But she was up front about the reasons she came: She wanted to hear me teach and to plug in to the campus community.

We had so much in common — a love of literature and plays, the outdoors, running, campus life here in Avenell — that we never struggled to make conversation. Consequently, I had not actively pursued personal theology or inquired about her regard for Christ. Of course, I knew that the closer we became, the more difficult it might become for me to risk topics that might divide us. Honestly, I didn't doubt for a moment that she had a faith, but I resisted applying any pressure on her to change for my sake or to conform her spiritual beliefs to my particular denomination's.

Obviously she had to be at least sympathetic to the Christian faith to have agreed to come to Avenell in the first place. And as I shared my day-to-day routines and problems, she certainly heard plenty about my faith. I was a parish priest, after all. The topic was unavoidable.

I could put it off no longer; I would try to talk with her as soon as possible. Perhaps the Lord was using Joan as a catalyst despite the old widow's intrusive style.

I dialed the English department and the department secretary connected me to Caroline's office extension. Her voice mail picked up on the fourth ring and I left a brief message, suggesting that we have dinner together over the weekend.

I hung up and quickly sifted through my sheaf of phone messages. The day was getting away from me as I sat here mired in my morbid ruminations. Briskly dialing the Rockmont State Penitentiary, I felt lighter when John Greenwood's voice greeted my ears.

"Grif, so good to hear your voice. How are you?" he asked.

"Oh, just okay I guess today. A few glitches here and there. My schedule's picking up with Easter just a few weeks away," I replied. "Plus, I lost an old friend this week. Just yesterday, in fact — Simon Hostetler."

"The author of those books about different religious cultures? Why, I read his *Baptists in the South* book and thought he did a fine job of objectively capturing our strengths and weaknesses. I didn't know you knew him — I'm sorry."

I quickly summarized the prior day's proceedings.

He inquired about Peter and Leah's situation and how the Amish were responding to the tragedy before saying, "I wanted to let you know that I'm going to be down your way next week. There's a state chaplains' seminar in Chattanooga next Wednesday, and I wondered if maybe I could stay with you for a night or two. I know I'll still be commuting about an hour, but your company and Miss Bea's food beat out Motel 6 every time!"

"Of course," I replied, delighted at the prospect of being with one of my closest friends. John had helped me grieve my wife's death, and he kept me spiritually focused with his compassionate heart and wise ways.

We exchanged the details of his arrival and were about to wind up when John added, "I have something important I want to share with you while I'm there." Before I could ask him to explain, he said good-bye and hung up. Just what I needed, another mystery in my life.

I called to inform Bea, knowing that she would be just as delighted as I was. My sister had always seemed to have a secret crush on John, at least from my observation. She had never admitted to it, of course. Without playing matchmaker, I suppose that I, too, hoped that the two of them might find each other. Of course, now that Lyle Slater was in her life . . . I left her a message on the machine out of fear that I might forget to mention John's visit until the day he arrived. My memory had indeed changed since I turned fifty last year.

As I completed my calls and attempted to write a memo to Bishop Wilder regarding the summer missions trip to Mexico, Janine interrupted with letters for my approval and signature and questions about upcoming events. Before I knew it, it was almost noon and time for the PAC meeting just a few blocks away at Avenell's finest eatery, the Pepper Tree.

As I strolled down the campus sidewalk toward the cluster of small businesses and eateries we called town, the spring warmth cheered me along with the anticipation of good food and fellowship. There was something comforting, as well, about the predictable entrees and order of the meeting. Served in the private conference room, lunch would be buffet style with chicken and dumplings, meatloaf, and vegetarian lasagna. There would be a green salad, a wonderful chocolate dessert, iced tea, and a prayer from the PAC's oldest member, Pastor Billy Ray Compton of the Avenell First Baptist Church. Only today instead of the usual short devotional, a report on the monthly community prayer service, and personal prayer requests, we would submerge into the details of planning the traditional Easter sunrise service for the community of Avenell.

Last year was the Methodists' turn to host the service, and Brother Paul Parton had surprised us all with an unusually fine sermon and a contemporary drama from his youth group. The Free Will Baptist choir sang, the children of St. Mary's Catholic Church handed out Easter eggs with Bible verses inside, and I delivered the benediction. All in all a fine ecumenical service.

The members of Avenell First Christian Church, a nondenominational Bible congregation, seemed a little rankled not to have participated directly but were assuaged by the fact that they were hosting this year. In fact, as new senior pastor, Lyle Slater would be directly in charge of the planning. I was as curious to hear his plan for this year's service as I was to discover more about the kind of man to whom my sister was attracted.

The Reverend Lyle Slater had moved to Avenell from Virginia, where he pastored a similar church of size and stature. In his late fifties, he looked quite fit with his trim, athletic build and full, polished-silver hair. His anchor-man good looks and widower status had made quite a few ladies' heads turn in town. So it was a bit of a surprise when Slater asked my sister out back in February. It's not that Beatrice is not an attractive woman, but there were younger women who had set their sights on Rev. Slater.

He met my sister at a PAC-sponsored Valentine's social and asked her out shortly thereafter. They saw a movie and had dinner down at the Corner House in Harpertown. Bea had preened and primped like a peacock who'd forgotten she had feathers — quite a boost to her spinster self-image. They continued an amicable friendship, occasionally visiting each other's churches and their respective social events and fellowship suppers. I was happy for Bea, although honestly a little concerned about whether she might get hurt before it was all over.

Part of my concern was produced by the situation and part by the man himself. The new pastor seemed a little too polished, too perfect, too *something*. Today Lyle Slater looked as suave as an incumbent politician in his navy suit and red tie. He really was not classically handsome, but the combination of his swarthy complexion, large nose, prominent chin, and frequent smile were pleasing nonetheless. His voice boomed with the effluence of a radio announcer who never seemed at a loss for words. He was immediately popular with his congregation and the community at large. Although I'd told no one, certainly not my sister, my verdict was still not out on him and whether he would fit into our community. Something about Slater I still did not trust . . .

Lunch was predictably delicious and almost all twenty PAC members were in attendance. I sat next to Dr. Harry Snell, the founder and director of the Avenell Seminary counseling program. Once a popular Christian author and practicing psychologist, Dr. Snell was now in the twilight years of his career. He had an indomitable manner and enunciated every word carefully, like many professors do, as if no one else had ever put such a combination of words together. Although he was not officially a pastor in the community, he was included, like other para-church ministers on campus, in an attempt to facilitate true community here in Avenell. Today Harry was complaining about the lack of mentors in the modern church, the subject of his new book.

Other friends from the community chimed in with their perspectives, and soon it was time for the agenda at hand. Lyle Slater rose to the small podium at the head table and opened in a rather formal prayer. He then proceeded to share his outline of this year's service, including an outdoor sunrise vigil in the clearing between his church and the old Confederate Cemetery, worship service inside, and Easter egg hunt for the children that afternoon. Finally, it was time for questions and volunteering for contributions to the service.

I offered Peter and his Next Generation group of teens and college students to perform a drama. The Baptist choir — Southern, not Free Will — would provide selections from its Easter cantata, and on and on. Slim Graham from Campus Crusade volunteered to lead the traditional

Communion part of the service when the most extraordinary thing happened. It was almost two-thirty and we were growing restless. As the meeting was winding down, Slim said to Lyle Slater, "Of course, we will not be using white grape juice like you usually do at First Church."

The room went silent. Lyle looked puzzled, the eloquent orator suddenly without a response. Ironically, Slim seemed more embarrassed than Lyle.

"At least that's what one of the students mentioned when I told them I planned to volunteer to lead the Communion," Slim added quickly. "I thought she was joking, but then she went on to explain that First Church had just gotten new carpet and that the elders voted to switch to white juice to keep it new-looking. Is that true, or was my student pulling my leg?"

You would have thought that Slim had just exposed First Church for drug smuggling the way we held our collective breath. Lyle Slater regained some of his composure and adjusted the microphone to his lips. The mic was not needed for volume, but Billy Ray Compton's brother-in-law donated it to us — he owned the local Radio Shack over in Lewiston — so we felt obligated to use it.

"Yes, that's correct," Slater said. "Right before I accepted the call from First Church, new carpet was installed. Since it's cream-colored, one of the elders proposed that we could preserve it longer if we didn't have to risk so many stains from the red grape juice at Communion. The other elders, along with myself, approved the motion and we've been using white grape juice. It's cut our cleaning bill in half." Once more he seemed the smooth politician, this time fielding the slanderous reporter's accusatory question. "However, if you feel adamant about using red for Easter —"

"You mean to tell me that y'all use white grape juice for Communion so that you can preserve your *carpets?*" boomed Harry Snell.

Father O'Shaughnessy from St. Mary's chimed in, "Grape juice — rather than actual wine — is absurd enough without using white and making it more so."

"Well, I think it's a splendid idea," said Paul Parton. "I'm going to bring it before our council and recommend it as well."

"I agree," echoed Earl Don Feeley from the Avenell Faith Chapel. "We've replaced our carpet three times in the ten years I've been here. I don't think that's good stewardship!"

"Good stewardship!" smirked Ben Loudermilk from the Lutheran Church. "Is that what Communion's about? Good stewardship? What's more important, the mystery of Christ's body and blood in the elements or clean carpets?"

"I find white grape juice not only theologically repugnant but personally offensive!" proclaimed Dr. Snell. The room clamored with raised voices and defensive attitudes. Finally, Lyle Slater adjusted the mic again and it screeched a sharp acoustic feedback that silenced us all.

"Gentlemen, please. I had no idea this was such a crucial and divisive issue! Perhaps we can discuss it further at another time." He looked composed, but I noticed a thin film of sweat masking his smooth forehead.

"Lyle, did this issue cause any controversy when it was instituted?" I asked.

He smiled as if I were an ally. "No, not at all. Most of my congregants found it a logical, godly means of being good stewards of the resources God has blessed us with. With all due respect to our brothers and sisters who adhere to transubstantiation, we hold that the elements are merely symbolic. That's why we use juice in the first place, since alcohol has many different connotations in our culture today than it did in Jesus' time. Why, I once heard of some missionaries in Mexico who used tortillas instead of bread for Communion! Gentlemen, the form or color of the bread and wine do not matter. What matters is that we share in the Communion of Christ's death and resurrection."

"I agree that the elements are often symbolic, but still, the missionaries use those particular elements because they're familiar to new believers and available in the culture, not because they want to keep their carpets clean!" Ben started another volley of critical remarks that rose to a raucous din.

I glanced at my watch, eager to meet Dan and Peter back at the Divine Cathedral in a few minutes. Lyle Slater had abandoned his posture as leader at the podium and now spoke heatedly to Ben Loudermilk on his right. Harry Snell kept trying to engage me with his position, which I silently shared — I agreed with Dan O'Shaughnessy that juice instead of wine was bad enough — but another personal opinion would not settle the matter.

Finally, I could stand it no longer. "Gentlemen! May I have your attention! This is not accomplishing anything and has interrupted our planning for Easter service," I said into the microphone in its first required usage. "I move that we table our discussion for now and meet here next week to resolve this matter and finalize the community Easter service. Does anyone second?"

"Second!" exclaimed Rev. Slater.

"Those opposed? Good, then we will meet here next Friday at noon. See you then. Let me close in prayer." At least everyone seemed as eager as I was to end the meeting for now. I prayed a quick prayer of benediction, requesting wisdom, tolerance, and the love of Christ for each other and those in our charge. Amen.

At a quarter of three, I made a dash for the door but not before Lyle Slater cornered me.

"Grif, I didn't get a chance to mention it earlier, but I need to talk to you," he said. His voice was lower, almost a whisper, and his tone more humble than I was accustomed to. I assumed nonetheless he was already lobbying for support.

"Lyle, I'll be happy to discuss this Communion business with you tomorrow or next Monday, but right now I'm late for an appointment," I explained amidst the conversational voices and the knife-and-fork noises of busboys clearing our tables.

"I understand, but it's not about this business, although I'll probably want to talk to you about this as well. I need to talk to you about Simon Hostetler. I heard from Harry Snell that you knew him well." He watched my countenance carefully, a veteran at gauging the unspoken communications of reaction.

"Yes, Simon and I attended Union Seminary together many years ago," I said. Lyle nodded, wide-eyed for more information. "We hadn't kept in touch all that well, but then he showed up last month on sabbatical researching Tremont, the Amish community where he grew up. I'm sure you've heard of it."

Slater nodded. "I've heard Beatrice mention it. She's promised to take me there for this year's Summer Arts and Crafts Festival."

My impatience resumed. "So what do you need to talk to me about concerning Simon? Did you know him as well?"

"Certainly, his work," he answered instantly, smoothing his lustrous hair with his hand. I expected silver residue to remain in his palm. "Do they know who killed him?"

His question hung between us like a dangling spider looking for her web. I leaned toward him and said, "Did the paper say he'd been murdered? I must have missed that."

He laughed, suddenly becoming the venerable senator regaining control of the situation. "Grif, come on. Word travels fast. One of my members called me this morning and told me that Hostetler was hanging from some old spooky oak tree you people have around here. No need to play coy with me, Grif. I heard that you went down to Tremont last night to help handle the Amish. And everyone knows you're tight with Dan Warren."

"Lyle, like I mentioned, I have an appointment to keep. I really don't have time to trade rumors and gossip. I'll see you later," I replied sharply.

He gently grabbed my jacket sleeve as I was moving toward the door. Before I could rebuke the man's audacity, he whispered, "I may have been the last to see Simon Hostetler alive."

"What?" I moved closer to Lyle to make sure I heard him correctly. How could Slater have been the last to see Simon alive? I tried to regain my faculties. "If you have information about my friend's death, why are you telling me? You should talk with Sheriff Claiborne," I asserted as Paul Parton patted my back and several others filed past.

Rev. Slater paused until they were out of earshot. "In due time. I don't want to get my name in the papers or generate any negative publicity for First Church. Simon and I had lunch down at the steakhouse outside of Mumford just three days ago —"

"I thought you said you didn't know him," I said.

"No, only that I knew his work better," he smiled back at me. "You can imagine my shock this morning when I read that the poor man was dead. I had met Simon at a seminar several years back . . . we ran into each other on campus last week and decided to become better acquainted." He paused dramatically. "Since I don't know the man well, this is difficult for me to say. But if I didn't know better, I'd think that someone was after him the way he acted at our lunch. He was practically paranoid."

"Why paranoid?" I asked, eager to determine what Slater knew, if anything. I heard the Avenell Tower carillon bells peal three times.

"Oh, I don't know, Grif. Jumpy, looking over his shoulder, averting his eyes whenever someone passed by our table. Like we were in some kind of spy movie. When I asked him about his new project on the Amish, he remained vague, almost defensive."

That was certainly not typical of Simon's usual laid-back demeanor. Of course, I wasn't convinced of Lyle's story yet, either.

"Why were the two of you having lunch together in the first place?" I asked.

"As I said, I've always been a fan of his work. I simply wanted to get to know him better. Thought we might have some common interests . . ."

Slater seemed to be fishing for something as much as I was. I found it difficult to imagine Simon having much in common with this well-tailored gospel salesman. "You don't suppose he was planning to write something critical about the Amish that led to his death?" Slater asked.

"That's a nasty insinuation, Lyle," I said. "From what I know, the Amish of Tremont are incapable of violence."

"Grif, you surprise me. 'All have sinned and fall short of the glory of God.' As pastors, you and I both know that every man — and woman — is capable of doing whatever it takes to protect what they cherish," he said, that plastic grin back on his face.

"I'll mention your story to Sergeant Warren next time I see him. But I encourage you to call him yourself and tell it to him directly. Now I really must go," I said, checking my watch for effect.

"Thanks for your time, my friend." A quick pause. "Give my regards to Miss Beatrice," he said, smiling.

Chapter Five

Tangled Branches

I hurried out of the Pepper Tree and into the bright, humid spring afternoon, where daffodils and wild violets bloomed along Southern Avenue. I mulled over Lyle's disclosure. Definitely hiding something, that man. Or fishing for something himself. If I were Billy Ray Compton or one of the other local pastors, I'd attribute his oddness to the fact that Slater was a Yankee. And perhaps that was true, but I hated to be so stereotypically Southern. Maybe I'd talk to Bea about the good reverend and see what I could discover about his background. I wondered what kind of seminar had attracted Slater and Simon Hostetler — they weren't exactly peers in their profession.

Approaching the towering stone spires of the Divine, I found my curate on the steps fronting the sidewalk. Just as I was within a few yards of him, a Carroll County Sheriff's squad car came alongside us. Peter and I got in the back and were quickly introduced to John Corey, the State Bureau of Investigation agent specializing in forensic evidence. He shook our hands over his shoulder, clearly curious about the inclusion of two priests at a crime scene investigation. In his early thirties, I'd guess, with his brown hair military-short, Corey displayed an alertness that I associated with his profession. Amicable though and more talkative than some law enforcement people I'd known, Corey regaled us with details from his morning's court case.

As Dan sped down Highway 19's recursive trail, a brief lull occurred and I noticed the smell of mint gum — Dan's alternative to smoking. At the base of the mountain, our talk finally turned to Simon Hostetler's death. I recounted my strange, brief conversation with Lyle Slater and asked Dan if he happened to know any more about Slater's background.

"No more than you," he replied. "Although First Church is where the sheriff attends, *when* he attends."

Corey chuckled. "You mean when they'll let him in the door. Ornery as Sam is, I'm surprised any church would claim him."

"We'll be interviewing most of the people the victim saw this week, so I'll add Slater to my list," said Dan. "Interesting that his appointment was not listed in the deceased's Day-Timer."

"Any suspects yet?" asked Peter, shifting his long legs toward me on the expansive backseat. Corey looked curiously at Dan.

He returned the look and said, "It's okay, John. Sam and I would trust these two with our lives."

"Of course. After all, if you can't trust a priest . . ." the dark-suited agent replied.

Dan braked for a stoplight and began summarizing the case for us. "Hostetler was last seen Wednesday at the Miller farm in the afternoon. Mrs. Lydia Miller is his sister. He ate lunch there, helped his brother-in-law, Lucas Miller, with some plowing and planting that afternoon until four. Mrs. Miller believes her brother had an appointment or dinner date because he left shortly after five and told her he would not be joining them for dinner. He bathed and changed, and that was the last she saw of him. Naturally, she was very upset when we talked to her yesterday."

Peter leaned forward over the transom where a plexiglass shield could be raised when transporting prisoners. He looked boyishly eager for more details or for us to reach our destination — or both.

Dan continued. "Before his time at the Millers, the good professor had breakfast in Avenell with his research assistant, Mariah

Gates. They returned to the university library together and worked for a couple hours before he left for Tremont. Earlier in the week he kept appointments with Dr. William Lovejoy, of the Avenell sociology department, and with at least three of the Amish: Joseph Yoder, Bishop Zook, and Deborah Kaufman. Like I said, it's interesting that Hostetler's appointment with Slater was not in his appointment book."

"What about the autopsy?" I asked.

"Doc Graham and one of Corey's colleagues, a state medical examiner out of Nashville, were scheduled to perform it this morning. The report still wasn't in when I left to pick you up. Right now all we know is that the man had a noose around his neck."

"What about the Amish clothes he was wearing?" asked Peter.

Corey looked back at us. "That's why I'm here. If this looks like a hate crime, then the state can request a federal investigation."

Dan had already made the turn off the old Mumford Highway and onto Chigger Ridge Road; he had decided to avoid going through the small tourist-attracting downtown area of Tremont. It took a few minutes longer, but soon we turned onto a one-lane gravel road leading to the Schroeder farm.

Once there, the necessary explanations

and introduction of Agent Corey were made to Leah and her parents. While Leah gathered her bonnet, we all sipped iced tea. Corey murmured something to Dan and then headed back to the car. He returned quickly, having loosened his gray print tie and abandoned his navy blue suit coat. Carrying a dark case in each hand, he looked like a hotel porter. Just as I was about to inquire after Agent Corey's equipment, Benjamin Schroeder took Peter and me aside and looked at us sternly before speaking.

"I am charging both of you with the safety of my daughter. If you are truly men of God, then you must promise me that no harm will come to her. There is nothing about any of this procedure that pleases me."

Although I had seen Mr. Schroeder on a couple of occasions prior to last night, at that moment I saw him for the first time. The dirt-skinned work clothes, the blue suspenders that helped his brown pants meet the curve of his belly, the worried eyes and weathered wrinkles betraying his paternal vulnerability . . . his love for his daughter. He stroked his rounded salt-and-pepper beard, tracing the smooth skin above his upper lip with his index finger. Yes, the man was scared and likely with good reason.

"Do you accept my charge? It is the only way that I will permit her to accompany the English lawmen to the oak tree."

Peter seemed intimidated but I found myself sympathetic to his father's heart.

"Yes," I said slowly. "We will do our best to take care of Leah and make sure that no harm comes to her."

Peter nodded.

Just then the object of our discussion returned with her lovely copper-bright hair tucked beneath a tan bonnet.

"If possible, we would prefer Leah to return by suppertime — that would be six. You would all be welcome to stay," said Mrs. Schroeder.

"That's very kind of you," said Dan. "We will make sure she's back by then. But the rest of us will need to be going — we don't want to interrupt your mealtime together."

"We shall pray for you," said Mr. Schroeder.

As we headed out the door and through the yard, Leah waved to her two younger brothers who were chasing a squirrel up a newly green poplar tree. She quickly fell in beside Peter.

Agent Corey carried a small black suitcase in one hand and an expandable dark canvas briefcase in the other hand. Peter offered to carry one but the agent politely declined. When we reached the edge of the large, expansive yard, just beyond the clothesline draped with white shirts and other Plain clothes, John Corey turned to Leah.

"Miss," the agent said, "it's important that you show us the exact route you took yesterday morning. Also, anything else that you remember — anything that looks different than it usually does."

"I'll do my best," said Leah. "But as I said last night, nothing unusual happened until I got to the Judas Tree."

As we headed into the mouth of the woods, the worn trail could only accommodate two abreast. Dan asked Leah to walk alongside Agent Corey and asked me to follow alongside Pete. The dark-skinned, six foot five sergeant followed behind us, veering off the path to look for evidence. His khaki uniform camouflaged him among the full spectrum of spring green.

"I understand you're an artist. Were you carrying anything with you?" Corey asked Leah.

She blushed. "Yes, my portfolio. A collection of sketches and a few watercolors in my big binder. I'm saddened to say it, but I had hidden it behind the barn that morning so that my parents would not see me leave with it. They do not approve of my art."

"I see," said Corey. "And you were taking your work to show to Dr. Hostetler, correct?"

She nodded. Then twigs and branches snapped behind me. I looked back to see Dan searching to the right of us like a retriever seeking his fallen prey. I wished I'd thought to bring my hiking boots, although my Rockport walking shoes were holding up well amid the gravel and dust. Peter remained silent, engrossed in Corey's interrogation.

"Did you sing to yourself as you walked? Whistle perhaps? Anything to alert someone that you were coming?" asked the state agent.

"Well, now that you ask, sometimes I do whistle a hymn or two. But I don't think I did yesterday morning because I was in a hurry. I was already late. What a funny question," she said pleasantly.

Corey asked something I could not hear over the cawing of a crow.

I scanned the woods, officially part of the Cumberland Ridge Dolby Forest, and wondered where the Schroeders' property line met the military base's. Besides the hues of emerald, jade, and chartreuse, the smells and sounds of spring vied for our attention just as vividly. As pleasing and delicately balanced as a rare pipe tobacco were the blended scents of clover, sweet timothy, moss, moist earth, and the fecund smell of decay. Birds — certainly a robin or two — chirped music, trading songs celebrating winter's departure. Flapping wings and occasional rustles sounded in the underbrush. A squirrel chittered. Crickets found their voices while flies buzzed like boys with new hot rods. We were surrounded by every shape of leaf imaginable: the perfectly pointed ovals of beeches, the raggedly decorative tulip poplars, the elongated fingers of elms, the jagged green teeth of maples.

Could such a testament to the Creator's unfathomable penchant for beauty endure the intrusion that had begun so long ago and continued with our presence now? My mind spun back to the Martyr's Chapel, the way its rustic splendor had been violated and desecrated by the violence that had transpired there last fall. Was it easier, I wondered, for nature to heal the wounds that people inflicted upon it? Or did the essence of depravity linger among the trees the same way it seemed to haunt my beloved chapel? I did not like the idea of the Martyr's Chapel garnering legends and thrill-seekers the way the Judas Tree had and likely would continue to.

We stopped and I realized that Dan was nowhere to be seen.

"This is where I first thought I heard someone coming toward me. I thought it might be Dr. Hostetler, that he'd grown tired of waiting and was coming to look for me," explained Leah, almost whispering.

"If I may ask, Miss Schroeder, how do you know that this is where you first noticed the sounds?" asked Corey.

"Easy," she said, pulling back the brim of her bonnet. "This is where the blackberry bushes start — right over there. I happened to notice the buds when I heard footsteps in the distance." She pointed toward a stand of leafy bushes garnished with small white flowers and tight green fruits. Only a trained eye would have noticed it now, although come late June, the purplish jewels would attract everyone's attention.

"Did you stop to listen or did you keep walking?" asked Corey.

"Let's see. I stopped for a moment and debated on whether or not to call out. I decided against it since it was likely my brothers or the Yoder children playing. Again, I didn't want anyone to know where I was going," said Leah.

"How far away do you suppose this person was, based on the sounds? A hundred yards? Farther? Closer?"

The young Amish woman closed her eyes and placed her hands at her sides. "Maybe two hundred yards? That's about two football fields, right?"

Peter laughed, "Yes, it is. I'm glad to see that my tutorials last fall were not in vain."

Corey smiled and Leah added, "Actually, it's because of my brothers that I know about football."

Dan came up behind me without a sound. "I found a set of footprints that disappear in the creek about a quarter mile northwest of here. I staked them with crime scene tape — I'll send you over there with your kit on the way back to cast a mold. I'd guess a man's smooth-soled boot, size ten or eleven. Since there's no tread design or brand logo, I'm guessing they're handmade."

Corey nodded and jotted this down in a notepad. We resumed our hike, and I felt a bit nervous — the kind of feeling one has when viewing a violent movie for the second time. You know what's coming but still cannot prevent its effect on you.

"Where did the sounds stop? Or when did you notice that they were no longer coming toward you?" Corey asked Leah.

"Oh, maybe about here," said Leah. "I didn't mark the spot mentally the way I did when I first noticed it by the blackberry bushes. As I got closer to the clearing, I realized the sound never passed me and instead had veered off right."

"That would be consistent with the tracks you found," said Corey to Dan.

We approached an especially dense part of the woods, and I noted my first mosquito of the year. Pine branches embraced overhead, dappling the waning sunlight into splotches of shadow and muted gold. The smell of evergreen filled the breeze. As we neared the final fifty yards leading to the clearing, Corey stopped our procession.

"Miss Schroeder, please think back to yesterday morning. You're walking into the clearing to meet Dr. Hostetler. You're late for the appointment. You heard someone coming toward you on the trail who then veered off right. What did you see as you walked into the clearing ahead?" He offered her his most engaging expression, his head cocked toward his witness. Sweat soaked his white shirt beneath his arms. I wiped my own brow with the handkerchief from my back pocket.

Leah looked intently beyond Corey, over his shoulder, lost in recollection. Slowly her eyelids dipped and wavered as if she were about to sleep. She closed them, and I silently prayed for her memory to focus.

"Yes," said Leah quietly.

"Yes?" echoed Corey. "Do you see something? Remember something?"

"I remember thinking that someone had already pruned the clearing. I hadn't been here since January. Usually in spring, my brother Jacob or Mr. Yoder will clear the trail and cut back the brush around the Judas Tree. I knew that no one in my family had pruned yet this year."

"We'll check with Yoder and the Air Force base to see if either of them cleared this," noted Dan. "Seems like an awful lot of work unless this was something the perpetrator had been planning for a long time."

"Yes," said Corey. "But a lot of these guys are into planning the details, setting the stage. What else, miss?" Corey continued, turning back to Leah. "Tell me what you heard or any smells you noticed."

Leah's eyes were open again. "No, nothing. I'm sorry."

"You've already been very helpful," replied Dan.

"Tremendously," said Corey. "Let's go into the clearing now." He led us forward, then stepped aside so that Leah would be the first to enter the oval plane orbiting the hangman's tree. She stepped gingerly into a natural amphitheater carpeted with dandelions and wild clover. A few rocks, mostly sandstone and feldspar, dotted the smooth area. We paused and gave her a minute to look around.

"How do you feel?" asked the forensic scientist.

"Right now I'm very conscious of you all watching my every move. But I felt some of that yesterday as well. Like someone was watching me."

"Could it have been your peripheral awareness of the body before you realized it?" asked Dan.

"Perhaps," said the young Amish woman, loosening her bonnet and tilting it off her forehead. "But I don't think so. There's a difference between being watched by the dead and the living. . . . I sometimes sit up with our kinfolk, the older ones who are close to passing."

"Yes, I know what you mean," I said. " 'The dead see not with eyes of their own making, immortal vision passed on to those still waking.' "

"Keats?" asked Peter.

"No, Wordsworth," I said, feeling a bit embarrassed, like my old English professor who had a literary quote for even the most mundane events.

"So maybe the perpetrator was still here. Do you suppose he camped out to watch someone discover the body?" asked Dan.

"Perhaps. Or forgot something at the scene," said Corey.

"But if he was into staging things, deliberation, he may have waited and watched," said Dan. "Leah, how many people knew that you were meeting Dr. Hostetler?"

"Well, the only person I told was my best friend, Gerta Miller, and I don't think she told anyone, but you can ask her. Of course, I made the appointment when I ran into Dr. Hostetler down at the SweetHaus Bakery — I was delivering some of my mother's apple butter. I suppose someone could have overheard me."

"Do you remember who was present when you made the appointment?" asked Peter.

"It was a busy time. There were at least half a dozen people. A tour group had stopped in for lunch and had just finished up, so most of them were strangers. Jessie Stolzfus was working that day, and she might know."

Dan nodded and scribbled something down on his growing list.

"Show me where you stood and where you walked yesterday," instructed Corey.

Like an actor blocking her scene, Leah took several exaggerated steps left a few feet and then toward the center of the clearing. She then turned around sharply to her right and found herself facing the giant oak. She moved toward it as far as yellow crime scene tape permitted. About one hundred square feet surrounding the massive oak had been cordoned off with stakes and the yellow-and-black tape. With the hangman's rope absent, the tree looked as stately and majestic as any sentinel. It belonged more in an antebellum garden or on a riverbank than it did in a crime scene.

The Judas Tree. Its mighty trunk, at least five feet in diameter, extended for nearly ten feet before forking into twin boughs extending diagonally. The right bough, the infamous hangman's limb, leveled out to almost perpendicular several feet further up the tree. The left bough remained at an even diagonal giving the tree's primary frame the shape of a Y bent on the right side. Numerous other boughs, many as thick as my waist and thighs, shot tangled branches skyward. The wet spring had produced ample foliage in deep-seated hues of jade green. Except for being the site of three men's deaths in the last one hundred and fifty years, it was a gorgeous antique.

Although the scene had been covered by Dan's colleague, Jerry Wilson, I was surprised that no guard had been posted.

"Budget cuts," he explained. "Besides, unless someone else is in danger, there's usually no reason to post."

Meanwhile, Corey propped his two cases against a nearby pine tree and took out a large sketch pad. We watched attentively as he explained his procedure.

"While your local forensics team took reams of pictures, I like to map the scene," he explained. His wrist moved instinctively, naturally as his pencil formed wide arcs and small geometric shapes. Leah and Peter grew impatient and walked off toward the northern rim of the clearing, talking softly. Finally Corey asked, "Does this look about right?" and held up a crude map showing our location with the nearest state highways, Dolby Air Force Base, and the Schroeder and Yoder farms nearby. On the back he'd drawn a large oval with the Judas Tree represented by a large X just right of where the trail ended at the long west ridge of the oval.

"Yes, looks good to me," Dan said. I nodded.

Agent Corey placed his maps inside the

sketch pad cover and began donning latex gloves. He placed several paper and plastic bags in his hip pocket, assembled a large flashlight-looking device, and tucked two knitting needles into his belt.

"Careful you don't fall on those," Dan said, half-joking. "Working on an afghan?"

"If you don't appreciate my services, Sergeant Warren," Corey shot back, "I've got a waiting list of units who do."

"Easy, John, I'm only kidding," soothed Dan.

"I know," replied the calm agent. "I just like giving it back to you."

I said nothing but still wanted to know what the knitting needles were for. As Corey lifted himself over the crime scene tape he looked at me and said, "All criminalists have their own style and idiosyncrasies. Some of them like to use pencils to retrieve physical evidence, others use forceps or even chopsticks. I use my wife's knitting needles. The sharp points come in handy sometimes, too."

I smiled in admiration.

"Dan, this was already dusted for prints, right?" he continued, approaching the gnarled ganglia of above-ground roots at the base of the tree.

"Yessir. But we didn't find any — no finger- or footprints. Either someone swept up or enough time passed that the wind and squirrels did the job. Those you see there should be ours — mine, the sheriff's, and Wilson's."

"Next time, place a rubber band around your shoe, just to keep yours distinguished from the perp's."

Corey began scraping and prying, placing tree bark and soil samples in his paper bags. He methodically frisked the oak column, stopping three times to make notations.

"What's this?" he exclaimed.

Dan and I walked to the edge of the tape barrier. Peter and Leah joined us.

"That's the fresh-cut graffiti I told you about — the Bible verse," explained Dan.

"If I had to guess, I'd venture that this was done well after Hostetler was dead. Miss Schroeder, did you notice this when you first found the body?" Corey delicately explored the chain of gashes like a surgeon dressing a wound. He rubbed his gloved fingers together. From my distance, I couldn't make out the reference yet. "Would you bring me the polaroid camera out of the case on the left over there, Father?"

I hurried over and fetched the black- and pewter-colored camera, a fancier version than the old similar style polaroid I had.

Agent Corey told us we could remove the crime tape and join him. No one said a word as we approached the dark brown trunk and followed Corey's pointed finger. The marks were fresh, pale wood pulp carved where the bark had blanched away.

DEUT 32-43

We stood there momentarily silent, taking in the letters. Agent Corey looked up at me and said, "Father?"

Before I could respond, two men in steel-blue uniforms burst through the under-brush behind Agent Corey.

One appeared agile and young with his weapon drawn. The other, heavier and short, commanded like thunder, "Stop where you are — all of you! This is property of the federal government, and you're under arrest for tampering with a crime scene!"

Chapter Six

Hangman's Noose

"Who in the —" snapped Corey. Pete and Leah huddled around Dan and me.

"Lower your weapon, officer," commanded Dan. "I'm Sergeant Dan Warren, Carroll County Sheriff's Department, and this is Special Agent John Corey, Tennessee Bureau of Investigation. We are authorized by the county and state to be here. Now, what's this all about?"

The tall blond officer — his uniform implied Military Police — reluctantly lowered his gun. The short, squat one strode forward, his breathing ragged. He was older than I was, with thick jowls and puffy eyes. He lit a cigarette as he sized us up. "I am General Nathaniel Bledsoe, and this tree is part of the property of the United States Air Force Dolby Military Base. I don't know who authorized you to be out here, but I'm willing to let you off —"

"No, sir, you are mistaken." It was Leah's soft voice, the antithesis of the haggard general's husky throat and contemptuous tone.

"The Judas Tree marks the boundary. Just to the other side is where your military base begins. The Yoders' property —"

"This area is under the jurisdiction of Dolby Air Force. Who is she?" barked the general.

"Leah Schroeder," she replied before the rest of us could respond. "I am the one who found Dr. Hostetler here yesterday."

"We will want to question you then, my dear." Bledsoe exhaled a column of white smoke into the late afternoon shadows. "I'll also need the body and any test results that may have been performed on it. Tell your commanding officer." He motioned toward Dan with his cigarette.

Dan unfolded a square of glossy paper from his hip pocket. "General, with all due respect, this is our case. The property line for where Dolby begins is clearly marked — that fence is a good fifty yards behind you there. I'm sure you're aware of that."

"Are you disputing my word, Sergeant?" snarled the old general, mustering his best red face. He stepped forward until he was forced to look up into Dan's chin.

"Yes, I am," replied my friend calmly. "If you have a boundary dispute, you may take it up with Sheriff Claiborne. In the mean-time, I'm afraid I'm going to have to ask you and Beetle Bailey over there to head on back to the base." The dark giant spoke firmly yet without rancor. He looked down at General Bledsoe and returned the silent intimidation tenfold. I caught the corner of a smile from John Corey just as the blond guard suddenly charged forward as if unsnapped from a leash.

"No one talks to General Bledsoe in that tone!" roared the human Doberman. He pulled his mentor away and thrust himself within an inch of Dan's face, eager to fight.

"Easy, Lieutenant!" ordered his boss. "Perhaps we need to return to the base and secure the proper paper work before we assume this case."

"I think that would be wise," said Agent Corey, flashing his TBI wallet badge. "I think you'll discover that this is not your case. In fact, I can't imagine why you'd want it in the first place."

"Classified," Bledsoe shot back, grinding his cigarette butt into a patch of moist earth beneath his shiny boot. "You can trust that your superiors will hear about your behavior today," returned the lieutenant.

"As will yours," returned Corey.

The lieutenant glared at the state agent but followed Bledsoe back through the foliage. After several moments, when we could no longer hear the rustle of the underbrush, we all released a collective sigh. Leah looked pale and leaned into Peter.

"What was that all about?" asked Corey. "Who made him the temporary dictator?"

Dan stepped forward, his broad arms folded across his chest. "I knew the military and the Amish didn't exactly like having each other for neighbors, but I had no idea. What in the world were they doing out here? I'm with you, John — I can't imagine why they'd want this case in the first place. Man, that's strange."

"They wish to buy our land," said Leah. "They've been encroaching on the old boundary for some time and now they want to take more of our land. There's a belt of farmland — we call it Canaan's Way — that runs across the land farmed by three families. They wish to buy the property and further develop their weapons of war. It is also desired by several English farmers and local businessmen."

"Do you know for a fact that Dolby has approached the landowners to purchase this property?" I asked.

"Yes," she replied. "I heard my father talking to the bishop one day in the barn. There is likely to be a community vote after Easter regarding the property."

"But I thought you said it was owned by three families," said Peter, "not by the community."

"Yes, technically my father, Joseph Yoder, and Jonah Kaufman own the land, but the entire church would have to approve the sale," she explained.

"What percentage is needed to pass?" I asked, intrigued by the rules of communal living.

"Why, one hundred percent," said Leah. "It must be unanimous in order for it to pass."

Agent Corey whistled.

"You're kidding," said Peter. "Everyone has to agree before you make a community decision? So just one person's vote could prevent the land sale?"

"That is correct," she said, adjusting her bonnet. "We trust that God works in each of our hearts toward his common good for all our community, not just a few."

"A lovely view of community," I affirmed.

"We need to get back to work before the sun sets. Father, you were just about to reference this verse for me before we were so rudely interrupted," said Agent Corey, returning our attention to the investigation.

I glanced back to find the scientist once more gently inspecting the tree's message.

The blocked letters and numbers jeered back at me like a jack-o'-lantern: DEUT 32–43.

" 'Rejoice, O nations, with his people; for he avenges the blood of his servants, and takes vengeance on his adversaries, and makes atonement for his land and his people.' That's paraphrased from my memory, but it's definitely close," I explained after the words had pressed their cumulative weight in each of us.

"It's not the 'Vengeance is mine sayeth the Lord' verse?" asked Peter.

"Yeah, that was my guess, too," chimed in Dan.

"No, Father Grif is correct," said Leah before I could. "The vengeance-is-mine verse is in the same passage about ten verses back." She shuddered involuntarily and I realized that the afternoon was dissolving into evening. Shadows gathered quickly in the enclosed woods and the dense area took on an ominous, enchanted quality. This feeling crystallized as the Amish woman repeated the verse again: 'Rejoice, O Gentiles, with His people; For He will avenge the blood of His servants, And render vengeance to His adversaries; He will provide atonement for His land and His people.' "

Leah seemed embarrassed then, as if we

thought her prideful for demonstrating her fluency with Scripture. On the contrary, the natural recall of God's Word, embedded in her mind and heart, encouraged me in a way that offset the somber feeling from the darkening sky and the reason we were here.

"But this was definitely done after the murder," reiterated Corey. "I'd even venture several hours after the murder if your Doc Graham is anywhere close to correct."

"So someone may have carved this other than the murderer?" mused Dan. "If I were the murderer, would I risk waiting around or going back to the crime scene just to carve my favorite Sunday school verse? Maybe some Amish person concurred with the result here — no offense, miss."

"None taken, Mr. Warren," Leah said. "That would mean I was not the first to discover the body, then."

Corey nodded and aimed the beam of his PoliLight at the carving. Nothing coalesced under its bizarre glare.

"Dan, can you and Peter give me a boost here? I need to climb up and look at that branch where the rope was tied." Corey rolled up his white, Oxford-cloth sleeves another turn. "Father Grif, would you take these evidence bags back to my case over there and bring the canvas bag over?"

I made the switch and watched the criminalist fasten a thick shoulder strap across his back. Dan and Peter locked hands and boosted the stocky, athletic agent up into the matted branches of one of the oldest trees in our county. The agent proved adept at climbing, quick and strong, despite his dress clothes and polished leather wingtips. Stopping twice to gather more bark and tree samples into paper bags, he became so excited over the discovery of a fiber sample that I thought he would fall. Slowly inching forward to the forked trunk and onto the extended palm of the hangman's branch, John Corey reached a perch where a band of bark showed smooth scratch marks, as if someone had taken a two-inch strip of sandpaper and gently massaged the fat limb on top.

"Dan," Corey called down, "How was the rope removed? Please tell me it wasn't untied or cut from up here."

"Well, how else could we remove it? Actually, Jerry cut it right above the noose and right at the top where you are. 'Course, knowing you, we should have cut the whole tree down."

"You joke, but yes, that's what I would have done. I would've taken this whole branch I'm on now."

Pete asked, "But isn't that a little impractical? Let alone that Mrs. Philpotts and the County Historical Preservation Society would be furious. How did the murderer get the body up there anyway?"

"See, that's why I would've cut the tree down — with all due apologies to Mrs. Philpotts. There's no telling how much trace evidence we've lost already. The insects, birds, and last night's dew have all tampered with the scene now, not to mention any of our fine servicemen. We don't know how the murderer rigged the noose. I'm anxious to see if the victim was dead already, or if he was still alive. My money says that he was unconscious or already dead when the perp pulled the rope around him."

The words floated down to us like leaves, the remaining cache of last fall's dry parchment. The agent's casual tone more portentous than he realized. I didn't know whether to hope Simon Hostetler was alive or dead when he swung from the branch Agent Corey now embraced.

The sun was setting, the light already faded within our tree-enclosed ring. I checked my watch — almost five-thirty. "We should be heading back soon. I want to have Leah back in time for dinner with her family," I said.

Corey was already descending, his navy dress pants scuffed and wrinkled, his flawless black shoes nicked and scratched, as well. Peter offered a foothold again, but the nimble scientist snaked his way down and jumped the last five feet. He immediately began labeling and sorting his new treasures.

"Yes, we're all done here. Jerry already walked the grid for this entire clearing. It was obviously swept up — no tracks, no horse or mule prints, although I spotted manure just off the trail only a few days old. We didn't even have the victim's shoe prints — men don't go flying through the air into waiting nooses. We have a smart, thoughtful hangman on our hands." Corey returned to the remaining black valise a few feet away and began packing up. "I wonder if he prepared the scene before bringing the victim here. Maybe someone saw him. . . ."

"Mr. Warren, if I may respond? Many families take this trail as a shortcut. It saves about a mile from taking the Chigger Ridge Road into town. The Yoders, Zooks, Kaufmans, and Millers all live on this side of the woods. My younger brothers often play in these woods. . . ." Fear smoldered in Leah's eyes, betraying her informative tone. She had removed her sunbonnet and tucked it discreetly into the band of her skirt.

Dan said, "Miss Leah, you've been very helpful today. I know it's not pleasant to think that one of your friends or relatives had anything to do with Dr. Hostetler's death — and likely they didn't. But they may have seen someone or something that would help these gentlemen catch who did. Don't be afraid that you are betraying someone you care for. The truth will come out. Anything you can do to expedite it is better for all concerned."

Peter put his jacket over Leah's shoulders, and she offered a faint smile of acknowledgment as the five of us headed back to the trail leading to her home. We walked silently, and the dying light brought to mind an old Baptist hymn that I began to hum under my breath. "Softly and tenderly, Jesus is calling, calling for you and for me . . . Shadows are gathering, deathbeds are coming, coming for you and for me." No one seemed to mind, each absorbed in his or her own thoughts about the secrets of the Judas Tree. I didn't consider how morbid my chosen hymn was until the last few hundred yards when the path became obscured. Dan switched on his high-beamed flashlight for us, and finally the outline of the Schroeder barns came into sight. Leah sighed as we met her father and brothers on the front porch.

"Your daughter was very helpful to us, Mr. Schroeder," spoke Dan. "And we appreciate your cooperation, too."

"I hope that our Lord will reveal his justice in this matter as soon as possible. Leah Rebekah, please assist your mother with supper. Gentlemen, Sarah and I insist that you stay and share a meal with us. We feel that it might help you in your investigation to observe the Amish way of life. We have nothing to hide." His eyes shone sincerely, the flashes of anger I'd witnessed the night before now seemingly focused on justice. His two older sons, Jacob and Nathan, looked at each other stoically while the young boys, Noah and Luke, were delighted and ran over to tug at Peter.

"Dan, I really need to get back. I want to run some tests and consult with Jerry before I head back to Nashville tonight," said Corey, and then to the Amish man, "Your offer is most kind, but I think I am more useful back in the lab."

Benjamin Schroeder nodded in understanding. "The rest of you will stay?"

"You are being very generous, Mr. Schroeder, and I appreciate that," Dan replied. "But I need to accompany Agent

Corey back up the mountain; I'm still on duty tonight. Perhaps Father Grif and Peter could stay for supper. . . ." Dan penetrated my eyes with the unspoken message that it might be very helpful if the two of us stayed and talked with the Schroeders. I didn't need much encouragement, although my reasons were not necessarily Dan's.

"If you're sure that's all right," I offered, excited at the prospect of getting to know the Schroeders — and the Amish ways — better. I had envied Peter his handful of meals at the Schroeder table these past five months.

"Of course," replied Mr. Schroeder, who seemed relieved that the law enforcement agents would not be staying. "Luke, run inside and tell the women to set two more places at our table."

The boy took off with his younger brother beside him. Their footsteps thudded a hollow rhythm across the wood-planked porch. Jacob and Nathan drifted to the end of the porch, and I could hear them talking quietly within the creak of the porch swing.

"How will we get back?" asked Pete, reading my mind. I was already debating whether or not Bea would mind picking us up in a couple of hours. Dan offered a better idea.

"Since the Fathers came down as a favor to me, let me make a quick call. I'll bet the Mumford PD would be glad to run you home later." He dashed to his squad car and returned momentarily. "It's all set," he said. "Officer Doyle from MPD will pick you up here around eight-thirty, if that's all right."

"That will accommodate a fine meal," smiled Benjamin Schroeder, more relaxed than I'd seen him so far.

"Mrs. Schroeder is an excellent cook," added Peter.

After Dan Warren and Agent Corey left, Peter and I entered the beauty of the Amish home, elegant in candlelight and the last dying embers of a spring sunset through the wide-paned windows. We all gathered around the long cherry wood dining table and seated ourselves on benches that had rump-prints from a century of use. I offered to return thanks for the bounteous table.

"We pray silently before our meal," blurted Nathan, the Schroeders' second son.

"Of course," I said. I had a growing suspicion that he and his older brother did not trust me yet.

The boy's father tried to apologize, "Nathan spoke without cause, Griffin. You are welcome to give thanks for us."

I felt embarrassed now, but everyone bowed so I said a short grace. The awkwardness dissolved as bowls and platters of steaming food passed from person to person. Hearty scents laced the air. The men drank coffee while the young boys and women drank milk. There was a platter of pork roast, an alumnus of the pigpen out behind the grain silo I learned, smothered in onions and brown gravy. A dark blue bowl of boiled potatoes in their pale red jackets. Preserved peaches in a small white bowl. A small casserole with peas, carrots, and rice in a cream sauce. A bowl of chow-chow, a spicy relish dish made of pickled cabbage and peppers. Homemade biscuits with hand-churned butter and blackberry jam. It was such a fine meal that no one spoke until our first helpings had almost disappeared from our plates.

"You are an excellent cook, Mrs. Schroeder," I offered. "Everything on the table is simply delicious." The woman blushed and Leah beamed proudly.

"Everything on our table was made here on our farm," said eighteen-year-old Nathan. "Everything."

"Do not indulge in pride, my son," Benjamin Schroeder corrected. However, as the young man's enthusiasm wilted, his father added, "Although, it is hard when one cooks as well as your mother." Everyone smiled and the tension faded.

"Pride aside, Mr. and Mrs. Schroeder, yours is a remarkable life-style," I said, and Peter nodded since his mouth was full of another biscuit.

"I know it appears strange to the outside world why we do things the way we do." Benjamin paused and sipped his coffee. "Or else they think we are perfect. And we are not. We work very hard for our way of life, and it is not always easy."

Sarah Schroeder seemed surprised at her husband's disclosure. I remembered Leah's slip the night before about Simon Hostetler's visit to her mother and I wondered how Mrs. Schroeder had explained it to Mr. Schroeder. The woman cleared her throat, excused herself, and stated, "Many people view us as quaint and idealistic. But the truth is that we are human like anyone else. We are not stupid and backward. And we are not superior elitists. We are just like everyone else in some ways. And in others we have made different choices and commitments to honor God and live according to His ways."

"I will serve dessert now if it pleases you," offered Leah. Her mother rose to assist, but

Leah told her to stay seated, enlisting her two youngest brothers instead. They obliged without any fuss, almost eager to help. Jacob and Nathan asked to be excused in order to finish up some evening chores. Peter offered to assist, and to my surprise, they accepted. I tried to imagine my favorite curate absorbed within the Amish fold. It wasn't as difficult as I wanted it to be. Was Peter seriously considering making such a change?

Young Luke refilled my coffee cup while Leah served an oversized slab of delicious carrot cake with cream cheese frosting. Raisins and nuts laced the moist dessert. Soon I was stuffed, but I didn't want my overindulgence to cost me the opportunity to know more about the Schroeders and their way of life.

"How much land do you farm, Mr. Schroeder?" I asked.

He finished a morsel of cake. "We own about four hundred acres here. Right now we're planting a little over three hundred of them — mostly alfalfa, soybeans, some wheat, and corn. The first two to sell, the last two for us. The spring rains have been heavier than last year's — if only they'll keep us moist into the summer."

Leah had reseated herself and her two

brothers had taken cookies out onto the porch. "Mother grows a vegetable garden, as well. We have dairy cows, a few pigs, chickens, and goats."

"I imagine it's very gratifying living off the land. But also very frightening and frustrating at times with so many variables beyond your control — weather, market prices, and so on." I licked the last rich swirl of frosting from my fork. I wondered if Mrs. Schroeder would give this recipe to my sister.

"Yes, but it keeps us dependent on God," said the man who was not much older than I was but looked heartier, ruddy and weathered. "He is the only one who can control all those forces. He desires that we trust in Him."

"And on each other in the community," finished his wife.

"That's what is so wonderfully remarkable about Tremont — the way you all support one another, as well as the kindnesses you show to others. My wife learned to quilt from Miss Mary Lapp. How is she? I really must pay her a call."

"You know Miss Mary?" exclaimed Leah. "Isn't she marvelous! Why, I love her like my own grandmother."

"She is indeed a saint of great faith and

patience," pronounced Mr. Schroeder.

"She's still living with her daughter and son-in-law, Mr. and Mrs. Stolzfus, not far from the village. She had a tough winter with her arthritis, but she's doing better now that the weather is warmer," said Mrs. Schroeder. "I'm sure that she would enjoy your visit."

I sipped my coffee. "Perhaps you would come with me to visit Miss Mary sometime soon, Mrs. Schroeder?"

The woman looked at her husband, as if for permission, but he did not meet her eyes. "I am very busy, but sometime perhaps I can accompany you." She fidgeted her fork over most of the cake still on her plate. "Perhaps I can spare Leah to accompany you next week."

"I know this is awkward," I said, shifting the conversation closer to my concerns about my friend's death. "But I understand Mr. Hostetler grew up here. Did either of you know him?" I extended my long legs to improve my circulation after such an immobilizing meal and to appear more relaxed.

"Yes," Mrs. Schroeder replied tentatively. "I knew him when I was a girl. Simon Hostetler was my grandmother's sister's son. He spent a few years here as a boy." She pushed her dessert plate away as a barrier between us and fidgeted with her linen napkin. Her husband looked at her with an odd expression. Whether it was derision, anger, or fear, I could not be sure.

Leah broke the tension. "I'm going to see if Jacob and Nathan are ready for some cake." She looked from her mother to her father and back again. "Plus," she added, rising gracefully and smoothing crumbs from her dark skirt, "there's no telling what mischief they're pulling on poor Peter." She smiled nervously. "Please excuse me."

"So Simon was not born here? You sound like he merely passed through for a few years." I was eager to discover whatever I could about my old friend's ties to this community, but I had to keep my tone casual, interested but not demanding.

Mr. Schroeder replied, "The Hostetlers came to our village in the late '50s. Caleb Hostetler and his two children — Simon and Lydia — came here as outsiders and wished to join our community. Caleb was distantly related to some of our people here as Sarah mentioned. After Caleb's wife died in an automobile accident, he wished to simplify his life, to make a fresh start, so he said."

"I must clear the table," Mrs. Schroeder said abruptly. Was there lingering tension between the couple over Simon's recent visit to her?

"No — that can wait. We may as well tell Brother Reed what he wants to know — the sheriff will find out one way or another," said her husband firmly. Sarah Schroeder reseated herself. Outside I could hear Leah squealing, the younger boys laughing, and Peter's voice blending into the happy mix. Inside the candle-lit shadows grew deeper, like pools of black ink, across the smooth planes of the uncluttered room.

Benjamin Schroeder pushed his dessert plate away and leaned both elbows on the table. "Simon Hostetler's family almost destroyed our community."

Chapter Seven

Amish Hospitality

"What do you mean? How did his family almost destroy Tremont?" I asked.

Benjamin leaned back and stroked his beard. "Sarah mentioned that Simon Hostetler's mother died before his father moved the family here."

"Yes, how tragic. It sounds as if Simon's father decided to change his family's lifestyle in the aftermath of his grief."

"Yes," said Benjamin. "I suppose so."

"You sound tentative. Did the Hostetlers not fit into the community?" I asked.

Sarah Schroeder looked uncomfortable again. Her husband replied, "Too well, if you ask me."

Confused, I pressed him for his meaning. He shook his head and turned to Sarah. "You might as well tell him."

She nodded. "At first, the Hostetlers fit in just fine. Caleb was a hard worker, a simple man in many ways who was definitely burned out in his English life. The children were young enough that they made the transition without much difficulty. A few years passed and the bishop made a rare decision to allow Caleb to be baptized into our community —"

"And then he betrayed us," interjected Benjamin Schroeder. I looked from one to the other and neither would meet my gaze.

"Simon's father committed adultery with someone in our community here," Sarah said quietly, her eyes downcast.

A low whistle escaped my lips instinctively. "Adultery? One doesn't think about that kind of problem occurring among the Amish," I said.

"We do not like the world to know our dirty laundry. It is between us and God, within our families and community," said Benjamin angrily.

"We are human, Griffin, all too human. This kind of sin does not happen often. But it can happen — and it did with Caleb Hostetler," added Sarah.

"What happened? Who was she? I don't wish to pry, but you realize that this might have a bearing on Simon's death," I said.

Benjamin nodded. "Anna Kaufman," he whispered. "My aunt. The Kaufman place borders what used to belong to the Hostetlers. In fact, they lived with the Kaufmans for the first year they were here.

Aunt Anna had her own husband and family but took very kindly — too kindly — to the poor widower and his motherless children."

"It was not her fault, Benjamin," said his wife. "Caleb Hostetler simply did not share the same convictions we do."

He scowled. "I'll say."

"And so the affair became public and Hostetler was forced to leave?" I asked.

"Yes. It broke her husband's heart. She confessed to him and to the bishop, was disciplined, and forgiven. But the Hostetlers were forced to move. They should never have been allowed to become part of us in the first place," Benjamin explained.

"But some in the community thought they should be disciplined and allowed to stay just as Anna was," added Sarah. "Caleb did not wish to leave, nor did Simon and Lydia, who were teenagers by this time. He begged to stay but it was in vain. Finally, as a kind of compromise, arrangements were made for Lydia to stay. She moved in with the Millers and eventually married their oldest boy. She is a good woman and has managed to put all this behind her."

"But Simon?" I asked. "He obviously chose not to stay."

"Yes," emphasized Benjamin. "He was angry that his father was forced out of Tremont and that his family was separated. He harbored great bitterness for many years, especially when Caleb died shortly after the two of them moved away."

"So in one sense, Simon blamed the Amish here for his father's death?" I asked, suddenly overwhelmed by this new data. No wonder Simon never liked to discuss his ties to Carroll County when we were in seminary. It was one of the bleakest chapters in his life. So had my friend truly been here to research his latest anthropology book? Or was he trying to exact revenge for something that had happened over three decades ago?

My hostess nodded vigorously. "I always liked Simon, and Lydia is one of my dearest friends now. But with Anna being Benjamin's aunt and all, you can see why many in the community were upset to see Simon return after all these years."

"It felt like one more bad omen," declared Benjamin, shaking his head. "I was not pleased to see Simon Hostetler one bit."

"What do you mean by 'one more bad omen'?" I asked.

The Amish man traded glances with his wife. "It sounds superstitious — and I'm not a superstitious man. I strive to be a man of faith, but . . . well . . ."

"We've experienced several setbacks in

the community these last few months," explained Sarah.

"Peter told me about the fire last fall," I said, recalling the barn burning experienced by a nearby farm family. Although the bishop did not want local law enforcement to investigate, arson was suspected. "Was the cause of the fire ever determined?"

Benjamin shook his head. "It was no accident. I know that," he said. "The Kaufmans are one of the finest farm families in our community. Jonah would never be so careless as to leave a lantern lit or a candle burning. No, we all suspect that an outsider set fire to his barn."

"The same Kaufmans as Anna's family?" I asked, making the connection.

They both nodded. "Her oldest son," explained Benjamin, "my cousin."

"Were there other setbacks?" I continued.

"Our entire hundred acres of soybeans were trampled last fall — destroyed. It is one of our main cash crops," replied the farmer. "We lost several thousand dollars overnight."

"Trampled? By whom?"

"We do not know, Brother Reed," replied Sarah. "The bishop suggested that some of our teenagers might have caused it accidentally. The ones in *Rumspringa* often gather down by the river, not far from our west field."

"But our Jacob and Nathan spoke with their friends, and no one was even at the local spot by the river the night before the crop was destroyed," added her husband.

I shook my head and began absently folding my discarded napkin on the table. "It certainly doesn't make sense," I pondered.

"Then there's the Yoders' cattle," said the Amish woman.

"Now, we don't know that those cows went down from anything more than a virus like Jessie said," countered Benjamin.

I looked up at him for an explanation.

He continued. "The Yoders run a dairy not far from here. After Christmas they lost half a dozen of their best producers to a cattle virus."

"Well, Felicia thinks that someone poisoned their milkers," huffed Sarah. "No matter what old Jessie Stolzfus says."

"Three losses all within six months of each other. Thank goodness no one was hurt," I said, thinking through the implications. "Do you believe that these events are related? Perhaps they are hate crimes from someone outside Tremont. Did you contact the sheriff about these events?"

"No, we do not like outside interference, as you have seen. Many of our people think that they are trying to scare us into selling our land," said Benjamin.

"They — who?" I pressed. Leah's comments from that afternoon came to mind. "Who would want to scare you into selling your land?"

"Take your pick," he said. "It seems that we suddenly have much attention from many groups. Local farmers want to buy our land, the military base would gladly buy us out, and several corporations have approached us, as well."

"Is it likely that you would ever sell out?" I asked. "Do any of the Amish wish to move their families away from Tremont?"

"Yes," said Sarah. "One has left already. Others are considering it. Even Benjamin and I have discussed the possibility. And now it seems a man has been murdered in our midst." Her voice faltered at the end as if a hidden grief suddenly buoyed to the surface. Whether she lamented the loss of life or the potential loss of her community, I could not tell.

"Yes. So when Simon showed up six weeks ago, did you somehow think he had something to do with any of these events? What did you mean earlier when you said that his arrival seemed like a bad omen?" I tried to make sense of it all, but the connections became more oblique, elusive.

Benjamin stood and squared his shoulders. He stretched his suspenders with his thumbs and forefingers before turning back to my questions. "Like I said, I'd have to be superstitious to think that there's any connection. No, I didn't think that he had anything to do with our lost soybeans or any of the other losses. It just seemed like another odd coincidence . . . another cause for dissension in our community. A reminder of a hard time from the past. And now he's found with a noose 'round his neck."

"Had either of you seen Simon since he left Tremont all those years ago?" I asked.

Silence ensued, each of them troubled by the odd occurrences they had just articulated. Finally, the husband and wife looked at one another. Sarah spoke in terse syllables. "Not until two weeks ago when Simon showed up at our door. He wanted to see Benjamin . . . to make peace over what happened between their families all those years ago. . . . I suggested he come back another time. I had decided it best not to mention it until Leah spoke last night." Mr. Schroeder appeared sullen and silent until Sarah began to clear the dessert plates and coffee cups from the table. Benjamin lingered, and I sensed he might still be willing to talk.

"Forgive my ignorance," I changed the subject, "but how would you describe your community here? I know a little about the origins of the Mennonites and the Amish, but it's mostly historical. I also know that there's a great deal of diversity even within particular sects. Is Tremont an Old Order Amish community?"

I feared my interrogation would exhaust the man, but I was quite grateful for the abundance of information. Benjamin returned to the table and, still standing, drained the last of his coffee. When he spoke, he sounded relieved to move on to other topics, but his thoughts were clearly preoccupied by our conversation.

"It was at first," he began. "Tremont was still Old Order when my grandfather came here after World War I. The folk were strong and righteous. God honored those first dozen families and blessed the fruits of their labors. In the last few decades, however, we have become lax. Too many compromises with the world's ways. Too many sins go unpunished or unnoticed. Shunning is rarely done in our community any more. We are farming less and turning more to home businesses and tourism. I do not think it bodes well for our community or our way of life here." He lowered his voice, "As Sarah mentioned, we have discussed moving to Lancaster or to Indiana, but it is a hard decision to make. We continue to pray. . . ." He shifted his weight in the ladder-back chair, a solid piece of furniture likely hand-crafted by himself or some family member. We could hear Sarah in the kitchen scraping plates and gathering utensils as well as the suddenly louder sounds of the children playing in the yard.

"I am most grateful for what you've shared with me tonight. I only have one last —"

My final question would have to wait; the outside voices were not only growing stronger, but several of their owners clanged through the screen door in an urgent din. The two young boys and Leah all spoke at the same time, each trying to overcome the others' voices. In the tumble of sentences, I made out the words "stranger," "barn," and "after him." Sarah ran from the kitchen to join us in deciphering the mayhem.

"Children — silence! Now, Leah, please tell us what is so earth-shattering," said her mother calmly. Mrs. Schroeder's face looked gaunt and pale in the light of the candle before her on the table. By contrast,

Leah looked fresh and ruddy, her freckled nose and cheeks burning with color even in the dim light. She inhaled deeply before beginning.

"We were playing in the front barn, showing Peter the new calf, when Luke here thought he saw someone hiding behind the wagon. We thought he was only fooling but Jacob went to see, and sure enough, a man darted out from behind the feed chute. He jumped the gate and took off across the pasture and into the woods. Jacob, Nathan, and Peter took off after him!"

"Could it have been someone playing a joke?" asked Mr. Schroeder.

"It was not one of us," blurted Luke. "It was an English man."

Benjamin and I rose from the table. "You all stay inside the house," he ordered. We dashed out the door and down the porch steps toward the lantern's glow inside the barn about a hundred yards away.

Just as we reached the barn, I heard a car rumbling down the gravel road from the highway. Was the intruder escaping in a car he'd stashed nearby? The crunch of tires on spattering gravel seemed to grow louder. Restless animals, whether uneasy from the excited, familiar voices or from the presence of an intruder, bawled and snorted from shadowed stalls. The air smelled of last summer's hay bales, mildewed grain, and manure. Mr. Schroeder unhooked the Coleman lantern from its nail post, splaying more distorted shadows across the cavernous barn. A cat slinked across my ankles and darted into the hay loft.

A car door slammed and I looked out to see a patrol car. Had Mrs. Schroeder already called the police? No, there was no telephone. My momentary disorientation lifted as I recalled the means for our ride home. It couldn't have been better timing.

Benjamin began surveying his tools and possessions, looking to see if anything was amiss. He muttered something in German under his breath. Voices drifted toward us like snatches of radio songs on a rotating dial. A uniformed officer spoke to Mrs. Schroeder on the porch before turning and jogging our direction.

"What happened?" he called out, still a few yards away. "You've had an intruder?"

"Yes," I said. "The children were playing in the barn and saw someone who ran off. The older boys went after him."

"Nothing was stolen," concluded Benjamin, once more his stoic self. "Perhaps it was merely the Yoder boy playing a prank. He is the same age as my Nathan."

"Did he try to harm the children?" asked the officer, his eyes shadowed by his uniform's cap. He was perhaps six feet tall, barrel-chested, thick shoulders. His right hand rested gingerly next to the weapon at his side.

"Not that we know of," I said. "Perhaps spying on them."

"So more of a trespasser than an assailant. Did the kids get a good look at him?" He stepped forward in the dim light and Mr. Schroeder held the lantern toward him. He wore a dark navy policeman's uniform with Mumford Police printed in yellow-gold letters over his badge, bright even in the shadowed barn hall. Motes of hay dust suspended themselves like stardust in the lantern's beam. I knew what was coming — the tingling in my nose — and sneezed.

"I do not think so," said Benjamin. "We will see what the older boys have to say when they return."

"I'm going to call it in, just to be on the safe side, what with that hanged man and all not far from here," the officer said matter-of-factly. I realized he hadn't introduced himself. He trudged back toward the patrol car, and the animated voices filtering from the porch.

A horse nuzzled me through the stall gate

while Benjamin and I waited. He returned the lantern to its post, and the shadowed images of plow, thrasher, buggy, wagon, and other unidentifiable objects took on large, abstract shapes, mysteries of some foreign geometry. I adjusted my wire-rimmed glasses just as someone's hand gripped my shoulder. Jumping involuntarily, I turned at a right angle to find Peter standing before me.

"Sorry!" he boomed, panting. "Did you see him? Did he come back this way?"

"Where are Jacob and Nathan?" demanded their father, just as the Mumford policeman returned to the scene.

"They kept going — wanted to make sure it wasn't Mark Yoder pulling a prank on them. But we're all pretty sure it wasn't an Amish man. He was wearing a black T-shirt and camouflage pants, hiking boots, maybe. Not your traditional Amish-wear." His face flushed from his evening run across the wooded fields. Even in the dim light his khakis appeared mud-splattered and matted with burrs and thistles. He nervously ran his fingers through his wheat-blond nest of hair.

"But he didn't try to harm you or the children?" the officer asked again. "And nothing was stolen?"

"No, he just seemed to be spying on us. You know, Leah thought she heard something when she first came out on the porch. Luke was teasing her about it. Maybe he'd been trying to spy on the house and then when we came out, he hid down here," Pete ventured.

"Why would anyone want to spy on our dinner hour?" asked Benjamin, angry at the violation of privacy. "Strangers and more strangers," he muttered, lapsing into German again.

"Perhaps he knew that your daughter discovered Simon's body," I said.

The officer scratched his ear before replying in his gravelly voice. "Maybe he wanted to see who your visitors here were. I called it in to the station. Dispatcher said he'd send a patrol car out this way later tonight. Probably nothing — just a kid or hobo passing through."

"Yes, perhaps," I said, distracted by something trying to push its way to the surface of my consciousness. "I'm Griffin Reed, rector of Avenell Parish, and this is my curate, Father Peter Abernathy. This is Mr. Benjamin Schroeder."

"Officer Steadman Doyle." Firm handshakes all around.

"I appreciate you taking Peter and me

back up the mountain," I said.

"No problem, no problem at all. I'm ready whenever the two of you are."

By the time we left ten minutes later, Jacob and Nathan had returned. Peter and I had been saying our thank-yous and goodnights when the two young men came sprinting up from the dark silhouettes of cottonwood trees between the house and barn. Mark Yoder had been home with his family the entire evening, either at the dinner table or with his father tinkering on their van.

I recalled hearing that the Yoders were one of several Amish families who owned automobiles in Tremont, where mostly buggies ruled the roads. I had been surprised but Peter told me that, while controversial, more and more Amish families used them for non-Amish jobs or to run home businesses — distributing the crafts, canned goods, and furniture that balanced the decline of farming income. I returned to one of my earlier questions and wondered if Mark Yoder, or whoever the spy was tonight, had a car parked nearby. The ridge road really wasn't that far away.

But Benjamin's question certainly seemed more urgent: What was so important at the Schroeder household to compel someone to spy? Did Leah know more than she realized about Simon's death? Had the murderer followed us to the Judas Tree this afternoon? Were the Schroeders in danger? As a recipient of my new Amish friends' hospitality, I worried that someone would take advantage of their generous spirit, their willingness to trust.

As we pulled away in the Mumford squad car, I in the front seat next to Officer Steadman and Peter in the back behind the protective plexiglass shield, I decided to call Dan when I got home and ask for extra protection for the Schroeder farm. I felt a familiar discouragement, an awareness that this was only the beginning to something more dangerous and malevolent; it was the same feeling that haunted me throughout my involvement with the murder in the Martyr's Chapel five months ago. A feeling that I had hoped to never experience again.

The police band radio crackled numbers and letters in low male voices as we made our way through the tiny village square with its bakery, restaurant, three craft stores, two furniture stores, feed mill, buggy shop, blacksmith, leather goods, and livery. All was quiet and dark this night, the quaint strip a forlorn ghost town. As we hit Highway 19 winding upward to Avenell,

Officer Doyle asked perfunctory questions about my role as priest and about university life, then shifted the conversation to the man found hanging from the Judas Tree. He seemed very curious about Peter's and my connection to the crime. Even though he was in law enforcement, I found myself uncomfortable disclosing my friendship with Simon. Instead, Peter revealed that he was hoping to marry Leah Schroeder and the officer grinned.

"Good luck," said Doyle. "The Amish aren't the easiest folks to get along with."

"Why do you say that, Officer?" I asked.

"Well, that hangman's tree is reason enough. I hear Hostetler grew up down there, then moved away," Doyle said, neither fact nor query. "I wonder who would've held a grudge for thirty-something years. Sure looks like one of them Amish people did it." His southern drawl bit the end of his speculation, emphasizing the clear distinction he made between us and them.

"I disagree, Officer Doyle," I replied, wishing I could see his face in the dim lighting from the car's interior, see the eyes behind his animosity. His uniform cap still shadowed his thin, sharp nose and jawbone.

"Well, who else then? Not many other folks roamin' around the outskirts of Tremont." It was clearly a forgone conclusion in his mind. " 'Course, you know them people, right? You must have some idea, else you wouldn't be helpin' Sheriff Claiborne and all," he said, agitated at my defense. "Didn't I hear that some special forensics hotshot was coming down to check the crime scene today?"

It was silent as we rolled into a sharp curve. "Yes," I finally said as we entered the next rolling arc in the road. "That's what I heard, too." My turn to do a little fishing. Maybe there was more reason for his prejudice than just small-town small-mindedness. "Do you know much about Tremont or the people who live there?"

"Well, just what everybody knows that's grown up here. That they dress funny and keep to themselves, mostly. Heard rumors all my life that they would harbor fugitives from the law if they felt like the government was being unfair. They don't have much to do with us outsiders, I know that. 'Course, that keeps the crime rate lower in that part of the county."

I wondered if his rumors were local superstitions or had some actual basis, so I asked, "Do you know of any fugitives the Amish have harbored?"

He thought a minute before replying,

"Well, back in the '60s, I heard that they hid draft dodgers because they themselves don't believe in violence. Something like that. 'Course, there was that trouble back then with the boys over at Dolby next door to 'em."

He adjusted the dial on his scanner, and soon I heard Maria Alvarez's voice from the sheriff's office sending Dan to help a stalled motorist stranded on the other side of Eaglehead Mountain.

"What was that trouble all about?" asked Peter.

"Well, the base needed more land to expand its airfields and all. They tried to buy the land they needed from the Amish, but the Plain folk didn't want to sell. So the Air Force took over a stretch of land by way of eminent domain. Upset the Amish to no end. They even protested outside Dolby's main gate. But it didn't do no good. What the government needs, the government takes, I reckon. Heard rumor that Dolby might be expandin' again."

We passed the familiar landmarks of the small stretch of downtown Avenell — the Diner, Kwik-Stop, and Walt's Barbershop. As we paused at the stoplight, I could see several figures in the pale light inside the Diner. One pair I recognized as my sister and Lyle Slater, smiling and nodding over cups of coffee.

Weary and unsettled from a long and puzzling day, I was eager to be home. Peter and I exchanged our good-byes as the squad car turned at the corner of Southern Avenue and Maryland. I thanked Officer Doyle and walked the remaining few feet to the rectory. Lingering on the porch, I inhaled the moist, mountain air, crisp and clean as spring water. It was almost ten-thirty and the living room lamp had been left on for me.

As I locked the door behind me, something I had seldom done before the murder on our campus last fall, I sensed something brewing inside me, an uneasiness, something that was not conducive to sleep. I thought back to Simon's expression during our lunch barely a week ago now. Had he really said, *"I'm on to something that must be exposed in Tremont"*? Would he have told me more if we had not been interrupted? Was his discovery directly linked to his death, or just a *post hoc* coincidence? No, there were simply too many coincidences piling up in Tremont.

It seemed as if Simon was about to confide in me prior to his death. Despite the pain of his father's affair and expulsion from the community, I found it hard to believe that my friend had returned to exact revenge on the Amish. And yet, what could he have possibly discovered that would precipitate such a violent end? The perpetrator behind the destruction of Amish property? Or did such crimes against the Amish belie darker secrets?

The Judas Tree loomed as large as my questions in my dreams that night. Tangled and brackish, thick limbs snared me as I tried to climb to the top of its boughs, closing in on me tighter and tighter. Perhaps these same visions haunted Simon Hostetler on his way out of this world.

Chapter Eight

Fear and Trembling

Despite my fitful sleep, Saturday morning found me energetically explaining the previous day's events to Caroline Barr, fresh-faced and springlike in her powder blue blouse and denim skirt. We met at the Diner where Willadean, her curly pile of hair the antithesis of Caroline's straight, supple bob, took our order for the 3-2-1 Tiger's Paw breakfast: three pancakes, two sausages, one egg. The place was crowded with students — some up early to head to the library, some who had partied all night and were just now heading back to Fraternity Row. I waved to Vera and Tom Welch, dear parishioners for some time — he worked in University Admissions — seated in a booth in the far left corner. Our waitress's husband, Willie, with his thick lids and heavy jowls, sliced bacon and poured waffles at the large grill behind the counter. The general noise level provided a kind of intimacy since everyone was forced to concentrate on their own immediate conversation in order to hear and be heard.

Caroline had accepted my apologies for not calling yesterday, especially considering my trip to Tremont. She simply smiled, nodded, and adjusted the silver charm bracelet gracing her left wrist. So natural, so understanding. It was one of the things that I appreciated about her, the sense of no game-playing, no hurt feelings, no false expectations. We were friends with two full, busy lives of our own. When we could be together, we simply enjoyed each other's company. While I found her attractive and vital, I certainly was not about to rush into any kind of romantic entanglement. Joan Dowinger's affront came to mind and I sensed my blood rising. Perhaps such a conversation with Caroline was necessary, not for Joan's or anyone else's sake, but for my own. But here was surely not the time or place. It was much easier to focus on the loss of my friend and the subsequent investigation and my small part in it.

I shared some of my grief with her, explaining more about my friendship with Simon and how surprised I'd been to rekindle our common interests after all these years. Describing the Judas Tree, the scene of Simon's death, proved more difficult.

"My dreams were so vivid and surreal last night, with the tree looming above me, encasing me, that I know my description sounds exaggerated. But there really is something . . ."

"Malevolent?" she offered.

"No, it's more complex than that. Maybe it's the old legends coloring my emotions. The feeling I had at the Judas Tree was more bittersweet — poignant even. I don't know how to explain it. And then to have this intruder at the Schroeders. I'm afraid this business will only get darker before it's over. Perhaps malevolent is the word to describe it after all."

Caroline listened attentively as I recounted other impressions surrounding my friend's death: his mysterious allusion to a certain discovery among the Amish; the encroachment of the military base; the desirability of Tremont land by several other interest groups; Simon's family history in the Amish community.

"So tell me, what *are* the Amish like?" she asked. "I know next to nothing about them — just the popular culture image of the aloof, pious, happy farmer. You say they respect your common faith, so are they Christian, then?"

The volume picked up as a table of young women burst into a crescendo of laughter. A burst of smoke and the scent of bacon grease wafted from Willie's grill, and I saw him scowl. I took my last bite of eggs, scrambled hard, and cold by now.

"Yes, they are definitely followers of Christ. Historically, they evolved from the Protestant Reformation in the sixteenth century, from a group known as Anabaptists. While baptized as infants in the Catholic church, they believed one had to be rebaptized as a faith-committed adult. They eventually became known as Mennonites after one of their strident leaders, Menno Simons.

"By the end of the seventeenth century, the Amish emerged as yet another distinct group in this denominational chain. They followed the teachings of Jacob Amman, who called for a much stricter separation between their church and the outside world — including shunning. The various Mennonite and Amish groups emigrated to our country in large concentrations during the mid-seventeenth to late nineteenth centuries, mostly of Swiss, Dutch, and German ancestry. They settled in Pennsylvania, of course — Lancaster County is probably the best-known Amish settlement — but also in Ohio, Indiana, and smaller pockets in Kentucky, Tennessee, and Georgia. From what I've read lately, they continue to struggle with technology, with urban sprawl, with the pressures of modern society . . . just like the rest of us, I guess." I wiped my mouth with a paper napkin and folded it next to my empty plate. "Forgive me for going on so long. I didn't mean to lecture you."

"No, no, don't apologize," Caroline looked at me intently and smiled. "I'm very impressed — you'd make a good professor." She rested her napkin on the table just as Willadean brought our ticket and placed it next to my water glass. "And what about Tremont? How long has it existed?" Caroline asked, as if to prove her interest.

"I think a group of about a dozen families from Lancaster settled here right after World War I. I don't know if they were dissatisfied with life in Pennsylvania, felt too crowded, or simply wanted to move to our beautiful area. A second wave of families came in the '50s. I guess they have over a thousand people down there now. And like the other Amish communities around the country — at least according to what Simon told me — they've had to adjust to a reduced agricultural economy. Carroll County still leads the state in alfalfa and soybean production, largely because of the Tremont Amish, but the national market reached a plateau years ago. So they've taken up entrepreneurial businesses — crafts, baked goods, furniture, tourist-attracting types of things."

"I've only visited once, right after I moved here. I had lunch at that little restaurant next to the bakery and bought some quilt designs as gifts for some friends back in New York. A very quaint little town." She sipped the last of her tea, and I noticed that many of the students were starting to filter out.

"Enough about me and the Anabaptists," I said, tired of my troubling preoccupation. "Thanks for indulging me, but I want to hear about your week."

She smiled. "I'm always happy to listen to you." Caroline poured more hot water over her tea bag until the inside of her cup shimmered a dark jade tone. "Well, on Tuesday — did I tell you this already? — I talked with the director of the Louisville Festival about how my play will be staged. He wants me to consider letting them produce it in the round, something I hadn't even considered . . ."

Despite my best efforts, my mind remained lost in the missing details of the last hours of Simon Hostetler's life. I sipped more coffee in an attempt to focus my attention on my present company.

" . . . So then yesterday I told Dr. Lear that

we'd have to wait to produce the Brecht play until the fall. He wasn't too happy about it, but most of the committee trusts my judgment more than his, so the motion passed. Anyway, that's what's consumed me all week. Very mundane by comparison to yours. Grif? Are you okay?" She speared a triangular bite of pancake for emphasis, while I, returning to the conversation at hand, stirred more sugar into my black coffee. It tasted good and rich, unusual for Willadean's brew. I was glad I had given up chocolate for Lent instead of caffeine.

"Forgive me, Caroline," I said. "I can't quit thinking about Simon, and the effect of his death on the Amish. I was listening."

"It's all right," she smiled. "As I was saying, my week pales in comparison to yours." She patted my hand casually for reassurance, and I felt blood rush to my face. "Do you plan on remaining involved with the case? What's next in the investigation? Is there anything I can do to help you?"

Her words, perhaps innocuous enough, inflamed me to speak without thinking. "Why does everyone think I enjoy playing detective? You know as well as anyone that I didn't like being involved with that murder in the Martyr's Chapel last fall . . . and now this. No, I am not involved with the case.

But I am troubled by my friend's murder," I concluded.

"Easy, Grif. I wasn't implying that you enjoy getting dragged into this kind of thing," she said. "It's only, well, as you put it so often, God uses us if we're willing to be used. He certainly used you as His instrument of justice last fall. Perhaps you should examine whether or not you're willing to be used by Him in resolving the death of your friend Simon."

The blush that arose at her touch moments before had slowly become indignation. Her words were spoken sincerely enough, but carried the slightest edge of instructive rebuke. How ironic, I thought, that I was concerned about the status of her faith and here she was giving me spiritual counsel. My silence must have seemed conspicuous.

Caroline continued. "I'm sure Bea has already said it, but let me tell you again: Be careful." She could not hide the concern in her voice. "I've grown quite fond of you, and I don't want some Amish-hating psycho . . . you know what I'm saying."

I remained resistant to her worry. "I'm sure God will protect me if He is indeed calling me to be His Sherlock Holmes. Better yet, Chesterton's Father Brown."

"Grif, you're taking this the wrong way," she said, trying to find my hand again but not before I withdrew it. "I'm only saying that I see God using you in numerous ways in people's lives, but that I want you to be careful nonetheless. That's all I meant."

"Thank you. I guess I'm not used to receiving spiritual counsel from you —" I stopped short but the damage was done; my words made quick, sharp stabs to her heart. "I didn't mean . . . that came out the wrong way," I offered.

Her jewel-blue eyes telegraphed unexpected hurt.

"How *did* you mean for it to come out, Grif? Because I don't have a degree in theology or belong to the Episcopal Church, I can't speak about God? I've never heard you so pious — I . . . I thought you were different." She paused and cocked her head before continuing; I could smell the lilac scent of her lovely auburn hair. "You sound as if you resent the fact that I care about you. Are you backing away from me?"

Anger flared in her voice now, and my stomach knotted the drawstring around my breakfast.

"Caroline, I'm sorry. I . . . didn't mean it the way it sounded. I'm not backing away. It's just that —"

"It's just that we're starting to care for each other and that makes you uncomfortable. You're afraid for me to expect anything — any advancement — in our friendship. But I wish you'd just say that instead of making remarks about my qualifications to speak about God."

"Caroline, I agree we need to talk about the direction of our friendship," I said, suddenly defensive.

She gathered her small leather backpack as if to leave. "I thought you were different, Griffin Reed. I thought you were not intimidated by someone just as strong and smart as you are. I thought you weren't hung up on denominations and rules but on the heart. Maybe I was wrong." Her words were weighted as smoothly and clearly as round stones in a riverbed. "Call me when you know what you want."

She got up and left me sitting there a bit dazed until just as she was opening the door and its jangling bell punctuated her exit, I said, "Wait! Caroline —" But she was gone. Looking around, a few people stared at me while others continued eating and talking unaware. I drank my cold coffee, the dregs etched into the bottom of the cup, and signaled Willadean for a refill.

"Hey, it happens to the best of us, Father

Grif," said the street-smart waitress, smacking her gum.

"What are you talking about, Willadean?" I demanded.

"Fight with the girlfriend. I could read her lips clear across the room. Like I said, it happens to the best of us," she replied, filling my cup.

"Dr. Barr is not my girlfriend," I said.

"Well, all I'll say is, you sure did look happy when she walked in here this morning." She left me to offer her advice-column counsel to some other unlucky patron. I poured in extra sugar and stirred my coffee until a dark amber vortex swirled in the center of my cup.

I suddenly felt very old and foolish and angry. What if Caroline was right? What if I was merely throwing up defenses to keep from growing closer to her? What if I was afraid of confronting her about the true status of her faith? What if I was afraid of loving someone again the way I'd loved Amy?

Chores and errands took my mind off the tangled skein of emotions and self-recrimination. I got out the lawn mower, which had been winterized and in storage for the past six months, replaced the plug, changed the filter, and sharpened the blade. I then cleaned the garage, sorting through boxes of old sermon notes and parish records. I was well into cleaning my tools and clearing my workbench when Bea came out to find me.

"There you are! What in the world has gotten into you? Spring fever? Isn't it a little early to be getting the mower out?" she said.

I had purposed not to let my sister in on my morning's frustration. She stood there in jeans and a sweat shirt, her silvery hair hidden beneath a red kerchief like a domestic pirate. "No, I was just in the mood to clean up, get some order out here." I tried to sound nonchalant, just another typical Saturday afternoon.

"Well, I don't know what it is, but something's going on with you. Did you tell Caroline what Joan said? You two didn't break up over that, did you? Oh, Grif, tell me you and Caroline didn't break up!" She stood there anxiously with hands on her thick hips.

"Bea, we did not discuss Joan's problem and we didn't break up. Besides, we're just friends. There's nothing to break up." I held up a ratchet screwdriver as if it were the most fascinating object I'd ever seen.

"Is it Simon's death? You're sad, aren't

you? An old friendship is renewed and then snuffed out before you know it. I know how hard that must be," she said, extending her hands. "If you want to talk about it, I'm always glad to listen."

I nodded and murmured, "Thanks, sis."

"Oh! That's why I was looking for you. Dan called and wanted to see if you could meet with him and Sam down at his office in about an hour. I told him you'd call him back only if you couldn't make it." She pushed a stray hair back under the scarlet kerchief. "Will you be home for supper tonight? I don't know what your plans are, but I assumed you and Caroline would be —"

"I thought maybe I'd invite Peter over for Scrabble or maybe cards," I said.

She looked me up and down. "You *did* have a fight with Caroline, didn't you! Oh, Grif, I'm so sorry."

"It's not important. Now, what were you saying about tonight? I assume you and Lyle have a date."

She giggled. "Yes, he's taking me out to dinner. I couldn't remember if I told you or not. I just want to know if you want me to fix you something or if you want to eat out. Maybe you and Peter could order a pizza?"

While I should have been happy for my sister, I was annoyed that she was violating our old unspoken Saturday night routine: Garrison Keillor on the radio, homemade pizza, and Scrabble afterward. Plus, I still had my misgivings about the Reverend Slater.

I tried to sound upbeat. "No, don't cook anything, sis. A deep dish from the Pizza King is a fine idea. I'll call Peter before I go meet Dan and Sam. Where's the suave pastor of Avenell First Church taking my favorite sister tonight?"

She smiled. "Well, it's a surprise. He promised me it was someplace I'd never been before. I have to confess, he makes me feel like a teenager sometimes."

I turned my back to her as if to return to my tools and rolled my eyes. "Just be careful, Bea. Just be careful."

"Oh, don't worry, Grif. I can take care of myself. You know that. Just because Lyle can make me feel like a schoolgirl doesn't mean that I am one."

She turned to go back into the house and I yelled, "Have a good time!"

Life suddenly felt very messy, very out of my control, without rhyme or reason or the secure predictability that I so appreciated about Avenell in the first place. As I cleaned up in preparation for my meeting at the sheriff's office, I acknowledged all the fear that had wedged itself inside my soul. Fear of change, fear of getting too close to Caroline, fear of getting hurt — either by her or by losing her to some outside force like Amy's cancer. I was afraid that I was about to lose Peter, either to the Amish faith of the Schroeder family or to the leadership hierarchy of the Episcopal Church. My exchange with my sister made me realize that I was afraid of losing her, as well. Oh, not losing her for good, but losing the familiarity of her presence in our home. What if she were to marry Lyle Slater? So many possible changes and so much fear of all of them. Things that were once unimaginable were now concrete possibilities.

Changing into jeans and a cotton sweater, I went through my mental index of Scripture verses on fear: *The* LORD *is my strength and my shield; in him my heart trusts; When I am afraid, I put my trust in thee; There is no fear in love, but perfect love casts out fear; For you did not receive the spirit of slavery to fall back into fear, but you have received the spirit of sonship.*

And then as I was tying my walking shoes, a troubling verse came to mind, one I found every bit as unsettling as the one carved into the Judas Tree after Simon Hostetler's death: *Therefore, my beloved, as you have always obeyed, so now, not only in my presence but much more in my absence, work out your own salvation with fear and trembling; for God is at work in you, both to will and to work for his good pleasure.* Even though I knew the context of the verse was different than my present grumblings about change and the uncertainty of my future, I still did not like what it required of me. The reminder that my fears should lead me to greater dependence on God. The reminder that God was not nearly as concerned with my comfortable security as I was. Was I even afraid of how God might want to use me to bring justice in the death of Simon Hostetler? I did not like this question most of all.

As I was about to head out the door, the phone rang. I paused, expecting Bea to answer it, but then I recalled that she had walked over to Berthy Weismuller's. After a moment's debate, I picked up the receiver and heard an unfamiliar voice ask for Griffin Reed.

"This is he," I responded, annoyed at what I presumed was a sales call.

"We have not met before, Brother Reed. But my brother spoke of you. This is Lydia Miller . . . Simon Hostetler's sister . . . I . . ." Her voice grew weaker as if she were about to faint or to hang up based on second thoughts.

"Yes, Mrs. Miller. I . . . I'm so terribly sorry about the loss of your brother. He was a good man, a good friend to me. Did he tell you that we attended seminary together years ago?" I asked.

"Yes, and that is why I am calling you. Your sheriff came by this morning and told me that the body would be released in another day or two. As Simon's only living kin, I am the one to bury him. . . ." Her voice dissolved into tears. "I was wondering if you would conduct a service for my brother, Brother Reed. Bishop Zook has granted me and my family permission to attend such a service but not to have it in our church here in Tremont. I wondered if you would conduct Simon's funeral at your church there on the mountain. . . ."

The poor woman, I thought to myself. I understood why the bishop would not wish to conduct the service in his church, or presumably have Simon buried on Amish property, but it seemed rather petty at the moment in the wake of Lydia Miller's grief.

"Yes, of course. I would be honored to conduct Simon's funeral. When did you wish to schedule it?"

We exchanged several details about the time and order of the service then. Simon Hostetler would be celebrated and laid to rest the following afternoon, Sunday, after church. Lydia's brother had left instructions to be buried in a private cemetery in Pennsylvania, close to his home. She would have his body shipped to a funeral home there first thing Monday morning.

"Thank you, Brother Reed," concluded the woman. "I suspect my brother trusted you for a reason. When I come to the service tomorrow, I have something my brother left for you."

"What? Something Simon left for me?" I blurted. "I don't understand. How could he have known he was going to —"

"I do not know that. Wait until tomorrow and I will bring it to you. Thank you."

"Bring what with you? I don't understand," I said, but it was too late. She had hung up. I stood there for a moment, lost in thought or prayer or both before recalling my mission prior to her call.

On my way down to the station, I prayed for God's peace and comfort for Lydia Miller and her family, for assurance of His sovereignty. I prayed for the wisdom and compassion to conduct a fitting service to honor my friend.

And after an image of the Judas Tree sprang to mind, I prayed for protection from the Evil One, who, I was convinced, prowled even now like a roaring lion, hungry to devour a community of sheep.

Chapter Nine

The Brethren

I arrived late and out of breath to the sheriff's office but quickly explained about the phone call from Lydia Miller regarding the funeral service for Simon. The sheriff and Dan nodded and asked me to be seated in the confined office.

"I hope you don't mind my giving her your number," said Dan. "She seemed pretty distraught when she learned the body would be released to her as next of kin. She should've been expecting it."

"Grief blindsides us," I offered. "And I'm guessing her loss is compounded because of the controversy surrounding her family in the community." I summarized what I'd learned from the Schroeders the night before.

"Yes, indeed," whistled Dan, pouring me a cup of coffee.

Sam Claiborne told Dan to make a note about Caleb Hostetler's affair with Anna Kaufman and to see what he could find out. Then the short barrel of a man launched into reading strings of medical and forensic jargon. As he finished, he pushed a white bakery bag toward me. Inside the bag were thumbprint cookies from Trudy's Bakery. They're the sheriff's favorite, so she usually sends over a dozen when they're fresh. Today the center icing was tinted pink, and I chuckled to myself about three grown men eating the dainty cookies in whole bites. Hearing about the way poor Simon ended his final hours, however, soon made me lose my humor as well as my appetite for the rich shortbread cookies.

"So what you're saying is that Simon Hostetler was likely dead *before* he was hanged?"

"Yep. Not certain, but likely. Head injury, brain contusion, hemorrhaging. Then in his weakened state, he couldn't put up a fight when the rope was placed 'round his neck." Sam Claiborne had grown a close-cropped beard over the winter months that now accentuated his thick jowls and deep-set eyes. The truth of the matter was the beard only reinforced his nickname, "Bulldog." He concluded, "Likely incurred by a blunt instrument — anything from a tire tool to the butt of a Beretta. Doc Graham's betting on the latter."

"Wouldn't the blow to the head have done

the trick by itself and killed the guy? Why string him up, too? To send some kind of message? Seems like overkill to me," Dan reflected, adding, "No pun intended."

"Any other wounds or health problems?" I asked, grabbing the white bakery bag for another cookie.

"See for yourself, Grif." Sam tossed Doc Graham's report toward me across the industrial metal desktop. I could hear the faint whir of a fax machine and the low music of Maria Alvarez's voice at the dispatch desk up front. The place had certainly calmed down and returned to its small-town pace since the commotion last fall. But since that was when I met Caroline, I was reminded of my morning's conversation with her, and I didn't want to replay that again. I took the manila file as Sam added, "The victim had severe cuts and scratches, several bruises and lacerations — likely from hitting tree branches on the way up — but nothing else in the fatal category. Between the head wound and the noose, it's not like he needed anything else."

Something in me churned each time I heard Dan or the sheriff refer to Simon Hostetler as the "victim." I did not like the idea of reducing my friend's life to nothing more than a generic role, especially in death.

I realized, however, that like a medical professional treating a patient, law enforcers had to distance themselves and objectify the harsh brutality of the crimes they investigated. Still, it did not keep me from thinking about the unique individual, the human being made in the image of the Creator, who had memories, hopes, desires, and fears. I reminded myself then to remember always the total person, not just the final role he played.

"Doc doesn't mention any indication of terminal diseases or conditions here," I said, scanning the medical jargon in the tersely worded report. "Further reinforcement that this was not suicide."

"Not that we need it," said Dan. "If Hostetler had strung himself up, he couldn't have cleaned up the scene afterward."

"Yep," Sam confirmed, "definitely a homicide. By the way, we sent word for a patrol car to keep watch over the Schroeders. Any ideas who might've been spying on y'all last night?" He bit into his third cookie, the sandy crumbs sticking to his lips and beard. "More coffee?"

"No thanks," I said, thinking how best to characterize my impressions. "No, I don't. Dan told you about our run-in with the officers from the Air Force base. Maybe Bledsoe put us under surveillance since he's so eager to take over the investigation."

"I hope that won't happen. Something fishy about the good general's eagerness to relieve us of the case. He hasn't returned my calls," replied the sheriff. "But I've got several friends down at the Dolby base. I'll see if I can schedule an interview with Bledsoe first of the week, find out what's going on."

Speaking of friends down at the base, I made a mental note to call my old colleague Leland Finch, the base chaplain at Dolby. It was a long shot, but perhaps he could shed some light on the base's relationship to the Amish of Tremont. I decided not to mention it to the sheriff or Dan until I'd talked to Leland myself.

Sam continued. "In the meantime, we'll beef up security around Tremont, especially the Schroeders' farm and the Judas Tree. What else did you find out over dinner last night — anything useful?"

I recapped the rest of the information Sarah and Benjamin Schroeder had shared with me. Sam seemed particularly interested in the recent acts of vandalism around the Tremont farms and the interest by several parties in buying out choice Amish property. He half smiled and said,

"Good work, Father Grif."

I bristled at his praise.

"Yes," he continued, "our list of parties interested in a sector of land known as Canaan's Way grows by the hour. We've got local farmers, the Dolby base, as well as two corporations — one backed by the Carroll County Industrial Recruitment League. But what's really interesting here . . ." the sheriff paused as he retrieved a pair of bifocals from underneath a cluster of loose papers on his desk. He rested the glasses on the bridge of his nose, wiped another crumb from the corner of his mouth, and scanned a document from the stack on his desk. "Well, you tell him what you found among Hostetler's effects, Dan."

My tall friend sauntered to his superior's desk and braced his seat against the corner. He shuffled through a bulging file of his own and grabbed a sheet that looked like a bank statement from where I was sitting.

"This is a quarterly investment report," explained Dan, "from a company known as the Omega Group. Not much we can tell about what kind of business they do. But we do know two things: the Omega Group has approached at least three families in Tremont, and according to a letter we found in his personal effects, Simon Hostetler was connected to the company."

"What?" I asked incredulously. "Simon? Part of some corporation trying to buy up Tremont land?"

"You seem surprised," gauged Sam.

"Well, yes. Simon claimed to be here on sabbatical, working on his next cultural anthropology book on a religious group. He never struck me as a businessman. It's hard for me to imagine why he'd be involved with a company trying to buy up Amish land."

"Revenge, maybe?" offered Sam. "Getting back at the Amish families who threw his father out and split up his family all those years ago? That seems the obvious possibility."

"And maybe someone in the community found out about Simon's ties to Omega and decided to put a stop to his attempts at buying up their land," Dan added.

"Wait — both of you! You don't understand. Simon Hostetler was not a bitter man. Nothing he displayed indicated any kind of bitterness or spitefulness whatsoever. He seemed content for the most part, dedicated to his work. . . ." Perhaps I rushed to his defense too quickly.

"But people can change over the years, Grif," Dan added, as if reading my thoughts. "Maybe Hostetler had a lot of secrets. . . ."

"I'm still not convinced. What else did you find in his effects? Did Agent Corey turn up anything noteworthy from the scene?" I asked.

Sam and Dan exchanged glances, as if willing to change the topic for my benefit. "Nothing unusual. He's still running some of the evidence. But he and Jerry both think that the hanging was clearly premeditated since the scene was relatively clean and swept up. It seems likely that whoever did this knocked out Hostetler, dragged him to the Judas Tree, tied the rope around his neck, then climbed the oak and tied the other end around that forked branch. Then they left him there while they cleaned up and walked away."

"What time did this likely take place? Sometime Wednesday night, correct?" I asked, thinking of the seclusion of the dark clearing.

"Probably between midnight and four A.M. Doc Graham's betting closer to midnight based on body temp, but he acknowledges that could be off since the body was outside all night," the sheriff replied.

"What about the Amish clothes? Any idea why Simon was wearing them? Could he have been mistaken for an Amish man and killed in a random hate crime against the folk in Tremont?"

Sam scratched his bearded chin. "I suppose so," he mused, rising and pacing a worn path in the yellowed linoleum. "Especially considering the wave of damaged crops and such that the Schroeders told you about. Hostetler could've simply been in the wrong place at the wrong time."

"In the wrong clothes," added Dan. "Although this does seem awfully elaborate to have been a random hate crime, don't you think? We still have plenty of other leads we're following up."

"May I inquire what they are?" I asked.

Sam nodded. "I know you're eager to believe the best about your friend. And we appreciate your help on this in any way you can provide. It's crystal clear that the Amish trust you more than us. Dan, tell him what else you've got."

Dan shuffled through his notes. "Well, we've got his research assistant, Ms. Mariah Gates, a grad student from Penn State. She's young, pretty, very intellectual, and seemed quite shook up about this. She reluctantly handed over Hostetler's journal, his notes, and the manuscript for his new project, *Judgment and Justice Among the Amish*. In fact — what do you think, Sheriff? — I'll bet Father Grif here might be able to make more sense out of this than you or I can. What if I send a copy of all this home with him to look over for us?"

"Good idea," Sam affirmed. "I know you have other responsibilities, but anything you could tell us from looking over his effects would be appreciated."

I nodded.

"Here, Grif, I'd definitely like your opinion on this section right here." Dan handed me a thick sheaf of what looked like research notes. "This appears to be an outline and notes for one chapter that could've clearly got Dr. Hostetler in trouble. Look toward the middle of this page," he directed.

My eyes scanned the page as Sam summarized the contents. "The Brethren. A legendary vigilante type group that tried to prevent the Amish from settling in the Cumberland Valley almost a hundred years ago. Locals thought them strange and were afraid they would take over the farming economy — which they pretty much did. But not without overcoming numerous setbacks: burned houses, dead farm animals, poisoned wells. Three men were finally apprehended and convicted of malicious intent to harm property. They got off with a slap on the wrist. But supposedly the group continued to exist until World War II, when they consolidated with the local chapter of the KKK."

I took a deep breath and translated the handwritten notes before me. "So Simon thought that the recent vandalism was a resurgence of the Brethren?"

"Or else he was somehow involved in the vandalism himself," Sam said softly.

"No. I don't care what happened all those years ago with Simon's father and the affair he had. Simon was not the kind of man who would hurt others. He must have suspected one of the vested-interest groups trying to buy up Amish land of using Brethren-like scare tactics."

"Perhaps. As you can see, he doesn't indicate who he thinks was behind it. Of course, we mustn't forget that Hostetler himself was part of one of those vested-interest groups."

I shook my head, now eager to go through my friend's notes and journals in an attempt to clear him of any criminal association. Sipping the last of my now cold coffee, I tossed the paper cup into the plastic-lined trash can. Just the very notion of a Klan-like organization trying to scare off the Amish — whether a hundred years ago or this week — made me queasy. My sugary indulgence of thumbprint cookies churned in my stomach.

"The only other real lead we have here," explained the sheriff, "is that Hostetler was poking around a lot into old wounds between the Tremont folk and the base at Dolby. Look at all the government documents he's accessed here. Some have only become public record within the last year or so."

I flipped the pages in my packet and found the reference to which he alluded. "The Department of Defense invoked eminent domain in order to purchase over two thousand acres when the Air Force base expanded back in 1969. There were marches, demonstrations, mostly passive kinds of resistance. That would've been right before Simon moved away from Tremont. He probably remembered the conflict, may have even participated in the demonstrations," I said.

"Possibly. He may have been digging up the past for his book. In fact, Ms. Gates said that she'd never seen Hostetler so 'personally motivated' on a project before," added Dan.

"I'll make sure I ask my contacts at Dolby if they'd ever heard of Hostetler before," replied Sam. "And I hope to see how Bledsoe reacts when I mention that the dead man had been doing research into the topic."

I clenched my jaw just thinking of the smug, authoritative general. "I'll look over all this and see if I have any ideas," I offered. "I want my friend's reputation cleared. And I want whoever killed him to be brought to justice."

"So do we, my friend," echoed Dan. "So do we."

"Before we wrap up here," said the sheriff, "I wondered if you could tell us what you know about the Amish and particularly about ours in Tremont."

I nodded and began to rattle off my limited knowledge of Amish history, traditions, and customs, much like I'd done with Caroline that morning. We concluded by coming up with a list of Amish folk that Sam wanted to question.

"Well, that makes a little more sense," Sam said, running his thick finger down the handscrawled list of names. "We've got reports that several dozen young people use the Judas Tree site from time to time for all-night partics. In fact, Don Slocum down at Mumford PD faxed me over a couple of arrests of Amish teens he made last year for public drunkenness."

"Yes, the Rumspringa, or 'Time Out,' as it's often called, is a time for young Amish men and women to indulge in worldly pleasures, to work outside the community, to decide for themselves if they truly want to join the church and commit to the Amish way of life," I explained. "The Judas Tree does seem like a perfect spot for an all-night party. There's also a spot down by the river that the Schroeders mentioned."

"We'll call in the teens for questioning, as well, but I don't expect much," said Sam.

Dan looked over the sheriff's shoulder and urged, "Let's concentrate our efforts on key players here: Hostetler's sister, Lydia Miller, and her husband, Josiah —"

"Any idea of where Simon went after he left his sister's place?" I interrupted, recalling what had been discovered so far about his last day.

Sam answered. "No, not exactly. We have a notation in his appointment book that simply says 'Meet J., eight.' While Hostetler interviewed about a dozen Amish in the past month, most were done anonymously — he simply noted initials. We'll see what we can come up with for J.'s identity, but you keep your ears open as well."

"At least we have a starting point," encouraged Dan. "Four names appear in his appointment book: Bishop Thomas Zook, Joseph Yoder, Sarah Schroeder, and Deborah Kaufman."

I took the list from the sheriff's hand and scanned the curious pairings of biblical first names and Swiss-German surnames. I wondered if one of these Plain folk was a murderer.

This day had definitely not turned out like I would have hoped. My spat with Caroline, my growing list of personal fears, and now the questionable reputation of my deceased friend. Nevertheless, as I returned home late in the afternoon, the spring sun sliding its way down the slope of Eaglehead Mountain and shadows gathering in cool, dark pools beneath the eaves of ancient-looking brownstones and majestic pines, my anger and frustration melted like the winter snow. It was hard to be angry in spring, I decided, driving back from the sheriff's office. Winter was an entirely different story. But a confetti of colors celebrated the landscape: yellow jonquils, white clover and Queen Anne's lace, lavender violets, pink dogwood, and the full spectrum of greens from the gold-toned chartreuse in the leaves of the tulip-poplars to the ebony jade of iris stalks. One could not sustain anger in the face of such beauty.

Parking my LeSabre in its usual spot in the drive, I noticed a navy Mercedes sedan

pull up behind me. A glance at my watch —
almost five — and I knew that my sister's
suave, silver-haired date was here.

"Grif, good to see you again," said Rev.
Slater, clasping my hand firmly with both of
his.

"And you," I smiled. He smelled like pine
solvent, a sweet turpentine kind of smell
that probably cost quite a bit of money. His
tan gabardine trousers and navy blazer con-
trasted with my jeans and casual sweater.
Ah, the world of dating. I wondered if my
colleague had any serious intentions of
moving toward marriage with my sister. It
was a matter I might have to take up with
him soon.

We walked inside together, and I called
out to Bea who replied, "Oh! Just a minute,"
from the direction of her bedroom. Lyle and
I could both tell by her tone that it would be
more than "just a minute." However, I
didn't have to work to come up with conversation topics. I recalled the brouhaha over
First Church's use of white grape juice for
Communion in order to keep the carpets
cleaner. And more importantly, Lyle's almost cryptic mention of his lunch with
Simon Hostetler the day before his death.

As if his thoughts paralleled my own,
Slater said, "Grif, I was wondering where

you stand on this communion issue? Surely you understand that we're simply doing what we feel is in the best interest of the church? Why can't the PAC members show First Church the same respect that they show the Catholics or Pentecostals?"

"Well, Lyle, it's one thing for us to respect your congregation's practices and another to ask us to partake in them, as well. I think we could all agree to disagree if this were merely about minor doctrines or interpretation. But the joint Easter service is something that unites us, despite our many differences, as a community of shared faith."

My voice revealed the weariness that had crystallized from my day of conflicted desires and frustrating fears. Though not surprised, I suddenly felt annoyed that Slater would try to win my allegiance while here to pick up my sister for their date. Despite my desire to share my day's discussions with Bea, I looked forward to having the house to myself that night.

Rev. Slater pulled a dark thread from his tailored jacket with tweezer-like precision. His eyes matched his name; they were the color of slate, a steely blue that now focused on the watercolor print above the mantel. "I see," he sniffed. "But surely this is not the first time this issue has come up. What do the Catholics do during Communion at this beloved community service? I don't imagine they view it quite the same as the Baptists, or even you Episcopalians, for that matter."

I was growing impatient for Beatrice to retrieve Slater and be on their way; I had had enough confrontations today. "You're right. The Catholics typically do not partake in our Communion at the Easter service. That's why we have a sunrise service — to give believers the opportunity to return to their individual churches for worship and Communion if they so desire. Many churches cancel their own services and direct their entire congregations here. Others encourage attendance at our sunrise service, the Easter egg hunt, and so forth, but still hold services of their own. It's worked fine for several decades now, long before the PAC was formed officially."

Slater had seated himself comfortably on the love seat near the fireplace, crossing his long legs and extending his arm along the back of the settee. He exuded casual elegance and a familiarity with my home that I found contemptuous.

"I understand, Grif," he nodded and smiled, patronizing me. "Well, we'll see what my elder board says about the Communion issue. We're meeting tomorrow after the service."

"If I may change the subject," I said, turning on the reading lamp and seating myself in my favorite armchair, an old oak William Morris that had belonged to Amy's parents. She'd had it re-covered for me in a hunter-and-tan print tapestry. "I'm curious about what you said concerning Simon Hostetler. At the Pepper Tree the other day, you mentioned that you thought he was acting strangely?"

Lyle cocked his head toward me inquisitively. "Ah, so the sleuthing continues." He smiled to himself again. "Evidently, poor Dr. Hostetler discovered more than he should have about the Amish. . . ."

"You still believe his paranoid behavior was connected to his research on the Amish?" I questioned.

"Yes. I'm telling you, the man couldn't sit still for a minute when we had lunch just five days ago." He uncrossed his legs and glanced surreptitiously at his expensive looking chrome-faced watch. Of course, now I hoped my sister would continue to primp for at least another five minutes.

"What did you talk about? You said you'd met him at a seminar a few years ago? What was the seminar about?" I tried to sound casual, curious but ultimately unconcerned.

Slater sounded nervous himself. "I met Simon about five years ago at a pastors' seminar called Perceptions of Religion in the Media. He had just come out with a book about the way the media and the public at large perceive church leaders. I reconnected with him afterward, and we've stayed in touch. My great-grandparents had been Amish. It's always been an interest of mine."

"You reconnected with him? I thought you said you met him at the seminar for the first time. Had you known him before?" I couldn't hide my growing interest.

Slater scowled at his slip. "Well, we had run into each other once or twice." He hesitated, clearly out of his scripted control zone, unsure how much to disclose. "We both taught at the same small Bible college out west for a brief interval. But that was ages ago. Like I said, we really didn't connect until that seminar a few years ago." He was clearly eager to move on.

"Oh, really? I didn't know you'd been an academic, Lyle. Bea had mentioned that you had your Doctorate of Divinity, but I didn't know you'd taught."

"Well, I quickly realized that I preferred the pastorate," he shot back.

"What was the name of the small Bible college where you and Simon taught?"

His delayed response was interrupted. Just then Beatrice glided into the room with a poised grace that summoned a small intake of breath from both of us. She wore her silver hair pulled back in a lovely cascading chignon. Her violet skirt and white blouse, along with the supple strand of our mother's pearls, matched the understated élan of her companion. Despite her self-consciousness, she beamed pleasure in the light of our appreciation. Slater had jumped to his feet like a palace guard before the queen while I slowly rose and complimented my sister.

"Sorry I took so long, Lyle," she said and smiled nervously.

"It was well worth the wait, my dear," he returned. "But I suppose we should be going."

Ah, yes, I thought to myself, *trying to make the quick exit.*

"Grif, did he tell you where he's taking me? I simply love surprises!" Bea gushed.

"Not a word. But he was just telling me that he knew Simon. They even taught together back at — what was the name of the school?" I asked, smiling.

"United Brethren Bible College," he answered sharply, as if he'd already told me.

"Well, it's certainly a shame about poor Simon. You'll have to tell me more about your friendship with him, Lyle. Grif, I put the pizza coupons by the phone in the kitchen, and in case you change your mind there's still some leftover Mexican casserole in the fridge. There's also some —"

"Go! I'll be fine. Lyle, take this lovely woman away from here and have a wonderful evening!" I commanded.

He smiled at me one last time before guiding my sister toward the door and saying, "Good night. Enjoyed talking with you."

I heard their voices, giddy and distant, as he helped her into his Mercedes. They drove off into the cool spring evening, and I was reminded of Miss Dickinson's carriage that held "but just ourselves and Immortality."

I tried to shake off my somberness of heart by shuffling through pizza coupons from our two local choices. Instead, I felt a new pang of fear suction itself to my insides. It transcended the emotions of protective possession and brotherly love for my sister and compounded my worry that I could not fully define it.

From the other end of the phone line, a young female voice promised me a pizza within the half hour. I kicked off my shoes and dialed the digitized radio until I heard Garrison Keillor's rich bass booming a gospel tune on *A Prairie Home Companion*. I slumped back in the Morris chair, propped my feet on the matching oak ottoman, and waited for my medium pepperoni, mushrooms, and green peppers to arrive. Avenell had always reminded me of Keillor's fictional hometown of Lake Wobegone with its sundry characters and humorous crises. But all of that had shifted for me during the past six months. I had come to Avenell in part because it was home, a safe place to heal after Amy's death, and in part because it was benign and familiar. A place where students lingered outside ivy-covered brownstones, debating amicably with one another and their black-robed professors. A place where every cottage promised a glass of iced tea on the porch swing and a drowsy spaniel or retriever at your feet. Where people seldom locked their doors and where I knew all my parishioners by first name.

But so much had changed since last fall. Not just the actuality of one black-hearted crime, but even the possibility of it in our small community seemed to open a Pandora's box of twenty-first century, postmodern ills that made us no different than Nashville, Atlanta, Memphis, or Charlotte. Or anywhere else for that matter. There were no safe havens left in this world.

"You're an old man, Griffin Reed," I said out loud.

Perhaps my odd, unnamed fear was simply powerlessness in the face of danger. The feeling of watching my wife die of cancer. The feeling of watching someone point a nine-millimeter barrel at me in the Martyr's Chapel. The feeling of watching my sister drive off into the night with a man I did not like nor trust.

That's when it hit — the peripheral source of my latest fear. Lyle Slater had said that he and Simon had both taught at United *Brethren* Bible College. The *Brethren*. Could Slater somehow be involved in the tangled nest of secrets slowly emerging from Simon's death among the Amish?

The Brethren connection might have been simply coincidence, but I knew I would not sleep until I heard my sister return. I knew I could never give her my blessing to marry Lyle Slater until I knew the full truth behind his relationship with Simon Hostetler.

Chapter Ten

Ashes to Ashes

Sunday morning I was up bright and early to put together the brief order of service for Simon's funeral in the afternoon. I called Peter and asked if he would help officiate, and he agreed. The Schroeders were already planning on him picking them up so that they might come in support of their friend.

Yesterday Lydia Miller had chosen three o'clock for the service time. The casket would not be present at the service; instead, Drinkwine Family Funeral Home would be preparing it for shipment to Pennsylvania. Mrs. Miller expected a small, quiet service, and concluded with "perhaps that's the way Simon would have liked it."

With this in mind, I pared down the order of service to a simple time of reading, praying, and singing. Whether it was the violence in the way of his passing, or the sense that he had few friends and family, I felt compelled to focus on passages of Scripture that emphasized the comfort and intimacy of our relationship with God. As usual, I was likely preaching to myself as well as anyone else. Finally, with a rough outline and several selections made, I showered and dressed for morning services.

The celebration of the Eucharist in the Cathedral of the Divine went smoothly enough. Because of the week's commotion with Simon's death, I had not prepared a homily so I was forced to wing it. "In light of the tragedy among the Amish in Tremont," I said, standing at the top of the chancel in front of the great marble altar, "and in light of the Lenten celebration of our Lord's suffering and death, let us commit to one another to bind and heal one another's wounds and thus preserve the body." Although I do not enjoy the pressure of extemporaneous speaking, I must say that it usually goes very well. Such was the case this Sunday as many parishioners commented on specific points I'd made about community and unity in the body of Christ. Even Peter complimented me as we changed in the vestry after the service.

"I don't know what Bea's planning — or if she's even home for lunch today — but you're welcome to come back to the house and grab some lunch. I know there's leftover pizza," I said.

He grinned out the corner of his mouth.

"It sounds as if Miss Bea's romance has thrown a wrench into your domestic life."

"Not necessarily. I was cooking and keeping a home of my own long before Amy or Bea assumed those duties," I replied. "But certainly, one does become a creature of habit the older one gets. That reminds me — here are the car keys." I tossed him the set and he caught the jangle of silver with one hand.

"I appreciate the lunch offer, but I guess I better take off if I'm going to pick up the Schroeders and be back in time for the service. It's almost twelve-thirty now."

"Yes, of course," I said, hiding my disappointment.

Watching him drive off a few minutes later, I found that my anxious fears of the previous evening had transformed themselves into a kind of self-pity and moroseness. My network of relationships was becoming distant and elusive. Caroline had not attended either service at the Cathedral of the Divine. I was not surprised, but felt annoyed nonetheless since her absence would only add fuel to Joan Dowinger's "concern" about her faith. Beatrice, still floating on Lyle Slater's surprise of dinner theater reservations in Chattanooga for *South Pacific*, had agreed to attend her suitor's church. When I returned to a quiet rectory, I was not surprised to find a message on the answering machine informing me that she and Lyle were lunching with a couple from his church. This, too, annoyed me because I wanted to suggest that Lyle attend Simon's service since he knew him, and also because his presence would afford another opportunity to discover the true nature of their friendship. Why hadn't I invited him last night or asked Bea to invite him this morning? I dialed Slater's number and left a message on his machine with the time of Simon's service.

I felt rather sorry for myself with three of my dearest friends — Peter, Caroline, and Beatrice — absent from my presence. So I ate a slab of cold pizza just to reinforce how truly lonely I was and then looked over the order of Simon's service. Mrs. Willamet was unavailable to play the glorious pipe organ this afternoon — her granddaughter's bridal shower — so any hymns we sang would necessarily be a cappella. Such singing would likely honor Simon's Amish roots more appropriately anyhow. I chose "Abide with Me" over "In the Cross of Christ I Glory" and Mendelssohn's "Cast Thy Burden upon the Lord" rather than "My Faith Has Found a Resting Place."

I tried to nap in the hour remaining before the service but could not put my mind at ease. At first I assumed it was just the usual performance anxiety of conducting another service, but as I sat on the back porch steps with my glass of iced tea, I found myself trying to sort through the odd variety of information I knew about the late Simon Hostetler. Whether or not he was involved in exacting vengeance on the Amish who had banished his father, I sensed that the cause of his death was connected to his character.

I recalled how Simon's quiet demeanor belied a thoughtful, gentle man with a quick sense of humor and a compassionate heart. While we had not always agreed theologically back in school, I never doubted his faith. I'd been a bit surprised that he'd pursued academia rather than the pulpit, but his introverted personality seemed better suited for research and classroom interactions with students. I remember finding him out in the small courtyard at Union one late evening, smoking a pipe of rich tobacco that smelled of cloves. He seemed troubled but not upset, and I assumed he was debating some aspect of Calvinism or Luther's treatises. Was he secretly ruminating over the bitterness of his lost father and blaming the

Tremont community for that loss?

Somehow I found it hard to believe that Simon was such a vengeful thinker. I remember him being much more intrigued by concepts of grace and hope in our theology classes. He was not one of those who relished divine judgment and damnation like some were. Why had Simon come back to Tremont after all these years? Surely, it was more than just his desire to research Amish culture and concepts of justice.

My thoughts scattered like pollen on the wind this spring afternoon. Thin lines of clouds aligned like rows of gray-clad soldiers on the distant horizon above the mountain; it would rain by nightfall, perhaps before.

The service was simple and sacred. Afternoon clouds continued to gather forces until the light was filtered gray through the mosaic windows of colored glass. The loneliness of fifty people mourning the murder of someone they all knew resounded like thunder in the cavernous cathedral.

The somber tone was offset by the support I observed for my friend's sister. I was delighted that over two dozen Amish accompanied Lydia Miller, her husband, Josiah, and their three children to the service. The Schroeders were there of course, along with the Yoders and the Stolzfuses. Miss Mary Lapp did not make the trip, nor did Bishop Zook. The former I easily excused because of her arthritis and age, but the latter disappointed me. Even if he distrusted Simon's motives for returning home, the leader of a flock should nonetheless set an example of grace and compassion. Could there have been another reason for Bishop Zook's absence, I wondered as I focused on a striking blonde several rows behind the many Amish men and women. Mariah Gates, Simon's research assistant, glared back at me.

The forty-minute service passed quickly. I had restructured an Episcopal order of service to accommodate both the Amish in attendance as well as Simon's lack of denominational affiliation. I quoted from one of his earliest books about the significance of faith in holding a community together: " 'It is only the shared celebration or corporate lament that binds the faith of community together. The circle that clings together in all the many forms of worship, then also celebrates the human experience.' " Lydia Miller's husband read a psalm and Benjamin Schroeder — much to his credit — recalled a boyhood anecdote of fishing Turner's Creek with Simon many years ago. We sang and I prayed and the service ended. Outside, nature heaved its collective sigh in the form of a gentle shower, the pathetic fallacy of heaven's grief, pattering against the high-arched roof and stained-glass windows.

I had arranged for coffee, tea, cookies, and cake to be served in the Fellowship Hall downstairs. The Schroeders and Stolzfuses also brought pies and puddings, and Mrs. Schroeder and Leah began serving the mourners. Like the service, the gathering evoked a certain pathos, a feeling that this man's life should have come to so much more than this. I quickly made my way to Lydia Miller and offered my condolences. I was eager, as well, to discover what she had alluded to at the end of our phone conversation, the "something" she wanted to show me.

A lovely, heavyset woman with dimples and wide eyes, Mrs. Miller bore a faint resemblance to her brother. We exchanged pleasantries and I shared some of my favorite memories of time spent with Simon. As she thanked me for the service, I could tell that she felt uncomfortable in this setting, away from the normal routines of her Amish life. I suspected she would wait until a more private moment if she indeed had something for me from Simon. Just as I was about to move on, Lydia Miller said, "Let me introduce you to my good friend, Mrs. Deborah Kaufman."

I turned to see another woman similarly dressed, likewise without makeup or jewelry, but with more gray at the temples than Lydia at the edge of her kapp. Mrs. Kaufman smiled demurely and nodded. Surprise must have registered in my eyes because the woman quickly said, "I do not know what you may have heard about the past, Brother Reed, but I assure you that all has been forgiven between our two families. I love Lyddie as if she were my sister."

I nodded and said, "I'm glad that you are here, and I know your presence would have meant a great deal to Simon."

"My younger brother, Adam, is around here somewhere. I would introduce him — oh, there he is," said Deborah, pointing to a tall, thin young man with a scraggly goat's gruff of beard on his chin. He was cramming a piece of chocolate cake in his mouth with both hands but released one of them long enough to wave back when he caught his sister's gaze. "Forgive him, Brother Reed — he is like a child. I will introduce you later."

I nodded and she then turned to help her brother, who probably looked younger than he was, wipe his mouth of buttercream frosting. Lydia Miller had returned to the table of desserts and the other womenfolk. Something about Adam looked vaguely familiar, but I could not imagine when I would have met the young man before today.

I nibbled a molasses cookie and continued mingling through the small clusters of conversations. As I looked for Benjamin Schroeder and Peter, to my surprise Mariah Gates strode into the room and came directly toward me.

"Ms. Gates, I'm glad you came. I know how much we'll all miss Simon." I offered my hand. She wrapped her dark raincoat around her lithe frame tighter in reply.

"Thanks for calling this morning to inform me of the service, Father Reed," she said crisply. "Can you point out Simon's sister to me? I have not met her and wish to offer my condolences." Her words were sharp, businesslike.

I nodded and directed my eyes toward the back of the Fellowship Hall. "Perhaps we could have coffee sometime before you return to Penn State," I said. "I was very intrigued by what Simon had shared with me about his work."

For the briefest of seconds, something

akin to surprise, fear, or discomfort registered in her iris-blue eyes. "I did not know Simon was in the habit of sharing his work with many people," she countered. "But, yes, perhaps sometime before I leave we can arrange an appointment. Now, if you'll excuse me." She marched directly toward Lydia Miller and leaned in to the circle of women surrounding the Amish woman. A few words and nods passed between them until Mariah Gates extracted what appeared to be a business card and left it with Mrs. Miller.

"Spying or eavesdropping?" asked a familiar voice.

"Bea?" I turned sharply and found my sister, out of breath, at my elbow.

"Oh, Grif, I feel just horrible about missing Simon's service. Why didn't you mention it last night or this morning? You know I would have wanted to attend. Lyle and I heard your message when we returned from lunch." She collected herself and smoothed a wisp of silver behind her ear. "Quite a turnout from the Amish. Which one is Simon's sister?"

I tilted my head and she followed the trail of my eyes. "Over there," I said, "talking to the . . ."

Mariah Gates was nowhere to be seen.

Within the moments of Bea's arrival, the attractive research assistant had quickly exited. She definitely had a reason for wanting to meet Simon's sister, I concluded, but it seemed more than merely offering her condolences. "Mrs. Miller is over there talking to Leah's mother. I'll introduce you in a moment. Where *is* Lyle? Didn't he want to pay his respects, too?"

My sister made a chortling sound within the back of her throat. "Well, of course, he did. Poor thing had a migraine, though. I made him go straight to bed and told him I would pass along his prayers and sympathy to Simon's sister."

Very convenient, I thought to myself, suddenly aware of how much I disliked my suspicious mind. Still, the thought of my friend's body dangling like a snared animal . . . Perhaps I was justifying my skeptical nature, but it seemed to me that murder changes everything, and that suspicion remains one of the only recourses against the fear of the unknown.

I bid the caravan of Amish families goodbye shortly before five o'clock. Peter drove the Schroeders in my car and the rest piled into two minivans. Beatrice took it upon herself to clean up the Fellowship Hall and I let her. Before her departure, Lydia Miller thanked me again and I seized the opportunity to inquire about her reference to something Simon left for me.

"Oh yes," she said. "I nearly forgot. You know — it's nothing really . . ." She searched hidden pockets within the folds of her voluminous deep violet skirt. "Well, goodness . . . I know I brought it with me. Excuse me one moment." She retreated and conferred with her husband and one of her children. Then Beatrice began talking to her, and Mrs. Miller did not return. On the phone yesterday her tone seemed urgent, but perhaps my imagination had simply exaggerated it. Evidently, the item was not as significant as I had hoped.

But then I recalled my intuitive notion that Mariah Gates was not just making a social call, the feeling that she was after something, a falcon scanning for prey. Of course, Simon could have left some of his notes and things at his sister's house and Gates was simply inquiring after them. Was there something in the dead man's notes to incriminate his beautiful research assistant?

My musings continued as I headed back upstairs into the Divine Cathedral. I had left my Bible and the service notes up by the altar, and as I listened to my footsteps echo on the marble floor and the spring rains pattering on the windows, I suddenly felt a delicious moment of peace. There was something sublime about an empty church, the sheer size of it, the beauty of so many details converging to afford a place devoted entirely to worship. I strolled down the chancel, savoring my moment. The restoration was almost complete; only a few tile replacements and finishing touches remained. The large scaffold that had nestled alongside each section of the interior was now gone, its job of supporting the detailed cleaning and window repairs finally fulfilled.

Inside, the gray-and-white marble walls and floor held the cool relief of a mountain spring. The Lord's palace was empty, row upon row of cherrywood pews guarding the chancel and altar. The long, silver pipes of our massive organ graduated along one side. Flying buttresses rose high above, like the arcs of fallen stars captured in stone. Such neo-Gothic splendor cut through the confusion and malevolence of Simon Hostetler's murder and reminded me of who I was. I released the tension of my fears and uncertainties, grateful for this moment's respite. Yes, I was definitely suited for the contemplative life, for serving the spiritual needs of others, for teaching the divine story of God's love for us through the gift of His Son. It was only during the moments when I lost sight of this that my fears encroached.

I knelt and prayed. I asked my Father for divine assistance with all of my duties and responsibilities, for my parish and the lives entrusted to my care. I prayed for those in need of comfort in the loss of Simon Hostetler, for his sister and Mariah Gates, and for the safety of all the Amish in the Tremont community. I prayed for my own sister and for Lyle Slater and their growing relationship. I prayed that I would not get in the way with my suspicions and petty criticism of the man. Finally, I offered a prayer for those responsible for Simon's death . . . my requisite need for justice softened by the remembrance of our Lord's dying words on the cross: "Father, forgive them; for they know not what they do." Grace offered in the midst of His own suffering.

The quiet relief of unmarked time filled me. Looking up at the stained-glass windows and the depictions of miracles, I noticed the tableau of the Last Supper in bright-colored shards. I marked the empty chair at the table where Judas had once sat. I reached down for a pew Bible, seated myself, and flipped to Matthew 26.

When it was evening, he sat at table with the twelve disciples; and as they were eating, he said, "Truly, I say to you, one of you will betray me." And they were very sorrowful, and began to say to him one after another, "Is it I, Lord?" He answered, "He who has dipped his hand in the dish with me, will betray me. The Son of man goes as it is written of him, but woe to that man by whom the Son of man is betrayed! It would have been better for that man if he had not been born." Judas, who betrayed him, said, "Is it I, Master?" He said to him, "You have said so."

It filled me with great sadness sitting there in the dim light of the cathedral. Judas is one of those players in the passion story who often seems nothing more than a cardboard villain, someone easy to hate because of his betrayal. But perhaps we make him one-dimensional because he is so much like ourselves; we, who are so quick to act on our own fickle hearts, so premeditated and selfish in the midst of our minuscule suffering.

With my finger still marking the place in Matthew's account of Jesus' last days, I turned the page. There in chapter 27, while Jesus is being led away before Pilate, it reads:

When Judas, his betrayer, saw that he was condemned, he repented and brought back the thirty pieces of silver to the chief priests and the elders, saying, "I have sinned in betraying innocent blood." They said, "What is that to us? See to it yourself." And throwing down the pieces of silver in the temple, he departed; and he went and hanged himself.

It's so easy for me to dismiss Judas as inhuman, as evil, apostate. Or even to pity him, which still manages to diminish his humanity. It's much harder to face the Judas in my own heart and beg mercy from the One I betray daily.

I knelt again and prayed more, the thick needlepoint tapestry cradling my knees.

How much time passed I do not know, only that when I opened my moist eyes, Lydia Miller was sitting next to me, her head reverently bowed. Judging by the inky shadows filtering through the colored windows, the day had drawn to a close.

"Forgive me for disturbing you, Brother Reed," she whispered. "But I found the gift Simon left for you and returned to give it to you. I had left it in the van. My brother Adam had been playing with it."

"Mrs. Miller . . . I . . . why, you didn't have to return this today," I stammered, wiping my eyes.

"The others are waiting for me, so I will make this short," she began, unwrapping a small swath of black cloth. "Simon left this with me the day he died." She handed me a wooden box with rounded corners. About four by six inches, it appeared solid without an opening and was stained dark in color. I turned it over and over, looking for a latch or opening but could not find one. Each surface plane was identical to the others, the two end squares forming a congruent set. It appeared handmade and reminded me of a small cigar box or jewelry case. There were no hinges, no apparent opening whatsoever as I upended it in the dim light of the cathedral once more. Shaking it produced the sensation of a hollow core, but no rattle, only a slight shift of weight as if sand were packed inside.

"What is this?" I asked.

"It's an Amish puzzle box — one that's very old, by my guess," said Lydia. "Fathers often make them for their children, but usually they are much easier to solve than this one."

"So it does come apart, then? What is inside?" I held the box reverently in the palm of my right hand.

"It's supposed to come apart, but Simon did not show me how to open it. He told me it contained something special and that he needed a safe place to keep it. I told him I would hold it for him. He was reluctant but finally agreed. The last thing he said about it was, 'If something should happen, this belongs to Griffin Reed.' I asked what in the world he was talking about, but he just smiled and went outside to join my husband in the barn. They were getting ready to plow. That was the last time I saw him."

The emotion she had suppressed during the afternoon service now emerged in a torrent of tears. I placed the puzzle box between us and offered Mrs. Miller my handkerchief, which she accepted with thick, work-worn hands. After a few moments' release, she composed herself and murmured, "I'm terribly sorry."

"Oh, please, don't apologize. I know how much you must have loved Simon. He was a good man," I said. "But I must confess, I've never seen this puzzle box before."

"Well, he must have had some reason for wanting you to have it," she said.

"Yes," I concurred. "I suppose you're right. Did Simon say anything else about his work? Did he talk about what he'd discovered since he'd been in Tremont these past six weeks?"

She shook her head and refolded my handkerchief to return it. "No. As you can imagine, Simon and I did not know each other all that well. We wrote occasionally, and he'd come to visit only once before. The things he writes about — wrote about — do not interest me, so I actually know little about my brother's work. But he did ask an awful lot of questions about the history of Tremont while he was with us."

I nodded. "But didn't he know most of that from growing up there himself?"

"Some of it, I suppose. But you know how we all are as children — in one ear and out the other." She thought for a moment, her face pale in the shadows of the sanctuary. "He had many questions about recent history, too. He was very concerned about the acts of vandalism — the barn burning and all."

"And you and Josiah answered his questions? Did most of your neighbors and friends answer Simon's questions?" I asked, although I suspected the answer already.

"I tried as best I could, and Josiah humored Simon for my sake. I'm afraid some of the others would not give Simon the time of day. They still think of him as siding with our father and all . . ." She looked over my shoulder toward the rood screen that guarded the small side chapel to the left of the altar.

"Do you have any idea who would do such a terrible thing to Simon? I know the police have asked you, but is there anything you've remembered, anything that might help them catch the person capable of such an atrocity?"

Lydia Miller thought for a moment. "No, I really cannot imagine anyone who would hate Simon, or any human being, enough to take his life." Anger crackled in her tone. "I suspect it is one of the parties vying for our land."

I thought aloud: "Why would someone after Amish farmland kill Simon? I don't follow. . . ."

"Nor do I. But the way so many people come to us about Canaan's Way, you'd think it had buried treasure," she said. "For all I know, it does." She took a deep breath before standing. "I really must be going — the others will think I've converted, I've been here so long." We shared a smile at her attempt at humor.

"Thank you for bringing this to me. I'll let you know what's inside as soon as I find out," I said.

I offered to walk her out, but she declined and I listened as her leather-soled shoes tapped down the marble chancel to the massive oak door. In my hands the puzzle box looked like a wood scrap, a leftover block from some cabinetmaker's floor. But I suspected then that Simon did indeed believe himself to be in danger, and that whatever was inside was worth risking one's life for.

Chapter Eleven

Box of Puzzles

When I ventured out into the chilly air Monday morning, there stood my curate, dressed in heather-gray sweats with an Avenell tiger charging across his muscular chest. Peter shivered in the new dawn air.

"Been waiting long?" I asked.

"A man could freeze to death out here waiting on you," he teased, running fingers through his blond sleep-creased hair. "Wait till you hear what happened yesterday in Tremont."

"Didn't know you were out here or I would've been up sooner. What happened?" I asked.

"I'll tell you once we take off," he said cryptically.

Annoyed and impatient, I tied my Nikes, the cement porch piercing cold through the seat of my sweat pants. If he could be secretive so could I, I thought to myself, eager to tell him about the puzzle box from Lydia Miller.

It seemed like a long time since the two of

us had run together, at least several weeks. We both began to stretch against the front porch steps, extending our arms and legs like curious statues. Our warm breaths cast faint white films in the lingering cold as we silently took off up Maryland Avenue toward the heart of campus.

We had covered almost half a mile when I could stand it no longer. "So what happened?" I asked between ragged breaths.

The man I loved like a son inhaled deeply and replied, "Break-in at three homes in the community. Yesterday. All three during Simon's service. The Millers, Yoders, and Schroeders. Whoever that was spying on us Thursday night must've come back." His words were sharp, telegraphed with staccato precision between his deep exchange of breaths.

"That's terrible! Robbing someone during a funeral!" I exclaimed. "What did they take?"

Stray beams of gold protruded through newly green branches as we turned off Southern Avenue onto Poplar Circle. The morning burned its way through the blanket of cool mountain air. We waved at two student joggers before Peter turned toward me and mouthed, "Nothing."

"What? I thought you said there were

three burglaries."

"No, just break-ins. Nothing was stolen at the Miller farm, the Yoders', or the Schroeders'. 'Course, Jacob surprised them at his house. He didn't come up to Avenell with the rest of the family for Simon's service — he'd just gotten in from a road trip to visit his cousins in Georgia. He surprised the intruders up in his parents' bedroom — two men in black and ski masks — but they knocked him down and took off. They sure made a mess."

We had paused near the university baseball field, where several team members ran laps inside the park. Bleachers faced the back sides of both dugouts. The red clay dirt encircling the pitcher's mound and each base had been freshly raked. White chalked lines connected the earthen circles to form a near-perfect diamond.

"Is Jacob all right? Was he hurt seriously?" I asked.

"No, thank goodness. He's got a nasty bruise, but he's okay. More than anything, the Amish are all shook up now. Since theft was apparently not the motive, Mr. Schroeder and Bishop Zook seem to think that someone's trying to scare the Amish." He paused, then said, "Let's keep going," and dashed off again before I could object.

"Scare them — into selling their land? Wouldn't the intruders have left a message if that's what they were trying to do?" I asked.

"After we returned to the Schroeders' last night and all the excitement died down, Mr. Schroeder showed me a surveyor's map of the Canaan's Way property. He told me that a representative from Dolby Air Force Base had made an appointment with him and Bishop Zook for this week — tomorrow, I believe. Benjamin also told me that he, along with several other property owners, had received a letter yesterday from a corporation called the Omega Group. They manufacture computer software. Ever heard of them? Both Dolby and Omega upped the amount of their offer since their previous attempts. Benjamin is afraid the generous offer will persuade his neighbors to sell off Canaan's Way or other parcels of land adjacent to the river. So far the Amish have held out, but some of them are beginning to want to sell." Peter's breathing was now regularly paced to the cadence of his stride and his words.

"Yes, I've only recently heard of Omega," I said, momentarily debating whether or not I should tell Peter about Simon's shares in the corporation. Certainly I trusted him, but he did have a vested interest in the welfare of the Amish community now. Whatever Benjamin Schroeder and the other elders decided would likely affect the future of Peter and Leah's relationship. I proceeded to explain that the sheriff and Dan had found paper work indicating that Simon had invested in the software corporation.

Peter stopped next to a public drinking fountain on the perimeter of Rivendale Park, where several faculty walked their Pomeranians and Old English Sheepdogs amid students enjoying coffee and the *New York Times*. The large green courtyard was complemented by bursts of color from blossoming trees.

As a thread of water dribbled down his chin, my curate squared his shoulders and said, "So Simon Hostetler was a secret shareholder in the same company that's trying to buy up half of Tremont? Does his sister know this — or anyone else, for that matter?"

The edginess in Peter's voice included anger, perhaps even betrayal. "I don't believe anyone else knows about this unless Simon told them. And I don't think his purpose in coming back to Tremont was merely to help with a buyout."

"I guess we'll find out eventually, won't

we? Don't you find it too coincidental that Simon Hostetler owned shares in a company that wanted to buy out the place where he grew up, a place that rejected his father? Surely the two are related," Peter concluded.

After my own drink of water, I simply said, "Perhaps." The two of us resumed our pace, slower this time, and left the park and its profusion of pink-and-white dogwood trees behind us. I turned over Peter's accusation, one that had troubled me for its merit about Simon's dual relationships with Omega and the Amish. Could the deceased professor have been hired by the Omega Group to persuade and negotiate the purchase of an industrial site in Tremont? It sounded like something a corporation might do; hire an expert on the culture with whom it was negotiating. I recalled reading an article about how IBM had done just that with a recent Japanese computer deal.

By the time we returned to the rectory, I had decided to tell Peter about the Amish puzzle box that Lydia Miller gave me. I had attempted to call Dan Warren the previous evening to tell him about the cryptic little artifact, to see if he thought it as significant as I did. However, a four-car pileup just off the interstate on the other side of Eaglehead kept Dan and Sam tied up most of the night according to Andy McDermott, who was running dispatch to give Maria the night off. Consequently, I had locked the puzzle box in the small safe in the church office where we kept the parish checkbooks and petty cash.

"I want to show you something," I told Peter. "Lydia Miller gave it to me after Simon's service yesterday. Apparently, he told her that it should be returned to me."

"What is it? Something that belonged to you?" he asked.

I fumbled for my keys beneath the ornate planter that Bea had already adorned with spring fern and mountain ivy. "No, that's just it. I never saw it before. Which makes me wonder if Simon suspected that he was in danger prior to his death," I replied, leading Peter across the expanse of lawn to the vestry door at the side of the church.

It was only eight-thirty, so Janine was not in yet as we descended into the basement of the dark fortress. "Funny," I muttered. "The office door's unlocked. I could've sworn I locked it last night. . . ."

Immediately the same thought dawned on both of us simultaneously. I rushed in, Peter literally edging my heels, and proceeded to find nothing amiss. Everything appeared to be in its usual place, just as I'd left it the previous night.

However, our first fear proved true nonetheless. The safe door was closed but unlocked. Inside, the petty cash box was there with all of its eighty-seven dollars and some odd change. Both parish checkbooks were there, no checks missing or unaccounted for. But the puzzle box was gone.

"Are you sure you put it in here? Maybe you just thought about putting it here but decided instead to put it somewhere at home. In your office, maybe? Locked in your desk?" Peter struggled to prompt me.

"No," I shook my head. "I know I'm getting old and forgetful, but I definitely left the puzzle box here last night."

"A puzzle box? Like the Schroeder boys play with? That's what Simon left for you?" he asked.

I nodded, then described the wooden toy and its refusal to open for either Lydia or me.

"Well, don't touch or move anything," Peter instructed. "Let's call Dan and see if he can dust for prints."

The rest of the morning became a montage of odd, almost surreal details. Janine arriving and jumping three feet when she found Dan Warren and Jerry Sharpe inside the office. The taste of coffee on my tongue as I defended my memory, as sure as I could be about depositing the puzzle box in the safe the night before. Bea coming over to the Divine when she saw the squad car and her shrieking, "A burglary!" before I could explain. She quickly decided that food would aid the investigation and returned to the rectory to bake cinnamon rolls. I felt totally responsible for the loss and expressed as much to Dan.

"Don't be discouraged, my friend," he said kindly. "Obviously, we're dealing with a professional here who knew exactly what he was after and where to find it. He must have followed Hostetler's sister when she came back and gave you the box. He hid in the church, watched you put it in the safe here, and then retrieved it after you locked up for the night."

I shook my head, puzzled. "I'm usually fairly observant, but nothing seemed amiss last night. Nothing. Now I've likely lost a vital clue to Simon's death."

"Don't be so hard on yourself," said my curate. "I'm sure the truth will come out in the end." I detected Peter's earlier tone of suspicion that Simon's death may have been his own fault because of his ties to Omega.

"Perhaps it's too obvious," offered Dan,

sipping coffee that Janine had made for us. "But what if the break-ins yesterday in Tremont are connected to the puzzle box? What if they — whoever they are — were looking for the puzzle box all along? I mean, all the families that were broken into had ties to Hostetler."

"I suspect you're right," I said. "And I feel even worse. Why didn't I take the puzzle box by your office last night and let Andy lock it up there? You can't imagine how sorry I am."

"Don't apologize," Dan said, resting his large hand on my shoulder. "We're going to find out what's going on in Tremont with or without the puzzle box."

"It's a perfect symbol for this whole business, isn't it?" asked Peter rhetorically. "Simon Hostetler's murder and this whole business with the Amish — nothing but a box of puzzles."

By eleven o'clock, Dan and Jerry had dusted and scanned every inch of the office and half the church. Nothing turned up, and it seemed likely that any possible forensic evidence that had remained from our thief was likely destroyed inadvertently by Peter and me when we first discovered the puzzle box missing. Janine, Peter, and I tried to restore some sense of normalcy.

I was sorting through the morning mail when I heard Janine retrieving messages from the answering machine. She bounded over with a half dozen messages. Still no word from Caroline, but instead a confirmation call from John Greenwood about his visit this week, two prayer request calls, two sales solicitations. The last one was a short, direct message from Mariah Gates. I quickly dialed her number and was surprised to hear her request a meeting with me as soon as possible.

"Is something wrong?" I asked, wondering if she could have somehow known about the stolen puzzle box.

"I have to fly out tonight to do some other field research, and I'd simply like to speak with you about Simon before I go," she said.

"I see." Looking over my afternoon schedule, I found that I was free after premarital counseling with Katie Johanssen and Joshua McEwen at one. Ms. Gates instructed me to meet her in one of the private research rooms at the main library on campus at three.

And that's where I found her shortly before the carillon bells on campus pealed their three echoing notes. Mariah Gates stood with her back to me in one of the small offices usually reserved for graduate students in Avenell's Eastman Library.

A tall, imposing woman with nervous blue eyes, Ms. Gates couldn't have been much over thirty. With her youthful features, trim taupe suit, and well-cut mane of straight blond hair, she looked more like a network anchor than a Ph.D. candidate in cultural studies. We exchanged pleasantries, and she seemed much warmer and more relaxed than the day before. Then she invited me to be seated at the table where an imposing mountain of research materials had accumulated.

"How long had you worked with Simon?" I asked, scanning the collage of books, photographs, handwritten notes, and computer printouts.

She turned to face me once more, her pupils scanning mine. "Not long. Only since last fall, really. I was hired fall semester at the last minute when Simon's former assistant left the program."

"Did you know his former assistant?" I asked.

"Jeff? No, like I said, he left before I arrived. I think he just burned-out. He was ABD, all but dissertation. Simon was disappointed because he was all set to go on sabbatical and do field research. So Simon saw my areas of specialization and asked me to assist." She walked over to the table and sat opposite me in a hardwood chair.

"A fortunate break for you, I suppose. What areas do you specialize in, Ms. Gates?" I scanned an opened book before me: *The Effects of Hydroponics on Amish Farming Practices in the 1980s.*

"Mariah, please. I'm a forensic anthropologist specializing in environmental practices of religious cultures. Basically, I like to examine how religion affects attitudes about the earth." She fidgeted with her hands and then began shuffling through a stack on the table until she pushed a thick, bound document my way. "Here's my master's thesis. University of Virginia, Charlottesville."

The black hardbound manuscript was titled *Stewards of the Earth: Agricultural Environmentalism in the Old Order Amish Community of Lancaster, Pennsylvania, circa 1849–1900.* I scanned the table of contents and read the abstract. Turning to the bibliography in the back, I noticed that all of Simon Hostetler's books and most of his published articles were included on the list.

"Very impressive," I said sincerely. "Looks like you were familiar with Simon's work long before you came to Penn State. Had you ever met him before last fall?"

"No, unfortunately not. Neither of us could believe that we hadn't crossed paths before last fall. I knew his work, of course. He . . . well, he was very intrigued with my research interests. . . ." Her voice carried a pleasant, no-nonsense tone. She shifted her weight in the chair and unbuttoned her jacket. Our mood seemed to be that of a job interview that, while contrived, was nonetheless going well.

She continued. "I wanted to ask what Simon had told you about his latest project. You mentioned yesterday that he'd spoken of our work."

I paused to choose my approach, remembering many of the pages of souvenirs Simon Hostetler had left behind. What would I be able to tell from reading his descriptions, notes, and outline for his manuscript? Would his character emerge even in the jagged curves of his right-slanted handwriting?

Although the glass windows were nearly soundproof, the murmur of student voices, rustling papers, and occasional laughter drifted back to us. "Simon and I were old friends from seminary days back in New York. It was such a delightful surprise to have him around again. He told me that he was working on a project involving concepts of justice among the Amish, their ambivalence for organized political bodies, and that sort of thing. He never really went into much detail —"

"He seldom discussed his works in progress until his first draft was complete," she said.

I seized an opportunity. "I know he grew up in Tremont. Did he ever talk much about his childhood? From what he told me, I sensed he wasn't suited for the Amish lifestyle and left Tremont as soon as he could."

She leaned into the table and folded her hands to reveal thin fingers with shell-pink painted nails and several gold rings. I hated to be sexist or influenced by stereotypes, but Mariah Gates was an interesting blend. A beautiful woman who obviously took pride in her appearance. A keen, academic intelligence that clearly demonstrated its capacity for informed analysis. It's not that these seemed mutually exclusive or even paradoxical, only that I rarely saw such a blend in one person. Of course, there was Caroline — she was certainly beautiful as well as brilliant. No, it wasn't the combination. There was something incongruous about Mariah Gates I couldn't quite articulate.

"Simon didn't talk about his personal life much. Occasionally, he would mention something, but usually, he was the dedicated social scientist — pleasant, amicable, but singularly focused."

"Did he have other family besides his sister, Mrs. Miller?" I inquired.

"Not to my knowledge."

"I know the sheriff has already asked you, but could Dr. Hostetler's current project have endangered his life? This business about laws and discipline of the Amish . . ."

She sighed. "No . . . and honestly, I'm just as shocked as you are about what happened to him. While his topic was certainly controversial, I can't say that it endangered his life. As you know, the Amish are a peaceful people consistently committed to nonviolence. Why do *you* think Simon was killed?" Her question sounded agitated, a scratch in the polished veneer.

"I wish I knew. Was there anything else that might have endangered Simon's life? Did he ever speak of his outside interests — his involvement with the Omega Group, for instance?" I could not resist a little fishing trip of my own; it was difficult to tell who was interrogating whom here.

Her eyes registered recognition at the name, but she immediately shook her head. "No, I have no idea about Simon's business dealings. He was always focused on our work when we were together."

"Could his speculation about the Brethren being the ones behind the recent Amish vandalism in Tremont have gotten him killed?" I wondered aloud.

"The Brethren? How in the world did you hear about them?" she asked.

"Simon may have mentioned them — I can't recall," I hedged. "What do you know about them?"

She sighed. "Well, they're more mythic than historically supported. The Brethren supposedly existed here at the turn of the century when Tremont was being founded. Locals who opposed and perhaps even feared the unfamiliarity of Amish ways formed a Klan-like vigilante group committed to intimidating the new Amish settlers. In the early '50s, two brothers and their cousin were arrested for setting fire to an Amish barn, but that's about the only historical support for the group. I imagine the locals simply talked about the Brethren to the Amish more than they actually were involved."

She uncrossed her legs and shifted once more before continuing. "We have a few mentions in a handful of other academic sources throughout the past century and the testimony of maybe a half dozen Amish that such a vigilante group exists. Most Amish, however, view the Brethren as a tangible body committed to religious persecution. That's about all there is." Her voice pressed the strain out of its delivery and shifted into the expository mode of the professor.

"But Simon had enough information that he planned to include a chapter on the Brethren in this new book?" I prompted.

"Yes, Simon had become more and more convinced of its re-formation. He had found two people in Tremont who supplied him with more information than our previous interviews in Pennsylvania and Ohio. He hoped to discover or access a handbook from the 1920s known as the *Golden Rule*, supposedly the Brethren's code of operations."

"But he hadn't found it yet? Would someone be willing to kill him to keep him from publishing the *Golden Rule*?" My voice became animated; finally, a potential motive was emerging.

"Not to my knowledge. Would someone kill to protect the Brethren? If you had asked me two weeks ago, I would have said no. But now, who knows? It's just all so, so . . . unbelievable. If the Brethren are indeed motivated to hang a man as kind and intelligent as Simon, then it's all the more reason they should be exposed and brought to justice." Her passion inflated the volume of her last words.

I nodded and wondered aloud, "Will you continue the project alone? Or will the publisher abandon the manuscript?"

"To the best of my ability, I'm the only one who can finish what Simon started. I will complete the project," she said without hesitation.

"Are you concerned about your safety if you continue?"

She locked eyes with me, her dark pupils shimmering with some kind of strange determination. "No, I am not afraid. It's worth the risk." As if she instantly regretted the second admission, she pressed her lips together quickly.

I said, "I don't know what happened to Simon, but I don't think it's over yet."

She leaned forward across the table until she was only inches from my face. She lowered her voice and spoke more gently than ever before: "Father Grif, you have no idea what's at stake here. Please, do not endanger yourself."

The conviction in her voice sent needles along my spine, the acupuncture of fear.

Chapter Twelve

Spring Storm Rising

"What do you mean," I asked, "that I don't know what's at stake here?"

She hesitated, her lips like wilting pink blooms. "Nothing — forget it. It's just . . . nothing. Just be careful as you go around posing your innocent questions about Simon's death. You may ask the wrong person at the wrong place. Simon did."

"Who? Where? What are you talking about? Listen, Ms. Gates," I said, growing annoyed. "If you know something about why Simon was knocked on the head and hung from a tree branch, then you need to tell Sheriff Claiborne." I paused for a moment before adding, "I'm not going around investigating Simon's death — you asked me here, remember?" My blood pressure had probably spiked at least twenty points by now.

"Do you know why the commanding officer at Dolby Air Force Base is trying to take over the investigation of Simon's death?" She reduced the volume but not the intensity of her voice. "Don't forget about the military buyout of Amish land in 1969."

"How did you know about Bledsoe? You tell me — why *does* the Air Force want jurisdiction over Simon's investigation?" My patience had been suspended several exchanges prior.

"History repeats itself — that's all I'll say. Unchecked, history repeats itself." It was almost as if she were talking to herself then.

"So you're saying that Simon's death has something to do with the military trying to buy up more property from the Amish," I prompted. "The Canaan's Way property?"

She shook her head, straight blond hair falling into her face. Then she smiled and I knew our interview was over. "Please," she concluded as she rose from the chair, "just be careful."

Back in the office, Janine was packing up for the day and left me with several urgent messages even as my mind continued to comb through the odd conversation I'd just completed with Mariah Gates. As I'd marched back from the library, I analyzed my distrust for the attractive woman and wondered what she might gain from her mentor's death. Perhaps as his graduate assistant she would inherit his research and be the one to complete the book that he had planned. But treatises on justice among the Amish hardly became best sellers.

Why did she bring up the Air Force base, clearly trying to cast some suspicion on their involvement in Simon's death? It seemed too pat, too obvious. What could Simon possibly have had to do with Dolby? More likely, his ties to the Omega Group influenced his presence in Tremont. Could Omega have something to do with the military base, perhaps government contracts for defense software? I would definitely mention the idea to Dan and see what he thought about it.

Then another possibility crossed my mind, one so obvious I couldn't believe I had not considered it before. Had Mariah Gates and my friend Simon ever been romantically involved? She was an intelligent, attractive young woman. He was a single, mature bachelor. Both shared a passion for the same academic discipline. Perhaps it was only my Calvinistic view of sinful human nature, but I wondered if Mariah's businesslike façade hid a deeper grief for the loss of her mentor.

So many questions, so many unknown variables.

As I sat at my desk in the basement office,

I wondered if Dan had turned up anything from his morning's investigation of my break-in. Phoning him at the sheriff's office, I thumbed through the messages and saw one that surprised me and one that I had been dreading: one from Caroline with the formal message *call at your convenience;* the other — the one I had anticipated — was from Bishop Wilder in Nashville. Before I could think through further implications of either call, Maria patched me through to the burly sergeant.

"No luck so far, Grif," Dan began. "No prints, nothing. Like I said, it looks professional. The door lock was pristine, same for the safe. Someone knew what he was doing."

"Shame we didn't get to find out what was inside that puzzle box first," I said.

"I told you, you can't blame yourself for this. It's all going to work out. How's the rest of your day been? Better, I hope." I could hear the sheriff's voice in the melody of background noises.

"Funny you should ask, Dan," I replied. I tried to summarize my intense exchange with Mariah Gates for him but found myself struggling to convey the emotional undercurrent I'd experienced with Simon's assistant.

"I'll run a deeper check on her background," Dan offered. "Preliminary one looked good. She's divorced, no children, MBA from University of Virginia, began work on a Ph.D. at Penn State last year —"

He was cut off by Janine's interruption: "I'll see you tomorrow, Father Grif — unless you need me to stay." She turned the corner to my desk and said, "Oh, I'm sorry, I didn't hear you on the phone." She adjusted her glasses and waited.

I thanked her and sent her home. "Sorry, Dan. Now, what were you saying about Gates?" I asked hopefully.

"Well, it's interesting that Gates mentioned Dolby in conjunction with Simon's death. I spent most of the afternoon in General Bledsoe's office down at the base. We agreed to cooperate with Lieutenant Northrop in our investigation. Of course, we're not off to a good start, because Sam released the body to the custody of the victim's family, Mrs. Miller. Northrop wanted one of their boys to go over the body before it's buried, but it's too late now."

"Why all this interest from the military about Simon's death? As you explained last week when we were out there, the murder didn't even occur on their property." I swiveled back and forth in my ergonomically designed chair, silently trying to answer my own question.

"General Bledsoe says that because of the close proximity of the crime to the base, they're afraid that it may involve some highly classified project there," said Dan.

"They think Simon was a spy?" I inferred. "Granted, there's evidently a lot about Simon I didn't know, but I find that a bit far-fetched."

"Same here," Dan said. "But for all we know, Hostetler could've been up to something no one else knew about."

"Did Bledsoe say anything else? Did he give you any idea what kind of secret project was at risk?" I asked.

"Nope. Bledsoe's a tough one. Sam did some checking with his friends at the base before I went down there. It seems Bledsoe's respected by most of his peers. He graduated top of his class at the Air Force Academy and served in Vietnam before he returned to Dolby, where he quickly became commanding officer. Why, he's been there over thirty years. Most people act like Bledsoe *is* Dolby Air Force Base."

"So he was there back when the base bought out some of the Amish land," I concluded. "Wonder if General Bledsoe has anything personal at stake with the folks at

Tremont? At the time, there was sure some bad blood on both sides. What about the classified project?"

"Are you kidding? Bledsoe's tighter than the lid on a frozen jar of molasses," Dan boomed a bass laugh. "Sam's checking into it to see if anyone in Mumford knows. Listen, Grif, it's great to compare notes, but Sam just motioned me to the parking lot, so I guess I'm taking off."

I bid my friend good-bye and simply sat at my desk, staring at a large rectangular print that hung on the wall just left of my desk. A large Ansel Adams print, actually signed and numbered, not just a reproduction. Entitled "Spring Storm Rising," it captured the solemn plane of the northern New Mexico mesa in the foreground being eclipsed by intricate swirls of gray clouds over the Sangre de Christo mountains. The tension between the smooth, peaceful expanse of flat earth and the roiling energy of the approaching thunderstorm had always intrigued me. In many ways, it was an excellent metaphor for the Christian life, the calm center of God's Spirit within us, which is often surrounded by the tumultuous circumstances of life. At the moment, it also seemed to symbolize my intuitive sense that the secrets surrounding Simon's death would only continue to mount before any clarity emerged.

I moved on to my other business at hand. It was a little after five o'clock, but I tried the bishop's office anyway and he answered the phone himself.

"Grif, thanks for calling me back. I know how busy we all are," said Thomas Wilder, one of the most gifted combinations of servant leaders I'd ever encountered. "I know I'll see you soon at the going-away party for Philip down at St. Anthony's, but I wanted to get your input on an important decision before then."

Here it was; I knew what was coming. "Of course, Tom," I replied. "I'm always happy to help."

"Tell me, Grif," he said, his tone relaxing a bit, "what do you think of that curate of yours replacing Phil down in the valley. He's young, I know, but he certainly seems to have thrived under your leadership."

"Yes, indeed," I said. "Father Abernathy would make a wonderful rector for St. Anthony's. He's energetic, mature, compassionate, intelligent — I cannot think of a better candidate." Any other time, I would have basked in my pride for Peter's character and ministry accomplishments. But just now the sadness of imminent loss impinged upon my loving pride for him. I was determined not to reveal my personal feelings to Tom. This was an incredible opportunity for my curate to advance.

"Well, technically, as you know, he'll have his own parish, but it's so small that he will continue to rely heavily on you. I'm glad you recommend him so highly, Grif." He paused as if choosing his words carefully. "But let me ask you this: Are you sure his age isn't a factor? I mean, being single and all, perhaps I should wait to advance him until he's married and a bit more . . . seasoned."

"I understand your rationale, Tom," I said. "But Peter is very mature beyond his years. And, between you and me, he is practically engaged to a young woman that I highly respect. There might be a wedding in my parish this summer."

"Who is she? One of the students there at Avenell?" he asked.

"Well, no. Actually, she's a local woman from the valley, from down in Tremont." I had hoped to reinforce Peter's candidacy, but I may have indeliberately raised a new qualification in the bishop's eyes.

"The Amish community? She's not Episcopal? Doesn't that pose some problems for the two of them?" he asked. "I'm not sure Peter's ready to lead a flock if he's sorting through such crucial relational issues."

"Well, they're sorting those issues out right now. Their relationship may or may not lead to marriage; we'll have to wait and see." My shoulders slumped in my chair as I feared that I had inadvertently dented Peter's appointment to the Parish of St. Anthony's.

"I'll certainly need to speak to Peter about this, but I trust your judgment, Grif. He's always impressed me, and I know how highly you think of him. For now, he's my first choice for Father Jackson's replacement. I'll wait until after Easter, however, to make my final decision."

We chatted for a few minutes longer, catching up on denominational news and plans for next month's synod, before I hung up. Had I unconsciously undermined Peter's advancement by bringing up Leah? My impulsive response to the bishop's concern about Peter's bachelorhood certainly raised new questions in Tom's mind. Of course, he would find out when he interviewed Peter anyway, but I certainly didn't want my curate to feel that I wasn't endorsing him one hundred percent. More storm clouds to complicate my life.

I tried to call Caroline then and felt something inside me relax at the sound of her voice on the answering machine. I missed her. Even though it had only been a couple of days since our blowup, I missed talking to her and sharing some of the minutiae of our days. I left a message and glanced up at the lovely photograph to my left. Yes, all sorts of spring storms loomed on the horizon.

Great relief flooded over me as I stepped across the short alley of lawn from the church to the rectory. Late, inky-green shadows of the massive oaks and beech trees looked like pools from some hidden underground spring. I looked up into the massive branches of the nearest leafy oak and involuntarily shuddered at the thought of the Judas Tree. But I could not entertain further thoughts about Simon's death or the complicated web accreting around various questions. I needed a nice quiet evening at home: no break-ins, no murder suspects, no tensions over relationships or the impending move of a good friend.

By God's grace, Lyle Slater had a deacons' meeting, so Bea was home for the evening and feeling quite domestically inclined. Her chicken tetrazzini had just come out of the oven when I entered the rectory. The smell of parmesan, onions, and mushrooms had greeted me from the porch, and I felt such relief to be home that an audible groan accompanied my deep sigh. Bea had invited Peter to dinner, and much to her delight, he had brought some just-picked buttercups. Inspired by his gesture, Bea insisted that we eat in the dining room, not in the breakfast nook within the warm blue-and-white kitchen. The sunny bouquet graced our table along with our mother's rose china. Fresh spinach salad, the chicken casserole, homemade yeast rolls, and iced tea nourished my soul as well as my body and helped dissolve the mind-numbing questions and tangled emotions of my long day.

While Peter did not discuss the break-in or speculate about Simon Hostetler's death, his conversation nevertheless focused on the Amish way of life. "Did you know that the reason they don't use telephones is because it detracts from face-to-face contact? Leah said that several families installed them in order to fill dairy and produce orders, but discovered that too many other calls were being made. The Tremont community really struggled to know what to do. On one hand, they need a phone to stay up to date with their buyers. On the other, it diminishes the personal way they like to do business, as well as their close-knit life-style."

"So how did they resolve it?" asked Bea.

"They decided to keep one phone for every three families — usually in the barn! The bishop implored them to use it as sparingly as possible."

"So they're not opposed to all technology," concluded my sister.

"Right. Not at all. Mr. Schroeder explained it to me this way: The Amish simply do not believe that progressive technology is automatically beneficial. The English, as they call us, assume that if technology makes our lives run smoother and faster, then it has to be better. But the convenience that comes with phones, cars, and computers often takes us away from dependence on God, family, and community."

"That's true," I affirmed. "From what I've read, many Amish societies incorporate various forms of technology — from tractors and telephones to advanced software to help them manage their home businesses. Of course, these issues often divide communities, as well. There's a fine line between being a good steward and using technology for the common good, and being worldly and using it to promote self-sufficiency." I grabbed another roll and slathered it with butter.

"I admire the commitment they demonstrate to the faith," concluded Bea. "I'm grateful that I'm not called to their lifestyle, but I appreciate its appeal." She took a small bite before adding, "Do you think you could ever be Amish, Peter?"

He looked up from his plate quickly. "Yes, I think I could." There was a moment's silence while my sister and I took in the repercussions. "Actually," he continued, "it's something that I'm honestly considering right now. Grif, I've been meaning to talk to you about it. I value your perspective."

I tried to nod and smile but my ambivalence was clear.

"Of course, we can talk later, after dinner," he responded.

"Yes, let's do," I said.

Peter nodded while he chewed. The awkward moment passed as Bea folded her napkin alongside her plate. She had barely touched her dinner.

"Aren't you hungry, sis?" I asked. "This is delicious."

Peter concurred, "As always."

"Oh, I'm fine," she smiled. "Just trying to cut down a bit. It's no secret that I could afford to lose a few pounds." My sister filled out her large frame with a graceful ease that Rubens would've appreciated.

"It wouldn't have anything to do with

your new boyfriend, would it?" I teased, eager to move on to a more light-hearted subject.

"Are you still seeing Rev. Slater?" Peter asked innocently, picking up the game.

"You two stop it," she replied good-naturedly. "Nothing wrong with a lady wanting to improve herself. I'd like to think that I'm dieting for my own benefit and no one else's."

"But you are dating Rev. Slater?" my curate repeated.

"Well, yes, Lyle and I are still seeing each other. He surprised me with the most fabulous treat last Saturday. We went to the Chattanooga Choo-Choo Dinner Theater and saw *South Pacific*! We had a marvelous time. Bali Hai!" she sang out and laughed.

"So can we expect a June wedding?" Peter continued. "I hear there's a parish pool on which one of us three will get hitched first."

We all laughed and Bea responded for both of us. "My money is on you, Father Abernathy. We old folks are only out to have a good time!"

The meal seemed complete even before my sister promised a special dessert. This was the familiar life I loved: the amiable banter, the warmth of a well-set table and delicious meal, the grace of God in giving such bounty. The troubles of Tremont, as well as my personal conflicts, seemed only speculative ramblings from a weary imagination, the dreamer awakened by the reality of what he holds dearest.

"No, no. Leave the dishes until later. You both sit right there," Bea commanded.

While she bustled into the kitchen humming to herself, Peter whispered, "Is it a special occasion or just the power of love behind Bea's good mood?"

"I think she's got spring fever, which often includes the latter," I whispered back as my sister reentered. "Here's coffee for you both. It's French vanilla decaf." She placed cream and sugar from our mother's silver service on the table before our china cups and saucers. In the brief moment it took to adjust the rich, fragrant brew, Beatrice returned with a crystal-stemmed cake stand and a bowl teeming with rubies.

"Fresh strawberries!" she announced. "Mr. Spradley just got them in today — they're from California but he expects a Florida crop in by the end of April. Here's the whipped cream and angel food cake." She served portions and placed them before each of us.

The angel food cake dissolved in smooth-as-cream mouthfuls, the berries sweeter than most for the first of the season. " 'It's food too fine for angels; yet come, take and eat they fill! It's Heaven's sugar cake,' " I declared, quoting from *Sacramental Meditations*.

"I don't think Edward Taylor had my angel food cake in mind when he wrote that. Honestly! You and Philip Jackson are always risking sacrilege in your praise of food," exclaimed my sister, proud, I suspected, nonetheless.

"Who do you think I learned from?" I kidded, winking to my curate.

"That reminds me," Bea said between small bites. "I'm assuming that we're all going together to Philip's retirement party next week. Would either of you mind if Lyle came along? He hasn't met Philip yet, and I want to make sure he does."

"It's hard to believe Father Jackson has been in the ministry for over forty years," said Peter. "I hope I can last that long."

"I suspect you will, and then some," I offered, wishing Bea had not introduced the topic.

"Do you know whom Bishop Wilder has in mind for the position there?" asked Bea.

I decided I might as well get it over with sooner than later. "As a matter of fact, I talked to Tom today. Peter's definitely on his short list," I said and smiled up at my curate.

He looked startled but not surprised. "No, I'm too young," Pete replied. "He needs someone with experience for St. Anthony's."

"I don't know why it didn't occur to me," said Bea. "Of course! Peter's perfect for the job. St. Tony's is growing by leaps and bounds, mostly young families and singles. They just finished their building program last year. It would be a perfect match!" She seemed pleased with herself that the matter had been resolved so easily.

"It would be hard to leave Avenell," said my curate.

"Peter, you have the experience, and better yet, the maturity to make an excellent rector for St. Anthony's. This afternoon I told Tom that he won't find a better man for the job. Despite my fear of losing you, I know you can't stay here forever." Our convivial interlude had abruptly shifted back to the sober tone of Peter's announcement about considering the Amish faith.

"Aw, you can't get rid of me that easy," he said, his voice attempting humor but failing the stretch.

I decided to voice my fears and end the attempt to linger in my denial. "Peter, it seems that I'm going to lose you either way you go. If the bishop offers you St. Anthony's, you'd be foolish not to take it. Or if your heart compels you to join Leah's family in Tremont, then you should follow. Either way, I will always love you as a son." My voice became thick with emotion. "Go or stay with my blessing as our Lord leads you."

Bea seemed about to make a quick jibe, but then sipped quietly from her cup when she observed Peter's eyes mist over. He nodded and excused himself from the table in a hushed voice. My sister looked sympathetically over at me, the prospect of loss apparent in her own eyes, as well. And I knew what she was thinking: If it should work out that she and Lyle Slater married, then I would be all alone. Of course, in Bea's perfect world, Caroline and I would share a double ceremony with her and Lyle. Why not throw in Peter and Leah and make it a triple? Such fantasies worked well for television and romance novels, but hardly in real life.

The phone rang, startling me to immediately answer it rather than deferring to the answering machine. I half hoped it was Caroline returning my earlier message, but a male voice greeted me instead.

"Grif? It's Leland Finch — down at

Dolby. Hope I'm not interrupting your supper." His voice reverberated through the receiver and my mind cartwheeled to catch up to my old friend.

"Lee! Good to hear your voice. It's been a long time," I said, swallowing my last bite of strawberry. "Thanks for returning my call."

"No problem. It's been too long since we got together. We've got to plan to meet for one of those greasy breakfasts you love so much down in Lewiston. I meant to catch you at the office today, but then the time slipped away from me. Now, what can I do for you? Your message said something about a friend of yours dying," he said. "Do you need an assist for the funeral? Was he a military man?"

I tried to remember how long it had been since Lee and I had gotten together. Over a year, at least. We had first met years ago when we jointly helped a young airman kick a heroin addiction. Lee and I shared similar philosophies of ministry, and I had appreciated his sharp sense of humor and his blunt faith.

"Well, Lee," I said after explaining about Simon's death and the close proximity to the military base. "I was hoping you could tell me what you know about the relationship between the Amish and your folks there at Dolby."

Dead silence for an awkward few moments. "Grif, I'm afraid I can't help you out there. That's not something for you to get involved in." And he abruptly hung up.

Chapter Thirteen

Weight of Glory

"Lee? Lee — you there? Hello?" I stammered. But the line was dead and clicked into a dial tone as I replaced the receiver.

"Who was that?" asked Bea. "You look as if you've seen a ghost — is anything wrong?"

Ignoring my sister's questions momentarily, I flipped through the address book and found Leland Finch's number. But when my return call went through, only a recording greeted my ears, my friend's sonorous voice instructing me of his office hours on the base. I didn't have a home number for him and local directory assistance had no listings for his name.

For the second time that day — by two different people — I was being warned not to question the triangular configuration among the Amish, the Dolby military base, and Simon Hostetler's death. This time by someone I knew, someone I trusted. What in the world was going on?

Peter and Bea were engaged in their own conversation as I stood cradling the phone in my palm. Finally my sister offered, "More cake?"

I shook my head. "No, thanks, sis. But that meal was absolutely the highlight of this day."

"I was just telling Miss Bea that I better be going. We'll talk tomorrow in the office about St. Anthony's," Peter said diplomatically.

We said our good-nights, and I helped my sister wash the good china by hand.

I could not quit thinking about Leland's abrupt warning about Dolby and the Amish. He had always been the kind of man who spoke frankly and directly, but he had also always displayed compassion and gentleness. I felt I knew him well enough, even if we had not connected in some time, to demand further explanation. But I also considered other contacts to the Dolby Air Force Base; several parishioners were retired military people. Perhaps I'd pay some long-overdue ministry calls this week.

My frustration and mild anger found release in the comfort of warm, soapy water surrounding the circular scrubbing motions and the clean squeak of fine china as the dish towel dried the smooth surface. Halfway through, Bea touched my elbow at the sink and asked, "Are you okay? You seem troubled. Anything I can do?"

I shook my head and forged a weak smile. She let me keep my silence until bedtime, then only asking what time John Greenwood would be arriving the next day. I'd almost forgotten! My chaplain friend was traveling down from Rockmont State Penitentiary.

When I told her that he'd arrive in time for dinner, Bea clapped her hands together. "Grif, perhaps we could have a little dinner party. You could invite Caroline — a kind of peace offering — and Lyle could come and I could even invite Roberta Montoya. She remembers John; they met at last year's harvest festival."

"Bea. I know you mean well, but this is not a singles cruise for John. How about if we just kept the party small? I'm not sure Caroline will be free, or if she will want to come," I said, shaking my head at Bea's matchmaking instincts. "I'll call and ask her tomorrow morning, though. But let's just keep it the five of us for now."

I welcomed the opportunity for John to meet Lyle Slater and gauge whether I was being too hard on my sister's beau. And I had wanted my dear friend to meet Caroline for some time, as well. The thought of John's visit cheered me, and I told my sister as much as I hugged her and said goodnight.

While Bea read in the living room, I retired to my room and went through the motions of my bedtime routine. Caroline had not called and I momentarily debated trying her again, but now it felt too late, my energy and focus all spent. Afraid to admit how overwhelmed I felt by the odd convergence of so many conflicted feelings, I began looking for something to read. I picked up a notebook from my bedside table, written in Simon Hostetler's strong masculine script. Despite the case's contribution to my fatigue, I found myself thumbing through Simon's notes, focusing in particular on the Brethren.

Apparently this book contained notes from several of Simon's interviews with both Amish and "English" about the existence of the ominous fraternity. The last entry in the journal arrested my perusal: a testimony from an anonymous source that I did not recall from my cursory oncethrough earlier. Must have overlooked it. A non-Amish woman from Mumford, identified as an eighty-six-year-old widow and homemaker, recounted her husband's participation in the clandestine group of vigilantes back in the early years of their marriage. She recalled thumbing through a book called the *Golden Rule* discovered in her husband's desk after their honeymoon but did not remember specifically what she had read. However, she did recall once hearing her husband telling another man "to meet at the Judas Tree at the usual time." When she confronted her spouse, he dismissed it as a hunting trip until she produced a black robe from the back of his closet. When he confessed his distrust of the Amish in Tremont and his participation in "just scaring them off," as he put it, the wife made him promise to quit immediately. Apparently, he gave it up, for the wife never found any evidence of his continued membership. When asked if the Brethren resisted the husband's resignation, the wife did not know — only that her husband seemed frightened for several weeks before he finally "came back to himself."

Simon concluded his write-up by asking the woman if she believed the Brethren continued to exist after her husband left the group. "Oh yes," she'd told him, "I know they still exist to this day. Look at all them bad things happening to them poor Amish people down in Tremont. Fires and ruint crops and such — ain't nobody but the Brethren would do such meanness. I don't understand it, though. If they ain't scared them Plain folk off their land in the last eighty years, why they think they gonna do it now?" Simon asked what she thought had inspired this sudden streak of Brethren activity against the Amish, but the woman did not know. "I've said too much already today. You be careful now, you hear? You didn't hear it from me."

She had never told anyone, not even her grown children, about her knowledge of the Brethren until a few weeks ago when she agreed to talk with Simon Hostetler. How he found her, and her true identity, no one might ever know. But Simon believed her, and now he was dead.

A sound too shrill to be the alarm clock punctuated the silence.

"Grif? I want to apologize," Caroline purred through the phone. I had drifted off amid a packet of Hostetler's notes on church organization and management within the Amish. Answering the bedside phone instinctively alert for the latest death, crisis, or need within the parish, I still felt mired in the quicksand of sleep. "Caroline?" I echoed, confused by some dream just out of reach.

"I'm sorry to call so late. Hope I didn't

wake you," she continued. It wasn't quite eleven o'clock yet. "I just got in from a poetry reading and didn't want to continue playing phone tag for the rest of this week. I want to apologize for the way I acted Saturday. I think we still need to talk about where our relationship is headed, but I wasn't very kind."

Her words rolled like marbles in the dusty circle of my weary mind. I struggled to form a coherent response. "I understand." While I was not surprised at her apology, I was selfishly encouraged that she offered first. But I knew my part in this friction was just as much a contributing factor, if not more so. "Caroline . . . I need to apologize, too. I'm afraid I haven't been very connected to my feelings. My responses at breakfast Saturday surprised me as much as you. I'm sorry . . ."

I paused for her response but only the quiet electric pulse of telecommunications responded. So I kept talking. "You're right, we do need to talk about where things are headed. I'd like that very much. In fact, Bea was hoping you could come to dinner tomorrow night. There's someone I'd like you to meet. My old friend John Greenwood is in town for a couple of days. You don't need to bring anything."

"That would be nice," she said. "Although you and I may not get to talk very much — it sounds like a dinner party."

I confirmed her observation, adding that Lyle would be there and that I'd thwarted Bea's plans to ambush John with a blind date. Caroline laughed and I was moved by the echo of her voice inside the cavernous space in my heart.

"Well, I certainly want to meet John," she concluded. "Perhaps we can just enjoy the company and then plan another time when you and I can get together and talk about us."

As I hung up the phone, I felt grateful that the pressure had been taken off our relationship for the moment. The Lord was gracious. Now I could look forward to a pleasant evening with dear friends — except for Slater. But I would at least tolerate him for my sister's sake.

As my faculties resumed consciousness, I opened my planner. I found tomorrow morning scheduled with my hospital and retirement center visits — a light week, thankfully. In the afternoon I could catch up on correspondence, approve the mock-up for this Sunday's bulletin, and meet with my sexton. If time permitted, I could work on my homily for this weekend and the order of service for the Lenten service Wednesday.

Then tomorrow evening I could relax.

But what if the dinner party was not such a good idea, after all? It would be good for Caroline to meet John finally, and I was eager for his approval of her. But what if they didn't like each other? What if John shared Joan Dowinger's concerns about Caroline's faith? I didn't need another complication before the present ones were resolved.

I longed to return to sleep, but my mind bloated with complications: the brutal murder of my friend among the Amish; my odd participation in the investigation; my fears of loving another woman; my concern over that woman's faith and how others perceived her; my fears of change, of losing Peter and perhaps even Beatrice.

I released them then, like caged birds free of their bars, all in the breath of prayer, realizing that today I had left very little to God. I picked up the old, battered, faded Bible from my bedside. Turning to Psalm 86, I savored favorite verses: *Incline thy ear,* O LORD, *and answer me, for I am poor and needy. Preserve my life, for I am godly; save thy servant who trusts in thee. Thou art my God; be gracious to me,* O LORD, *for to thee do I cry all the day.*

From my bedroom window, I greeted the

day and offered it up in another psalm-based prayer. Restful sleep had delivered me from many of the troubles of last night. Pulling back my curtain, I found it was difficult not to hope. This day shimmered with the dew-breath of spring — a robin heralding his return, apple blossoms promising fruit by June, the moist breeze pollinating the mountainside. Sleepy students rustled across lawns in cut-off khakis and T-shirts, wet grass slicked to the toes of their Birkenstocks and cross-trainers.

Not only had I slept like the proverbial baby, waking with a rest and zeal that I had not experienced in weeks, but I accomplished a great deal in a short time. A quick check-in at the office shortly after eight revealed that Janine was in early to finish the bulletin.

Only two hospital visits were on my schedule. Mrs. Ruby Jean Modell had slipped on her porch steps back at the first of the month and had been slowly recovering from a broken hip. Her spirits were high since she would finally be going home this week. Her daughter Flora, a friend of Bea's from the Parish Ladies' Auxiliary, had baked a sour cream coffee cake just for my visit.

My other call was to one of our stalwart

members of Peter's Next Generation group, a junior history major named Billy Tomiko who underwent an emergency appendectomy the previous morning. He was recovering smoothly and would be back in his classes by next week.

Mr. Cantrell, an Alzheimer's victim in the Eagle's Nest Retirement Home down in the valley, was in high spirits, as well. He clearly recognized me, asked if I'd read Psalm 23, and prayed with me for half an hour. He seemed to fade as I told him good-bye and promised to return next week. Heavy hearted, I lingered in the ammonia-drenched corridors of the retirement center and found myself tracing a familiar route to the west wing. Room 4-B was empty now, the walls pared down to the beige wallpaper, the room bared of antiques, photographs, and paintings, back to the bland impersonality of a hospital room. Aunt Olive Merriweather, a relatively new acquaintance of mine from the fall, had died in February. When she took pneumonia with the first snowfall in January, she called to invite me down and we had a great visit. I had assumed that she wanted prayer and attention from a new friend, but instead she had a gift for me: an autographed, first edition of *To Kill a Mockingbird*. She had no way of knowing, but it had been one of my favorite novels since I read it as a freshman here at Avenell.

Her gift had caught me by surprise, giving as she did out of her own pain and suffering. *Our choices have so many unseen repercussions,* I thought to myself as I departed the sunny building this day. That dear woman's unexpected kindness would always linger with me. Just as the brutality of Simon's death would always linger with me. Yet the hidden heart always reveals itself. Had I already encountered someone burdened by his or her involvement in my friend's lynching? Or worse yet, someone without conscience? I wondered how far the ripples would extend from Simon Hostetler's death. How many of those unseen repercussions, like underground streams feeding natural springs, would ever reveal themselves?

My worrisome thoughts led me back to my friend at the military base down at Dolby. Returning to the office after lunch, I made a call to Leland Finch and he answered on the second ring.

"Look, Grif," he started. "I apologize if I was rude last night. It had been a long day, and I didn't have the energy to go into the complex relationships between us and the Amish in Tremont. I hope you understand."

His words sounded scripted, premeditated for the eventual call from his old friend who asked the wrong question at the wrong time. I chuckled into my receiver. "Lee, of course I understand. You don't have to tell me about how demanding ministry can be. Well, listen, I'm going to be down your way later this week and I wondered if we might have lunch. I could even meet you on the base if that's convenient."

"Well, I don't know, Grif . . ." His script failed him. "I mean, sure, I'd love to see you and all, but it's shaping up to be a pretty busy week."

"That's exactly why you need to reconnect with an old friend," I countered. "I'll meet you at your office this Friday at noon. No excuses now, you hear?"

"Grif . . . well, all right," he said, squeezing out his compliance. "I'll see you then. You're hard to refuse, you know that?"

Now he sounded more like himself, like the old minister I'd known for some time. But I was still oddly troubled by his reluctance, his change of tone and character from what I'd known for so long. What could be behind the tension in his voice?

Similar questions still lingered when John Greenwood arrived in my office around four. I had just finished meeting with Joe

Brewer, my sexton, about the plans for Holy Week services in three weeks when a familiar smile rounded the corner. He chatted amicably with Janine while I wrapped up. John's beard looked fuller than I recalled from our last meeting, only thinning out at the sideburns. His hair formed a fringed halo atop his bald crown. Dapper looking in a chambray shirt and tan jeans, my friend seemed younger than his sixty-six years. A banker for the first third of his life, John Greenwood retained an air of efficiency packaged in a down-home style.

While he and my sexton exchanged greetings, I closed the computer files on my desktop PC, marked the passage I was considering from St. Augustine with a sticky note, and signed the letters Janine had placed on my desk. I then welcomed him with a handshake and bear hug. He told me he'd already dropped his bag off at the rectory and shared a cup of coffee with my sister. Bea had informed him about our dinner plans — and about Lyle Slater — and he asked me if we had time for a walk around campus before then.

We followed the sidewalk running in front of the cathedral, up Southern Avenue toward the University Center, the Avenell Seminary, and the Tiger Bay Pub. A group of students played volleyball on the quad while a golden retriever chased a Frisbee. Late-day sun bathed the campus in a golden suspension similar to its auspicious arrival that morning. A grounds crew weeded a flower bed in front of the vacant President's Manse, anticipating the perennials ahead.

Many annuals, however, had already budded and bloomed. John marveled at the beds of profuse color and compared them to his flora two hours away in Rockmont. I basked in the company of my friend and mentor, eager for his counsel on the various swirling currents in my life. After we had peeled the surface of our lives away by exchanging details of our day, I described in more detail what I knew about the death of Simon. My summary included the cultural anthropologist's ties to Tremont and the shadows that seemed to be collecting on his reputation: his bitterness over the shunning of his father; his fascination with the anti-Amish group known as the Brethren; his investment in a corporation eager to buy up Amish property.

"Could Simon have changed that much from when you knew him twenty-five years ago? You have to admit, Grif, that's a long time," said John.

"Yes, I know it is," I replied. "But he sure seemed to be the same old Simon these last few weeks. Quiet, intelligent, funny. I guess I don't like the prospect that he might not be what he seemed." John's question resonated with my thoughts about Leland Finch earlier that afternoon.

"I'll continue to pray for you and for Simon's family and friends," concluded John. "I'll pray that the Lord's truth emerges, and that He prepares you all to appropriate as much of it as you can handle."

We walked in silence for almost a block. The air was loaded with the smell of burgers and onions sizzling over coals, the scent of an eager cook inaugurating his barbecue grill. John and I looked at each other and acknowledged our own growing appetites.

Then, as we turned up Harvard Lane toward the music center auditorium, John asked about Caroline. I didn't waste time since my friend would observe for himself very shortly the dynamic between Dr. Barr and me. I quickly described my visit from Joan Dowinger and my own concern about my friend's spiritual state. He took it all in stoically, like a thoughtful courtroom judge.

"Do you think she's a Christian?" he finally asked point blank.

"That's such a complex question — and who can judge whom? I want her to be, but honestly, I don't know," I admitted.

"Well, she must have some kind of interest in God or you wouldn't be interested in her," he said as we passed a group of joggers. "Although, sadly enough, until I got to seminary, I can't recall many of my professors who displayed a brilliant intellect as well as a deep-seated faith."

"That's what Bea said, too — about me being interested in her." I waited until a robed faculty member crossed in front of us, headed toward the Eastman Library, where an oversized bronzed tiger statue guarded the academy. Dying sunlight glanced rays off the weathered metal creature as I recounted to John the little spat Caroline and I had over breakfast on Saturday. He nodded and smiled, and I stopped abruptly at the corner of Poplar and Princeton.

"Why haven't *you* ever remarried?" I asked suddenly.

"Hey, wait a minute, I thought we were talking about you! We've been over this before, haven't we?" he said, leading the way across the oak-lined street.

"Not really. You always dodge the question. I know the loss of your wife was incredibly painful — and then to have it compounded by your arrest for her murder. But after you were acquitted and all the dust settled . . . haven't you met anyone you wished to know better?" I ventured.

"Of course. And I've been out a few times. But . . . I don't know. Just haven't met the right one, I guess. 'Widowed Prison Chaplain' isn't the greatest hook for the classifieds," he grinned. "Of course, it sounds like some wedding bells may be ringing down here for Miss Bea. Is this Slater fellow serious about her, you think? What's he like?"

"Unfortunately, I believe he is serious," I said, explaining my impressions but trying to withhold my bias.

"Well, guess I missed my chance with your sister. Another one slips away," he joked.

But was he joking? The two of us had never discussed his feelings toward Beatrice. I shared his smile and tried to imagine John and my sister together. He certainly wasn't as polished and cosmopolitan as Lyle Slater, but a hundred times more authentic. I realized then that I would not mind giving up my sister if she married a man I trusted.

"We better head back," I said, checking my gold-rimmed Timex. We headed toward Fraternity Row and the intramural fields, the back side of campus from the way we had walked so far. It would take us back along shady, cracked sidewalks and open expanses of bluegrass and clover.

"Grif, I certainly don't want to come across like Joan. But I'm afraid we both know that you need to talk to Caroline sooner than later about whether or not you share a common faith," he said. "While I suspect you share similar sensibilities, you could both get hurt if things . . . well, you know what I'm trying to say."

"I know that, John, but . . . it feels so intrusive, so evangelically correct. As if I should write her a note reading 'Are you a Christian? Willing to sign the Apostles' Creed and the statement of faith? Check Yes or No.' It's like I cannot date a woman and trust the Lord to work in both our lives. Instead, I have to hold her up for a parish vote and see if everyone approves." The directness of my anger didn't seem to surprise John as much as it did me.

He nodded in understanding, then cleared his throat before quoting: " 'It is a serious thing to live in a society of possible gods and goddesses, to remember that the dullest and most uninteresting person you talk to may one day be a creature which, if you saw it now, you would be strongly tempted to worship or else a horror and a corruption such as you now meet, if at all, only in a nightmare.' "

"Ah, the *Weight of Glory*," I whispered, cooling the internal conflagration. "One of Lewis's best sermons."

"We're all moving one direction or the other," he said. "I have little doubt that you and Caroline are moving in the same direction toward God. But I do think it requires a conscious movement much of the time." John patted my shoulder. "I'm looking forward to meeting your Caroline tonight."

We walked in the intimacy of silence the remainder of the way. Although I did not like the reinforcement of his counsel, I appreciated his concern. And once again I wondered about the prudence of our dinner plans, whether or not conversation would be strained or politely aloof. Or perhaps, despite everyone's attempts, a generation gap would strand us. After all, Caroline was a dozen years younger than I, and over twenty years younger than Bea, Lyle, and John. She was an academic scholar, a poetic playwright — much more attuned to her youthful students than a stodgy quartet of aging Christians.

In the soft gauze of twilight, I paused and simply asked the Lord's presence to grace us this night.

When we arrived back at the rectory, Bea and Lyle Slater were sitting on the porch casually. My sister introduced John and he shook Slater's hand.

"I have a surprise for you, Grif. We're going to Caroline's for dinner!" Bea announced.

"What? I thought you were cooking lasagna? When did this happen?" I asked.

"I thought you'd be pleased, excited even. She and I talked this morning. I called to ask if I could borrow some oregano from her herb garden. It was her idea — she practically begged me. Thought it would be fun for us to have a change of venue. She said she'd been meaning to do it for some time —"

"Enough, already!" laughed John. "We're convinced, Miss Bea."

I tried to warm up to the idea, but my prior concerns lingered. "What time is she expecting us?"

Slater quickly scanned his chrome Rolex. "We should be on our way even as we speak. I'll be glad to drive us all."

The next thing I knew, we were assembled in Lyle's luxury sedan for the short ride across campus. He and John made small talk about the latter's ministry to state inmates while I gave Bea a look that meant to say, "I hope you know what you're doing."

She smiled back reassuringly.

Chapter Fourteen

Kidnapped

The little white cottage with blue shutters nestled comfortably between the edge of campus and the sloping north face of Eaglehead Mountain. Lyle brought Gerber daisies as pale as pink salmon and Bea had insisted on bringing a jar of homemade marmalade. On the doorstep awaiting our hostess, John joked about bringing her one of the pocket New Testaments he gave to inmates, but then reconsidered the implication of his remark.

Caroline greeted us with the warmth and familiarity usually extended to family members who have driven many hours for a short visit. It was good to see her, and I was affected by the warmth of her quick hug as she greeted each of her guests.

"You make a good Southerner, despite your Yankee roots, Miss Caroline!" I declared playfully.

She laughed and served us blue corn crackers with a dill vegetable dip while we chatted and waited for dinner. The cherry dining table, as plain and beautiful as one in an Amish home, was set with white china and linen napkins. Bea complimented every aspect of Caroline's home and good taste.

The marinated chicken came off the gas grill on the flagstone patio — its inaugural burn of the season Caroline announced — smelling of rosemary and red wine. I mentioned the other grill John and I had smelled on our walk around campus.

"It's that time of year!" said Lyle as the meal was assembled.

A layered salad, baked zucchini casserole — "last year's crop," our hostess apologized — and French bread completed the collation.

Around a dessert of cheesecake — New York style, courtesy of Caroline's Italian grandmother — we sipped coffee and discussed the upcoming premier of her new play, tentatively titled *Shelter from the Rain*, this summer. Caroline and John clearly liked each other, each responding naturally to the other's questions about family, career, and upbringing. The conversation flowed with the natural ease of a mountain stream, all of us treading the current with an unforced rhythm.

Our discussion had come around to parish news, the retirement of Philip

Jackson, the likelihood of Peter's nomination for the rectory of St. Anthony's — something he and I had not gotten around to discussing as we had planned — when Caroline quietly stated, "That reminds me — I had a caller today. Mrs. Joan Dowinger, treasurer of the Avenell Parish Ladies' Auxiliary. She said the Auxiliary is trying to call on all the 'young, professional women of the university' in hopes of attracting new members."

I almost choked.

"Oh yes — Joan," said Bea, as if unsure of how to grasp Caroline's disclosure in light of my last tangle with the wealthy widow. "Well, I hope she didn't scare you off. You know you'd be more than welcome to attend any of our meetings, dear."

"What else did Joan say? I hope she didn't question you about our friendship," I said, clearly annoyed. I could just imagine the politesse of Joan's pointed questions; her nerve transcended my categories.

Caroline smiled, her radiant eyes live blue coals. "Not directly, of course. But when I mentioned that I'd been attending Cathedral of the Divine, she said, 'Ah yes, I thought I had seen you there before! Welcome, my dear! And didn't I see you with our rector at the last potluck dinner?' " Her lovely voice cracked at the near perfect falsetto imitation of Joan's prim warble. We all laughed.

"And what did you reply?" I asked, wiping the tears from my eyes.

"I told her, 'Yes, since Griffin and I share custody of our children, we do try to get along with some civility in public.' " An impish grin betrayed her jest.

"It would serve her right if you had said that!" laughed Bea, obviously impressed with Caroline's quick wit.

"You're a daring one, that's for sure!" echoed John, equally amused.

"I told her, 'Yes, I attended with my friend, Father Grif,' " Caroline corrected, her smile fading. "She took the hint and did not press me."

As our laughter faded, I regretted that Caroline and I were not alone. This would be the perfect opportunity to delve into the subject below the surface of Joan's intrusiveness. Obviously, my friend had some idea of the subtext for Joan's visit. And in light of our disagreement at breakfast a few days ago, I wondered if she had seriously considered the implications. Now was not the time, however, as she refilled coffee cups and we all let out contented sighs from full stomachs and warmed souls.

Bea proposed that we play a game, cards perhaps, but then Lyle pointed out that there were five of us. We discussed various options, but finally John begged off, content to kibitz and sip more decaf. Caroline and I sat across from each other at the now cleared table, opposite my sister and Lyle. We played Spades, the card game of bidding and trumping.

Several hands went pleasantly enough until about the sixth or seventh round. Caroline and I had dominated, and I was consequently teasing Bea and Lyle a bit. It was during this hand that I believe the Reverend Lyle Slater cheated. Caroline led the king of hearts — the ace had already gone. Bea followed with the red seven of kind, and I played suit with my ten since I had bid low and did not want to catch any tricks. That's when Slater played a trump, the four of spades. He took the trick.

That would have been fine except at the last hand, when Caroline thought she'd take the trick with the jack of hearts, Lyle played the queen. Instantly, I knew something was wrong. Bea seemed not to notice.

"Oh, I must have miscalculated," Caroline offered demurely. I gently pointed out the error.

"I'm sorry, Lyle," I began. "But when

Caroline led hearts, didn't you trump with a spade? And then you ended up holding the queen of hearts on the last hand."

But it was too late. Even as I spoke, the smooth operator had discreetly begun shuffling the deck, no doubt to make sure we could not reconstruct the hand and his violation.

"Oh, come now," he laughed. "That's the first hand we've made our bid on and you accuse us of cheating? Really, Grif. I thought you were bigger than that."

Bea looked uncomfortable, and I honestly believe that she knew what had happened, as well. Nonetheless, she defended her date. "Grif, you must have miscounted. Maybe it was the hand before this one? Surely, you're not going to try and take away our only good hand!"

"John?" I asked. "Did you see what happened? I'm sure it was an accident."

"I'm afraid I didn't, Grif," he replied, stroking the large ginger cat on his lap.

My eyes met Caroline's and her expression indicated that I was dead-on correct but that perhaps I should let it go. Fortunately, I suppose, the phone rang then, breaking the tension and disrupting the game.

"Grif, it's for you," said Caroline, handing

me the cordless phone and pointing toward the empty hallway for privacy.

"Hello?" I asked. Some undercurrent of fear already possessed me since I had told no one where I'd be tonight, especially since I had not known myself that we were coming to Caroline's.

"Grif, thank the Lord," breathed a familiar voice. "I've been looking all over for you. I — you've got to help — it's Leah — she — they can't find —" The staccato syllables of my curate's usually composed voice broke into sobs.

"Peter, slow down," I said. "Take some deep breaths. It's going to be okay."

He sniffled and tried to recollect himself.

"There now," I said. "Tell me what happened."

He took in deep breaths like a thirsty man drinks water. "Leah — she's disappeared. She was helping a neighbor, Mrs. Yoder, with some quilting and stayed for supper there. Afterward —" he swallowed hard, "Leah left for home, right as the sun was setting. But she never arrived."

I thought he would release the torrent of fear once more, but he inhaled it and continued. "Grif, that was over three hours ago. Her father called me and Sheriff Claiborne just a few minutes ago. I was hoping you'd go down to Tremont with me and help me look for her."

"Of course," I said. "John's here with me, too. I can bring him and Bea if you think they can help."

"No — I don't know — whatever you think." His voice plummeted to a husky whisper. "Grif, I don't know what I'd do if I lost her." Another series of sobs wracked the young man's body behind his voice.

"I'm sure she's fine, Peter," I said. "Let me pray for her and for you." I offered up a few sentences asking for protection, safety, and peace, then concluded, "Please bring Leah back safely to us, dear Father. Restore her to her family and those that love her. Deliver her from the enemy. In your Son's name, Amen."

A moment of silence passed before I added, "Peter, are you at the dorm? I'll pick you up in ten minutes — I'll have to return to the rectory to get my car."

"I'll meet you at the rectory, then," he said.

I returned to the jovial card party and found John had been convinced to take my place.

"Everything all right?" he asked looking up.

"No, I'm afraid not," I said and explained the situation.

Bea shrieked and muttered, "Oh! I can't believe humanity!" Everyone else, even Slater, looked genuinely concerned.

After a moment for the news to sink in, John said, "Well, we best be going down the mountain to help in the search."

Caroline offered to come with us to Tremont as well, but I discouraged her. Slater offered the use of his car to save time, but I told him that Peter was meeting me at the rectory anyway. After hasty thanks and farewells to our hostess, the four of us roared back home in Lyle's large Mercedes. Peter stood out front, his pacing silhouetted by the porch light and stray beams from the streetlamps. There was no moon tonight.

I decided to take John up on his offer to accompany us, but I instructed Bea and Lyle to stay behind. As well intended as they were — and as arrogant as my decision felt — I did not believe they could be helpful in an already tense situation.

I did, however, accept Slater's offer of an extra flashlight and roadside flares from his trunk. Bea ran inside and came back with three flashlights and a package of unopened copper-topped batteries. Before I knew it, the three of us — Peter, John, and I — were careening down the mountainside toward

Tremont and the unknown fate of Leah Schroeder.

My old Buick had never made it down to the valley in such record time. During the surreal journey, Peter relayed the sketchy details of Leah's disappearance at least twice while John and I listened and asked questions for which my curate did not have answers. Finally, John prayed a prayer similar to what I had offered when on the phone with Peter, and we remained silent all the way from Mumford to Tremont.

Finally arriving at the Schroeder farm, we would never have guessed the suffering going on inside by family members save for the single Coleman lantern flickering from a stout nail on the front porch post. Without knocking or waiting for permission to enter, Peter ran inside the home of his surrogate family. John and I lingered behind but were not surprised to find a tear-streaked mother and wide-eyed brothers inside. They welcomed Peter as one of their own; even restrained Benjamin Schroeder wrapped a broad arm around my curate's back.

"No word yet," said the Amishman. "Your friend from the sheriff's office and the police from Mumford are out in the woods right now."

"Dan Warren? I'm glad he's here — he'll

do everything he can to find Leah," I offered. "You have my hope and prayers that she is safe and on her way back to us all even as we speak." I introduced John Greenwood to the Schroeder family and they acknowledged him with nods and wan smiles.

"Should we start looking ourselves?" I asked. "What route did Leah usually take from the Yoders'?"

Silence. Finally, the oldest son, Jacob, spoke up, voicing all our fears. "She usually cut by the Judas Tree and took the footpath home."

Sarah Schroeder cried out a mournful wail and buried her face in her husband's shoulder. Candle flames intensified the horrific effect of her fearful cry and I shuddered at the thought that no one could bear to voice: Had Simon Hostetler's murderer abducted Leah?

"I should never have permitted her to go to Mary Yoder's quilting party," said Benjamin stoically. "It is all my fault."

Peter shook his head. "No, Mr. Schroeder. Do not blame yourself. You couldn't have known. We must not lose hope. Now, I want Jacob to come with Grif, John, and me while the rest of you stay here. We're going to find her." My curate's fear had crystallized into anger that needed to find a target for its energy.

"Can't I come, too?" asked eighteen-year-old Nathan.

"No, you stay here with your mother. I will assist in the search," said his father.

We filed out of the candle-lit glow of the house and gathered our flashlights from the car. Benjamin decided we should stick to the trail and move toward the police search being conducted from the Yoder farm toward us. "Surely, we will find her before we meet in the middle," he said.

Jacob Schroeder proved a worthy guide, leading us with the Coleman lantern deeper into the dark wood. None of us spoke until our eyes had become accustomed to the murky light, the dark underwater-like world of rustling shadows and elongated trees sighing in the path of our feeble light. The moon continued to be hidden behind inky banks of stratus clouds and the wind smelled of fresh water.

"I'm sorry to drag you into this," I whispered to John finally.

"Don't be silly," he whispered back. "I'm glad I can be of some use."

Benjamin looked back at us like a professor regarding unruly pupils in the back of the classroom. We returned to silence, the only sound being our gentle footfalls on earth and the occasional snapping of twigs. I tried to recognize shapes and landmarks from the trail that I'd taken just days before on my way to the death scene. Nothing looked familiar; black silhouettes dotted the landscape where bushes were collected in daylight, vertical streaks of indigo where trees had embraced the sky. A pair of luminescent eyes caught the beam of my flashlight, taking all of our breaths away until an opossum materialized and slinked its silver-grayness back toward a large persimmon tree.

Finally, we paused. Jacob stood with an open hand toward us like a ghostly crossing guard to signal our halt. After several moments, we all instinctively turned off our flashlights and lanterns. As my eyes adjusted once more to the pure darkness, I recognized the mounds of blackberry bushes that Leah had pointed out as a halfway point on our prior hike. I half expected to hear her whistle a hymn or come singing from around the bend up ahead. Perhaps this was all a huge misunderstanding. Maybe she stopped off at another friend's house on the way. I cocked my ear toward the darkness ahead.

Nothing. The conspicuous absence of night sounds in the woods signaled that the woodland creatures were well aware of human presence. Had someone been here before us? Someone bringing Leah back to the scene of Simon Hostetler's hanging? I couldn't bear to think about what might await us at the clearing of the Judas Tree.

"Should we spread out and try to cover the woods off-trail?" I asked Peter.

"I was wondering the same thing," he replied.

"No," cautioned Benjamin. "These woods are much thicker and more dense than they look. If you don't know them, you would only get lost. Let's stay on the trail until we get to the Judas Tree."

Jacob nodded and relit his lantern. We trudged along, briars and ragweed tugging at our cuffs. An owl resounded his only chord throughout the treetops above. I recalled the old superstition about an owl's song signaling imminent death and responded with a silent psalm of courage: *He who dwells in the shelter of the Most High, who abides in the shadow of the Almighty, will say to* the LORD, *"My refuge and my fortress; my God, in whom I trust." For he will deliver you from the snare of the fowler and from the deadly pestilence; he will cover you with his pinions, and under his wings you will find refuge; his faithfulness is a shield and buckler. You will not fear the terror of the night . . . nor the pestilence that stalks the darkness . . .*

"Look!" shouted Peter. From the gnarled branch of a sycamore tree hung an Amish woman's kapp, the traditional head covering of white cotton fabric. The ties dangled from the rounded kerchief like flailing arms in the breeze. Not one of us said a word as Benjamin proceeded several feet off trail and retrieved the pale cloth.

"Yes," he said soberly. "It is my Leah's. I would know her mother's stitches anywhere." He held the kapp like a wounded bird, delicately inspecting it for an indication of its mistress's whereabouts. Other than a reddish streak of dust and a slight tear at the corner, nothing indicated what might have precipitated its removal.

"Perhaps we should wrap it in something so that the police can fingerprint it," John said.

"Yes, here," I offered, extending my own handkerchief. Peter took it from me and then took the kapp from Benjamin and enshrouded it inside. Leah's father looked forlorn standing there in the darkness with his hand open-palmed toward heaven. He looked weary and afraid, ancient; a prophet of old sent to foretell the future based on the direction of the wind and the meaning of the hidden stars. I thought he, too, would break down and sob when he turned and recomposed the tight lines holding his tears behind his eyes. He took the lantern from his oldest son and led us up the last several hundred yards of the trail to the clearing where the Judas Tree reigned.

Despite the eerie landscape we had encountered thus far, nothing could have prepared us for the spectacle of the tree itself, forlorn and alone. Nothing but the rustle of leaves from its branches greeted our scrutiny. Crossbeams of light and the odd elliptical glow from the lantern encircled us in the clearing as we gravitated toward the ancient tree. Nothing hung from the hangman's bough, and we all reflexively released our breaths. As the dramatic effect of the night-shrouded tree diminished, I wondered where Dan and the other police could be. Surely they had managed to cover the ground between here and the Yoders' dairy farm by now.

As if my thought had conjured them, we heard rustling and saw the penetration of several stiletto beams. I could hear the crackling of walkie-talkies and the murmur of male voices. A giant emerged leading the brigade, Dan Warren himself, and he called out to us to identify ourselves. Peter yelled in return and soon a half dozen uniforms were upon us as we all gathered around the oak tree. The bright lights from the officers' torches lit the clearing like a stage on opening night.

"Grif! What are you doing here? Never mind — I'm glad to see you all," said Sergeant Warren.

"Have you found my daughter?" implored Benjamin.

"Not yet, sir," replied Dan. "But we've got another dozen men scouring off-trail and down by the river. Sheriff Claiborne himself is on his way down here."

"We found this," said Peter, extending my handkerchief with the kapp inside. "Mr. Schroeder's sure it's Leah's."

Dan called another officer over who seemed to produce a paper bag from nowhere and deposited the potential clue inside. "We found a few boot prints just off-trail not far from Yoders'," continued Dan, "but nothing else has turned up so far."

I suppose that's good news, I thought to myself, translating Dan's oblique communiqué. Leah's body had not been discovered.

Just then a uniformed officer who looked young enough to pass for a teenager jumped to the forefront of our pack and thrust a cell phone toward Dan.

"Sergeant Warren, sir, it's for you — Sheriff Claiborne!" he announced.

Dan seized the black cordless device and began murmuring into the receiver. He turned his back to us and I feared the news was not good. I glanced around as silence descended on the band of men gathered beneath the Judas Tree towering above, a mocking turret of nature's silence. The moments seemed like years as Dan continued conversing. I looked from the Schroeders to Peter to my friend John. I knew we were all praying the same prayer.

"They've found her!" boomed Dan, whirling around to us. "She's alive!"

Chapter Fifteen

Amish Secrets

By the time the five of us made it back to the Schroeders' farm it was nearly one o'clock in the morning. Leah, wrapped in an old blue quilt, sat in her mother's kitchen sipping strong, hot tea. Her eyes spilled tears as she rose and hugged her father and then Peter. I was moved by the way the two young people clung to each other, the way Peter inhaled her presence amid his own tears of joyful relief, and the way Leah clasped her hand on the sharp blade of his shoulder.

Sheriff Claiborne was drinking coffee and talking with Mrs. Schroeder. The mood was different from that first, formal interrogation last week. The two talked in animated conversation as if they were kin. Mr. Schroeder expressed deep gratitude to the sheriff for responding so quickly and bringing Leah back safely. The two men shook hands like gentlemen who had recovered the same shared treasure.

"If you don't mind," said Sam. "I was hoping that Leah might feel up to telling us exactly what happened tonight. Other than the fact that she was grabbed off the trail leading from the Yoders' to the Judas Tree, we still don't know."

"Yes, that is necessary," said Mr. Schroeder. "But first let us offer a prayer of thanksgiving to our gracious Father for his loving-kindness in returning Leah Rebekah safely to us."

Without knowing the protocol, we all naturally joined hands with one another — even the sheriff — there in the candle-lit kitchen. Moments of silence passed and then Peter spoke aloud the gratitude and relief we all felt: "Thank you, Lord, for your goodness in protecting this dear woman."

"Amen," we concluded in unison.

"Now, Miss Leah," began the sheriff, "start at the beginning and tell us everything you remember. What time did you leave the Yoders'?"

In the flickering glow of oil lamps and beeswax candles, Leah's long coppery hair shimmered like red gold. Her pale beauty and troubled eyes reminded me of the lovely subjects in many of the pre-Raphaelites' paintings, a Rosetti or Millais, perhaps. As she sipped from her mug of tea before launching her tale, she could easily have become Ophelia or a Victorian princess.

"Well," she began. "I left Mary Yoder's just after supper. I didn't even stay for dessert because I promised Momma that I would be home by dark. So it must've been around five-thirty when I set out. I knew I'd be cutting it close, but figured I had a good hour of partial light, and besides, I know the trail like the back of my hand."

We all leaned in toward her, eager to learn the details of her abduction. John Greenwood wisely took out a piece of paper and began jotting down notes from Leah's narrative.

She continued. "I had just passed the last dairy barn — the long, flat gray one — when I heard someone behind me. At first I thought it was one of the children or Mary with something I'd forgotten. But when I called out, no one was there, and I continued on my way. I started through the woods, following the trail that runs parallel to the river before it crosses that little footbridge and comes out by the road not far from where the Judas Tree stands." Her words became tighter in her throat as if it were becoming difficult for her to breathe. I wondered if she might hyperventilate as her mind reapproached the shock of her attack.

"I wasted no time as I came to the clearing beside the old tree. It was a little spooky —

the way you feel when someone you cannot see is watching you. But I figured it was my imagination combined with the first evening shadows. That's when — I — I felt someone grab me from behind, a man. I fought him but he was too strong. . . ."

She confined tears to the corner of her eyes as her voice trembled. "While he held me, another man gagged and blindfolded me, and then the two of them took me back to the highway from the way I'd come." Leah paused and sipped more of her tea.

"That must've been where we found your kapp," said Peter. His forehead was scribbled with faint wrinkles at his temples, his anger visible.

"Did the two men say anything to you?" the sheriff asked. "Give you any indication why they were doing this or what they wanted you to do?" He scratched his chin with his left hand.

Leah shook her head and her mother wrapped her arms around the girl's shoulders. "They said nothing," Leah continued, "just tied my hands and put me in a car that was waiting. It was close to the highway, I'm sure, because it didn't take us long to get back there. I think someone else — a third person — was driving the car. Still no one said anything. It wasn't until we'd driven for what seemed like fifteen or twenty minutes that one of them said, 'We just want to ask you a few questions. Tell us the truth and you won't be hurt.' Then the car stopped and they took me inside some kind of building. We had to climb some steps."

"Good, Leah," encouraged Sam. "Any details you can remember may help us find the place. Go on."

She nodded and said, "They sat me in a chair and bound my feet. When they removed the gag, I thought about screaming but was too afraid. And then someone else came in and asked me questions." A long anguished silence passed before Leah spoke again. "They asked me questions about Dr. Hostetler . . . about what I saw when I found his body."

"What? They kidnapped you to ask you questions about the outsider!" exploded Mr. Schroeder.

"What did the man asking the questions sound like?" asked Sam.

"His voice was disguised — it sounded mechanical, like a machine was talking to me," she said.

"An electronic scrambler — you speak into it and it reconfigures the sound particles into synthetic impulses. Someone went to great lengths to interview you," murmured the sheriff, jotting down his own notes. "What exactly did he ask you? And what did you tell him in return?"

She seemed to look right through the sheriff as if extracting her replies from the shadowed corners of the room. "First, he repeated the thing about me not being hurt if I answered their questions truthfully. Then he told someone to give me a drink of water. After I drank a few sips, he asked me what I remembered about finding Dr. Hostetler. I told him all I could remember — pretty much what I told you and your deputy last week, Sheriff.

"He asked me then if I knew why Dr. Hostetler had been killed, and I said, no, I didn't. He said, 'Someday the truth about Simon Hostetler will come out and the Amish will see that he deserved to die.' His words sent a chill up my spine. I started crying — I thought they were going to kill me." Leah pulled the quilt around her more tightly and began to sob. Peter stepped forward and gently placed his large palms on her shoulders while her mother refilled her mug of tea. All of us in the room released our collective breath and tried to imagine the motive behind Leah's interrogation.

When Mrs. Schroeder placed a piping hot mug before her again, Leah sipped from it and then concluded. "The last thing he said was, 'Tell the outsiders to stay out of your people's business. And tell your people to sell their land and move away from this place — unless they want the Brethren to string them up like Hostetler.'"

"The Brethren!" I whispered. "So they're taking credit for Simon's death."

"But who's behind the Brethren?" asked John.

The sheriff turned back to Leah, "What happened then, after the interview was over?"

Color had gradually infused her neck and cheeks. "They placed the gag on me again, untied my feet and led me back outside. I heard low voices — real voices, not from the machine — talking in the distance as they led me back to the car. We rode for a little while and then they stopped, tied my feet again, and left me in the ditch." Anger was beginning to replace the fear in her tone as she concluded.

"And that's where we found you. You're a brave young woman," pronounced Sheriff Claiborne. "We will find the people who did this to you. Is there anything else that stands out? Smells? Sounds?"

Leah shook her head, flecks of her reddish-gold hair catching candlelight. "It did seem like they were extra careful with me when they laid me in the ditch."

"What do you mean?" asked Sam.

"Well, one of them said, 'Make sure she can breathe.' And just the way they placed me on my side. It wasn't rough or careless," she explained. "Odd, really, considering I'd been scared for my life the entire evening and then they were concerned about my well-being."

"Maybe this whole thing was just a scare tactic," I said. "Maybe the Brethren — whoever they are — simply seized the opportunity to exploit Simon's death and Leah's discovery of the body by scaring her tonight."

"Well, it worked, then!" exclaimed Sarah Schroeder. "I cannot imagine that any of us will remain in Tremont for much longer."

The mother's fear had transformed into indignation, apparent in the sudden redness of her pale cheeks. Her husband cautioned, "Now, Sarah, let's wait until we hear what Bishop Zook has to say. Let us just be thankful that no harm was done."

"No harm done! Why, Benjamin Schroeder! Leah will never forget the fear for her life that she experienced tonight. I say that we heed the message given and convince the others to sell their land, as well," said Sarah. "We've always talked about moving out to my cousin's in Indiana."

"We shall see what the Lord reveals," Benjamin replied, surprisingly calm after his earlier outburst. "In the meantime, the hour is late and these gentlemen are far from home. Peter, Brother Reed, John — I would be honored if you would stay with us this night. We could put you up in the *Dawdi Haus*."

None of us knew quite what to say. I was surprised at the offer and didn't know whether it was extended out of fear or courtesy.

John Greenwood spoke first. "That's a mighty generous offer, Brother Schroeder, and I thank you. But I'm afraid that I've got a conference in Chattanooga to get to this morning."

"Yes," I said. "Forgive me, John. I forgot all about your conference —"

"Well, I'd be glad to take John back up the mountain with me," offered the sheriff. "Why don't you think this over for a moment." His eyes beckoned Peter and me over to where he stood next to John. In a hoarse whisper he said, "This would be a good chance for you to get to know some of these people and find out what you can about Hostetler's death. I'd consider it a favor if you'd stay."

"But, Sam, I've got a guest here and parish responsibilities to attend to in the morning," I countered. "I can't just take a whole day to —"

"Grif," whispered Peter. "It's a big deal that Mr. Schroeder would make such an offer. Personally, I'd like to stay."

"We don't even have our toothbrushes or a change of clothes," I countered.

"I'm sure the Schroeders can rustle up something to get you by," said the sheriff.

I looked in my visiting friend's eyes for direction. John smiled up at me in return. "You're outnumbered. Now, Grif, I'll be fine. If time permits, I'll stop back by on my way home after the conference on Friday. I'll at least call and let you know. I agree with Sam and Peter; I think the Lord wants you here for the night."

"Well, I guess that settles it," I said. "Peter and I will stay."

While I called Bea from the sheriff's cruiser and updated her on Leah's situation and the impromptu plans for Peter and me to spend the night, Sarah quickly made up the beds in the small addition attached to the main house, which had originally been built for Benjamin's parents. As Jacob led us to the Dawdi Haus, or grandparents' cottage, as it was called, the external darkness smothered the farm in black geometry. Silhouettes of the rectangular barns and the rounded arcs of trees and their vertical trunks filled my line of vision. I wondered what I had agreed to by spending the night here.

Inside our guest quarters, Jacob opened the windows to air out the tiny dwelling. "If you get too cool, feel free to close these," he instructed, setting the Coleman lantern on a small pine table. Shadows lingered but the place smelled just-cleaned. There were two chairs, companions to the table, in one corner; a fireplace with a cast-iron kettle on the hearth; two rocking chairs beside an old blue sofa; and a doorway leading presumably to a bedroom and bath.

"Would you like me to light a fire? It's no trouble," offered Jacob, brushing his straight dark locks across his forehead.

"We'll be fine," I responded. "The cool night air will be like a spring tonic. Thank you."

The young Amish man left us to get settled for the night. Since Peter and I had not anticipated staying, Leah's mother had sent over some of her husband's old nightshirts along with a basket of toiletries, including toothbrushes and paste. Peter was thoroughly keyed up, a combination of the intense relief over his beloved's safe return and the excitement at being so close to her here.

"Don't get any ideas of sneaking out to visit Juliet on the balcony," I said as I helped Peter pull out the fold-up bed inside the blue sofa.

He chuckled, "Don't think the thought didn't cross my mind. I almost asked Leah to meet me behind the barn for a good-night kiss, but I know how exhausted she is. No, I'll be on my best behavior."

"You love her completely, don't you?" I observed, tucking the last corner of the wind-scented sheet around the foot of the small bed.

"Yes, more than I ever thought possible," he replied soberly. "During those few hours when I didn't know if something had happened to her . . . well, I didn't know what I would do without her. I . . . I can't explain it."

"I know what you mean," I said softly.

After an awkward silent moment, he said, "I'm sorry, Grif. You know much better than I do what it's like to lose the person you love more than any other. Honestly, if tonight's any indication, I don't see how you bear it."

"I'm not sure myself sometimes . . . you just do. God provides just enough grace to squeeze you through the tight places," I replied. "But I'll always miss Amy."

Leaving Peter with a flashlight, I retired to the full-sized bed anchoring the next room. The lantern offered its steady, even glow around the cedar-paneled walls. I found a few old books — a German Psalter, a *Farmer's Almanac* from 1983, a book of quilt patterns — on top of a small bedside table. The bed itself was centered on the wall facing the double windows, homemade shades raised halfway. A simple slatted oak headboard embraced a worn, but no less lovely, quilt in a log-cabin pattern.

I pulled the shades down and began undressing, amused at the effect of Benjamin's nightshirt on my large frame. What a day this had turned out to be. I tested the mattress, tentatively sitting on its edge. Firm, just the way my fifty-year-old back liked it. Stretching myself diagonally across the solid comfort, I sighed deeply and tried to discover sleep. After several restless minutes I opened my eyes and scanned the exposed rafters in the darkened room. Despite my body's willingness to rest, my mind sprinted in innumerable directions.

It was a chaotic race — like French taxi

drivers — as questions competed with speculations. One conclusion floated free: Whoever was behind Leah's abduction tonight must also have been responsible for Simon's death. Or was it too conveniently obvious? It seemed likely that whoever these people were, they desperately wanted the Amish to sell their land. And they were likely posing as a rekindled Brethren in order to achieve their purposes.

But then another question popped free: If one group was behind this, and they did convince the Amish to sell the Canaan's Way property, how did they know the Amish would sell it to the right group? It seemed like there were still too many parties vying for the land — the military base, the Omega Group Corporation, local farmers, and the county commission on industrialization. Did one of them know something about the value of the land that the others didn't? Something that would drive them to murder and kidnapping in order to obtain it?

I began praying to quiet the inner chaos as more questions emerged. Our Lord's words rose from amid the swirling undertow of my uncertainties and fears: *For there is nothing hid, except to be made manifest* . . . Now where was that? Drowsiness set in once the sea of my mind calmed. He was preaching to the multitudes by the sea, I believed. Yes, the fourth chapter of Mark's gospel: *Nor is anything secret, except to come to light. If any man has ears to hear, let him hear.* I prayed to have ears to hear whatever might be significant within the prior din of questions.

I awakened to the sound of the younger boys, Luke and Nathan, clanging milk pails beside the barn. The morning sun told me it was going on seven o'clock. I stretched like a bear emerging from hibernation and splashed tepid water across my face from the washbasin.

In the next room, the sofa-bed had been hidden away, and Peter was nowhere to be seen. My watch confirmed that it was indeed shortly after seven, and I tried to remember what my schedule looked like for the day. Wednesday, March 23. It was a rather slow day, if I recalled correctly. A planning day to map out the parish summer calendar and the missions trip to Juarez, Mexico, in August.

I would certainly enjoy my Amish breakfast more knowing that nothing urgent was awaiting me up on the mountain. As I crossed the clovered expanse of lawn, the morning sun sent a sheen of reflected light across the farmyard. Judging by the sounds from the barn and the shirts billowing in the breeze on the clothesline, the Schroeders had been up for some time. I stood for a moment and simply marveled at the beauty of the landscape, the shape of the wooded slopes beyond the barn, the empire of green trees guarding the farmstead, the smell of morning sunshine and fresh cut grass. It was enough to take away the nightmare of Leah's abduction the night before.

In fact, one would never have imagined the prior night's turmoil based on the smiling faces inside around the Schroeder dining room. Leah, Peter, and Mrs. Schroeder welcomed me and bid me to sit and eat. On the table were stacks of griddle cakes, a small pitcher of syrup, fresh butter, homemade granola, fresh yogurt, canned apples, and blackberry preserves.

I thanked the Lord for such bounty and took my first bite just as Sarah filled my coffee cup with a strong chicory-scented blend.

"Where is everyone else?" I asked. "I thought I heard the younger boys a moment ago."

"School," said Leah. "They eat right after chores so they can change before they go into town for school. I hope they didn't wake you this morning banging their pails and cutting up."

Peter smiled. "Grif sleeps through anything. I'm surprised you all didn't hear him snoring in here!"

"Okay, you're asking for it, Father Abernathy," I returned, pleased to see the lightheartedness. "See if I help you make your bed up again." I spooned creamy yogurt over my bowl of dried oats, raisins, pecans, and wheat germ. "So what about your other brothers, are they still in school, too?"

Leah giggled. "Oh no," she said. "Although, sometimes I think they should be. Jacob has a job with Tenleco. He works construction for the new plant they're building. And Nathan's with Father out planting."

"Tenleco? The paper factory over in Lewiston? I didn't know they were building a new plant," I said.

"Yes, they had to shut down parts of their existing plant in order to comply with EPA standards," offered Mrs. Schroeder, returning from the kitchen.

"Oh yes. I do recall that they were fined some time ago for polluting the Jackson River," I said.

"The new plant will certainly be larger than the old one," said Leah. "Jacob's been working on it for several months now."

"Benjamin is sorry he missed you this

morning," said Mrs. Schroeder, passing me more hot cakes. "But he and I were hoping you would stay for lunch and supper."

"That's very kind of you," I said. "But I guess Peter and I had better return home now that everything has settled down. I have some planning to do, and I know Peter leads his young adult Bible study tonight. Sheriff Claiborne said he'd be sending extra men to patrol the area, so I'm sure you'll be safe."

"Well, surely you can both stay until lunchtime," said Sarah. "I'm baking fresh bread and there's a rhubarb pie in the oven."

"You're making it very difficult," I said. "Peter? Okay with you if we stay the morning?"

He smiled at Leah, whose eyes were equally electric.

"Who am I kidding?" I chuckled. "Did I even need to ask?"

"Perhaps by then," said Leah, "we can convince you to stay for supper — or longer."

"Yes," agreed her mother.

I thought to myself that the Amish seemed slow to warm up to one, but when they did, the hospitality was incomparable. Of course, the tense circumstances of the previous night certainly afforded a bonding experience.

"Thank you, we look forward to it," I said,

wiping a trickle of syrup from the corner of my mouth.

"We look forward to more of your cooking, Mrs. Schroeder!" said Peter sincerely.

"I'm glad you're enjoying yourself, Peter." She smiled as she retreated into the kitchen with a stack of plates and saucers. "Leah, when our guests have finished, would you join me please?"

Leah's words trailed behind her mother, "Yes, ma'am." Then turning to Peter, she giggled, "You know that I can't cook half as well as Mother does."

He smiled and whispered back, "You don't have to."

Moments later, I finished my last bites and left the two of them lingering over the last hot cakes. With my utensils bridged across my blackberry-smeared plate, I found Mrs. Schroeder in the kitchen, drying a skillet with a dish towel in a spotlight of brilliant morning sunshine.

"That was simply delicious," I said, stacking my things next to the sink. "I appreciate your hospitality."

"After the way you helped us search for Leah last night? Why, it's the least we can do," she said. "I only hope you have been comfortable."

"Absolutely. Your way of life certainly has

much to recommend it. I can see why most people tend to idealize it," I replied.

She nodded, folded the dishcloth over her apron, and refilled my coffee cup without asking. "Yes, our way of life — living in the presence of God's goodness and the family He provides — is truly a blessing." She replaced the coffeepot on top of the gas stove. "Certainly, with all the commotion lately, you have seen for yourself that we are not without our problems, though."

"After what happened last night, do you still wish to move?" I asked.

She hesitated as if I had asked something too personal, which perhaps I had. "Yes, in some ways. My desire to move does not seem as urgent this morning as it did last night. But certainly there are many factors that go into that decision . . . and ultimately, it is not for me to decide." I sensed a shift in her tone, the core of her words becoming heavy within the gravity of fear. "In fact —" She stopped abruptly, reconsidering her words or the timing of what she was about to request, or both.

She wiped her hands on her apron, then looked up at me. "There is something I wish to ask you, Griffin Reed, something that I have no right to ask. Something that will ultimately change all our lives."

"Please," I replied. "What is it? Certainly, I'll do whatever I can." My mind flurried with the possibilities of her request. Perhaps she was about to entrust me with some secret about Simon's death, about their relationship, or about some other aspect of the past that would illuminate the ominous pall since my friend's murder. Little did I know that what she would ask of me was much more personal and much more arduous to oblige.

Chapter Sixteen

Potter's Field

I voiced my speculation by asking, "Does it have anything to do with Simon Hostetler's death?"

Moments passed and I studied the delicate wrinkles at the corners of the Amish woman's mouth. Pale freckles laced the undertones of her cheeks, picking up the reddish hues of her hair. She adjusted the cream-colored kapp firmly centered on the bun of hair pulled back from her face.

"No. As I said, it is something personal." Her slate blue eyes did not leave mine. "It has to do with Peter. I want you to give him your blessing to join my family as an Amishman."

I couldn't believe what I was hearing, although cognitively I was not surprised. Certainly, the breakfast scene from moments ago — even Peter's request that we stay last night — pointed to his interest in the Amish lifestyle. I felt almost as if Sarah Schroeder had asked me to sever my hand, and she seemed immediately to recognize my anguish.

"My daughter has observed you and your fatherly love for Peter for almost six months now. Please know how much she respects and admires you and your faith. She has repeatedly told me that you are Peter's spiritual father."

I did not wish to trust her praise but prayed nevertheless that what she observed was in some way true.

"You must know as well how much I love my daughter and long for her happiness. Leah is not like other Amish girls. She cannot bear to leave her family and the Amish way of life, and yet she is pulled by her art and now by her love for Peter out into the world." She lowered her voice as if remembering the young people were only in the next room. "At first, I thought her interest in Peter was only a curiosity, the leftover restlessness of youth . . . but the more that I have observed the man, well, the more I have liked him. The more I have realized that he may be worthy of her love."

She shifted her feet and glanced out the window into the simmering sunlight. "Peter is steadfast and sincere. He clearly loves Christ with all his might. And now he loves my Leah, as well. I believe he would be happy here among us, as part of our family. Benjamin feels the same way, although I'm not sure he would say it as directly. He's not too keen on the idea of anyone marrying his only daughter."

"Has Leah had many other boyfriends?" I asked, stalling as my mind whirled with the significance of her request. "Are there Amishmen who have wished to marry her?"

She regarded me cautiously before responding. "Several have tried. None have won her heart, just the silly attempts of boys who would try to be men. No, I have never seen her care for anyone the way she regards Peter. She told me she would've married him if she did not have to choose between him and us, her family. Just last week, before all this matter with Simon started, Leah said to me, 'I feel so' — how did she put it? — 'storm-tossed inside.' She went on to say, 'Everyone has always teased me about how picky I am when it comes to dating. Last fall I had decided to begin catechism and join the church, even though most girls do not commit until they are practically engaged. But I decided that I wished to commit to Christ and to the Amish way of life with or without a husband.' That's what she said."

"She is a very courageous young woman; she and Peter are much alike," I observed.

"Yes, they are. That is why I wish to see them married, if possible. That is why I am asking you to allow Peter to join us here. . . ." She took out a white handkerchief from an apron pocket and traced the embroidered letters on it between her fingers. Her eyes formed a mist as gentle as the breath of spring rain.

I was honored that she would share her burden with me, but I was equally disheartened because I didn't know what to tell her. "Mrs. Schroeder, I grieve this dilemma as much as you and your husband. You are correct — I do love Peter as my own son, and I pray for his happiness. And I know that nothing would make him happier than to marry your daughter. But I'm not sure I can encourage him to leave all that he's known behind. Why, he might be offered his own church by our bishop."

Sarah retreated within herself for a moment before echoing, "So he's been offered his own church, eh? And so young. I did not know." She moved the linen square from hand to hand nervously, as if weighing my curate's options for him.

"Well, he has not officially accepted it yet," I explained. "I'm not even sure that he will."

"I suppose you believe he should take this opportunity the Lord has blessed him with?" she asked.

"I . . . I'm not sure how to counsel Peter right now. It is difficult to separate my own desires for him to stay on as my curate from what is best for his future," I said.

"Well, I suppose all we can do is pray." Leah's mother dabbed her eyes and recomposed herself. "Thank you for listening to my request, Brother Reed." She wiped her nose and put her handkerchief away before continuing, "I appreciate your honesty. And I understand that you want the best for Peter."

An awkward tension then ensued, and I wondered if I had mishandled the Amish mother's request. We stood anxiously together for several quiet moments, each lost in our hopes and fears for a future that would likely unfold in ways neither could fathom. Finally, I thanked her for breakfast again. She smiled and said, "Lunch will be at one o'clock. I'd best get busy. If you see Leah, would you send her in?" The distance of polite formality had returned.

When I passed through the dining room and onto the porch, the young couple was nowhere to be seen.

Since it was now going on nine o'clock, I decided a walk into town might be good exercise for body and spirit. Plus, I wanted to use a telephone and check in with Janine at the office, as well as with Bea. John Greenwood should be arriving at his conference with other chaplains and ministers about now; I hoped he did not mind last night's intrusion. Of course, I knew that he didn't, but I couldn't help but feel responsible that our pleasant dinner together had ended so abruptly.

I opted to take the long way via the trail leading to the Judas Tree. It connected to Chigger Ridge Road and circled north back into town. Schroeder father and son waved from the far horizon of a red-brown field as I headed for the other side of the barn and the trail leading through the woods. I considered asking Peter along, but opted for the privacy of solitude. I wanted to release my conversation with Sarah Schroeder into prayer. Plus, some of my questions from the night before wanted to start transforming themselves into hypotheses about the life of Simon Hostetler, and I wanted to let them do so without interruption. Hikes and jogs have always helped me solve my problems.

The lush green undergrowth seemed higher today than last week, even more untamed than the dark tangles underfoot last night. Could light of day really affect a setting so dramatically? Perhaps it was being alone this time that made me more observant and alert, more on guard to the bird calls and chittering around me. Perhaps I was feeling a bit paranoid. The impetus was certainly there.

I continued stamping along the path in my black Rockport walkers, feeling old once again as I wished for my hiking stick and a drink of water. All of the previous week's mud had dried, forming tan, dust-coated lips at the trail's edge. My mental map told me that once I hit the road just past the Judas Tree's clearing, it was only another couple of miles into the cluster of shops and services forming the heart of Tremont commerce.

Without the entourage and the deliberation to notice every detail as we had done with Dan Warren and Agent Corey, or in last night's search for Leah, I shaved almost ten minutes off the time taken to reach the clearing where the giant oak yawned and stretched. I had abandoned my paranoia of being watched at the halfway mark, feeling rather annoyed with myself. There were no signs of the young woman's abduction the previous night, no signs of struggle or of the figures waiting prior to Leah's ambush.

The clearing was much the same as it had been in the fading light of last week's visit, isolated and peculiar but rather benign. It looked much more like a deserted camp site than like last night's brooding crime scene. The fire pit had not been used recently, or if it had, the user had taken great care to scrape all ashes from inside the ring of stones. The Judas Tree loomed watchfully over the smooth forest floor, leaves and acorn tops its only charges.

I approached and touched the bark, as fiercely dry as an old man's callused feet. Around the other side the carving remained, almost as fresh looking as before. I wanted to talk with John Corey, the state forensics agent, and see if he knew what kind of knife had been used to leave such a verdict. DEUT 32–43 glared back at me with the same inanimate ferocity as a jack-o'-lantern's smile.

I acknowledged to myself that I had chosen this route deliberately, searching for something that had eluded me since Simon's death a week ago to this day. *What was I looking for? What did I expect to find here?* I scrutinized my memory as much as the area surrounding the old tree. Perhaps this was where Simon kept secret appointments with Amish men and women who wished to remain anonymous, or perhaps this is where he suspected the Brethren of holding their meetings. If only I could find someone willing to talk about the group, let alone someone who could tell me if there had been a meeting the night Simon was killed. Perhaps my visit to the military base on Friday would yield results to those hopes.

Above me the light shifted, the sun momentarily displaced by clouds. I looked around me. Odd. The only thing I noticed now that I had not noticed before was a half dozen small holes in the earth scattered along the trailing misshapen roots of the oak. They reminded me of prairie dog holes from the Southwest and great plains, but we did not have those critters here. Probably gophers or field mice, I concluded.

The sky became darker still, and I found myself worrying about the possibility of a spring thunderstorm. Despite my first impression of normalcy, the place suddenly appeared even more dismal than on either of my prior visits. I stood there a few moments and the clouds shifted once again. There was more light now, but the mood lingered. The mammoth oak arched high above me, green leaves seducing midmorning shadows, filtering out most of the light, admitting only scraps of dull sun. It appeared ominously indifferent, a kind of silent witness to the horrors it had generated . . . a tree of knowledge of good and evil that became complicit in the aftermath. An outcast, like our original parents of sin.

I shuddered. Crickets violined the same lonesome notes over and again. The day was not half gone, and I suddenly felt very foolish for letting my imagination run away with me. Detaching myself from the odd tricks of the place, I tried to refocus my hypotheses about Simon's death. Yet I had no clear idea about how Simon Hostetler died, about why he was here in the first place last Wednesday night, about who would want him dead. He was a college professor, a former member of this community, the son of an adulterous father shunned by that same community, a bachelor, an author, a scientist of religious cultures. Which of those roles had cost him his life? Had any of them?

I made my way across the clearing, parting branches and overgrown evergreen shrubs until I found where the trail resumed. Sunlight washed over me once again as if I had just exited a darkened room. Chigger Ridge Road, spread out like a white ribbon bordering a green gown, lay just a few hundred yards before me. I had never noticed that it bordered the Yoders' property, but now I could make out the tiny post-age-stamp-sized barn far across the hillsides. Looking west, I heard the low drone of a plane and followed it until it darted behind the dense tree tops toward Dolby Air Force Base. A routine flight, I wondered, or some secret military operation?

Perhaps Simon had ventured too close to some military secret. Even if he had, surely even General Bledsoe himself wouldn't choose to hang a man and implicate the Amish. Or would he? What if Simon had stumbled onto something, perhaps even some secret from the past? Maybe the military were vandalizing Amish farms to pressure them into a land deal. Like all of my morning's hypotheses, it seemed too tenuous, with too many missing pieces.

Walking toward the gravel road, I passed through the thinning forest until I stumbled over a shoulder-sized walnut branch. Catching myself with my hands, I nonetheless slid to the rocky, dry trail, cushioned by pine needles and new saw grass. I leaned against the dark-skinned bark that had caused my fall and caught my breath.

Around me stood a large grove of mature black walnut trees — perhaps as many as a hundred. Intermingled within were scrub pine and evergreens, naturally shaped like hearty Christmas trees. Weren't black walnut trees prized for their hardwood? Didn't I hear something on NPR about their worth escalating in the past few years? Why, some groves were valued at millions of dollars. Was this one of the parcels of land presently being sought by outside farmers and the government? Were there black walnut groves on the property that Dolby had purchased thirty years ago — and had they cleared the land for profit? No, that land was mainly farmland. Surely there would have been an outcry from the press, if not from the Amish themselves, if the land had been so obviously lucrative. Nonetheless, I would have Dan Warren check it out.

I rose and continued down the trail, retrieving my tinted sunglass clips from my jacket pocket and snapping them into place over my spectacles. By now it was after ten, and I really wished that I had some water. But I figured I would be in town soon and could rest and have a drink before taking the more direct route back to the Schroeder farm.

Scanning the area roadside, I spotted various groves of small saplings and low-lying shrubbery that could easily provide convenient hiding placing for cars like the one used by Leah's abductors last night. Had

Simon been captured the same way? Or had a car been used to bring him here?

I tried to imagine the scenario that led to my friend's death. Perhaps the person driving the car had an accomplice who left Simon's body and then returned. Could it have been someone from Tremont, even one of the Amish? I had not allowed myself to seriously consider this possibility since most Amish were so opposed to violence. However, they were human, and if threatened enough or perceiving a threat, perhaps . . .

Then something important occurred to me. It seemed likely that whoever kidnapped Leah and killed Simon was not from within the community, but knew his way around the community. Knew the trail between the Yoders' and the Schroeders' farm, and more importantly, knew that Leah would be taking it last night. Did an outsider from the English world have an Amish contact or accomplice? Could someone have betrayed Simon Hostetler from within the very group he sought to understand and define?

More questions plagued me as I tromped through the last quarter-mile of trail and reached the road. As the morning sun neared its apex, the pastoral scene took on the quality of an overexposed photograph.

Bright light underscored every tree and leaf before bleeding brighter at the sky's edge. Pausing to catch my breath, I heard a whippoorwill echoing its lonesome call backed up by a chorus of cicadas. Today was an excellent reminder of the Tennessee summer that lay ahead of us: humid, muggy, incandescent.

In the distance, white gravel dust rose like smoke as a black buggy approached on the backwoods road. The one-horse hitch slowed as I stepped back to avoid the dust plague bearing down on me. A familiar face peered out from beneath a straw-brimmed work hat as the driver said, "Whoa!" and brought the rig to a stop.

"Headin' into town? You're welcome to ride if you like," said Joseph Yoder.

"Mr. Yoder, it's nice to see you again. Thanks for the offer, but I'm enjoying this fine day," I replied, wiping the film of sweat from my brow.

"Visiting the Schroeders, are you?" he asked. Flies buzzed around the chestnut mare's tail and mane, and she quivered ferociously to shake them off.

"Yes. I came down last night to help search for Leah. Thanks be to God that we found her," I said.

"Yes," he returned. "Thanks be to God.

Who knows when this business will end. Sure I can't give you a ride?" The man was growing as impatient as his horse.

"It will likely end when the truth comes out, don't you think?" I asked, squinting into the sun-drenched rig. "When Simon Hostetler's murderer comes to justice."

He shook his head and his graying beard waved gently in the light breeze. "Outsiders are not my concern," he said sternly. "Now, I've got milk to deliver."

"Good day," I said.

He was about to send the horse flying like Pegasus into clouds of dust when he caught the reins short in his hand. "Here," he offered. "If you won't ride with me, then at least take this hat. You will be sunburned if you're not careful. It may only be March, but the sun keeps its own calendar." Before I could respond he tossed a brimmed straw hat similar to his own down toward me. My thanks were drowned out by the spattering gravel under horse hooves as the gruff Amishman went on his way.

I was grateful for the hat and intrigued by his demeanor. He seemed totally unflappable, grateful at Leah's return perhaps, but not particularly concerned that she was abducted coming from his farm in the first place. I stood watching the trail of pale dust settle along the road ahead of me, then resumed my place on the weed-choked median inside the tire tracks.

The sun beat down mercilessly as it neared the noon hour, and I prayed thanks for the serendipitous gift on my dark-blond head. Yes, I admitted to myself, it was foolish to be out here on a spring day that had to be at least seventy-five degrees without water or sunscreen. I adjusted the straw brim and swiped at the sweat that threatened to trickle into my eyes.

Movement shimmered in the shade of trees up ahead of me, off the road to the left. Someone just bending at the edge of the woods.

Like a mirage in the desert, the person lingered over what looked like a series of stumps and boulders next to a grove of cedar trees. I stopped and almost called out. It appeared to be a woman, tall, draped in dark homespun fashioned in a kind of cloak with a hood. Surely she was seeking to disguise herself on such a warm day. I could not discern the feminine form with certainty, and then I thought of the Brethren. Didn't they wear robes with hoods?

Stepping slowly off the gravel road, I moved to an island of trees between us. Still a good hundred yards from the figure, I leaned behind a large maple and watched. She, or he, was looking down at something, talking to herself or someone lying in the tall weeds on the ground before her. No words were discernible, only a low, hushed tone. I moved from trunk to trunk in my small grove until I was almost within earshot. More details sharpened: the silhouette of the speaker's face revealed a broad forehead, thin, upturned nose, slight lips, and a distinct chin. Tufts of blond hair poked at the hood's edges like straw from a barnloft. It held the soft contours of feminine features. If I didn't know better, Mariah Gates stood before me!

As my eyes penetrated the wooded shadows, I could discern flat, pointed stones like old teeth rising up around the hooded figure among the weeds. Not tree stumps, but gravestones. Perhaps an old Amish cemetery. I stepped forward, darted to another maple several feet in front of me. The figure seemed unconsciously aware of my presence, head cocked my direction before looking back down.

I stepped forward again and snapped a splintered branch in the pasture. The figure struck the same head-tilted pose for a moment, glimpsed my form, and dashed away from me. I rushed forward and called out,

"Ms. Gates? Is that you? It's Father Reed! Ms. Gates?" But there was no reply except for the faint cracking of brush and twigs.

The woman ran along the tree line, edging the pasture to maintain speed. At first I thought the swirling cloud of dark fabric would veer toward the road and perhaps some waiting buggy or car left up ahead in the ditch on the other side. But after several hundred yards, the figure disappeared into the woods with the grace of a diver, plunging effortlessly into a sea of shadows. I could not catch her and headed for the collection of gravesites instead.

Could I have been mistaken? Was that woman really Mariah Gates? What in the world would she be doing down here in the middle of a weekday in an Amish cemetery? I trudged the last few yards and scanned the tombstones and wooden markers. Perhaps the person was a local Amish woman, someone from the Yoders' even, who had every right to be here and viewed me as a threat, an interloper. Perhaps she was just being extra cautious after hearing what had happened with Leah the night before.

I proceeded forward and came upon haphazard rows of jagged gravestones, most looking older than the eighty-odd years the Amish had been here. An old Confederate cemetery, perhaps? In the shade of massive cedars, I crouched to try to make out some of the moss-choked names and dates. Thick skeins of kudzu smothered many of the markers, a dozen or so dating back to the War Between the States. Another handful were from the last few decades of this century. I stepped carefully across the weed-strewn memorial to the spot where my mystery figure had stood only minutes before, the tall grass still depressed.

There in the upper left of the loosely-formed rectangle of the cemetery a pale, weather-streaked marker:

CALEB HOSTETLER
1928–1969
The Lord Have Mercy

Chapter Seventeen

Exhuming the Past

The late morning sun blazed its way to the center of the sky, penetrating even the shady resting place where I stood among the dead. A rust-eaten, spiked fence buckled and balked around the perimeter of gravestones. Some sections were missing, others so obscured by weeds, chokecherry, dandelions, and thistledown, as to be invisible. I knelt and rubbed at the thin film of moss edging its way across Caleb Hostetler's tombstone. The stone was handcut, the letters crudely carved, *The Lord Have Mercy*, a mocking epitaph. The rectangle of sod in front of the stone had been cleared by hand recently, tufts of grass and deep-rooted weeds blown onto other markers.

It seemed odd that Simon's father had been ostracized but was still buried close to the community. Of course, this did not appear to be where most Amish families buried their own. Was my mystery woman the caretaker? Someone who had known Caleb and pitied him? Or an avenging angel, someone remembering the sins of the father that had now been revisited upon the son? Perhaps it was Simon's sister, Lydia, paying an anonymous visit to her father's gravesite. But why would she run from me? She trusted me enough to ask me to conduct Simon's memorial service and to hand over the now-stolen puzzle box.

I glanced around at knee-level, where names and dates gave silent witness to the agony of those who had been abandoned and forgotten. Some of the oldest markers simply read *Unknown Adam* and were dated through the 1870s. Several strides to my right, just a few feet from a tree resembling the notorious oak in the clearing, leaned an odd-shaped stone. I had to scrape with my thumbnail to clear away more patches of moss and lichen. ROBERT WALLACE, b. 1832 – d. 1863.

The poor Confederate who allegedly had betrayed his brother and his cavalry company because of his convictions about slavery. Although I'd heard about such a cemetery somewhere off the backroads of Carroll County, I had never discovered it for myself. Supposedly, it was where Yankees from the war had been buried, and before that where those too poor were put to rest. My guess now was that this was where the

Amish buried their own who had not merited a decent, Christian burial. Potter's field.

I could only marvel at the attending symmetry. Only days before I'd sat in the Cathedral of the Divine and pondered poor Judas. The end of his story reverberated in this place as if whispered by the trees, an eternal refrain: *But the chief priests, taking the pieces of silver, said, "It is not lawful to put them into the treasury, since they are blood money." So they took counsel, and bought with them the potter's field, to bury strangers in.* Was that where Judas' hanged body found final peace? In this same kind of place as I now stood, haunted by blood money and betrayal?

As I walked away, I could only hope that Caleb Hostetler found peace in this shady grove. I wondered if his desire for a married woman thirty years ago had anything to do with his son's death last week. Somehow I believed it did. There was a maxim by St. Thaddeus of Risalt from the sixteenth century: "Exhuming the past sanctifies the future."

The remaining three-quarters of a mile glided by in the dust and heat of a midday spring sun. It was almost noon by the time I reached the small row of shops on either side of the road that passed through Tremont. I would have to hurry if I was going to make it back to the farm in time for Sarah's lunch. Several cars were parked diagonally next to a dozen black buggies, most with red-orange reflectors on the back. One battered pickup with TENLECO stenciled in fading paint on the door caught my eye. Perhaps I would run into Jacob Schroeder on his lunch break.

My walking shoes thudded across the planked walkway in front of the bakery, and I scanned the remaining shops: craft stores, a quilt shop, another baked goods shop, an apothecary, a cobbler, and down the road, a livery. I could smell leather and manure even from this distance.

But that scent was quickly enveloped by the aroma of an apple pie fresh out of the oven as I made my way into the most-frequented place, the SweetHaus Bakery and Amish Café. It was cool inside, with electric fans oscillating an artificial, but no less welcome, breeze. A handful of Amish were eating on one side of the room along with an equal number of tourists and a couple of men who appeared to be construction workers; no familiar faces. I ordered a ginger ale and made my way to the pay phone at the back of the shop next to the restrooms.

The phone was in use; a tall, burly man dressed in tan Carhart work pants and a paint-spattered gray sweat shirt wrestled the two-foot phone cord like a dog on a leash. The nearest table was vacant save for a few crumbs from someone's cheese straws. I sat down, thoroughly enjoying the sensation of the cold ginger ale washing down my parched throat. The confetti of mingled conversations created a lively atmosphere.

"Yeah, I know . . . Judas tree . . ." said the phone man.

I swallowed hard and the carbonated bubbles rushed to my nose; I grabbed a napkin just before a resultant sneeze. Careful not to stare, I edged my metal chair closer and leaned into the table as if resting my arms. The phone man glanced over his shoulder toward the other two workmen I had noticed. They were two tables over from my right.

". . . Brethren . . . be there," said phone man gruffly.

Had I heard correctly? What did this stranger know about the Brethren? I wasn't sure I could edge closer without arousing suspicion.

"Excuse me, sir? Could we take your picture?" Someone tapped my shoulder from behind. "I know you people don't usually do that kind of thing, but it would mean so much to my wife," said a heavyset man in jeans and a T-shirt celebrating the Tennessee Volunteers' national football championship.

I stared at him blankly. Then scanning my gray trousers, pale blue oxford shirt, and black jacket, I realized he was talking to me. Of course, my borrowed straw hat was on the table. I smiled politely and said, "I'm sorry, but I'm not Amish," hoping he would leave quickly.

Phone man turned and looked at us over his shoulder before spinning back into the receiver. But for a moment, I saw his face. He had a short forehead crowded with dark brown bangs, a long narrow nose that formed a small bulb on the end, and a black Vandyke beard and mustache combination around his mouth and chin. ". . . gathering tonight," he mumbled.

"What? You sure are dressed like the Amish," my thick-accented admirer continued. "Please, my wife is right over there — just one quick picture. We're visiting my sister Vera Jo in Mumford — we're from Lowater, Mississippi. You know where that is?"

"No, you don't understand — I'm a tourist like you," I replied, annoyed at his persistence. I wanted to hear more of Vandyke's phone conversation.

"Yeah, right," the heavyset man smirked. "At least you didn't have to lie about it. I thought Amish people were supposed to be honest."

My indignation flared, but I let the man waddle back to his table and point me out to his wife. Was this the kind of thing the Amish were forced to endure every time they came to town? And this was Tremont — what must it be like when they ventured into Mumford or Lewiston? I shifted back in my chair and cocked my head slightly toward the pay phone.

". . . livery . . . tonight . . . midnight . . . see you there," Vandyke said and slammed the phone into its cradle. He strode past me and over to the table where his buddies waited. Both of them wore jeans and yellow-tan work boots, one in a torn flannel shirt, the other in a brown T-shirt. As I stood and deposited silver into the still-warm phone, I strained to filter their words from the low chatter of other tables. It was much more difficult than intercepting the phone conversation.

"You can say that again," Flannel Shirt said. He tilted his empty tea tumbler and crunched the cubes like broken glass. His face was non-descript, with a firm jawline, deep-set eyes, broad forehead, and curly brown hair.

". . . messed it up . . . who cares," murmured the other. His nose hooked over a dark-blond mustache, and he wore a blue baseball cap with a logo that I couldn't make out. The phone man with the Vandyke was impatient to leave now. He tossed a couple of greenbacks on the table and stood to leave. The other two followed his lead.

The flat operator's voice informed me that I needed to dial a number or hang up. Should I follow them out of the restaurant? Had I really overheard them planning some kind of secret meeting at the livery tonight? What if they were the ones who had abducted Leah? Perhaps they were plotting another scare-crime tonight — perhaps they were planning to burn down the livery. I slammed the phone down with the same force as my predecessor and raced past the sandwich counter and out the door.

Harsh sun blinded me momentarily. The three workers were just pulling away in the Tenleco truck. I could not wait to talk with Dan Warren and Sheriff Claiborne.

Back inside the tiny restaurant, I tried to recall the handful of words I had overheard: *tonight* was repeated several times, *Brethren, the gathering, livery,* and *midnight.* At the pay phone once more, I inserted correct change and dialed the sheriff's office. Maria Alvarez picked up on the first ring, and I identified myself.

"Oh, I'm sorry, Father Grif," she said. "Sam's in a meeting all day with the county commissioner, and Dan just left to respond to a call for an assist with Munroe County Sheriff's Department — they had a big rig carrying hot asphalt jackknife on the interstate."

"Well, just tell them I called," I said, wondering if I should try to explain my suspicions to Maria. Perhaps I was jumping to conclusions. Maybe those construction workers were merely gossiping about the Judas Tree and the string of recent vandalism preceding Simon's death. Or perhaps they were responsible.

"Would you like one of them to call you when they return?" the dispatcher asked.

I explained that I was in Tremont and would not be close to a phone until I returned to Avenell this afternoon. Thanking her, I hung up as a plan began to form in my mind. I fed the phone slot more change and dialed the church office.

Janine answered on the first ring. "Cathedral of the Divine, Avenell Parish, this is

Janine. How may I help you?"

I greeted my faithful assistant and explained where I was. She replied that Bea had called this morning and informed her of my impromptu trip to the Schroeders.

"So what's happening around the office? Anything urgent?" I asked, half expecting some crisis to be brewing but praying that none were.

"Well, there's Joan Dowinger's latest emergency. Her DAR ladies needed a place to meet this week because the Pepper Tree accidentally double-booked. So she wants to meet in the Fellowship Hall — I told her I'd check with you but that it was likely just fine. Other than that, Miss Bea drove Miss Berthy Weismuller to the doctor in Lewiston. Her rheumatism is acting up."

"In other words, Janine," I replied, "I'm not missing anything."

She giggled mischievously, "You could say that. Are you enjoying the Amish country?"

"I'm hardly on vacation," I replied. "But yes, thanks, I'm making the best of the situation. No one else called?"

"No," she said. "No one other than Mrs. Dowinger and your sister."

"I had planned to return this afternoon, Janine," I said, "but now I may stay down here a little longer."

"That's a great idea," she said genuinely. "Enjoy yourself — you need to get away more. I've got everything under control."

"I'm sure you do. Thanks, Janine," I said. "I'll see you tomorrow, then."

I hung up and deposited more coins. The answering machine picked up at the rectory, and I left Bea a message letting her know I planned to say in Tremont a little longer. At least until midnight.

While there was plenty of time before then, I realized I did not have much before returning to the Schroeder farm for lunch. But since I was here in town, there were two more stops I wanted to make. I strolled down the narrow boardwalk until I reached the small shop on the corner, the Oak'n Barrel.

Lydia Miller stood wide-eyed behind the wooden counter in her crafts store as a tinkling bell signaled my entrance. She scanned my dark casual clothes but did not make the same mistake as my persistent friend in the bakery. Before I could remove my straw hat, she said, "Good day, can I help you?"

"Mrs. Miller? Father Griffin Reed — from Avenell. I was in town and thought I would stop in and see how you are doing," I said.

"Oh, Brother Reed. How good to see you! Thank you for thinking of me." She came around the corner of the glass display case that supported her current sewing project and offered her hand in a firm clasp.

"A very nice shop you have here," I complimented.

"Well, please, look around," she said, clearly pleased.

Around me shelves and tables displayed eye-appealing merchandise of everything from hot pads to quilts and hand-carved baby cradles to homemade preserves. I smiled and went straight to the glass counter where faceless dolls in Amish garb sat guarding an old-fashioned cash register. Next to them a bank of glass jars offered a rainbow assortment of hard candy — peppermint, spearmint, cinnamon, horehound, licorice, lemon, cherry. I chose a sour apple stick with light- and dark-green stripes.

"How are you and your family doing, if I may ask?" I placed a dime on the counter and unwrapped my candy. The sharp smell gave way to a tangy sweetness that was not unlike a green crab apple.

Lydia Miller nodded and adjusted the small white kapp covering the bun of faded, dark hair, her eyes even wider. "We are doing very well, under the circumstances," she offered. "I continue to grieve my brother, but it is in the Lord's hands at this point. I have done all that I can." She shifted her heavy frame from her left to her right foot and regarded my enjoyment of the candy with amusement. "Have you solved the puzzle box yet?" she asked.

"No," I replied. "In fact, that's the other reason I wanted to stop by. You see, the puzzle box was stolen from my church office the morning after you gave it to me. I reported it to the sheriff and he's investigating, but there are no leads yet. I'm terribly sorry. I feel responsible."

There had been a sharp intake of breath when I first mentioned the theft, but after that Lydia Miller merely nodded. "It is not your fault," she said. "If it is important enough for someone to steal, then I am sure that it will come back to us."

"Any idea what might have been inside? Do you remember anything else that Simon might have said about it?" My apple stick now looked like a sharpened pencil on top. I crunched into it with sounds that would have sent my dentist cringing.

She shook her head just as a non-Amish couple, both clad in denim, entered the store — an older man with thick, white sideburns and presumably his wife with a neat stack of frosted blond curls on top of her head. We suspended our conversation while Lydia tried to assist them. I wrapped the remainder of my candy in its clear plastic sleeve and took in details toward the front of the shop. Bea's birthday wasn't long after Easter; perhaps I should look for her gift while I was here. I wandered to the other side of the room, examining various bric-a-brac. Picture frames, carved trivets and coasters, bonnets and pinafores for children. A pull train and an interlinked family of ducks. Noah's ark with a dozen pair of different animals.

As I scanned children's rattles and Amish cookbooks, my eyes were drawn to a familiar sight. Neatly displayed near the window were three-dimensional rectangles without hinges — puzzle boxes. One looked almost identical to the one that Lydia had given me from Simon. While the proprietress continued answering questions about the bird's-eye stitch, I picked up the block and turned it over. The seams were much clearer on this box, the workmanship not nearly as skilled as Simon's. Here a small square of white paper adhered to the bottom of the box with tiny printed directions about how to open it. I followed them by pulling on the top while sliding the right side. The wood chest opened like an envelope that had been slit at one end. Inside another paper square stated: *Congratulations! You solved the Amish puzzle box! A favorite with kids of all ages, it's the perfect gift!* I snapped the end shut and slid the top back in place and then repeated the procedure. *If only the box that Simon had bequeathed had opened this easily,* I thought. *If only I still had the puzzle box, or better yet, knew what was inside.*

It looked as if the couple would be buying a quilt. Lydia rang them up and I was surprised to hear how expensive the purchase was. After the front bell had marked their departure, I said, "Big sale? I couldn't help but overhear."

"Thankfully, yes," she said. "Business has been down considerably since Simon's death. In truth, things have really been slow since Christmas."

"In your shop or throughout town?" I asked. "After Simon's death, I was afraid just the opposite would occur — a lot of curiosity seekers."

"Oh, there were a few morbid types, kids from the high school, a couple of reporters. But people who like to shop and enjoy our community are definitely staying away.

Mostly the older, retired folk." She paused and reached for a candy stick of her own — rich brown horehound. My grandfather had loved horehound, the odd sorghum taste that reminded me of root beer. "However, the auction this weekend should draw tourists back down to our valley."

"What auction?" I asked, alarmed. "Has someone decided to sell his farm?"

"No," she replied. "It's my friend, Deborah Kaufman — you met her at Simon's service. Since her mother died last fall, she and her brother Adam have been planning to move in with their other brother, Jonah. He will farm the land that had been their parents' and probably rent the house to another family. The auction is just for a lot of their parents' old things — furniture, a few quilts that Deborah and the boys do not wish to keep, some tools, those sorts of things. Perhaps you could come?"

"Well, I'll certainly consider it." We stood there for an odd moment's silence before I continued, "If I may ask, did you and Simon ever discuss what happened with your father?"

She looked at me curiously. "Simon . . . well, it's funny that you ask that. Most of our lives, we have avoided talking about what transpired all those years ago. Simon had his life and I had mine . . . very different lives at that. But during this visit, Simon had many questions. He spoke frequently of our parents and asked me many questions about our mother's death — if I remembered her, what she was like, the exact circumstances of how she died."

"Where did your family move here from?" I asked, eager to continue.

"From Oak Ridge," she said automatically, referring to the small city in east Tennessee famous for its Atomic Energy Lab. "My mother died when I was eight — Simon would have been ten — and the following year we moved here."

"I'm sorry about your mother. It must have been hard growing up without her," I offered. "How did she die?"

"Poison. She was accidentally exposed to a toxic chemical in the lab. A freak accident it seems — my father always blamed himself."

"Was he exposed, too?" I asked.

"No. And it was never explained what mercury resinol was doing out in the lab in the first place — evidently, it was not something typically in use." She paused, as if lost in the embrace of a loving mother known more from memory than from life.

"How terrible . . . I'm very sorry." I tried

to imagine any possible connections between what Lydia was sharing with me and the death of her brother.

"Father was very disillusioned with being a scientist after Mother's death. We had cousins on her side of the family here, so we moved down on a trial basis. We liked it and decided to stay. . . ."

"Until . . . your father's indiscretion," I said.

"Yes. Please excuse me for a moment," she said, looking over my shoulder. A woman in chartreuse shorts and tank top entered and began browsing. Lydia strode over to help her, and the two began discussing quilt patterns. After another five minutes and dozens of suggestions, the customer ended up with a matching set of placemats and napkins.

When Lydia returned I asked, "So Simon was what, about eighteen or nineteen when your father died?"

"Yes, that's about right, I guess," she replied. "Simon had not joined the church yet and was very hurt when Father was shunned for his sin. So Simon decided to leave and go to college. I stayed and got married. . . ." She paused, looked as if about to say something, then pressed her lips together. "It's been such a long time."

"Where did your father go? Did he stay in the area? I happened to notice his tombstone in the little cemetery just off Chigger Ridge Road when I was walking into town this morning."

"Father only moved to Lewiston . . . got a job at the paper factory for a while before he had a heart attack. Honestly, I think his heart broke in two. He was still hoping Anna Kaufman would leave her husband and children for him."

"So she was not shunned, as well?" I asked.

"No," Lydia said. A spark of bitterness singed the single syllable. "She was allowed to repent and resume her life here, although she was the one who had initiated the affair."

The words flared out of the Amish woman with the force of a spontaneous conflagration. However, she immediately tried to douse her anger. "I am sorry," she said. "I should not have said that."

"It's quite all right, Lydia," I offered. "I know how difficult it can be to let go of anger."

"Despite her staying with her husband in Tremont," she whispered, "poor Papa still believed they would be together some day." She looked up at me. "That's why he chose to be buried as close to town as possible. In the potter's field. Not in Oak Ridge, where Mother is buried. One more disappointment . . ."

The pain of losing both her parents to different toxins, one chemical and the other of passion, created small wrinkles around Lydia Hostetler Miller's eyes.

"Were you out at your father's grave this morning?" I asked. "I thought I saw someone from the road as I passed by."

"Really?" she asked. "That's odd. I usually try to keep the weeds from overrunning that place, but I haven't been there since Christmas."

"I hope I'm not prying. I appreciate your honesty with me," I said. She nodded and I waited a second before I asked, "Do you think Simon harbored a grudge? Could he have come back here now to try to get back at the Amish who shunned your father?"

She shook her head vigorously. "I don't think so. As I mentioned, Simon asked many questions about the past, but he seemed . . . well, not surprised, impassive about it all. As if he already knew it but needed someone else's version of it to make it real. Am I making any sense?"

"Yes, you are," I said. Glancing at my watch, I realized that there was no way I could make it back to the Schroeders in fifteen minutes. At least not on foot.

"Well, I suppose I should be going. I appreciate your trust and candor, Lydia. You remind me a lot of Simon in those ways. If there's anything I can do, promise —"

"Thank you, Brother Reed," she interjected. "I am pleased that you came by today. It's not often that I speak of the past, but it seems right that I should do so with you."

I turned to go, the door pull in hand and the bell tinkling over my head, when Lydia Miller called out, "Brother Reed?"

"Yes?" I turned, looking back at her.

"The Lord bless you and keep you, and protect you from the enemy who prowls like a hungry lion waiting to devour His sheep."

"Amen," I said, grateful for her blessing as I ventured outside into the bright spring afternoon. If I was going to carry out my plans for the rest of the day, I would need protection from the enemy, indeed. I strode across the boardwalk and headed up the street to the barnlike structure with the sign reading, *Tremont Livery and Smith Shop.*

Chapter Eighteen

Kindred Folk

The bright sunshine had not diminished and now flared full strength directly above the small strip of Amish businesses. Glancing down the road, I saw something that made me even more eager to carry out my plan: The three Tenleco construction workers whom I had overheard in the bakery stood talking to an Amishman just inside the door of the livery.

I wasted no time and walked the couple hundred yards briskly. But just as I was within earshot, Vandyke and his cohorts packed themselves into the cab of the beat-up Ford pickup and pulled away. I caught my breath and scanned the whitewashed two-story building with its numerous hitching rails and water troughs out front. Several saddled horses were hitched to the nearest post alongside two mule-drawn buggies. The Amishman who had been talking with the Tenleco crew watched me curiously. Finally, after I had leaned against the nearest hitching post for several moments, he limped out from inside the barn.

"How can I help you?" he asked. His white beard reached mid-chest and flapped in the breeze. He must have been in his early seventies, but his eyes shone clear and familiar. Perhaps I had met one of his kin.

"Do you rent horses? I'm Griffin Reed — a friend of the Schroeders. I was hoping I could rent a horse to ride out to their farm and back," I explained, offering my hand.

He took it and shook it gently. "Albert Yoder. Ah yes, Brother Reed. You are the English visitor who helped Benjamin look for poor Leah last night. You are also the elder of her young man, Peter, are you not?"

"Yes, I suppose you could say that. Pleased to meet you, Mr. Yoder. Are you related to the Schroeders' neighbors who run the dairy?"

He laughed. "Everyone in Tremont is related to a Yoder! So you've met my brother Joseph, have you?" He spat on the ground beside us. "Now, you wanted to see about renting a horse? Do you ride?" he asked. His eyes regarded me warily, or perhaps it was simply his squinting into the sun above my shoulder.

"I used to, when I was younger," I said, instantly recalling happier times with Amy, a brook-side picnic up in the Smoky Mountains. We had rented horses and followed mountain trails the entire spring afternoon. She loved the way the wind felt in her honey-gold hair, and I loved watching her.

"Well, I'll be glad to loan you old Callie. No charge. She's an older mare, but still has plenty of life," he said, leading me into the cool shadows of the livery. The smell of manure and winter hay rose from the barn floor. He retrieved a large ebony mare with a white starburst between her eyes and methodically began to saddle and bridle the beautiful creature.

"I'll be glad to pay you," I offered.

"No, sir. You'll be doing me a favor by giving her some exercise," he replied.

"Thank you, Mr. Yoder. I'm much obliged to you," I said. He nodded and proceeded to position the bridle comfortably over Callie's head. After a moment I asked, "Mr. Yoder, those Tenleco men who were here when I walked up — they looked familiar. Do you know them?" I tried to sound as casual as possible.

He looked up and blinked thickly. "Don't reckon I know them," he said. "They were asking directions is all, said they knew my brother. Seems everybody knows the Yoder Dairy."

"I see."

"I did know Simon Hostetler, though," he volunteered as he tightened the cinch without looking up. "He was a good man. A shame what happened. I hear he was a friend of yours."

"Yes, sir," I replied. "We went to seminary together many years ago. Yes, he was a good man. I can't imagine who would want to take another man's life the way someone took Simon's."

"Don't think there's no meanness afoot just 'cause you're in Amish country," he said and handed me the reins. "We got all kinds of trouble of our own."

"What kind of trouble, Mr. Yoder?" I asked. The horse whinnied and I patted her soft, dark head. We led her outside to the front of the livery.

The old man stood and looked at me intently as if he were awarding me consideration for my patience. He scratched his chin, his fingertips lost in the white cotton beard. "I fear the English warmongers are up to their old tricks." He leaned against the side of the barn, spit, and planted a brown boot about two feet off the ground against the barn wood.

"What do you mean? The military over at Dolby?" I bit his bait.

He nodded. "Back when that good-for-nothing airplane base was wantin' to take our land thirty years ago, we had some problems with crops being ruined, fields torched. Joseph was just startin' out then. Lost a couple of his best dairy cows — throats slit. Someone took two of my best mules. Never did catch anyone, and it sure was not one of our people. It's extortion, that's what it is." He leaned back to gauge my reaction. What did he hope to accomplish by sharing his contempt for Dolby with me?

I took out my handkerchief and blew my nose. "If the government's responsible for Simon's death, what's the motive? What do you suppose they want now?"

"How should I know? He's been 'round here pokin' his nose in all our business for the last month, asking questions better left alone. Maybe he asked the wrong question to the right person, if y'know what I mean. Y'know what they say about letting sleeping dogs lie."

"I'm afraid I don't know what you mean. What kind of questions?" I prompted. "Was Simon asking about the Brethren? Were they responsible for his death?"

"So you've already found out about them. Word of advice, Brother Reed. The same sleeping dogs that bit Simon might bite you just as well."

I laughed nervously. "Is that a threat or a warning?"

"Only a word of wisdom to someone who don't know our ways, that's all. Plain and simple. I got to get back to work now. Good day." He turned and limped back into the livery, toward the low hush of other voices of both men and horses. "Enjoy your ride," he called out over his shoulder.

"Mr. Yoder?" I called out.

"Yes?" he spun around and moved toward the gate.

"What time do you close this evening?"

"Why do you ask?"

When I pointed to Callie, he chuckled and said, "Oh, I'm usually here until suppertime, 'round six o'clock, I guess. Bring her back when it's convenient for you, Brother Reed. Good day."

He seemed to have been caught off guard for a second there. Did he know about the clandestine meeting scheduled in his barn for tonight? I could not decide. But if he were not in on the meeting, then why meet here? If I had my way, I would find out this evening for myself.

I gathered bridled leather around my palm and mounted the saddled mare. My straw hat crowned my head once more, and I shook out the reins and trotted the horse out into the spring sunshine. Callie seemed just as impatient as I was to leave the dust of this place behind and head out to the open countryside. *"Maybe he asked the wrong question to the right person,"* the old man's voice whispered amid the sound of my horse's *clip-clops* along the dusty shoulder of the road. What had Simon asked that could have cost him his life? And who was the "right person"? I recalled my lunch plans with Leland Finch at Dolby Air Force Base on Friday and made a note to find out if Simon had visited the base prior to his death.

I tapped the reins gently and Callie cantered off the road's shoulder and onto a gravel road. Riding across the open shoulder of the road, I relished the rush of wind against my face, the heat of the sun, and the smell of clean horse flesh. The countryside spread out before me like a quilt at a picnic in squares of green, brown, and tan.

Despite this glorious feeling, old Mr. Yoder's words bounced along inside me, alternately edged with menace and with concern. Perhaps he was trying to warn me as a liaison of the Brethren, as if he himself belonged. After all, I had already speculated that some Amish must be helping the

Brethren mount their attacks.

But could this old man possibly betray his community? I could not imagine it. So perhaps he was trying to be helpful after all, or simply venting his anger and fear about the military base's encroachment on his homeland. But what did a past land sale have to do with the present? Did Simon's father's affair have something to do with the military base? What could the two possibly have in common?

I felt the same feeling that used to accompany me during my calculus tests as a freshman at Avenell — a fascinated awe that this problem had a solution mixed with an uncertainty that I would ever find it.

As I rode Callie through the pasture running parallel to the gravel road, the Schroeder farm looked as serene and quaint as one of Leah's watercolor landscapes. In addition to questions I posed to Mr. Yoder back at the livery, I was simply grateful to ride quickly rather than walk slowly. My morning hike was drastically cut by taking Callie, not to mention the more direct route.

Even though my watch displayed one-thirty, Sarah Schroeder was just putting lunch on the table as I came into the house.

Benjamin and Nathan were already seated at the table, and Leah was bringing in a plate of sliced ham from the kitchen.

"My apologies for being late. I hope you didn't wait on me," I said, out of breath. "Let me wash up and I'll join you."

"No rush, Brother Reed," said Benjamin Schroeder. "We run on Amish time around here. Our clock is just now going on one."

I thought he was joking until I looked up at the small plain face of a wooden-cased clock on the mantle. Sure enough, it was a good half-hour behind my own.

"Yes," said Sarah, placing a loaf of fresh bread beside Nathan. "I forgot to tell you about Amish time when I mentioned lunch this morning. Please sit here when you are ready."

I hurriedly washed my hands in the bathroom and returned to the hearty meal spread out on the cherrywood table. "So you all actually have your own standard of time?" I asked. "How do you know what time it actually is?"

Nathan laughed and Leah seemed embarrassed as she explained, "It's another way we separate ourselves from the English world. We try not to be ruled by the clock the way many people are, so most everyone in Tremont sets theirs a half-hour behind the time you use."

After a silent blessing, we began passing around the plates of cold meats and cheeses to fill the fresh slices of delicious wheat bread. "Where's Peter?" I asked. "Isn't he hungry?"

"Oh," said Leah, swallowing her first bite. "He has gone back to Avenell to prepare his lesson for the Next Generation Bible study tonight. He caught a ride with Daniel Yoder, who came by on his way to deliver a rocking chair up on the mountain. Peter hoped you wouldn't mind. I told him Jacob could take you home when he gets in from work this afternoon."

"Of course," I said. "In fact, I had such a pleasant time this morning that I was wondering if . . . well, would it be too much trouble for me to stay another night?"

The two of them looked at each other and then a wide grin broke out across both faces. "We would be delighted, Brother Reed," said Benjamin.

"Honored," said Sarah.

Leah looked a bit surprised, but it was Nathan who asked, "What did you find to do this morning that makes you want to stay around this place?"

"Nathan," said his father, "is at the age where our way of life seems boring."

"Well, I took a long walk into town and stopped in at the bakery. I checked in on Mrs. Miller to see how she and her family are doing, and I had a delightful horseback ride on old Callie out there. Maybe it just takes a city slicker like me to appreciate the simple things, Nathan."

Everyone laughed and I relished my sandwich while making sure to save room for the rhubarb pie Sarah had mentioned this morning. My host and hostess whispered back and forth a few times before Benjamin announced, "We are going to invite Mary Lapp for supper. You mentioned that she was a friend of your wife's."

"I would like that very much," I said. "I had thought about paying her a visit this afternoon."

"Well, we will let you deliver the invitation for us, then," said Sarah. "Are you ready for pie?"

Moments later I bit into the tart, crisp fruit pie that was one of my official heralds of spring. I felt a twinge of guilt for the thought, but it seemed to me that the simple pleasures of Amish life, especially the food, were almost as compelling as the numerous questions piling up around Simon's death.

After lunch, I borrowed a change of

clothes from Benjamin and returned to my room to bathe. I had not seen Mary Lapp for over a year, as best I could recall, and while I was genuinely eager to renew our friendship, I was also curious to hear her describe some of the present tensions in the Amish community.

Although Benjamin offered me the buggy, I preferred to stick with Callie. The beautiful March day continued to unfold itself around the narrow roads and even narrower trails that sutured the Amish community from home to home. A cloud bank loomed on the distant horizon, reminding me that the prospect of rain always loomed around the ridges of the Cumberland Plateau in springtime.

Mary Lapp, Amy's dear friend from years gone by, was now living with her grown daughter and family, the Stolzfuses, on their farm about four miles from the Schroeders. When I rode up to the brick and white-washed clapboard farmhouse, Mary was on the sun porch working a loom. She didn't seem to recognize me at first, especially in Benjamin's brown homespun pants and chambray shirt — both a bit too short.

"Griffin Reed!" she exclaimed, as I approached the porch steps.

"How are you, Miss Mary?" I removed my

straw hat and bent to hug the dear woman. She clasped both her palms around my neck and gave me a wiry embrace. Smiling with the kind of gusto only those unafraid of dying can exude, her beautiful, lined face radiated contentment. She wore a dark gray housedress with brown apron and white kapp, almost indistinguishable from the sleek silver-white hair beneath it. I scooted my wicker rocker closer to the gifted artisan's loom. She offered to stop but I insisted that she continue. The graceful movement and gentle *drum-thrum-drum-thrum* sound were instantly soothing.

"Oh, Griffin Reed, what a sight for sore eyes you are!" she began. "I think of you often and pray for your comfort. Oh, I loved your sweet wife. She was an Amish woman at heart! Kindred folk, we call them."

Although I'd heard Mary praise my wife's sweet spirit and artistic talents before, I could not recall her ever speaking the words I'd just heard. I smiled and replied, "Why do you say that, Miss Mary? Aren't we all a little Amish at heart?"

She stopped weaving, and her hands retreated to her side like a turtle snapping into its shell. "Oh my, no! As good a man as you are, Griffin — and as good as you look in those fine working clothes," she laughed,

"I'm not sure you're cut out for Amish life." She paused, perhaps reflecting on what was below the surface of her casual comment.

My silence must have betrayed my momentary hurt, for she added, "No harm intended, Griffin." Her fingers began to work the dexterous magic of the loom again before she continued speaking. "Not all of us can be content with the simple things in life. Not all of us are willing to seek God in the everyday things — plowing a straight row, weaving a rug, cooking a meal. But I'm convinced that's where we find Him." She beamed a wizened smile full of straight dull pearls. "Just as you find Him in your cathedrals and creeds."

"I understand, Miss Mary," I said. "How are you feeling? You look as spry as ever."

"Thank you, young man," she chuckled. "To tell the truth, I've been under the weather these past months. Even went over to the doctor in Lewiston. High blood pressure's all he found. And a high level of something I never heard of, but enough about me. I'm out here enjoying this beautiful day the Lord has given us. What about you, Griffin? How is your heart doing? Have you been graced by the love of another?" she asked gently.

Her careful concern for the genuine good

of my heart moved me. I found myself telling her about Caroline and all that had happened last fall, about my visit last Thanksgiving to the Avenell Cemetery where Amy was buried.

She nodded and beamed her pleasure. "Amy is gone, dear, and we miss her. But love is a gift, one not to be refused when the Lord gives it. Your Caroline sounds like a lovely woman. I hope I get to meet her soon."

Words were inadequate, so I merely nodded, childlike, and we sat in the moist afternoon air, the scent of spring-rained earth rising to meet us. Miriam Stolzfus, a younger version of her mother, emerged from the house carrying two glasses of lemon refreshment. Introductions were made, and then she excused herself and returned inside.

I reflected on Mary's words some more until the sound of her loom brought me back to the present, back to my original intent for being here.

"Do you remember the Hostetlers, Miss Mary?"

She rocked her small body in time to the rhythm of her hands. "Oh yes, of course. They came here all of a sudden back in the spring of '59. One of the roughest springs we ever had. Hailstorm delayed spring planting. It was a hard time."

"They had moved from east Tennessee — Oak Ridge, I believe?"

She peered up at me. "Yes, Caleb's wife, Suzanne, had just passed on, and she was second cousin to the Knepps, who used to live down by the river. They moved back to Lancaster in '74."

"Were you surprised, Miss Mary, when the Hostetlers wished to join the Amish church?" I asked.

The old woman stopped her weaving and cocked her head. "Not really. I guess us old timers are always a little surprised when any outsiders wish to become permanent members of our faith community. But Caleb and his children had always fit right in. He worked hard, seemed to enjoy our way of life."

"Anything strike you as unusual about their relationship with their neighbors, the Kaufmans?" I asked innocently.

"I'm sure you've heard by now about Anna and Caleb — no one in Tremont can keep a secret. Oh, there were suspicions and gossip before it all came out. Caleb began to seem preoccupied. And poor little Anna. She never had been . . . well, quite right, if you know what I mean. She was always talking to herself out in that herb garden of hers, or dressing inappropriately, or shouting out 'Amen!' when the deacons prayed during church." Mary resumed her weaving.

"Do you think she could have been mentally ill?" I suggested.

The old woman nodded. "Perhaps. Her youngest boy, Adam, he's not right at all. Like a child. Sweet spirit, but he can't be left alone for a minute. He takes after his mother."

"Yes," I said, "I met him at Simon's memorial service up in Avenell. Lydia introduced us."

"I was sorry I couldn't make it to the service. Like I said, I'm not as limber as I used to be. But I heard good things about how you conducted things. What a good friend you were to Simon. How kind you've been to Lyddie and her family."

Blood rushed to my cheeks and I said, "Well, I do what I can. Miss Mary, let me ask you a hard question. What do you suppose brought Anna and Caleb together? Could they have known each other before he moved here?" I thought aloud.

The old woman's fingers nimbly worked the loom as if she were playing a harp. "No, I don't think they knew each other. I think the way of the flesh simply overcame them. She was a pretty girl, big brown eyes like sunflowers, blond hair. Perhaps she did feel sorry for him. Caleb was just a lonely soul unsure of himself after Suzanne's death. It happens — even in our world. Not often, mind you, but it happens. May the Lord have mercy on their poor souls."

My mind leapt at the phrase, so reminiscent of the epitaph on Caleb's tombstone. "So how did their affair become known?"

She paused again and sipped her glass of lemonade. "Well, it sure looked like the hand of God. Anna broke down in church one Sunday with her husband sitting on one side and Caleb sitting on the other. I'll remember it until I die. Poor thing. The bishop was reading Psalm 51 and the tears just started rolling down her face. Finally, she stood up and began confessing. Right there, before God and all of us. Her poor husband, Philip, learned the same as the rest of us. Later, the elders decided that Caleb would have to leave Tremont. Anna was allowed to stay, after she had spent a few months with her sister in Ohio. Saddest thing."

"I assume it must have been unbearable for both families. How did each family handle it?" I asked.

"Well, after Caleb moved to Lewiston, Simon left to attend university. Lydia moved in with Jed and Victoria Miller — he was a deacon in the church then — and ended up marrying their son the following year." She resumed her weaving, the sound accentuating her guttural voice. "The Kaufmans . . . let's see . . . Jonah married and got his own place, the old Keim farmstead. His sister, Deborah, never did marry, poor thing. She took care of her brother Adam and her father. Philip never was the same after Anna's death. A sad story, really."

"Had you seen Simon since he returned?" I asked. Warm afternoon sun filtered through a stand of beech trees in the yard beyond the screened porch.

"Yes. I ran into him in town one afternoon a few weeks ago. I had some quilts for sale in Lydia's little shop there. Simon was very sweet. Told me he had never forgotten how kind I was to him as a boy, how welcome I always made him feel in our home. He was friends with my nephew Timothy when they were growing up. I asked him if he might ever come back to Tremont to live, and he surprised me by saying that he just might do that someday — when he retired."

"Simon was planning to retire in Tremont?" I repeated. "Was he serious?"

She thought before answering. "Oh, I don't believe he had definite plans, but yes, I think he still loved Tremont."

"Would other people in the community have responded as kindly if Simon had mentioned this notion to them?" I asked.

"No, I'm sure there are some who would not have welcomed his presence. He reminded people of old wounds. Of what can happen when the flesh is weak."

"Doesn't Lydia remind people of those same things? She's managed to stay all these years," I said.

"Yes, she has. But she's different. She's always loved our ways and seemed very content with the Amish life. She never brought up the matter. In fact, she and Deborah Kaufman are the best of friends. Lyddie's one of us now." The old lady smiled up at me from her loom as if retrieving a thought from several sentences prior in our conversation. "That day I saw Simon . . . well, he asked me if I thought the military would be able to buy the Canaan's Way property. Or if the owners would sell it to a private corporation. He asked me if I'd ever heard about a group called the Brethren." Her voice sounded very matter-of-fact, matching the cadence of the loom.

I was stunned at what a wellspring of information my old friend was turning out to be. "And have you?" I volleyed back to her.

"Only as a girl. My papa used to tell me that most English were not like the people in Carroll County who tried to run our people off when we first came here. But that was a long time ago, right after Tremont was founded early in the century."

I ruminated on her words. "Did you tell this to Simon that day he asked?"

"Yes. I think the Brethren came to represent the concept of prejudice and fear more than the handful of old men who were trying to scare us away. I don't think they ever really intended to harm us." She pursed her lips in a thin, sympathetic smile, aware that I was disappointed. "Griffin, I'm afraid I'm not much help. And I so want to be. Poor Simon did not deserve to die like he did. We Amish usually accept everything that happens as our Father's will, but I have not had peace since this terrible deed was uncovered. Then those break-ins and what happened to poor Leah . . . What is the world coming to? Things like this do not happen in our community. We have tragedies and calamities, sin and suffering, but usually the outside world's hate and violence cannot thrive here. It feels like our way of life may be coming to an end. Oh, I'm going on again, aren't I? I'm just a foolish old woman, Griffin. May the Lord give you ears to hear any truth I may have spoken and grant you grace to forget my own prideful folly." She smiled again, sun-glossed eyes squinting in the light.

On that benediction I thanked the dear woman and offered her Sarah's invitation to supper. "Oh, I'm so sorry, Griffin. Today is my grandson's birthday and we're having a little party for him. He's sixteen — the beginning of his Rumspringa, our young people's time to explore and decide for themselves if they wish to be Amish. Please send our thanks and let us make it another time."

I rose and said my good-byes. However, as I hugged the old woman, she exclaimed, "I have something for you, Griffin. I believe it's finally the right time."

Miss Mary scurried off the porch and into the house like a field mouse in a children's story. I couldn't imagine what she might have for me unless it was something that had been Amy's. When she returned, a quilted garden of colors draped her arm.

"This is for you," she instructed, unfolding the exquisite quilt in a pattern I had never seen before. "Your wife designed this pattern. We had cut the pieces and started it together by hand and then . . . well, she wasn't able to continue. It hurt too much for me to see it after she passed, so I put it away in the cedar chest. Last fall I ran across it and decided it was time to complete it. I just finished it after Christmas. Amy called this pattern 'Garden of Eden.' I teased her about the loud colors, that they were prideful."

Each square featured an interlinked bed of flowers, row of trees, stream, or animal. The intricate pattern repeated itself both horizontally and vertically in bright print calicos and in solid primary cottons. A field of emerald framed the cloth landscape. I was speechless, but the well of tears seeping from my eyes must have conveyed my bittersweet surprise.

"I know it must be painful, Griffin. And I almost decided not to give it to you earlier when I heard about your friend Caroline. But I want you to have this, and I think Amy would, too. It's so cheerful and bright — a sign that the grief of winter ends and hope can bloom again."

I accepted the quilt in my arms delicately, as if my lost wife had somehow suddenly walked into the room and handed me the gift. It smelled of sweet cedar.

Chapter Nineteen

The Gathering

During supper back at the Schroeders, I could hardly contain my anticipation — and my fear — of what would transpire after midnight.

"Jacob, I hear you're working construction for Tenleco's new paper mill," I said, finishing the last of my sausage and cabbage kraut.

"Yes, sir," he replied. "It's good pay for working with my hands."

"Where's that new plant going to be? I saw several other Tenleco workers in town this afternoon eating lunch. Is the site close to Tremont?" I asked.

"Yes, sir, reasonably close," he said. "It's just on the other side of the military base, not far from the Jackson River. Most of us bring our lunch. Those guys must have driven over from the old plant."

"I thought Tenleco was trying to get away from the river. Isn't that what got them in trouble with the EPA in the first place? I'm surprised the military would let them build so close to Dolby."

The clean-shaven young man shrugged his broad shoulders. "I don't think Dolby was too happy about it, but there was nothing they could do. Tenleco's been wanting to move the plant for some time now."

Just as I was about to phrase another question, Sarah emerged with our final course. Over chocolate cake with sour cream frosting, Mr. Schroeder changed the subject and asked how my visit had gone that afternoon. I thanked him for inquiring and described my time with Mary Lapp in detail, concluding by showing the quilt on which she and my late wife had collaborated. Leah and Sarah fussed over its unique design and intricate beauty as I folded the quilt and draped it across the back of my chair.

I was about to excuse myself early to my guest room when Nathan almost blew my cover. He asked, "Would you like me to take Callie back to Mr. Yoder's for you, Brother Reed? I'd be glad to do it. Jacob could follow me in the buggy."

"Oh, I almost forgot all about poor Callie — and by the way, thank you for tending her this afternoon when I returned from Miss Mary's." I lingered over a frosting-laden morsel of cake. "No, thank you, Nathan. Mr. Yoder was in no hurry. I'll probably take her back in the morning before I leave. I've enjoyed riding so much today, and it would be nice to get one more in before I head back to Avenell."

His youthful enthusiasm wilted only a moment before he was off with the young boys, wrestling them on the living room floor. Although my impatience grew, I did not want to arouse suspicion. Consequently, we adults, including Leah, lingered around the table with final glasses of iced tea or cups of coffee. The living room roughhousing had evolved into a checker game between Luke and Nathan with their brothers kibitzing.

"Oh, I talked with Peter this afternoon," said Leah. "I called him when I was in town this afternoon. He seemed surprised that you decided to stay — and a little jealous." She glanced slyly at her parents before continuing. "He said he would pick you up in the morning. Also, he said that Sheriff Claiborne had called the office looking for you and would try back tomorrow."

"Thank you, Leah," I said. It was just as well that my law enforcement friends were tied up with other business. As frustrating as it was to be out of direct communication with Sam and Dan, I feared they would try to talk me out of believing that I had heard the Tenleco Construction men correctly, or they would want to begin searching for them and bring them in for questioning. In either scenario, we would not know for sure whether the Brethren were indeed meeting in Yoder's livery tonight, which was something I intended to find out for myself.

The conversation turned to the upcoming auction at the old Kaufman farmstead, and I pretended to yawn. Sarah had visited there this afternoon along with other Amish women to preview items before the public descended Saturday morning. Benjamin suggested again that I attend, and I agreed that I would likely be there.

"Bring Miss Bea and your friend Miss Caroline," encouraged Leah. "It's a very festive time. I think you all will enjoy it."

"That's an excellent idea, Leah," I said. "Perhaps we will pack a picnic lunch and make a day of it."

I yawned again and began making my exit — but not before two games of checkers with ten-year-old Luke. He won both of them, and my defeat made for a good excuse to retire. Benjamin and Sarah both thanked me for staying and wished me a good-night. On the porch I asked Leah what time most of her family went to bed under the pretense that I might want another piece of cake before bedtime but not if it might wake up anyone. She said the little boys would be in bed by nine and the adults by ten or so, but to make myself at home.

"Oh, one other thing, Leah," I said, again trying to sound casual. "Do you have a flashlight I could borrow? Sometimes I have to get up during the night, and it's too much trouble to light a candle or lamp."

"Of course," she smiled. "I'll be right back." She returned in a matter of moments with a medium-sized Magnalite. Perfect. I thanked her, said good-night, and strolled into the cool evening, a thin veil of light blue clinging to the western horizon. A dog barked and Callie whinnied from the barn, perhaps at her strange surroundings.

Inside the Dawdi Haus, I lit the oil lamps and read for a few moments, but I was as fidgety as a toddler in a Sunday service. I set the alarm function on my watch for an hour later and tried to lie down. Just as I drifted off, the tiny siren pierced my unconsciousness and I awoke with a start. It was finally time.

Peering outside, I found only two lights illuminating windows of the farmhouse. Treading quietly toward the barn, I felt nervous but also excited, as if I were a boy sneaking out of my bunk in order to go spy on a neighboring camp. But as I considered the consequences that might result from my plan, a cool shiver dripped down my spine. I knew it was foolish not to tell anyone where I was going. At least I had left a note on the table in my room, explaining my whereabouts and reason for being there. This reassured me as I made my way into the darkened hall of the barn to saddle Callie and wait.

It was nearly ten o'clock when the last light dimmed to darkness in the far left window on the second floor of the Schroeder farmhouse. Then, flashlight in hand — but used only once — I carefully led Callie to the edge of the woods parallel to the road leading into town. The worn leather saddle barely creaked as I swung into it in a grove of shadowy poplars down from the house.

The ride into the village square was exhilarating. The damp, clean scent of horse flesh, the moist night air, the yeastlike smell of rich earth upturned by daytime plows all created a potent elixir for my mission. A spattering of stars broke cloud cover. No moon, one of the few things the Brethren and I could both appreciate this night. That, and the absence of streetlamps lining the walkways along the shop fronts.

Right after I passed the dozen or so shops that lined the village, I dismounted and tied Callie securely to a hitching post a safe distance from the livery. I crept along, building to building, before checking my watch. Ten-thirty.

The livery was silent. No signs of a meeting scheduled for the place in less than two hours. Nonetheless, I was all prepared to explain how I couldn't sleep and decided to return Callie tonight rather than wait until the morning. The front gate where the old man Yoder had stood and warned me was latched and secured with a dense Yale padlock. The small corral behind the livery was empty and therefore not bolted, however. I returned to Callie, unhitched her, and turned her into the white-fenced oval. She seemed pleasantly surprised and trotted toward the dregs of a broken hay bale and a trough of water.

Cutting through the corral, I went directly to the back of the horse barn and found a window that easily swung out from the building when I pulled. Crawling in was a bit more of a problem, but headfirst I descended into the dark shadows and animal smells of the place.

I couldn't even remember the last time I had performed a forward roll, but that's the way I landed on the carpet of straw and spilled oats below me. The window slammed shut as my feet crashed over the sill. Nearby horses whinnied nervously; a mule brayed further down the line of stalls. My eyes adjusted to the interior darkness, even murkier than the leaden-clouded night. Still no signs of anyone else in the building.

This was the end where the office was located, and, after brushing myself off and stretching my back, I crossed the barn floor and turned the office doorknob. Locked. I tried to peer in but didn't want to risk the flashlight yet. From what I could distinguish through the dusty pane above the waist of the door, nothing seemed out of the ordinary.

I backed away and leaned against an oversized buggy wheel. No chairs were set up out here. None of the tools or buggy parts had been cleared from the barn hall. No indications that a group of men were supposed to convene here shortly. I suddenly felt very foolish. What if the meeting had been canceled or the location moved to a more secure site? What if I had misunderstood all that I had overheard? No, I had to go with what I'd planned and trust that this was where I should be.

After several minutes of nervous pacing and exploration of the various rooms and stalls off the main hall, I found a short, narrow staircase between two grain bins. The loft of the place was half-full with bales of hay and alfalfa; the other half was a potpourri of bridles, reins, saddle fixtures, and horseshoes. Inspired from memories of my boyhood, I searched the planked floor and then stacked several heavy bales like building blocks, forming a small igloo of hay. I heard the front gate being unlocked just as I hoisted the last bale into place.

I climbed over the smaller wall of my natural fort and deposited myself. Within the floor space defended by the stacked hay bales, I had included a floorboard with a large vacant knothole, one that provided an oval frame of vision directly toward the center of the barn hall below. It wasn't ideal, but I hoped it would at least allow me to see and hear most of the proceedings.

It was eleven-thirty, according to my illumined watch face. My adrenaline flow spiked as I heard the heavy front gate creak open and bootsteps thud in and close the gate behind them. Leaning back on a bale of clover hay, I fumbled with my flashlight and positioned myself as comfortably as possible above my knothole. Now I could only hope that the Brethren stayed in the hall of the barn. Elongated shadows rimmed the passage below with light from a handheld Coleman lantern.

"— shouldn't joke about that, Brother. What if the Leader heard you talking like that?" It was possibly one of the voices from the day before, but I couldn't tell. They tied up their horses, then unlocked the office door.

"You're right, but I just don't see why we can't meet in the usual place. No one's ever come close to finding us there. . . ." The voice trailed off inside the small office. After several moments, the two men emerged with at least one, maybe two more lanterns.

". . . same reason we're not wearing hoods tonight. We've got to think about what we're doing, or else the entire mission's for nothing. Is that the Leader?" Someone entered with a flashlight from the front gate, again pulling it shut behind him. So far I had seen only the tops and backs of heads. No voices were familiar.

Sounds of metal knocking wood, the office door creaking, the low murmur of horses disoriented by the presence of human voices at this hour. "Do you want chairs? It's a short meeting tonight, I hope," said the second voice. It sounded vaguely familiar. Could it be Vandyke or Flannel Shirt from the bakery? Someone else grunted. More shuffling and scraping sounds, but I still couldn't see much, only the misshapen shadows cast from their lanterns hanging on nail posts. Camp chairs formed a semi-circle directly beneath me.

"I hate the hours but the money is good," said voice two again, clearly the more chatty of the pair.

"We'll see how good the money is if we get caught and jailed, wise guy," said another voice. I still did not have an accurate count of how many different voices I'd heard. Three? Four? These last two seemed to be the Rosencrantz and Guildenstern of the Brethren, good for setting up meetings but not for keeping their mouths closed.

"Will you two shut up? This matter with Hostetler is almost behind us. If all goes according to plan we'll have everything we need by Easter." His voice sounded low and authoritative, the last to enter, the Leader. Somehow it sounded familiar, and I strained to see at least a silhouette, but he remained just out of the knothole's frame.

I checked my watch but couldn't make out the hands in the small wormhole of light and didn't trust the light-up dial. How many others were coming? Were they plotting something to cover up Simon's murder or some new act of vandalism intended to scare the Amish into selling their land?

"Yes, sir, I know. You're right," said a low, friendly voice. Familiar? Again, something almost familiar about the tone and cadence. Suddenly, about half a dozen male voices created a polyphonic chorus of greetings and half-statements, much as I experienced once a month at Rotary Club or the Pastors of Avenell Council. A couple of first names floated up — Bob? John? — but most of the men below me seemed to be more careful than those first two with their careless remarks. Low chatter and rough laughter. Was this truly the ominous-sounding meeting of the Brethren that so much had been speculated about? How could these men have had anything to do with Simon's death and then meet with such conviviality? Unless they were so callus that a human life meant nothing to them.

Abrupt silence. They all took a seat. I could see the tops of two heads, the clean-shaven silhouette of another. Dark clothes, but no robes or cloaks. Then in half-whispers the men leaned in and listened, presumably, as the leader spoke. They reminded me of football players clustering 'round their quarterback, except here none of his words were distinguishable. An involuntary shudder rippled gooseflesh down me like lightning across the open plains.

An invisible hand squeezed my heart, resetting its crescendoing rhythm. I suddenly felt as if I had made a grave error in judgment about coming here alone. The note I'd left had assuaged the poor logic of my decision, but I had not allowed myself to consider that by the time the Schroeders or anyone found my note, I might be dead.

Finally, whispered fragments drifted upward like ash from a burning building:

"— new site —"

"— he was not pleased —"

"— get it right this time —"

I placed my ear to the knothole and focused more intently. "He is concerned about the cops' investigation, as most of you know —" Someone interrupted to ask a question I couldn't hear. Oh, how I prayed I could remember all this. "No, the priest poses no serious threat . . . curious more than anything." His voice became softer again, faint like a familiar record that loses volume at the favorite song, worn from playing over and over.

"— Omega may try to —"

The Omega Corporation, the company

Simon owned shares in. How was it tied up in all of this? Was Omega behind the Brethren, or were they perhaps allies? My fears had plateaued to a heightened awareness of my physical surroundings. The bristling caress of hay and straw against my cheek as I pressed my ear to the floor. The smell of mildewed grain, dried manure, and oiled leather. The sound of male voices bantering about a murder investigation as if it were a lodge picnic.

"— who carved the verse then?"

"— a little spooky —"

"— don't be silly —"

So they did not carve the verse on the Judas Tree after Simon's death? Who, then, indeed? The leader stopped abruptly and a murmur of voices rose like a plague of locusts. *Come on,* I thought. Who carved the reference to Deuteronomy on the Judas Tree after Simon's hanging?

I turned and suddenly my leg began to cramp. Of all the times! I rolled over onto my back and involuntarily stretched out my right leg, but in doing so, I heard a metallic thump. My flashlight! I grabbed it and stifled its sound, but it was too late.

The voices rose and suddenly booted footfalls spilled upstairs. In the handful of seconds that had elapsed since I dropped the flashlight, they had begun searching the building. The men fanned out and were opening stall doors, spooking horses left and right. While some voices remained low, several others quickly shifted into their emergency plan. I heard a cell phone being used and a desperate voice asking for someone — or something — I could not discern. The splintering flare of pain had subsided in my calf, but there was nowhere for me to run. Perhaps my hay fort was not such a good idea after all.

By this time another pair of heavy footsteps had joined the one now at the top of the stairs only a few feet away from my hiding place.

One voice shouted, "Where is he? You think someone was really here?"

"Shhh," cautioned the other, moving closer to my fort of hay bales.

I had not moved for several moments, my back strait-laced to the bales behind me. At that moment I wasn't nearly as concerned about my safety as I was about what I would say if discovered. But before I could even begin to formulate a plan about why I was hiding in the loft of Yoder's livery at nearly one o'clock in the morning, a pair of hands like vises pinched my shoulders, and the edges of the world darkened around me.

Chapter Twenty

Highly Classified

I awoke in a strange room with a strange face peering over me. My glasses were placed on my face then, and I recognized Sarah Schroeder's heart-shaped face hovering over me. She placed a cool compress on my forehead. Strands of morning light outlined a window over her shoulder. Leah came into focus then, and her father alongside her. A strange man with a chest-level beard dangling from his chin held my wrist and counted under his breath.

"What happened?" I asked.

"You tell us," instructed the stranger. "You took a nasty bump on the head."

I pulled my hand back from the edge of the bed and touched my temple. Pain shot like a flare from a gun, tracing an arc of electric anguish down to my neck and shoulder. Memories of the day before floated by slowly, delicately, as if in a dream. The walk into town. The cemetery and poor Caleb Hostetler — yes, Simon's father. Talking with Lydia Miller. The livery.

"*Oh,* the livery," I said out loud. I recalled the conversation I'd overheard in the bakery, borrowing Callie from Mr. Yoder, and my midnight rendezvous. The last thing I remembered was being discovered in the barn loft.

"Is that where you got that knot on your head, Brother Reed?" asked Benjamin. "At the livery?"

"We've been so worried," exclaimed Sarah, "ever since we found you."

"Where did you find me? In town?" I asked.

"Why, no," replied Leah. "You were lying on our front porch when Jacob and Nathan got up to do the milking this morning at five."

"I sent the boys after Doc Miller here to come over and check you out," said Benjamin. "I hope you don't mind."

"No, of course not," I said. "Ohh." For a moment the room spun around like a cheap carnival ride. My stomach lurched to keep up.

"Do you remember how you got this bump on your head, Brother Reed?" asked the doctor. "I'd say you have a mild concussion."

I thought for a moment. Should I tell the truth or only part of it? Was this doctor trustworthy? Deciding that there was nothing to be gained from withholding information, I rambled through my story. "The last thing I remember," I concluded, "was being discovered in the barn loft."

Leah let out a deep breath and Benjamin looked from Sarah to Doc Miller.

"You are most blessed that you are alive," said the patriarch. "I appreciate what you tried to do for us, and for your friend Hostetler, but you could have gotten yourself killed."

Later that evening Caroline and I sat on my patio, sipping decaf amaretto roast while I filled her in on my entire visit from beginning to end. Bea had tried to play nursemaid at the rectory. She was more concerned than I had seen her in some time. She even started to break her date with Lyle, but then Caroline called and wanted to come over and see me.

Peter had driven me back up the mountain and stopped at Doc Graham's to have him confirm what the Amish doctor had diagnosed. My old practitioner concurred and prescribed acetaminophen with codeine for the pain, and plenty of rest.

"And no more gallivanting around!" he threw in at the end. "When you gonna learn that you're not Peter's age anymore?"

Either his playfulness cheered me or my head was feeling better. I had managed to go into the office, more to assuage my guilt at feeling useless than to actually get much done. Janine saw the bandage at the corner of my crown and insisted that I go home and take care of myself. Joe Brewer, our parish sexton, came by and reinforced her opinion. Finally, I returned to the rectory and slept most of the afternoon.

Bea hovered as much as possible, making me cups of hot tea, propping my feet, fluffing my pillows, or changing the discs in the CD player. It was a relief to send her over to Rev. Slater's for a deacons' dinner party. In the evening Caroline brought over her wok and made a delicious stir-fry for us. She was just as concerned as everyone else but didn't scold me for the risk I took.

As we sat outside in a pair of beat-up lawn chairs after dinner, I realized how preoccupied I had become with Simon's death and the consequent current of events in Tremont. I didn't want Caroline to feel neglected, especially at what felt like a crucial juncture in our friendship.

"What are you thinking about?" she asked, sipping from a mug that had been Amy's.

I smiled and said, "You." I looked up at the darkness above us and wondered how much of my heart to share. "I'm afraid I've been neglecting our friendship. I've gotten so caught up in the aftermath of Simon's death and what's been happening with the Schroeders."

She smiled but dodged the first half of my response. "Does Sheriff Claiborne have any idea who killed Simon? Or do you? Did this traipsing around last night reveal any new leads?"

Was she avoiding my desire to direct the conversation to our relationship or just sharing my concerns about the events in Tremont? I didn't want to force anything, and besides, Caroline was a shrewd thinker. Perhaps I simply needed to discuss my many speculations with someone objectively removed from the case. Turning toward her, I spent the next few minutes outlining my suspicions about the various stakeholders involved in the peace-loving Amish community.

"So you think the military base could have some secret that Simon stumbled onto?" she asked. "But then there's also this Omega Group that's wanting to buy Amish property for a new site, and since Simon owned shares in Omega, you think he could have been trying to pressure the Amish into selling. So perhaps someone discovered his true motive — if indeed that's what it was — and killed him?" She paused for a moment. "Grif, could Simon have been behind the Brethren? Could he have been using the historical precedent from the turn of the century to pressure the Amish into selling? That would allow him to profit personally, but it would also allow him to enjoy some revenge for what they did to his father. You said yourself that you think Simon's father's affair all those years ago ties in somehow."

"So someone discovered Simon's secret and killed him as punishment? I assume you're implicating someone Amish." Her hypothesis articulated an embryonic solution that had formed in my own mind, as well. One that I could not fully embrace. "I can't believe that Simon would be capable of exacting such calculated revenge. And I can't believe that any of the Amish I've encountered could be capable of murder."

"People are not always who they seem to be," she added. "We learned that the hard way last fall."

"But this is different," I countered. "I have to admit, though, that it might explain some of the missing pieces."

"I read in the paper that there's going to

be a public auction down in Tremont this weekend. Is it connected to any of this business?" she asked.

I explained about the Kaufmans' connection to the Hostetlers and summarized what little I knew about the auction. "I'm glad you mentioned it because I was hoping you could accompany me. We could take a picnic and make a day of it."

"Are you asking me for a date, Father Reed?" she teased.

"Yes, ma'am, I am."

"I would love to. It sounds like fun," she replied. "It would be good to spend some time together. I feel like there's so much we need to catch up on."

"Yes. Caroline, I — I think we need to talk about us," I said bluntly. "Like I said, I feel bad that I've been so preoccupied with Simon and the Schroeders that I've been neglecting our friendship."

She regarded me thoughtfully, then leaned toward me and touched the bandage on my forehead. "I understand. He was your friend and you would like to feel like you've done all you can to make sense of his death, to make something right out of all this. It's your calling. . . ." Her pale skin and rich hair seemed to radiate a cumulative reflection of the stars' light.

"Perhaps I have other callings, as well," I added, turning over her words.

"Grif, I've been thinking about our friendship, about what I want to happen in the future. Seeing this bump on your head makes me afraid that we'll run out of time . . . that something will happen to take you away from me. I guess what I'm saying is that I'm serious about us, about where I see our relationship heading. I need to know if you feel the same way." Crickets punctuated the quiet, steady rhythm of her words. She gazed into my eyes, as if trying to gauge some reaction.

"Yes," I said. "I would like to think that we are moving toward a life together . . . yet that frightens me. But I'm more afraid of losing your friendship than of facing my other fears."

"What about all the things you still don't know about me? What will your parishioners think — people like Mrs. Dowinger? I like coming to your church, but I'm not exactly Ladies' Parish Auxiliary material. . . ."

The sincerity of her concern lined the soft notes of her voice. An evening breeze sent a slight chill across us, but I did not want to lose the moment.

"I look forward to learning all those things I don't know about you. I look forward to learning more about your faith and seeing how it evolves. I'm glad you like coming to our church, and it doesn't matter to me if you're never LPA material. What matters is that you remain honest about yourself . . . about us . . . about God."

"Just for the record, I am a believer, you know," she replied. "I'm not ready to debate theological stances on the book of Revelation, but I have discovered a great deal about what truly matters in the past few months. It all started last fall in the Martyr's Chapel. . . ."

"Shh," I whispered. And I leaned over and gently kissed her.

The moment was worlds away from where I'd been the night before, but I liked to believe that I was following my calling — as Caroline put it — in both cases.

I had spent most of Friday morning talking with Sam and Dan over western omelets at the Diner. Willadean was in rare form, eager to eavesdrop on our conversation, but I managed to fill in my friends on my day — and night — spent in Tremont. They were both upset that I would take such an unnecessary personal risk, let alone risk breaking the law by sneaking into the livery after hours. However, since I was going to be all right, the bump on my head already fading, they were definitely intrigued by what I'd heard. Sam quizzed me tenaciously, hoping for a clue that would lead him to the identity of any members of the Brethren.

"You didn't see any faces? Or hear any details that made you think of another place or profession? Could it have been a construction crew from Tenleco, like the men you saw in town that morning?" asked the sheriff.

"It's possible," I replied. "But there was nothing they said to identify them."

We sat there and I finished my last bite of green pepper and eggs. Dan sipped his coffee and said, "Well, we discovered something you may find interesting. Mariah Gates, your friend Simon's assistant, is not who she says she is."

"What?" I asked. "How do you know?"

"FBI records came up void on parts of the background check we ran on her," Sam explained. "Usually, that means someone has set up a false identity. So we did a little more digging and discovered that her name is really Myra Gaither, techno-environmentalist and president of the Omega Group, a watchdog organization that often works with the federal government to shut down violators." Sam watched my reaction.

"That's it!" I said. "I knew something wasn't right about her credentials. Dan, you mentioned to me before that she had an MBA. That's rather strange for a cultural anthropologist, but I didn't remember it until just now. So what does this mean? How is she involved with Simon? And how is he connected to Omega?"

"That's exactly what we're trying to find out," said Sam. "We're hoping to bring her in for further questioning today."

They both wished me well as I departed, and I did not mention my expedition to see the chaplain of the Dolby Air Force Base, my old friend Leland Finch. An hour later I was turning my old Buick off Highway 70, the one all us locals simply called the Dolby Road.

The small town of Dolby, Tennessee, thrived due to its proximity to the base. Although the same kinds of homegrown shops that we enjoyed in Avenell lined the downtown strip in Dolby, an air of military precision and efficiency emerged from the overall effect. Fresh paint, the clean lines of the old Romanesque buildings, sun skimming the sidewalks. Men and women in the steel-blue uniforms of Air Force officers mingled with mothers and toddlers in front of the town market, barbershop, café, and hardware store. A model small town.

As if in military formation, twenty-foot pines lined the double lanes leading to the checkpoint at the air base guardhouse. I flashed my driver's license (I'd worn my cleric's collar for reinforcement) at the stiff-faced guard, who checked his clipboard and then gave terse directions before motioning me through the gate. I saw him pick up a phone as the gate's arm lifted to allow passage. It seemed ironic that a place like Dolby, which practiced the antithesis of the Amish commitment to peace and simple living, seemed so similar in effect.

Just inside the gate, an old Seahawk fighter plane, newly painted, was forever grounded alongside a stone marker near a battalion of flagpoles. Old Glory saluted crisply in the late-morning breeze. A half-mile down the pine-lined corridor I passed the commissary, a laundromat, and several small brick buildings housing civilian contractors' offices, mostly computer technicians and construction engineers.

I took two right turns into a labyrinthine parking lot, and five minutes later I wandered into the building where Chaplain Finch's office was located. He was waiting at the door and seemed both anxious and relieved to see me. Dark creases shadowed the hollow spaces around his eyes.

"Griffin Reed, good to see you!" he exclaimed and pumped my hand. "Come on in."

"Lee, it's been too long. Good to see you, too," I said, following him inside the small office. Plaster walls were covered with memos and photographs of various planes and their pilots. A small cross was centered like a bull's-eye on the wall behind his desk.

"Let me grab my jacket, and we'll walk over to the cafeteria," he said. "Tell me how you're doing. What's been going on in that church of yours up on the mountain?"

As we followed one long corridor into the next, I tried to sum up the activities in my parish during the past year. I concluded by describing the present conflict in the Pastors of Avenell Community group over the upcoming ecumenical Easter service. Finch chuckled and nodded. It wasn't until we were outside marching across a training field to the cafeteria that I broached the subject of Simon Hostetler's death among the Amish.

"I've been rather shaken by this, Lee," I explained, "and I'd like to help his family make sense of it all."

"Grif, I'd like to help you," he said as we

entered the expansive building that housed the kitchen and cafeteria. "But I don't see how your friend's death has anything to do with the base." The clattering of trays and drone of many voices filled our ears. From the smells of onions, tomatoes, and spices, it had to be Mexican day.

Lee sounded sincere, but an urgency in his tone begged me not to proceed. I recounted what I knew of the relationship between Dolby and Tremont, including the forced buyout years ago and the impending one now. Holding nothing back, I included the mysterious acts of vandalism prior to Simon's death, the break-ins, the Omega Corporation, and the Brethren. We were in line by this time behind a column of officers in steel-blue uniforms. I kept my voice low.

"I wish I knew more about any of those things," Lee said, shaking his head. "But other than the land deal thirty years ago and hearing rumors about the base's desire to expand now, I know nothing about this business. I suggest you leave it to the local police."

Was it my imagination, or was Lee's closed attitude too conspicuous? It reminded me of his strange behavior during our brief phone conversation. We both chose the chicken burritos, a green salad, and gelatin. I tried to pay but the chaplain insisted. We found an empty table in a far corner of the cavernous room and unloaded our trays. I offered grace and chose my next question carefully.

"Lee, do you know anything about the base's involvement in my friend's death?" I asked.

A moment's hesitation, and then he broke into a wide grin. "Grif, you haven't changed a bit — always the direct approach with you. That's going to get you in trouble someday." He laughed and bit into the end of his burrito before responding. "I'm still not clear what leads you to believe that anybody here at Dolby would have anything to do with your friend's death."

"Well, the past tensions between the two, the fact that the Judas Tree borders both properties, and the fact that General Bledsoe tried to take over the investigation — not to mention the fact that the base has made it clear that it wants a thousand-acre parcel of land presently owned by the Amish. Don't you think those are interesting coincidences?"

A voice over my shoulder thundered, "Yes, I do. Mind if I join you, gentlemen?"

Leland immediately wiped his mouth, rose, and said, "General Bledsoe, sir!" I also stood while the stocky commanding officer dragged a nearby chair to our table. *Speaking of curious coincidences,* I thought to myself, *how often did the general eat in the cafeteria?* Bledsoe's timing was curious.

"At ease, chaplain! Who's your friend, another padre?" asked the general.

Leland introduced me and his commanding officer said, "You look familiar, Father Reed. Have we met before?"

"Not exactly," I explained. "I was with some friends at the Judas Tree when you and your lieutenant arrived at the crime scene."

"Oh yes," he said. "Mind if I smoke?" He produced a pack of cigarettes before either of us could object. A No Smoking sign on the wall behind him apparently applied to everyone but the general. He lit up and emptied the table's small square container of sugar packets to use as an ashtray.

"So how're you involved in this case, Padre?" asked the general. With his thick frame, General Bledsoe was older looking than he'd appeared in the woods that afternoon over a week ago, definitely at retirement age judging from the grooved wrinkles punctuating his forehead and the corners of his eyes. His balding head nonetheless sported a short military cut covering his crown and temples; he was deeply tanned and sported heavy jowls and large white teeth. He reminded me of the big, bad wolf in the story of the three little pigs. Used to huffing and puffing to get his way.

I replied by sharing my relationship to Simon and to the Schroeders, explaining that Leah had discovered the body.

"So you are not involved in any *official* capacity here?" he asked, swirls of smoke claiming the air space between us.

I glanced at Lee but he seemed quite content to let Bledsoe rule. I wondered if this had been a set-up. But why would Lee be involved in any of this? And yet, how would Bledsoe have known to show up here if my friend hadn't told him where we'd be? Unless it really was a coincidence after all.

"That's correct," I said. "I'm only trying to help out an old friend. And to do what I can to protect some new ones." My appetite had fled with the tendrils of smoke ascending from our table, and I pushed the plastic plate of cold, greasy food away from me.

"That's very kind of you, Father Reed," he said. "But for what it's worth, it sounds like you're getting outside your area of expertise." He spoke in fluid syllables that seemed to roll out the corner of his mouth, his accent full of gravel from a southern quarry, a smoker's voice. "Seems to me that you're trying to use your old friend Lee to prime the pump since I haven't had time to talk with your local sheriff about his investigation."

"No, Grif and I were just —" began Lee before I interrupted.

"Since you're here now, General Bledsoe, why don't you take this opportunity to set the record straight. Why were you so eager to take over the investigation of my friend's death when it wasn't even on military property?" I asked.

"Grif, this may not be the time to ask the general questions," said Lee.

I watched the general's eyes shimmer with contempt. A rainbow of coded bars and medals framed his left breast. "What makes you think your crime has anything to do with us?" he demanded in a low whisper.

I met his bravado before he could continue. "General, you didn't answer my question. What interest did you have in assuming the murder investigation of Simon Hostetler?" My words were as low and deliberate as his own, just as forceful as the pillar of smoke he continued to thrust my way.

"Did you ever consider," the general said,

leaning back, "that while you're playing detective some of us are protecting our country to make sure you have a place to play in? Did you ever consider, Father Reed, that matters of national security may be at stake? Any time a murder takes place two hundred yards from a federal military installation, I believe we must *assume* it has something to do with the highly classified operations conducted at that installation. Am I making myself clear?" He stubbed the unfiltered butt of his smoke into his makeshift ashtray.

"Your clarity is unwavering, General Bledsoe. That's why there are so many unanswered questions drawing me here in the first place. That's why the Department of Defense confiscated thousands of acres of Amish farmland thirty years ago."

He laughed. "Don't tell me you've taken up their old grudges."

"General Bledsoe, were you here when the DOD took the Amish land in the sixties?" I asked.

Leland Finch looked to his commander and then squirmed uncomfortably. "Grif, we really should be going."

"It's all right, Lee. It's public record. Yes, I was on the base at the time. And the DOD didn't just 'take' anybody's land. They paid the Amish good money for land they weren't using." His impatience grew as he shook another cigarette from his pack and lit up.

"Did you have any direct dealings with negotiating that purchase?" I asked.

"Classified information, Padre," he said smugly. "But off the record, yes, I did. And it's no secret — I don't like people who aren't willing to defend freedom. They hide behind their religion so they don't have to fight for their country. Personally, I've never had much use for people who use God to get what they want." His eyes and tone shifted the latter accusation to me. "If you'll excuse me, gentlemen . . ."

He started to rise, but before he stood I played my last card.

"Ever have any dealings with the Brethren?" I asked. He wavered only momentarily, with only a second's betrayal of recognition in his eyes. But it was enough.

"Can't say that I have. Another cult like the Amish?" He asked impatiently, trying to return to his curmudgeon's role.

"No, not exactly. Thank you for your time, General Bledsoe."

Drooping, bloodshot eyes regarded me carefully. "I like you, Reed. You've got spunk. So let me give you some advice.

Sometimes things are not what they appear to be. And, as I said, a lot of information is highly classified — even from other government departments — for our country's best interests. My suggestion to you and your police friends is to leave Dolby out of your investigation. Leave the detective work to the professionals and get back to tending your precious flock of academics at Avenell up on the mountain."

"And if Dolby is not left out of the investigation?" I asked.

General Bledsoe laughed so hard I thought he might burst the seams of his tailored uniform. His heavy frame shook as he reached to deposit his second tobacco stub between us.

"Why, then you'll regret the day you ever laid eyes on the Judas Tree."

Chapter Twenty-one

The Highest Bidder

Saturday morning as Caroline, Bea, and I drove the familiar route down to Tremont, General Bledsoe's words continued to reverberate inside me. He had communicated his message loud and clear — he certainly seemed to have cowed Lee — but I still couldn't imagine why he was so defensive and intimidating. Were his ominous words a threat or a warning? The product of his authoritarian personality? Or was Simon's death really connected to a "highly classified" project at the Air Force base?

The questions and tangled skein of conflicted interest only continued to become more and more knotted together. I knew there was something that I was not seeing in the picture of clues connected to my friend's death. Between a Presidential Search Committee meeting and dinner with Caroline at the Tiger Bay Pub, I had spent the rest of Friday afternoon and evening ruminating on the odd variety of suspects and suspicions. Were those words derived from the

Latin *suspectare* or *suspicere?* I wondered. In either case, they shared similar denotations: to view from beneath. And that was definitely how I felt I was viewing Simon's murder and all the turmoil in Tremont.

However, the spring day now before us on Saturday morning heralded nothing but the prospect of recreative pleasure. Caroline and Bea had collaborated and packed a picnic lunch to feed the five thousand if the size of the hamper was any indication.

We were just negotiating the last curves of the mountain road when Caroline asked, "Now, why did you say Lyle couldn't make it today?"

"He had a lot of paper work to catch up on at the church," Bea responded. "Plus, he said he had a surprise for me later this evening."

"Did you tell him these auctions are special events? It's not every day that the public gets a chance to intermingle with the Amish like this."

"Actually, no, I only asked him if he wanted to double date with you two," said Bea, thoughtfully. "I should have stressed what an opportunity this is. I have to admit, he's seemed a bit preoccupied this week."

"Perhaps he's in love," I teased.

"Oh, Grif, please," she said. "Don't get

started. It's enough that I have to listen to wisecracks from Peter and half the Ladies' Auxiliary about my friendship with Lyle."

"Bea, if I may be so bold," said Caroline, turning toward my sister in the backseat of the big Buick sedan, "would you marry him if he asked?"

In the rearview mirror, I saw my sister purse her lips and smile. "That's a very good question, Caroline," she replied. "A month ago, I would have said yes without a doubt. Now, however, I'm not so sure he's ever going to ask."

"Why do you say that?" I asked.

"Just a feeling," she said, her voice turning sober. "I'm not so sure that God's not calling me to something else."

I cast my eyes on hers via the mirror again. I had not seen my sister so serious about her future in some time. Perhaps thinking about Rev. Slater had forced her to think through the next season of her life. Honestly, I suppose I thought we would continue sharing the rectory unless one of us were to marry.

"What might that something else be, sis?" I asked.

"Lately I've missed China," she said quietly.

"What?" I barely braked in time for a red light.

"You were a missionary there for many years, weren't you?" asked Caroline.

Bea nodded. "Please don't mention this to Lyle. I'm open to seeing where the Lord takes our relationship, but I'm also aware that some days my heart aches to teach and disciple others again."

The three of us retreated into a comfortable silence. Sunlight danced off the storefronts of the Mumford town square as we followed the state highway to the turnoff for Tremont. It was not quite nine o'clock and yet the county seat bustled with activity. Overalled farmers swapped stories on the steps of the courthouse, fathers led sons to the barbershop, and women shopped for necessities at the drugstore. We soon joined a caravan of pickups and station wagons packing the county back roads toward the Amish community and the farm auction.

Caroline and Bea clearly had their minds set on bidding. Both had visited our local bank's automatic teller machine on our way down the mountain. Caroline had mentioned her desire for an Amish quilt, and I considered the idea of showing her the one that Miss Mary had made from Amy's pattern. Yet the timing seemed off, and something in me held back.

By half past nine, when we turned up

Green Creek Road, an old whitewashed clapboard farmhouse, very similar to the Schroeders' but more dilapidated, sat framed by rows of buggies. Lining the gravel drive and the shady yard alongside it, they actualized what I imagined an Amish traffic jam to be like. In the yard between the house and the barn an auctioneer's tent had been staked, providing relief from unexpected spring showers or the intense heat of our clear, sunny day. Although the auction did not officially begin until ten, I recalled Sarah Schroeder explaining that such an event was more social occasion than business for most Amish families. She also mentioned that some native Tremonters were annoyed that it was opened to the public and wanted to come early before the English bidders arrived. Several dozen sedans, pickups, and sport utility vehicles were already parked in the field across from the house.

As we left the Buick in a similar spot of pasture, I marveled at the carnival-like atmosphere. Already older children had set up makeshift ball fields while their younger siblings played hide-and-seek among tractor tires and plow handles. The variegated red-and-white tent thronged with dark-clothed Amish locals talking, sharing breakfast, drinking coffee, laughing, and examining and discussing prospective items. Dozens of English people like us already mingled among them, immodest in their denim shorts and T-shirts.

As we approached the opening of the tent, one couple looked like what I imagined to be affluent antique dealers. He wore a crisp white buttoned-down shirt and starched khaki trousers, his black-and-gold enameled pen poised over a pocket notebook. He looked down through tortoise-rimmed bifocals, considering a smooth, salt-glazed pitcher his partner held. From behind dark, oval sunglasses, she passionately appreciated the workmanship behind it, either for its aesthetic beauty or the profit it might fetch. Her blond hair was pulled back in a sleek bun, and she wore a mint green skirt and sleeveless blouse.

Upon closer inspection, several other couples shared similar wardrobes and attitudes. A tall, burly man in polo shirt and navy blazer barked into a cell phone as Caroline, Bea, and I eagerly lined up behind a man in overalls to register for a bidder's number.

I smelled fresh cinnamon rolls and noticed a concession stand set up to the right of the auctioneer's tent. Young adults staffed the row of card tables where people stood munching everything from fresh fruit to candy bars. Sandwiches and soft drinks were available and the popcorn and hot dog machines were already running.

The auctioneer's line moved fairly quickly — it was nearing ten o'clock — as I stepped up to the long table where an older woman with chestnut-colored hair waved an enormous diamond-ringed finger my way.

"Please fill this out. You'll be number 237 today," she clipped.

I took the form from her peach-colored nails and jotted down my name, address, phone, and the all-important credit card number. "Thank you and happy bidding," she replied mechanically as I returned the form to her.

My placard read *Lomas Auction Co. Bidder No.* at the top with *237* cast in red numerals six inches high beneath it. While Bea and I decided to share our number, Caroline was number 238.

"Yoo-hoo, Griffin! Beatrice! There you are! I knew I'd find you here!" rang a familiar voice. Joan Dowinger's figure swam through a sea of dark, suspendered shirts and pressed blouses. She motioned us over toward a tent pole, out of the main thoroughfare of traffic from the auctioneer's sign-up table.

My sister whispered, "I thought I saw a white Cadillac taking up half the cornfield. Should've known that if there's something to be purchased, Joan will have her fat checkbook out."

"Easy, Bea," I said. "You know Joan's not my favorite parishioner either, but let's not be unkind."

Caroline giggled and leaned into me as we moved along the crowded floor of the auction tent. She looked radiantly chic in a dark blue, short-sleeved dress and a straw hat.

"Oh, look! Is that Peter?" she asked. I followed her pale finger across several rows of heads. It was indeed my curate, alongside half the Schroeder family. I assumed he would be here, but when he didn't return my calls about riding down with us, I suspected he might be coming down early and using the grandparents' house that we had shared earlier in the week. His front cowlick made his golden hair look like disheveled hay from this distance. I called out, but he did not hear me.

Joan Dowinger collided breathlessly into us next to a striped tent pole. The heavyset matron wore a powder blue skirt, blouse, and jacket bound by a blue topaz pendant that had to have been at least five carats.

"This is practically an Avenell parish pot-luck! I just ran into Dwight and Missy Taylor. Look, there they are." Joan pointed out one of our deacons holding up a kerosene lamp for his wife's inspection. We all waved.

"Joan!" I exclaimed, giving her a polite two-handed clasp. "I didn't know you enjoyed auctions."

"Oh heavens, yes," said the wealthy widow. "I love excellence in any form."

"Mrs. Dowinger, how nice to see you," said Caroline, her eyes gleaming mischievously.

"Hello, Joan," said my sister. "I hope you're not here to spike the bidding."

Joan giggled. "Of course not. I'll only bid on those items that I simply must have. I just saw your good Reverend Slater over at the bidder's table. Perhaps he'll bid on something for you!"

"Lyle? Here?" asked Bea. "But I —"

"Well, I just assumed you were together," continued Joan. "He didn't mention you, but I — oh well, anyway, enjoy the auction. I'm off to look for a friend down from Nashville. I'll introduce you all later." It was clear by her tone that we would indeed meet her friend.

"I wonder why Lyle told me he had paper

work to catch up on if he intended to come here?" asked Bea as soon as Joan was out of earshot. "He could simply have declined my invitation without fabricating an excuse."

"Didn't you say that he was planning a surprise for you?" asked Caroline. "Maybe he's here to buy something special for you."

"I suppose it's possible," said my sister.

I reserved comment and it was fortunate that I did, for the silver-haired preacher had made his way behind us to clasp his hands over Beatrice's eyes.

"I can't believe you're here," he said.

"I can't believe *you're* here," returned my sister as she removed his hands and turned to face him. "Joan Dowinger was just telling us that she saw you."

"Oh, Bea, I was hoping to surprise you. I wanted to find something special here for you . . . for our anniversary. We're coming up on three months, you know."

My sister blushed as I turned and rolled my eyes at Caroline. She smiled as Lyle moved on to greet us both. "Griffin, Caroline, how nice. I had no idea when Bea invited me for a double date that this was your destination."

"I'm sure you didn't," I replied. "Have you been to many auctions, Lyle?"

"Oh, a few," he said, smoothing a tuft of

white hair alongside his temple. He was impeccably dressed in tan trousers and a long-sleeved knit pullover sporting a designer logo over his heart. "But I had heard your sister say that she loved Amish crafts, so I thought this would be the perfect place to find something special for her." His gaze danced across my sister's broad face and the two exchanged syrupy grins.

"Well, this way you can't go wrong," said Caroline. "She'll be here to help you pick it out."

"I'll make sure she gets anything her little heart desires," said Reverend Slater.

Bea's cheeks fused even pinker and she whispered, "Oh, Lyle."

Oh, please, I thought to myself. Was there anything more unbecoming than sixty-somethings acting like teenagers? I would never have guessed that Bea had any misgivings about their relationship by the way they carried on in public.

"Attention!" A public address system crackled and we all jumped. "Good morning, ladies and gentlemen. The farm tools and implements will be the first to be auctioned off. Bidding will take place in the barn at ten o'clock sharp. Housewares, furniture, and everything else under the tent will go on the block in one half-hour. Thank you and happy bidding."

"Well, we don't have long to decide what we want to bid on," said Lyle to my sister. "Let's go look at the pottery. We'll catch up with the rest of you later. Maybe at lunch?" He didn't wait for a reply but merely guided my sister toward a set of china.

Caroline twined her hand into the crook of my arm and we strolled along the edges of the tent, stopping occasionally to pick up a bowl or tablecloth.

"Don't you think it's strange that Lyle was here without Bea?" I asked. "They've almost been inseparable these past few weeks."

"Perhaps he really did want to surprise her. People who care for one another do that, you know." She smiled an expression of implied contentment. I felt myself reluctant to fully enjoy her presence, and I couldn't explain it. Was I afraid of missing some significant detail that might aid in solving Simon's murder? Or was I, once again, afraid of growing close to her? Several times I found myself recalling that moment under the stars two nights ago when we had first kissed.

"Grif, there's something I want to propose to you," she began. "Something that relates to our conversation these past couple of nights. There's something I want you —"

The loudspeaker interrupted and drowned her words in a sea of booming syllables. I stopped and looked into her lovely sapphire eyes. Surely, she wasn't going to ask me — no, I couldn't even allow such a thought.

"I'm sorry. I couldn't hear you," I said.

"Yes. Maybe now is not the best time to talk about it."

A boy dressed in brown pants, white shirt, and straw hat ran past and jostled her arm. "Sorry, ma'am!" He called out over his shoulder.

"This is not exactly the best place for a private conversation," she continued. "Maybe when we have lunch — or perhaps dinner tonight?"

"Yes, that would be lovely," I said, hoping to escape the immediacy of my fear.

The loudspeaker hummed static again and then wailed high-pitched feedback before a man's voice came on and said, "Please take your seats, folks. Bidding will begin in fifteen minutes here under the big top. That's right, fifteen minutes."

Caroline lingered to hold up matching doilies from a wooden crate of crocheted and tatted pieces. The crowd now seemed about half Amish and half English, judging by those in our immediate vicinity. I was just about to motion for Caroline to join me in finding seats up front near the auctioneer's podium, when an old Amish woman leaned toward me.

"Excuse me, sir," she said politely. "But would you ask your daughter to hand me that white pitcher over there? The one on her right. Yes, thank you."

Caroline responded before I had a chance to ask. I was simply too stunned anyway. Caroline, my daughter? Did we look that mismatched? Did I look that old? Certainly she looked youthful and beautiful, her auburn hair shimmering in the light. The pale but not pallid complexion. Blue eyes like crystal lakes. Thin lips and sharp nose. Beautiful.

She picked up on my quiet inventory of her features. "Grif, she's an old woman. She probably couldn't even see you! There's no way anyone would ever mistake you for my father. Come on, let's sit up front."

She led me toward the front of the tent where the couple hundred folding chairs were quickly filling. I thought we would have to move toward the back when I spotted a pair of empty seats next to an Amish family.

I still had not gotten to speak with the

Schroeders or any of my other Amish acquaintances. And as much as I hated to admit it, most of the Plain folk looked alike under the crowded conditions within the tent — beards on the men, white kapps on the women, lots of children. Voices chattered, babies laughed and cried, dollar amounts bandied about as prospective bidders discussed what they'd give for their favorite antiques. In my cursory examination of items with Caroline, I had not seen any that particularly appealed to me. Nonetheless, there was a kind of thrill simply being here.

The place was already humid and flies buzzed around the crusts of sandwiches and discarded sodas at patrons' feet. The auctioneer, a stout figure with a large overhanging belly, made his way to the microphone at the podium. He was dressed in a short-sleeved blue shirt and black pants, and I couldn't decide if he was Amish or not. He began the patter that made us all smile at his fluency with language. "Now, who's gonna get us started this fine spring day? Who's gonna bid on this beautiful old chest of drawers right here on my left? Let's start the bidding at one hundred dollars. Do I hear? Thank you, ma'am. I've got one, do I hear one-twenty-five. Thank you, yessir, in the back. Do I hear one-fifty?"

After the first dozen items or so, the novelty of his skill wore off and became more tedious, something to be endured as part of the experience. Caroline had only bid once, on a maple nightstand that went for $110. "Too high," she said. "You can tell this is one of the first auctions of the season. Too many dealers here jacking up prices."

"I didn't know you were such an expert on antiques and auctions," I said.

She smiled knowingly and replied, "There are a lot of things you don't know about me yet."

I returned her smile and resisted the impulse to kiss her, surprising myself since I rarely showed affection publicly even when Amy was alive. Maybe I had changed.

Paying attention was getting harder and harder. I looked around and found my sister and her mysterious boyfriend — dare I even call him that? — sitting about ten rows behind to my right. I waved to Benjamin and Sarah, who sat even closer to the front than we did, and Peter and Leah to the right of them.

Item after item passed through the hands of the auctioneer and his assistants: crockery, kitchen utensils, canning jars, pots and pans, a handmade crib, faded quilts, oil lamps, milk pails, and wooden pull toys. When a three-legged maple stool came on the block, Caroline waved her numbered placard several times before winning the bid at forty-five dollars.

It was getting close to lunchtime when the auctioneer announced he'd be taking a thirty minute break at noon. I looked forward to the opportunity to get outside again on such a gorgeous day, to spread out the old wool army blanket beneath the shady embrace of a tree and unpack the sandwiches, fruit, and goodies from the wicker basket. Since we had left so early, my stomach rumbled at the thought of it.

"Shall I go to the car and retrieve our lunch? Maybe I'll beat the crowd."

Caroline nodded.

"Why don't you look for Bea and Lyle and the three of you grab a shady spot?" I suggested. "I'll find you."

Caroline nodded again, and I climbed over legs, shoes, and boots until I reached the left aisle and headed to the rear of the tent. Several large pieces that had already sold stood awaiting new owners. Small groups of individuals, mostly Amish farmers, stood talking among themselves. An elderly gentleman in a nylon warm-up suit, likely another dealer down from Nashville, scribbled on a pad.

Outside, a throng of people milled around the back and side yards, many with small purchases in hand. Several women held a quilt by its corners, admiring the beautiful workmanship that went into it. A few families obviously shared my hunger and were beginning to spread blankets and open baskets. Others munched on hot dogs or slurped soda from paper cups. The auctioneer's voice boomed across the grounds, feigning enthusiasm for a butter churn that was only up to fifteen dollars.

I walked briskly across the yard and toward the pasture that had been converted into a temporary parking lot. Finding my old sedan proved more difficult than I anticipated, due to the numerous uneven rows of "gas-powered buggies," as I'd overheard one Amishman refer to automobiles. The midday sun blazed overhead like a solemn flare. As I retrieved our picnic basket, small cooler, and blanket, I thought about how I could lead our lunch discussion back to Lyle Slater's relationship to Simon.

Soon I was traipsing back toward the large tent and its extended tentacles of people milling about. I didn't see the rest of my company among them yet, and as I listened carefully, the auctioneer was just about to put the last item on the block before the lunch break.

"Yessir, amuse your kids, amuse your friends, with this genuine, hand-carved, bird's-eye maple Amish puzzle box. It opens just like — just like . . ." and he fumbled with the end for a moment while snickers broke out across the restless crowd. He finally gave up and joined his audience in laughing at his attempt.

I hurried closer and heard him say, "Well, folks, I don't know how it opens. But I bet some smart bidder out there knows." The auctioneer shifted tones from the jovial conversationalist to the patter-spewing gavel rapper. "So what say we start the bidding at five dollars? Do I hear five? Who will give five greenbacks for hours of pleasure? Thank you, ma'am. We have five. Do I hear ten? Ten dollars for the perfect souvenir of your visit to the Amish countryside. Yessir, thank you, sir. We've got ten, do I hear fifteen? Yes, ma'am, I see your hand, thank you."

"Twenty," a familiar voice shouted.

I dropped our lunch spread in the nearest clearing and raced into the tent. Where was my bidder's number? I'd left it with Caroline. Fumbling and climbing through the throng of people, most swimming against me as they departed for lunch, I found my row and scrambled past knees and elbows.

"Grif? What's wrong?" asked Caroline.

"That puzzle box! What does it look like?" I grabbed my numbered placard and sat in the folding chair. A quick glance at the item in the burly auctioneer's hand confirmed my instinctive response. "Yes! That's our puzzle box — the one that Lydia Miller gave me from Simon! We have to bid on it!" My whisper rose to a normal tone amid the growing din of a weary crowd eager for lunch.

"We'll get it then!" Caroline responded, sharing my urgency. Meanwhile, the bid was now up to twenty-five dollars and momentum was building. A woman we could not see offered thirty, but her bid was quickly topped by an older gentleman, the well-tailored dealer I'd noticed before with the cell phone. Who else was bidding, I couldn't tell.

"Can you stop the bidding?" Caroline whispered. "Tell them that it's stolen?"

"But what if I'm wrong? What if it's not ours after all? I'm going to bid." I raised my placard and nodded at the loose-lipped man at the podium.

The bid was now at forty dollars and even the auctioneer was startled. Whispered voices began to murmur and rise. Seizing the momentum and the energy of the crowd, the auctioneer jumped the bid to fifty. I glanced over to my left side, straining to see Benjamin and Sarah Schroeder, who, once I finally spotted them, seemed to be working equally hard to catch my eye. They nodded vigorously and I held up my number again.

I had now identified four bidders: the woman we couldn't see, the older man who appeared to be a dealer, myself — and Lyle Slater.

"I've got sixty — who'll go seventy on this beautiful, mysterious antique puzzle box? It's a gem, folks. What a conversation piece it will be! Do I hear seventy?"

It had gone from a child's toy to a mysterious antique all in the space of half a dozen bids. The woman blocked by a handful of heads suddenly emerged from behind them. A striking blonde motioned her bidder's number like a fan. It was Mariah Gates! Or whatever her real name was. Somehow her presence did not surprise me. Had she bid on other items while I had run to the car for lunch? Or had she come today to bid on this one item? But how could she have known that the stolen puzzle box would turn up here? There was no time to consider those questions now.

"I've got seventy. Do I hear eighty? C'mon now, let's do it right. I've got eighty. Do I hear ninety?" In his staccato monologue, the poet of a salesman pumped more adrenaline into the escalating sale, quickly making it appear the most sought after item of the entire morning.

Lyle Slater motioned and I heard Bea squeal. "Thank you, sir," the auctioneer responded. "I've got ninety. Do I hear one hundred dollars? Who knows what might be inside? Let's take this to the next level now, ladies and gentlemen. Who will bid one hundred dollars for this beautiful, captivating puzzle box?"

"Two hundred dollars!" I shouted, jumping the bid beyond anyone's imagination.

"Grif!" Caroline whispered, as if I'd lost my senses.

Hushed awe spread through the crowd like ink in water. Whispers of admiration mixed with those of astonishment at my folly. My plan was to use one of Amy's tricks — to shock the crowd so much that no one else could continue the bidding. She would decide how much she'd spend on an item and then if the bidding seemed to be clipping along, she'd dramatically stand and announce her top dollar bid.

The gasps melted into hushed murmurs as everyone quieted to see what would happen next. I wondered if anyone besides the bidders knew the true reason behind this round of auction fever. Looking around with the other craning necks, I attempted to size up whether my ploy would work. Bea shook her head toward me as if to ask, "What gives?" Certainly she recognized this as my potential artifact as well, didn't she? Couldn't she call Lyle off? They had no idea what they were doing by escalating the bid.

Then it hit me. Was Slater simply trying to impress my sister, or did he know something of the puzzle box's true value?

After my two hundred dollar bid sank in, the other bidders were clearly shaken. Slater dropped his jaw and then shook his head. By the look on her face, Ms. Gates was contemplating how much higher she would go. Then she, too, shook her head. The old antique dealer was on his cell phone again, obviously consulting the buyer he represented. Lyle Slater seemed peeved that I had jumped the bid so high. He whispered something in my sister's ear. The auctioneer tried to give the dealer time to complete his call, but finally he proceeded to finalize my bid.

"Folks, who woulda thought it? This gorgeous, hand-carved puzzle box — who knows what secrets are locked away inside it? Surely this gentleman knows! It's a beautiful piece, let's take it to the next level. Do I hear two-fifty?"

No one moved. I held my breath and Caroline squeezed my arm. "Two hundred going once, going twice . . . SOLD! Item #938–4A, Amish puzzle box, sold for two hundred dollars to bidder number 237!"

The auctioneer rubbed his protruding belly as if he'd just enjoyed a large meal. "Next item!"

Chapter Twenty-two

Dust of the Earth

During our picnic lunch — turkey sandwiches, apple salad, and brownies — shared like the loaves and fishes among my sister, Lyle Slater, Caroline, and me, I passed the wooden puzzle box around the circle. I had waited in line at the purchase table for half an hour while everyone gathered outside. I was afraid someone might steal the puzzle box if I let it out of my sight, and no one seemed to question my urgency to hold the prized possession in hand.

Rev. Slater held the puzzle box gingerly, with Bea leaning on his shoulder to admire it. His smile seemed patronizing. "Honestly, Grif. Paying that kind of money for a child's toy! If it was stolen from you, why didn't you just stop the auction?"

Annoyed at the tone of his voice, I said, "I wasn't certain until just now when I picked it up. But it is the box that Simon's sister gave to me. I recognize the pattern of the wood on top and that little scratch mark. I couldn't risk going through the proper channels to try to stop the auction."

Just then the Schroeders, along with Peter and Leah, joined us and spread out their own quilt and picnic lunch. Benjamin asked me three times if I was crazy to pay such money for a little block of wood. The puzzle box was passed around once again, and I asked the Schroeders to try and open it.

"It is not a design I am familiar with," concluded Benjamin when the wooden rectangle would not yield to him. Sarah and Leah had no luck either.

"Do you have any idea how it might have turned up here?" asked Peter. "Why would someone go to the trouble of stealing the box from the church office up at the Divine and then put it up for auction down here?"

"That's a question I intend to pursue as soon as lunch is over," I replied.

"Did you recognize any of the other bidders?" asked Leah. "Besides Rev. Slater, of course."

"The blond woman in the pastel dress was Hostetler's research assistant. I'm guessing she knows something about what Simon put inside this box. The other bidder — the old man with the cell phone — was obviously someone's proxy. But I wonder whose?"

My question lingered in the air as we turned our attention to lunch on this beautiful early spring day. Around us, a checkerboard of Amish and English families were similarly engaged in socializing and eating. Children scampered across the wide yards, laughing and chasing, ducking through the auction tent only to emerge from the other side.

In the barn behind the auction tent, most of the farm tools and implements had been sold. Several buggy wheels remained along with two sideboards. A couple of dozen Amish men stood in the shade, looking pleased with their purchases. The field behind the barn had not been plowed, but it had been mowed and children and young teens swarmed around it, caught up in at least two or three different games. The older teens had claimed the northwest corner of the field and were using what appeared to be parts of an old milk crate to form an impromptu baseball diamond.

I was finishing the last bite of my sandwich when I realized that I might find the one person who could solve the puzzle box on the playing field. Around me, Lyle and Bea chatted about their options for dinner and a movie that night, Caroline was engaged with Sarah concerning quilt patterns, and Peter and Leah whispered back and forth. Benjamin Schroeder caught my eye and nodded toward the young couple approvingly. I smiled back at him before palming the puzzle box and excusing myself.

"Hey, wait up!" called Peter. "Where you headed? Mind if I join you?"

I turned to find my curate jogging to catch me as I headed behind the red-and-white auction tent. He caught up to me and said, "Can I talk to you for a minute?"

"Of course. I was just heading out to look for someone. You're welcome to join me. What's on your mind?" I asked, sensing the tension in his clenched jawline.

"I need to tell you something, Grif," Peter began as we strolled toward the barn and my destination of the playing fields beyond. "I received a call from Bishop Wilder yesterday. He asked if I wanted the rector's post at St. Anthony's."

"That's wonderful! Congratulations, Peter. I'm very proud of you. You'll make a wonderful rector." I stopped to face him and shake his hand.

He held my hand and said, "I haven't accepted it yet. Bishop Wilder gave me one week to make my decision. He stressed that I should pray without ceasing and talk it over with those closest to me. I told Leah last night. She wouldn't come right out and say it, but I know she wasn't exactly thrilled." He swallowed as we rounded the corner of the barn. "After supper last night, Mr. Schroeder asked me if I'd like to live in the Dawdi Haus this summer and take catechism to join the Amish church. He said Leah and I could be married in the fall then, after harvest."

I stopped beneath a poplar tree and leaned into its web of branches. "What did you tell him?" I asked, suddenly feeling like I had neglected one of my dearest friends during my preoccupation with Simon's murder.

"I thanked him and told him I needed some time to think about it. When I told Leah about her father's invitation, she was really excited. Evidently, it's pretty rare for an outsider to be invited into the community. Now I have two hard choices to make."

I had never heard him sound so despondent before. "Is Leah willing to join you at St. Anthony's if you don't join her in Tremont?" I asked, afraid of the answer.

"She's not sure yet," Peter said. "And if that's the choice I make, I'm not sure I want her to come with me. It would be too selfish of me to tear her away from her family and the only way of life she knows. I don't know what to do."

"Pray and then follow your heart," I said tenderly. "It will be all right."

"And if it's not?" Peter asked.

"Then trust God to redeem your choice anyway," I replied.

"Please pray that I'll know what to do," he replied.

"I will. Let me start now." I placed my hand on his shoulder as we stood beneath the poplar with a warm breeze blowing on our faces. Silent prayers ascended before I could find words to speak aloud my concerns and hopes for Peter as he now faced one of the most important choices of his young life. We concluded with a shared "amen," and he thanked me, his eyes moist with unshed tears.

We stood there for a moment watching the people, many reconvening in the striped auction tent. "Who are you looking for?" he asked.

"Adam Kaufman — or his sister," I replied. "I thought I saw him out here on the baseball field with the young people."

We strode toward the mown field and the chatter of older boys assuming outfield positions.

"Swing!" shouted a brown-haired boy adjusting his straw hat. "You can do it, come on!"

Adam Kaufman, although at least a decade older than anyone else on the field, was enjoying himself as much as Babe Ruth at bat. The man-boy swatted the baseball with the hand-carved broom handle he gripped and watched it pop up to a short kid who caught it barehanded behind second base.

"You'll knock it outa here next time, Adam!" one of the kids called while another batter took his place. Adam walked over to the sidelines toward us.

"Adam? Hi. That was a nice fly you hit there," I said, walking closer.

"Yeah? It woulda been nicer if Josh hadn't caught it!" he said, grinning.

"Maybe next time you'll hit it over his head," I replied. "My name's Grif. I met your sister when you came up to our church for Simon Hostetler's funeral. You and I didn't get a chance to meet, but Deborah pointed you out to me."

"Yeah. I'm Adam John Kaufman. This is where I live — well, where I used to live. My papa died, so Sister and I are moving in with Jonah. Simon Hostetler hung by a rope around his neck."

"Did you know Mr. Hostetler?" I asked.

"Yeah. I helped him sometimes with his collection. He paid me a quarter for every sample I brought him." He adjusted his hat and scrutinized Peter, who stuck out his hand and introduced himself. "Then Brother found out and made me stop. He didn't like Simon Hostetler none. Brother said he's a son of the devil."

"What kind of samples, Adam? What did you help Mr. Hostetler collect?" I asked, excitement rising in my voice.

"Adam, you get over here right now!" a husky voice interrupted. From the similar physical features — a more mature, refined version of Adam's broad face — and tone of voice, I guessed I was about to meet older brother Jonah.

He was taller than Adam, broad shouldered and strong from working his own fields. Probably in his late forties, his wavy hair only showed a few flecks of silver among the rich brown crests, making him appear younger. His beard contained little gray, but its length extended several inches below his chin.

"Adam! You know better than to talk to strangers. Get on up to the house now! Sister's prepared your lunch."

The gentle man-boy gaited off toward the barn, turning to wave to me from behind the auction tent. I waved back, then extended my hand to the older brother. "You must be Jonah," I started. "I'm —"

"I know who you are," he snarled. "You're the fancy preacher from up at Avenell who's helping the sheriff look for someone who doesn't exist. I saw you at the elders meeting that night after Benjamin's Leah found the body of that demon-seed, Hostetler."

"What do you mean 'look for someone who doesn't exist'?" I challenged him. "Does that mean that Simon Hostetler's murderer has already left Tremont? Do you know who killed him? You know, it's one thing for you to harbor your bitterness and anger toward Simon for what happened between his father and your mother, but it's another thing to poison your younger brother."

"Look, you have no right to tell me how to handle Adam. He may be a child in the head, but he needs to know who his enemies are."

"And Simon Hostetler was his enemy?" I asked.

"As much as Satan is mine," he countered. "Look, I don't know who wrapped that rope around Hostetler's neck and tied him to the tree, but I think it's clear that God punishes unrighteousness."

"Then I pray He's merciful to me and you."

Caroline and Bea were packing up the

picnic leftovers and Lyle was folding the blanket when Peter and I returned to them. The Schroeders had already returned to the auction tent, the women eager to bid on an old loom that had belonged to Anna Kaufman. As the others began to file toward the tent, I offered to return the basket, cooler, and blanket to the car while Caroline secured our seats.

"What did you do with the puzzle box?" she asked.

"It's right here," I said, patting my pocket. "I'll see you in a few minutes."

Caroline nodded, her auburn tresses caressed by the wind as she turned toward the auction tent. I quickly tromped across the yard and over the fields to deposit the lunch paraphernalia back in my sedan. The afternoon sun could have been imported from the month of July for all its radiant intensity, I thought to myself, returning toward the yard but not the auction tent.

While announcements had been made informing us that the farmhouse was off limits, I made my way toward the back porch. Late picnickers sprawled on blankets or the soft carpet of bluegrass laid naturally beneath the sheltering elms. Children continued to run about, often with hot dogs or cookies in hand, in search of the next freeze tag or kickball game.

I had observed handfuls of women and a couple of men discreetly enter the back screen door, presumably leading into the kitchen, most of the morning. Probably relatives checking on Deborah and Adam, or perhaps friends helping them pack or offering comfort at their plight. Fearing that Jonah would be waiting to banish me, I nonetheless sidled up to the bricked porch with its cheery pots of begonias and geraniums and knocked at the back door.

"Why, Brother Reed! How nice to see you," said Deborah Kaufman. "Please come on in. Adam and I were just finishing up our lunch."

"Thank you, Miss Kaufman. It's nice to see you again, as well. I spoke with Adam just a few minutes ago. I don't think your brother liked me talking to him."

She led me into the house. We walked first into a mud room, clean and neat, with only one pair of boots on the multi-hued rag rug. A row of hooks no longer held jackets or coats. Stacks of boxes lined the corner and another doorway led into a lemon-scented kitchen. It was clear that this kitchen had been packed away. More boxes, sparkling floors, no personal touches.

"Don't mind Jonah. He's all bark and no

bite," said the Amish woman, grinning. Her nose was slightly off-center above her large teeth but could not detract from the overall beauty of her countenance. She ushered me into a space that was once a dining room. Boxes now formed a makeshift table for Deborah's brother, who sat eating a sandwich and slices of apple that had been peeled for him. "I'm sorry I have no chair for you to sit in," she continued. "Would you like a peanut butter sandwich?"

"I just ate, thank you," I said. "Hello again, Adam. It's Grif, remember? We just met on the ball field?"

"Yessir," he said through a mouth congealed with peanut butter.

I removed the puzzle box from the hip pocket of my jeans. "Adam, have you ever seen this before?"

"Is that the puzzle box that belonged to Simon — the one that was stolen? Lyddie told me all about it," exclaimed Deborah. "Where did you find it?"

Adam bowed his head into his broad shoulders like a box turtle, and I thought he might cry. I definitely did not want him to become upset or think that I was here to accuse him.

"I bought it this morning in the auction tent," I said. "I was hoping Adam might help me solve it."

"Why, Brother Reed, you're welcome to let him try, but if you or Lyddie cannot open it . . ."

I walked over to Adam, who was slowly raising his head from his shell. He eyed me from beneath his brows and started to grin.

"Adam," I began. "Have you seen this before?"

He nodded vigorously. "Yessir. It's my puzzle box. My daddy made it for me. I didn't steal it, honest. It was mine." His eyes grew moist and his voice defensive.

"Why, I don't recall seeing you with it," said his sister. "Adam John, tell the truth now and I won't be angry with you. Did you take this puzzle box from Brother Reed's office up on the mountain?"

He looked around the room nervously. "Yes, Sister," he finally replied. "I took it when Brother Reed wasn't lookin'."

"When? How did you know where to find it?" I asked incredulously.

"I spied on Miss Lyddie givin' it to you in the big church, and then I followed you down the stone steps to your office. You put it in the safe without lockin' the door and then went to the bathroom. I snuck in, took my puzzle box, and then closed the safe door, so you wouldn't miss it right off."

No wonder there were no marks from the break-in! It was really so simple, I thought to myself. I probably returned from the restroom, checked to see if the safe was shut — which it was, but not locked. Then I went home. Next morning, the office door is unlocked, but I simply must have forgotten to lock it. So simple, really. A boy and his toy.

Deborah Kaufman simmered with maternal frustration. "Yes," she said. "While we waited in the van for Lyddie, Adam went to find a restroom. We wondered why he was gone longer than she was. Now we know!"

"Don't be mad, Sister," he begged. "I just wanted my puzzle box back."

"It's all right, Adam," I said. "You didn't know that Simon had given it to his sister to give to me. Do you know how to open it? Do you know what's inside?"

"I'll forgive you if Brother Reed does," added Deborah. "But how in the world did the puzzle box end up in the auctioneer's tent?"

"I put it there this morning," said Adam. "I heard Miss Lyddie's boys talkin' about the puzzle box and how it got stolen and all. I never meant to cause such a fuss, so I thought I'd just sell it with all the other doodads at the auction."

I nodded. "It's okay, Adam. We understand. You mentioned earlier that you helped Simon with his collection. Did you give him the puzzle box?"

"Yep. He could never figure it out until I showed him how. So I gave it to him because he was my friend."

"What did you help Simon collect?" I asked.

"I'll show you," said the young Amish man. I handed him the carved box and he deftly massaged one end. Next thing I knew, Adam slid back the top panel on a grooved track. "There's a spring in there," he explained. "Holds it in place unless you know where to press."

"What's inside, Adam?" asked Deborah Kaufman.

"Oh, just part of the collection," he replied, tilting the box for us to see. He held the box out to me and then rubbed a pinch of its contents between his fingers. Granules of dull bronze powder.

"Dirt?" I exclaimed. "Simon collected dirt? That's what's in this box?"

"Yep," replied Adam proudly. "Special dirt."

I ran the soil between my own thumb and index finger. "Why is it special?" I asked. "What makes this special dirt?"

"I don't know," said the young man, "but Simon said this was special dirt."

"Do you know where this is from?" I asked. "Where did Simon get this dirt?"

"Probably by the Judas Tree," he said. "Or maybe by the cemetery. Or maybe Yoders' creek. They's the places I helped him find dirt and put it in the little jars."

Why in the world would Simon be taking soil samples? I couldn't imagine, unless it had something to do with his ties to the Omega Group. But then why would he place this dirt in the puzzle box and give it to his sister with instructions to give it to me in case something happened to him? It didn't make sense.

"Thank you, Adam," I said, shaking his hand. "You've been very helpful. Would you mind if I kept the puzzle box for a little while longer? It may help us find out who hurt Simon."

"Don't tell Jonah that I helped Simon," he replied. "He doesn't like Simon, and he'd be mad if he found out that Simon was my friend."

"It's okay, Adam," said Deborah Kaufman. "I'll take care of Jonah."

Back outside in the hot afternoon, I worked to make sure I could indeed open the puzzle box myself. Each time I slid the top panel back from its hidden catch, the handful of dirt inside seemed to mock me. Regardless of how strange the contents, I couldn't wait to share my costly discovery with Dan and Sheriff Claiborne. Perhaps I could even persuade Caroline to leave now, and maybe Lyle could drive Beatrice home.

The inside of the stuffy auction tent was now practically unbearable. Like a living sauna, it had absorbed the weary consumers' energy and left them tired and depleted. Only the die-hards with specific items in mind seemed to remain. The auctioneer performed with his professional's flair for entertaining even as he conducted business. His corny jokes and puns kept the dissipating audience engaged. As I walked in he was introducing an antique sewing basket with the line, "Guaranteed to keep you in stitches, folks."

I spotted Bea, Lyle, and Caroline two rows further back than where we'd sat this morning. The Schroeders and Peter were not in sight, and I concluded that they were looking at the remaining farm tools out by the barn. My young curate's anguish over his impending decisions about his life's direction weighed on me. I lifted up a prayer for him as well as one for the odd clue now in my possession. Why in the world would Simon want me to have an Amish toy full of dirt? Would a chemical analysis in the lab by someone like Agent Corey reveal the answer? Instinctively, I patted the wooden box back in my pocket before taking my seat alongside Caroline.

"Everything okay?" she asked. "I was beginning to get worried."

I nodded and smiled. "Yes, I'm fine. Sorry to take so long. Did I miss anything?"

My sister interrupted, "You missed Lyle buying me the most beautiful butter churn you've ever seen."

"Well, I expect fresh butter on my toast in the morning, then," I chuckled.

"Did I see you going into the farmhouse, Grif?" asked Rev. Slater innocently.

"Yes, you did. I wanted to speak with Deborah Kaufman and her brother Adam. Looks like you've made my sister quite happy, Lyle." I left him wondering about the nature of my visit and could tell that he seemed uncomfortable. Perhaps I should show him the puzzle box and gauge his reaction? Then I had a better idea.

"Oh, and I solved the puzzle box. You'll never guess — well, I suppose I shouldn't disclose what was inside until I've talked to the sheriff," I said.

"Grif! You must tell us now. Was it something valuable?" asked Bea. "I'll bet there was a key inside to a lockbox where Simon stashed the photographs he was using to blackmail someone!"

"Blackmail someone!" exclaimed Lyle. "What are you talking about?"

I rolled my eyes and groaned while Caroline laughed heartily. "Bea has no idea what she's talking about. Simon wasn't blackmailing anyone — that we know of."

"So what was inside then?" asked Lyle. "Anything that might help identify Simon's killer?"

"I certainly hope so," I said and raised my bidder's number for a varnished egg crate that would make a lovely planter on my patio. Out of the corner of my eye, Lyle whispered something to Bea, who visibly paled.

By four o'clock we were more than weary. My sister and Rev. Slater had returned to their amorous, buoyant selves but I still wondered what he had said to her. Caroline won the best shopper award in our group with her purchase of a Morning Star quilt in dark solid colors, a three-legged stool, and an assortment of embroidered linens. I played gallant knight and carried her purchases for her in my egg crate while Lyle was forced to do the same and carry Bea's churn.

We had just stepped away from the purchase table and out of the tent into the much cooler afternoon breeze when I felt a tug at my sleeve.

"Father Reed?" inquired a feminine voice.

I spun around to see an attendant from the auction company moving briskly toward me, an older woman who had just helped me stack our purchases in my crate.

"Yes?" I said, thinking that I had forgotten my receipt.

"I have something for you," she said and extended a business sized envelope. "I almost forgot."

Caroline took the crate from me while I retrieved the message from the auction lady. "What is this?" I asked. "Did I forget something?"

"No," said the woman. "Someone left this for you just after lunch. Said to give it to you when you picked up your purchased items."

"Did this person leave their name?" I asked.

"No, Father. A blond woman — tall, thin, real pretty. Said you'd understand after you read it."

"What is it, Grif?" asked Bea and Lyle in unison. They crowded behind me and tried to look over my shoulder but I soon turned away. The auction lady returned to her post inside the tent as I looked at the crisp business envelope left in her stead. The return address was embossed in black: *OMEGA Group, Inc.*, followed by an address in Dover, Delaware. My name was penned across the front in black ink in a slanting, feminine script. When I opened the envelope, I found two sheets of matching paper with the same handwriting. It was dated with today's date and read as follows:

Father Reed,

By this time you probably have many questions about Simon's death and my relationship to him. As you may know by now, I was not Dr. Hostetler's research assistant. My real name is Myra Gaither and I work for the Omega Group, a corporation that develops environmental remediation for toxic waste sites. We often work with the EPA to catch violators of environmental laws and bring them to trial.

For several years now, we have known that large shipments of toxic wastes from the Tenleco Paper Company have been disappearing into the Dolby Air Force Base. All attempts to question leaders at the military base have been thwarted.

I enlisted the help of Dr. Hostetler several months ago, and he came to believe as I do that the Amish farms of Tremont are in danger. Under the guise of his research project, we have been attempting to gather evidence of our suspicions.

What we've found has confirmed that the military base has indeed been burying the Tenleco toxins on the property purchased from the Amish thirty years ago. In fact, the toxic waste is leeching into the soils and waters of Amish farmland along the bordering property.

However, when Simon was murdered, most of our evidence died with him. Our soil and water samples disappeared. While new ones can be gathered, I feel it is time that I take matters directly in hand and discover undeniable evidence of the crimes committed against the Amish people. By the time you finish reading this, I will be on my way to Dolby Air Force Base to uncover the conclusive evidence needed to stop the murderers from taking more lives.

Simon trusted you, and I'm taking a chance that the military brass has not bought you out like it seems to have everyone else. I know this must all sound *strange, but please believe me.*

Meet me after dark at the Judas Tree. If I don't show up by midnight with the evidence needed to bring the truth to light, then call the press and look for my body somewhere on the Dolby base.

Sincerely,
Myra Gaither

Chapter Twenty-three

Another Judas

"Grif, what is it?" asked Caroline. "Something important?"

"Perhaps," I replied stoically. "Just someone wishing to make an appointment with me."

"They sure picked a funny way of doing it," said Bea as we resumed our trek toward the pasture parking lot. Small clouds of reddish dust drifted down the road toward town. My mind danced with questions before I finally calculated an impromptu plan.

"Lyle? Do you have your cell phone with you?" I asked as we approached my Buick.

"I'm sorry, Griffin, I left it at home today. You know how it is — even pastors need a day off." He turned to Bea and they began discussing their plans for the evening.

"Thanks anyway," I said. After I loaded our purchases into the trunk, I handed Caroline the letter and whispered for her to remain discreet. Slater and my sister continued their animated chat.

"Wow!" whispered Caroline as she concluded the second page. "What are you going to do?"

I motioned for her to come around to the side of my car. "I don't want to say anything to Bea or Lyle about this until I — until I know if this is for real," I whispered. "What do you think of it?" I folded the letter and replaced it in the cream-colored envelope.

"It makes sense, I guess. Some of these things she mentioned should be verifiable — especially the true nature of this organization, the Omega Group."

"But not under the deadline she's set. It's almost five o'clock on a Saturday. I've either got to believe her or get played for a fool," I said. "Dan did tell me that he and Sam discovered the Omega Group is an environmental corporation. That part fits."

"Surely she doesn't think you would show up alone . . . or does she? It's too obvious for a trap, if Mariah Gates is Simon's murderer," said Caroline. "Maybe she thinks you know something because you won the bid on the puzzle box. Maybe she's afraid of what you found inside."

"I hadn't considered that," I said. Then shaking my head, I concluded, "No, I'm going to take her at her word. I'll show up tonight, but I'm also going to give Dan and Sam a call and ask them to be there, too."

"I'd feel much better if you did," Caroline said and squeezed my hand.

Lyle Slater came around to our side of the car and asked, "What are you two lovebirds over here whispering about?"

"Oh, probably the same things as you and Bea," I said. "We were just discussing plans for tonight. And as it turns out, I need to go out to the Schroeders' farm and help them out. Lyle, I was wondering if you might be willing to give these ladies a ride back up the mountain."

Caroline didn't like the fact that I was excluding her from the action; I could tell by the way her eyebrows arched and her jaw tightened. Nonetheless, I didn't see how she could help me in this. I looked up at the late afternoon clouds gathering from the east. Over our shoulder in the yard of the farmhouse, the striped auction tent was coming down. Children scurried out from under it and squealed at the spectacle.

"Why, of course," cooed Slater. "I'd be delighted. But is there anything we can do for the Schroeders? I hope their need is not serious."

Once again I sensed his curiosity straining at the leash of his civility. I shook my head and thanked him. "No," I said. "But I know we'd all welcome your prayers."

Caroline kissed my cheek and whispered, "I'm praying for you," as I deposited her in the plush leather interior of the luxury sedan. I was moved by her support and was immediately stricken with the thought that I might never see her again. What was it she had started to ask me that morning? What if it were something to do with her budding faith and I never had the chance to answer her? What if the meeting tonight were indeed a trap?

The three of them sped away in Slater's Mercedes, and I followed them as far as the row of shops lining downtown Tremont. Pulling into a parking space alongside a black buggy, I lifted my fears up in prayer in the words of the psalmist: " 'Be merciful to me, O God, be merciful to me, for in thee my soul takes refuge; in the shadow of thy wings I will take refuge, till the storms of destruction pass by. I cry to God Most High, to God who fulfils his purpose for me. He will send from heaven and save me, he will put to shame those who trample upon me. God will send forth his steadfast love and his faithfulness!' "

The SweetHaus Bakery and Amish Café was just about to close, having obviously profited from the influx of auction-goers. I made my way to the back of the small restaurant and quickly dialed the Carroll County Sheriff's Department. Andy McDermott answered on the second ring before putting me through to Sergeant Warren.

"Grif, it's good to hear from you," Dan said. "How was the auction today? Any new leads about what might've happened to your friend?"

I quickly explained about the puzzle box, and Dan whistled a long, low note after I described Adam's involvement and the box's contents.

"That's great that you recovered the puzzle box, although I can't imagine what dirt has to do with Hostetler's murder," said Dan.

"Well, I think I might know," I replied. "Just as we were picking up our purchases, the auction attendant gave me a letter from Mariah Gates — or Myra Gaither, I should say." I read Dan the letter, and this time the reaction was not even a whistle, only silence.

"So the dirt inside the puzzle box must be a soil sample," I concluded. Still no response from the other end of the phone. I panicked, "Dan? You still there?"

"Yeah, I'm still here, just taking it all in. You think this is for real?" he asked. "Where are you, by the way?"

"I'm still in Tremont, at the bakery. Yes, I think Ms. Gaither may be telling the truth. Simon certainly seemed to trust her."

"And he ended up dead," murmured Dan. "Well, you're not going alone. I'll give Sam a call and we'll head down right away. You want us to meet you at Schroeders' or on Chigger Ridge Road?"

I thought about accessibility to the Judas Tree and chose the former. "If y'all aren't there by dark, I may start without you. Of course, I'll have Peter to help me. He's visiting the Schroeders for a few days."

"Grif, did you tell anyone else about this?" asked Dan. "Lyle Slater, for instance?"

"Only Caroline," I said. "Why do you ask about Slater?"

"Because I just finished verifying his background check this morning. You told me that he claimed to have taught with Hostetler at some small Bible college out west, right? Well, the college no longer exists and Slater didn't list it on his vita when he applied for the pastorate at Avenell First Church."

"Perhaps he didn't think it was important," I offered. "Although it does seem odd. What are you getting at?"

"Well, another thing is that I can't find a

copy of Slater's doctoral dissertation anywhere. One of the Avenell reference librarians searched all day for me and couldn't find it anywhere — not even on the Internet. It's as if it never existed."

I shifted the receiver to my other ear. "I still don't understand what you're getting at, Dan," I said. "You think Slater's a fraud?"

"Well, after Ms. Gates turned out to be someone other than who she claimed to be, I can't help but wonder if Slater isn't hiding something, too," explained Dan. "Until we know for sure, be careful. You did the right thing by not telling anyone else besides Caroline."

"Thanks," I said. "I'll see you in a couple of hours, then."

"Grif, you'd better not start without us. You wait at the Schroeders until we get there — then we'll all go to the Judas Tree together and see if Myra Gaither shows."

At a quarter after eight, however, I could stand to wait no longer. Benjamin and Sarah Schroeder had been most gracious when I showed up unexpectedly on their front porch just as they were finishing supper. Sarah, in fact, insisted that I sit down at their table and let her fix me a plate. I complied and quickly devoured two thick pork chops buried beneath a spicy vegetable casserole of onions, squash, tomatoes, and rice. Benjamin struggled not to press me on my reasons for going to the Judas Tree after dark, but apparently sensed the firmness in my tone.

Prior to my arrival, Peter and Leah had just departed for a young people's social at her cousin Jessie Bontrager's home. Leah thought it would be good for Peter to meet other young Amish couples. I suspected, too, that she was doing everything she could to sway Peter's decision. Sensing my disappointment that my curate would not be accompanying me, Nathan offered to join me instead, or to fetch Peter from the social if I wished. I declined on both accounts and prayed that nothing interfered with Dan and Sam's arrival.

Yet after I finished my supper and sipped the remains of my iced tea with Benjamin and Sarah on the front porch, I grew worried. It was going on eight o'clock and the sun had already set. Although flat bands of pale light lingered along the horizon like the folds of sheets below a clothesline, darkness sailed in on stiff gray clouds from the east. The wind confirmed an imminent spring shower with its moist breath nuzzling the tops of beech trees in the yard.

By eight-fifteen I had decided to set out myself and hoped that my friends would catch up with me. Benjamin refused to let me go alone, but I insisted, downplaying the sense of danger that lingered in the clenched fist of my stomach. He compensated by outfitting me with his largest flashlight and the promise to assist Sam and Dan when they arrived.

As I descended into the woods, the darkness became palpable in the mist-laden night air. Using the flashlight as infrequently as possible, I thought back over all that had happened in little over a week. One obvious lesson stood out in my mind: rarely was someone whom he — or she — appeared to be. I thought back over comments Simon had made, wondering if he betrayed anything of his true mission to me in some oblique way. If Myra Gaither's claims were true — and I would likely know very shortly, one way or another — then Simon really did desire to protect the Amish way of life here. Perhaps he felt like he was atoning for the devastating consequences of his father's sin all those years ago.

The wind shifted and the mist turned into heavier drops sifting their way through the treetops. The deeper into the woods I crept, the darker the night enclosed itself around me. The ground seemed moist, and I took care not to slip as I climbed over a litter of fallen branches. I found the halfway marker, Leah's favorite blackberry bushes, the hard way, their thorny stalks clinging to my jeans along my calves and ankles. Up ahead of me, a toad warbled, blending into the chorus of cicadas already heralding spring's triumphant arrival. The air continued to smell rich and earthy, of loam and moss. I stopped to check my watch — then I heard something.

The crack of a branch. Someone was following me off the path. They must have realized that I stopped and so they waited, as well. I even imagined that I could hear their breathing, shallow and faint, across the darkness. My light-up watch dial revealed that it was just past eight-thirty. Perhaps it was simply Dan and Sam. But if I called out and it was not them . . .

I continued on toward the Judas Tree as quietly as possible. Yes, there — I heard it again. Footfalls continued after I paused and then halted again. Whoever it was, they did not wish to be known. I quickly walked the remaining few hundred yards to the clearing that framed the massive oak. Finally, just a few feet shy of it, I peered from behind the dense cover of a cedar tree. Whoever was following me would likely cross right in front of me.

Was it Myra Gaither, evidence in hand, coming to keep her appointment with me? Dan or Sam? Or someone with more sinister motives?

Footfalls continued approaching, although it sounded as if the walker was being more careful not to be heard. I glimpsed a dark figure take cover behind the trunk of a tall scrub pine just twenty yards away. The shape appeared to be clad in a long, dark overcoat and apparently male, judging by height. My decision to be here alone suddenly seemed more foolhardy than courageous.

The figure approached, slowly moving from tree to tree. I decided surprise was my only weapon — along with the heft of the deluxe Magnalite Benjamin had given me. Just as the dark-clad figure moved to within ten feet of my hiding place, I whirled out from the cedar's trunk and pierced the inky darkness with my spear of light. His hands went to his face to protect his eyes instinctively and glints of silver shone from his head in the artificial beam.

"Slater! What are you doing here?" I barked. My annoyance turned to fear as

Dan's warning from our phone conversation returned to mind.

"Grif! Get that horrible light out of my eyes. Please!"

I lowered the beam and Lyle Slater stumbled toward me. I repeated my question. "What are you doing out here? You could get us both killed!"

"I could ask *you* the same thing. Who are you meeting out here?" he demanded, leaning toward the cedar trunk between us.

"What makes you think I'm meeting anyone?" I returned, suddenly aware of why I had never trusted the Reverend Slater. He worked harder at creating an impression than at being himself.

"Look," he said, lowering his voice. "I read enough of that letter over your shoulder at the auction to know that you're meeting someone here after dark. If you think you're going to expose me because of what a dead man claimed —"

"Lyle, what are you talking about?" I asked. "Expose you as what?"

The smooth-talking pastor was at a loss for words for one of the first times since I'd known him, and only the sounds of the night woods hung between us. I decided to use the little knowledge I had to ferret out Slater's connection to Simon Hostetler. "What did

Simon know about you that made him so dangerous to you, Lyle? What did he threaten to expose about your past, something from when you were both at United Brethren Bible College?"

"Did he ever talk to you about me?" asked Slater, suddenly more desperate than I'd ever seen him before. "Did Simon tell you what happened? It wasn't exactly my fault. . . ."

"Why aren't there any copies of your dissertation in the university's library?" I asked, wondering if Slater's appearance had anything to do with Myra Gaither's absence. What was taking Dan and Sam so long?

"Quit toying with me, then, if you know," sneered Slater. "What do you want? Money? Well, I don't have any, contrary to the way I make it appear. Surely, if you love your sister, you'll keep quiet about all this. I really do care for her, you know."

"Do you? I'm not convinced of that yet. You may enjoy her company, but would you actually consider marrying her?" I asked. "But let's get back to the real reason you're here. Did Simon know that your dissertation was a fraud?"

Slater shifted his weight toward me, and I prepared myself to duck behind the cedar trunk separating us if necessary.

"Look," he said. "I don't know what Simon told you — but I never meant to hurt anyone. Kent Livingston would've understood. If anything, this is something between him and me. Simon was always so self-righteous, had to report it to the Dean of Graduate Studies. His 'moral duty,' he claimed. Without giving any regard to the consequences, to the ways it would affect my life. Fine for him to get his Ph.D. and write all his books —"

"Slow down, Lyle," I said. "Who was Kent Livingston? What's all this about?"

"You really don't know?" he asked.

Just as I shook my head, we both heard a snap. I immediately extinguished the Magnalite.

From the direction of the clearing beyond us, more twigs crackled. Then the crossed beams of flashlights hacked across the darkness of the clearing. Slater started to speak, but I held up my hand to command silence and hoped he saw it. We stood like statues as the low murmur of voices wafted toward us. A muffled sound like the wind wove itself among the voices.

Lyle moved closer to my side of the tree trunk, and then, very carefully, we both took slow steps toward the edge of the clearing and the safety of another large cedar. The voices were definitely growing closer, just audible enough to distinguish bits of the conversation. Only one beam of light shone now.

"— never said anything about murder —" A male voice, low and angry.

"— if you want to keep your farm, then you'll play by my rules —" Another male voice, but one so unique in its husky timbre, that I recognized it immediately. General Nathan Bledsoe.

"— gotten out of hand . . . more than I agreed to —" said the first voice again.

"— end up like poor Hostetler then . . . do as I say —" replied Bledsoe.

I lowered myself behind a bush near the base of the cedar tree where we hid. Peering around the trunk, I could barely make out four figures in front of the Judas Tree, one of them appearing to be a captive — Myra Gaither, I assumed.

Slater shifted down to my level and whispered, "Who are these people? What's going on?"

I placed my finger on my lips and turned to see if I could discern their purpose for being here. From the position of a rope being fastened to the Judas Tree, it appeared that the shadowy tableau before us was about to actualize the worst fear creeping into the back of my mind.

"We're ready to go here when you give the word, sir," said another male voice, knotting one end of the rope. A swath of light bounced across part of a clean-shaven face and blond crew cut, confirming my guess that the voice belonged to Lieutenant Brian Northrop.

"— take the tape off —" ordered Bledsoe and even from our distance I could hear the quick smack of duct tape being peeled off the woman's mouth. "— scream, my dear, then I'll just shoot you instead of letting you die like your friend Hostetler. This really is an efficient little plan, don't you think? We'll put that sweet note we had you write for us somewhere close by. Poor little Mariah, so grieved at the loss of her beloved boss that she couldn't bear it anymore. I think it will play just fine." He laughed in a full-throated way that made me shiver with contempt for his arrogance.

"They're going to kill her!" whispered Slater in my ear. "We've got to get out of here or they'll kill us, too!"

"We can't let them hang that woman! Besides, the sheriff is on his way," I whispered back.

"I'm getting out of here. If you want to

stick around and get yourself strung up, too, that's your business." Slater began to back away from where I crouched.

"Lyle, no!" I hissed. "Don't be a fool."

But it was too late. He tripped over a fallen branch and landed on his back, grunting loudly at the impact.

Bledsoe and company wasted no time. A sudden strobe of light illuminated us both and Brian Northrop lunged our way, brandishing his sidearm and shouting for us to halt.

To my horror, Lyle Slater managed to get to his feet and began crashing toward the dark curtain of forest behind us. Northrop aimed and fired in Lyle's direction. I instantly decided that my only chance was to hide and then try to sneak away for help. I dove into a mound of kudzu and lay motionless.

Two beams of light now cascaded from the Judas Tree toward me, and I saw the tall, athletic Northrop advancing toward where I lay outstretched on the ground. The moments then seemed to melt like ice in January — slowly, slowly, passing imperceptibly. Northrop held a pistol with both hands, his outstretched arms and thick shoulders forming a thick diamond-shaped silhouette. For a moment I thought I saw him smile.

Chapter Twenty-four

Omega

Myra Gaither screamed, General Bledsoe laughed, and the unknown third man cursed under his breath. I lay frozen to the ground, paralyzed by the anticipated fear of a bullet piercing my head or chest. It never arrived.

"Well, well, what do we have here," smirked Northrop. "Hey, General, looks like we caught us a preacher man." The barrel of his weapon was aimed directly at me.

I could hear scuffling from the area where Bledsoe held his hostage. The portly general cursed and struggled to contain Myra Gaither, who shrieked and screamed for help. The third man yelled something unintelligible and then crashed through the woods.

"You coward!" Bledsoe shouted at him. "We know where to find you!"

The fleeing man had dropped his flashlight and the beam shone along the ground, as if some black hole in the earth were attempting to swallow up the light. From the continuing sounds of struggle, I wondered if Myra Gaither might escape her captor. She was definitely distracting Northrop, which served my purpose just as well. As he glanced at his commanding officer's struggle, I rose to my feet.

"Easy there, Padre. Why don't you just head over to the Judas Tree, nice and slow," said Northrop. "We're through playing games here." He waggled the pistol menacingly.

"Northrop! Get over here! I need your help!" bellowed Bledsoe.

For the briefest of moments the lieutenant appeared indecisive. Almost without thinking I dropped to the ground again and rolled behind the nearest tree trunk. I wasn't sure how long I could evade Northrop, but I knew I didn't want to see a noose around Myra Gaither's neck. I had to get some help. But how?

"Freeze, old man!" shouted my assailant. He pointed the gun toward the base of the trunk that provided my only cover and fired at me, the sound reverberating in my ears.

Northrop immediately groaned and fell backward.

"Police! Give it up!" boomed a familiar voice. *Dan Warren.*

His words were quickly swallowed by the

sound of a chopper flying overhead. An accompanying search light bathed the scene before me in an artificial moonbeam of illumination. General Bledsoe had his hands around Myra Gaither's neck, trying to tighten the hangman's noose, just as Dan Warren sprang from behind the Judas Tree and ordered, "Let her go! Now!"

The general looked up with tired eyes and released his grip on the woman and the rope. His intended victim stood transfixed by the shock of her experience.

I checked myself but could find nothing moist except for mud caked to my knees and thighs. No blood. I regained enough strength to stand and ran over to where Northrop lay. Dark liquid pooled between his collar bone and his right bicep. Mechanically removing the gun from his hand, I checked his pulse and prayed "Thanks be to God" when I felt the steady rhythm.

In a matter of moments, the entire scene became a surreal landscape of men in uniforms descending on the clearing. Like a military battalion commanding a war-torn jungle, the dozen figures quickly contained the clearing. Rain fell softly now, the pattering drops falling on overhead leaves and sporadic patches of bare ground. The chopper circled like a hawk having spotted its prey, the whirring of its winglike blades adding to the transformed setting.

Sheriff Claiborne came up to me and removed Northrop's weapon from my hand and then patted my back. His lips moved and sounds came from his mouth, but I could not discern the language being spoken. He moved on to someone else then, and I saw Dan Warren striding toward me.

Two officers attended to Brian Northrop, where bright smears of blood gleamed from his right shoulder even in the muted light. General Bledsoe looked like an old man in the glare of the harsh search beam from overhead. It was a strange sight to see the dictator of the Dolby Air Force Base with his hands cuffed behind his back.

"Are you okay, Grif?" asked Dan Warren. He placed both his large hands on my shoulders and led me to the far side of the clearing where lanterns had been posted on extended branches. "Are you wounded?" he asked, rubbing a smear of blood between his fingers from where he had guided me.

"No, I'm alright, I think. That's Northrop's blood." Tears sprang to my eyes at the realization that it could have been my blood, and I suddenly felt dizzy, disoriented.

"Grif, it's okay. It's okay." He leaned me

into him like a parent holding a child who wakes up and doesn't know where he is. I rested a moment in his grip.

Embarrassed, I moved away from my gentle giant of a friend and followed him back toward the road on the other side of the clearing. The distant echo of the helicopter had long since faded back into the subtle rhythms of the cicadas and the low voices of men combing the scene.

On Chigger Ridge Road, half a dozen patrol cars bottlenecked the narrow lane. An ambulance had arrived to transport Northrop to Carroll County General, and Bledsoe had already been secured in the back of the sheriff's cruiser. A second ambulance had just arrived as I moved toward Dan's vehicle. Myra Gaither was being loaded into the back of it, but from the sound of things, she wasn't too happy about it. A fresh-faced officer ran over from the ambulance to Dan and me.

"Are you Father Reed?" he asked. "This lady says she won't let us take her to the hospital until she sees you. Do you mind?"

Dan looked exasperated and started to upbraid the young officer, but I nodded. Following him over to the ambulance, I realized that I hadn't seen Lyle Slater since the cavalry had arrived. Was he wounded? I inquired of the young officer, but he knew nothing.

In the eerie orange glow from the ambulance lights, Myra Gaither, long blond tresses streaked with dirt and blood, held out her hand to me.

"Father Reed, thank you. Thank you for believing me. I am so grateful. And I know Simon would be," she said. "I think we've got all the evidence we need now."

"You're welcome," I said simply and released the woman's cool hand so that she could finally be loaded into the ambulance bay.

Back in Dan's squad car, I glanced back at the tree line. Jagged, leafy branches littered shadows along the wooded perimeter. The dark sky's blues and teals lined the horizon like a damask tablecloth, swirls of rain clouds fading into the night, as we pulled away and journeyed toward home. Above it all, the giant oak known as the Judas Tree towered toward heaven.

The next morning as I sat in the conference room at the sheriff's office, the night before seemed even more vivid, a dream that came to life and punctuated itself with an intensity of details that overcharged my senses. Dan had picked me up this morning and we had stopped for coffee and dough-nuts at the Diner on our way. He seemed unaffected by it all, which made me even more self-conscious about my silent reverie.

Around the long, laminated table, we joined Sam and an officer in a steel-blue Air Force uniform. I reacted to the sight of the tall, muscular military man as if he were here to haunt me. But he turned out to be the second in command at Dolby, General Michael Phillips. I nodded and shook his hand as Dan distributed the styrofoam coffee cups and cruellers.

Sam began by informing us all that Myra Gaither suffered two broken ribs and nu-merous cuts and bruises, but nothing se-rious. She remained in the hospital in Lewiston for observation but would likely be released tomorrow. Brian Northrop re-mained in Carroll County General Hospital in stable condition, suffering from a bullet wound to his right shoulder. The shot exited the body cleanly and no permanent damage was done. Both a military and county officer guarded his hospital room.

I breathed a sigh of relief on both ac-counts and prayed aloud, "Thank God."

General Nathan Bledsoe had been placed in the state holding facility in Mumford under military guard until it was decided whether he would face the federal and state charges first or the impending military court-martial.

"Numerous executives from the Tenleco Paper Company are being served with arrest warrants even as we speak," concluded Sam.

"So all of this business with the Brethren and the vandalism to the Amish farms was just to scare them into selling their land?" I asked, finally sipping my warm coffee.

"Apparently so, Father Reed," replied General Phillips. "I'm terribly embarrassed by the severe breach of trust that General Bledsoe perpetrated on his fellow officers at Dolby. We were beginning to become suspicious of where all his money was coming from, but none of us had any idea that he was capable of such heinous acts."

Sam nodded his confirmation. "General Phillips here has provided us with enough documentation to sort out most of the puzzle pieces." He tapped several thick manila folders on the table before him. "Bledsoe has been making illegal deals with several state industries to dispose of their toxic wastes. Using his authority, he basically set up a secret network of chemical engineers and laborers on the base to execute his plans. He paid them on the side from the exorbitant fees he charged companies like Tenleco. Evidently, however, using Bledsoe's illegal operation was still millions of dollars cheaper than processing the wastes on their own sites or shipping them out of state and paying a legal facility."

"So exactly how did Simon Hostetler play into all this?" asked General Phillips, voicing my question, as well.

Sam replied, "Myra Gaither was on the level. She and the Omega Corporation had been working with the EPA to track down these missing shipments of toxic wastes for some time. A few months ago, an anonymous source tipped her off to check the military base at Dolby. About the same time, Simon came here to research his next project on the Amish and their customs. Ms. Gaither convinced Simon to assist them in their quest to discover the needed evidence to bust the operation. She says he was eager to help and viewed it as a way of 'making up for past sins.' "

"So all the time he spent in Tremont interviewing farmers about their agricultural practices was really just an excuse to take soil samples," added Dan. "Hostetler enlisted Adam Kaufman to help him and together they probably collected close to thirty samples, according to Ms. Gaither."

"But then one of the Amish farmers became suspicious," continued Sam. "And as it turns out, he was working for Bledsoe as well, keeping him informed of attitudes and decisions in the Amish community. Helping him arrange the acts of vandalism so that no one got hurt, but the message was received nonetheless."

"Joseph Yoder," I whispered.

"That's right," said Dan. "We caught him on foot about a half-mile from the Judas Tree last night. He's pretty much confessed to all the charges. Everything except conspiracy to murder Hostetler."

"What tipped *you* off?" asked the sheriff, as he leaned forward and placed his arms on the table.

"I wasn't sure," I began. "But it appeared as if business wasn't going so well for Yoders' Dairy. I knew Joseph owned part of the Canaan's Way property that Bledsoe wished to buy, but Yoder couldn't convince his kinsmen to sell their shares. As proud as the Amish are in their work ethics, I couldn't imagine that Yoder would ever acknowledge that his dairy farm was not turning a profit. He tried to warn me that first night we went down to Tremont to stay away." I paused to sip more coffee. "But you said that Yoder won't acknowledge playing a part in Simon's death?"

Both Sam and Dan nodded. The sheriff explained, "He claims that Northrop caught Simon snooping around on the Dolby side of the property line near the Judas Tree. He realized what Simon was up to by collecting soil and water samples and fought him to take them away. During the scuffle, Simon fell and hit his head on a rock. It killed him. Rather than leave the body there, Northrop was inspired to use Simon's death as another means of frightening the Amish. So he left Simon as Leah found him in the Judas Tree."

"Has Northrop confessed to any of this?" asked General Phillips. "Needless to say, these are more than serious charges."

"Not yet," replied Dan. "But Bledsoe reports the same story. He claims that he was upset with Northrop for acting on his own."

"I suppose it will all come out in the court-martial," sighed Phillips.

My mind raced to explain other odd details of my friend's death. "What about the carving on the Judas Tree? Who put the verse from Deuteronomy on there after Simon's death?" I asked.

The sheriff and his deputy exchanged looks. "We're not sure yet, but Yoder seems a likely bet."

"You might also talk to Jonah Kaufman,"

I suggested. "I'm not sure he's ever forgiven his mother for having the affair with Simon's father."

"One other question, gentlemen," said General Phillips. "How did this puzzle box fit into the story? I'm still unclear."

Summarizing how the box came into my possession, I recapped Adam's story and speculated that Simon was growing nervous about his involvement with uncovering Dolby's secrets. "I suppose he was afraid that something might happen to his soil samples, and he wanted a backup. I'm still surprised that he told his sister to give me the puzzle box and not Ms. Gaither."

"That was their plan," replied Sam. "She explained that they had not contacted local law enforcement because of General Bledsoe's influence. Evidently, the Mumford police had stonewalled her when she tried to go through them in months past. If something happened to Simon, he was afraid Bledsoe would be watching Gaither. So he needed someone who they would not suspect of being involved in the operation."

"He needed someone he could trust," said Sergeant Warren.

"Yes," I said. "It seems that we all need people we can trust. There are usually enough betrayals to last a lifetime."

We all four paused for a moment, and then Sam added, "We found Lyle Slater last night near the Schroeders' farm. We released him this morning without charges."

I nodded. "He had nothing to do with Simon's death. He was just afraid of his own guilt and the secret he has carried all these years."

"What secret?" asked Dan. "Why was he out at the Judas Tree last night?"

"I haven't verified it yet, but I suspect that Slater had plagiarized a dying colleague's dissertation all those years ago at United Brethren Bible College. Simon found out and turned Slater in, but not before he resigned. Nonetheless, Slater passed himself off as a Ph.D. rather than acknowledge the truth to those around him. He switched from academia to the church, where, unfortunately, degrees are often more important than the critical ideas to back them up. Slater had just taken this job when he ran into Simon. He feared that Simon would feel compelled to tell Avenell First Church the truth about its glamorous new pastor."

General Phillips leaned toward me. "Yes," he said. "We all experience enough betrayals to last a lifetime. And usually, the one we betray the most is ourselves."

"Amen," I said. "Amen."

Sunrise Service

Two weeks later the Judas Tree no longer loomed at the centerpiece of my dreams. I had managed to sort through most of my feelings about the treachery of General Bledsoe and his henchmen as well as process the unfortunate loss of my friend.

The community of Avenell had burst full force into spring by Holy Week, with pink-and-white dogwood blossoms adorning the vernal landscape. Despite the external appearances, however, the repercussions of the "Dolby Waste Dump" case, as the local and national papers were calling it, continued to unwind themselves in the lives of those around me. Perhaps most notably with the departure of Lyle Slater.

The week after the case was resolved, Rev. Slater resigned from First Church through a two-page letter that did not go into specifics. I tried to meet with Lyle to discuss what he planned to do next, but he did not return my calls. In fact, he took the coward's way out and left Bea a letter, as well, rather than face her and discuss his decisions. She let me read the five-page epistle, and it amounted to a rather rambling factual account of what I had hypothesized in the sheriff's office. Kent Livingston was a colleague of Slater's in graduate school; both were writing on similar topics. However, as Slater developed writer's block and lied about his progress, Livingston developed a rare form of cancer and died. While sorting through Livingston's books and papers, Slater found a completed copy of his friend's dissertation. *It seemed the perfect solution to my dilemma at the time, dear Beatrice,* wrote Slater. *I kept meaning to own up to my deception and make amends, but like so many things in this life that we intend to do, time simply ran out.* He concluded the letter by saying that he had enjoyed their friendship, but that he did not plan to ever remarry and consequently thought it best for both of them to go their separate ways.

My sister received the news with a mixture of shock, anger, and compassion. She was eager to forgive Lyle and angry with him for not leaving a forwarding address or point of contact. As we sat in the cheery blue-and-white kitchen of the rectory, I folded the letter and held my sister to my shoulder to try to absorb some of her grief.

She cried only for a few minutes and then, characteristically, jumped to her feet and began to fix us both a hot cup of tea. "Darjeeling or chai?" she asked, wiping her eyes with a dish towel.

"I've been thinking, Grif," she said moments later, "of going back to the mission field. Now seems like it might be the right time."

"Bea, don't rush into anything on the rebound. Take your time," I cautioned.

She nodded and sniffled. "I'll take some time, but I thought you should know that I'm seriously considering returning to China this fall."

"I'll certainly pray about it with you." We paused as she placed steaming teacups before us on the table. "Bea," I said softly. "May I ask you something? About you and Lyle?"

"Of course," she replied. "What is it?"

"That day at the auction," I said, "we were sitting in the tent discussing the puzzle box and then I changed the subject. What did Lyle whisper to you that made you so sober? He leaned over and whispered something to you and you turned as pale as cream."

She nodded. "Yes, I remember." My sister replaced the tea kettle on the stove and looked off into the expanse of green lawn separating us from the Cathedral of the Divine. "He said he loved me."

Since Slater's resignation left First Church without a pastor, and since there had been so much unresolved controversy over the Communion service, the annual Avenell Easter Sunrise Service was held on the grassy quad behind the cathedral. Peter and I officiated and we had a lovely morning service, with well over six hundred in attendance. The choirs lifted voices like angels and the notes of favorites such as "He Arose" and Handel's "Messiah" floated across the campus. Drowsy children clutched chocolate eggs and stuffed bunnies while the eclectic body of Christians took Communion together from a common table.

Caroline was there, sitting with John Greenwood on one side and Joan Dowinger of all people, on the other. My sister was at John's other side and Leah Schroeder was next to Bea. As the sun greeted us with penetrating strands of red, orange, and gold, we rejoiced together at the resurrection of our Savior. In my homily I compared Judas and Peter and each man's betrayal of his Savior. But more importantly, the variant responses to the guilt and shame each man experienced.

"St. Peter embraced his human frailty as greater need for Christ's love and mercy, while Judas anguished in the solitary confinement of his own limited conscience. We all fail, we all betray one another, but through the power of Christ's resurrection, we have the grace we need to forgive and remain in the body of Christ."

Afterward, as clusters of folk gathered to chat and enjoy coffee and refreshments, Peter and I stood and watched the variety of children scramble across the lawn to find pastel-colored eggs hidden in the bushes. That morning as we had dressed together in the vestry, I knew that Easter was Peter's deadline for making his choice. The silence between us then weighed heavy, and some of its gravity returned now.

"I've made my decision, Grif," he said, looking up at me.

I placed my hand on his shoulder. "Know that I will always love and support you regardless of what you are about to tell me."

He nodded. "This is the hardest decision I've ever had to make. I hope I never face another like it again. I . . . I've decided to join the Schroeders in Tremont. I think the Lord is calling me to the Amish way of life. Leah and I will be married this November. I called and told Bishop Wilder last night."

I clasped my hand to his shoulder more firmly and nodded my head. Tears sprang to my eyes, but I couldn't keep from smiling. "Peter, I trust the Lord's will for you and know He will continue to hold you in the palm of His hand."

"Are you disappointed? I will miss you more than anyone else," he confided.

"No, I am not disappointed. And as you've discovered these past few months, Tremont is not that far away!" We embraced in a firm bear hug before we headed over to greet the others.

An hour later, our party sat around the dining room table to a sumptuous brunch prepared by my sister and me. White linen tablecloth and napkins, polished silver, and fine china even met Joan Dowinger's standard. Baked ham, fruit ambrosia, hot cross buns, spring vegetable quiche, and planter's punch anchored our delicious feast. Peter shared his news with the rest of the group and everyone applauded.

"Well, I have another kind of announcement to make myself," said Caroline, "and I think someone else at the table does, as well." To my surprise she eyed John Greenwood, who smiled back at her.

Caroline looked radiant in a bright cobalt dress and wide-brimmed white hat with matching blue bow. She tucked a strand of auburn hair behind her ear before continuing. "I would like to join the Episcopal Church. I've already signed up for Joan's new members' class for the summer."

I sat there with my mouth open while everyone else clapped and cheered again. Stunned to say the least, I knew this would be a matter that Caroline and I would need to discuss further. Before I could recover, however, John Greenwood picked up his knife and chimed it delicately against his water glass to get our attention.

"And I," he paused dramatically, "I am retiring from the ministry and moving here to Avenell. That is, if my friends here will have me."

"What?" I laughed. "Well, the Lord truly does provide. He takes one friend away" — I nodded at Peter — "and provides an old one in his place. John, that's wonderful news!"

"Indeed!" chimed in Joan and Beatrice in unison.

"Well, let us offer a prayer of thanks for these happy occasions," I said. "In the spirit of the Amish tradition, I ask that we pray silently and humbly before our God."

We clasped hands and the table fell quiet

and we sat there comfortably for several minutes. The carillon bells tolled twelve noon, then began reverberating in rich peals of silvery notes. It was a hymn we all knew, and spontaneously several of us said "amen" and began to softly mouth the words to the song of celebration:

Jesus Christ is risen today, Alleluia!
Our triumphant holy day, Alleluia!
Who did once upon the cross, Alleluia!
Suffer to redeem our loss. Alleluia!

The employees of Thorndike Press hope you have enjoyed this Large Print book. All our Large Print titles are designed for easy reading, and all our books are made to last. Other Thorndike Press Large Print books are available at your library, through selected bookstores, or directly from us.

For information about titles, please call:

(800) 223-1244
(800) 223-6121

To share your comments, please write:

Publisher
Thorndike Press
295 Kennedy Memorial Drive
Waterville, ME 04901